The Avenging Parrot

A
James "Bonnie" Dundee Mystery

By Anne Austin

Originally published in 1930

Murder Backstairs

Published by Resurrected Press

This classic book was handcrafted by Resurrected Press. Resurrected Press is dedicated to bringing high quality classic books back to the readers who enjoy them. These are not scanned versions of the originals, but, rather, quality checked and edited books meant to be enjoyed!

Please visit ResurrectedPress.com to view our entire catalogue!

For updates on future releases, LIKE us on Facebook: http://www.Facebook.com/ResurrectedPress

ISBN: 978-1-943403-20-2

Resurrected Press Books in A. E. Fielding's *The Chief Inspector Pointer* <u>*Mystery*</u> Series

RESURRECTED PRESS CLASSIC MYSTERY CATALOGUE

Journeys into Mystery
Travel and Mystery in a More Elegant Time

The Edwardian Detectives
Literary Sleuths of the Edwardian Era

Gems of Mystery
Lost Jewels from a More Elegant Age

Anne Austin
One Drop of Blood
The Black Pigeon
Murder at Bridge

E. C. Bentley
Trent's Last Case: The Woman in Black .

Ernest Bramah
Max Carrados Resurrected:
The Detective Stories of Max Carrados

Agatha Christie
The Secret Adversary
The Mysterious Affair at Styles

Octavus Roy Cohen
Midnight

Freeman Wills Croft
The Ponson Case
The Pit Prop Syndicate

J. S. Fletcher
The Herapath Property
The Rayner-Slade Amalgamation
The Chestermarke Instinct
The Paradise Mystery
Dead Men's Money
The Middle of Things
Ravensdene Court
Scarhaven Keep
The Orange-Yellow Diamond
The Middle Temple Murder
The Tallyrand Maxim
The Borough Treasurer
In the Mayor's Parlour
The Saftey Pin

R. Austin Freeman
The Mystery of 31 New Inn from the Dr. Thorndyke Series
John Thorndyke's Cases from the Dr. Thorndyke Series
The Red Thumb Mark from The Dr. Thorndyke Series
The Eye of Osiris from The Dr. Thorndyke Series
A Silent Witness from the Dr. John Thorndyke Series
The Cat's Eye from the Dr. John Thorndyke Series
Helen Vardon's Confession: A Dr. John Thorndyke Story
As a Thief in the Night: A Dr. John Thorndyke Story
Mr. Pottermack's Oversight: A Dr. John Thorndyke Story
Dr. Thorndyke Intervenes: A Dr. John Thorndyke Story
The Singing Bone: The Adventures of Dr. Thorndyke
The Stoneware Monkey: A Dr. John Thorndyke Story
The Great Portrait Mystery, and Other Stories: A Collection of Dr. John Thorndyke and Other Stories
The Penrose Mystery: A Dr. John Thorndyke Story

Anybody but Anne
The Bride of a Moment
Faulkner's Folly
The Diamond Pin
The Gold Bag
The Mystery of the Sycamore
The Come Back

Raoul Whitfield
Death in a Bowl

And much more!
Visit ResurrectedPress.com
for our complete catalogue

For updates on future releases, LIKE us on
Facebook:
http://www.Facebook.com/ResurrectedPress

FOREWORD

Anne Austin is one of the many writers that flourished during the 1930's and then disappeared as times and tastes changed. She got her start as an author writing romance novels, but switched to mysteries starting with *The Black Pigeon* in 1929. Many of her novels first appeared in serial form in syndication to various newspapers in the US and Canada. In all, she authored six mysteries and six novels in the romance genre.

Five of the mysteries feature James "Bonnie" Dundee, a young detective who becomes a Special Investigator in the District Attorney's office, with *The Avenging Parrot*, published in 1930, being the final installment in the series. There would be a gap of seven years in the series between *One Drop of Blood* (1932) and the last book in the series, *Murdered But Not Dead* (1939). This may have been the result of Austin's involvement with Hollywood as a result of the filming of one of her non-mystery novels, *The Wicked Woman* as a movie of the same name.

The Avenging Parrot deals with the murder of a woman who is a lodger at a boarding house, an institution with which many of the members of the intended audience would have been familiar with. Much of the action takes place within the confines of the house, and most of the suspects are either current or former lodgers there. The woman, who had been confined to her room because of a medical condition, was believed by her fellow lodgers to have had a sizeable fortune hidden somewhere in her room. The only witness to her murder is her parrot, Cap'n. It is not giving too much away to say that the parrot holds the vital clue to revealing the identity of the murder. The parrot would go on to make cameo appearances in several of the later books in the series.

As with several of the other mysteries in the series, much of the story deals with the small town attitudes of Hamilton. While the location of this mid-sized city is never exactly specified in the later books, in *The Avenging Parrot* it is revealed that it is in the state of Missouri.

As an author, Austin was concerned with the psychology of her characters, which play a larger role in her books than the actual mechanics of the crime. In *The Avenging Parrot*, the focus is on the residents of the boarding house, their aspirations, their romances, and the clashes of personality that occur whenever people live in close proximity to one another. The method of detection followed by Dundee is to understand the motivations of the various suspects rather than concentration on the clues. Yet, despite this focus, the mystery is supported by a chain of evidence intricate enough to please most mystery fans.

It is quite clear that Austin's mysteries were targeted towards a feminine audience, especially working women in their twenties. The detective Dundee, young, handsome, and considerate, was certainly designed to appeal to this group as the model boyfriend. The setting, a small, industrial mid-western city, reflects the realities of the times; prohibition and the middle of the Great Depression. The subject matter involves areas that would have been relevant and of interest to women of the period, the problems of making a living during difficult times, relationships with the opposite sex, and the personal failings of the men around them. One of the strengths of Austin's works is that she does deal with these matters in a realistic manner. As the series progressed, the tone of the books would become more mature and darker, the failings of the characters, both victims and suspects, more pronounced and believable, but in *The Avenging Parrot*, both Dundee, the hero, and Austin, the author, are still experiencing the flush of youth.

Though not well known today, the mysteries of Anne Austin are well worth reading. It is with pleasure that Resurrected Press presents this new edition of *The Avenging Parrot*.

About the Author

Born in 1895, Anne Austin began by writing romance novels about young women in the mid 1920's but soon turned her talents to producing a string of mysteries through the 1930's, some of which appeared as serials in newspapers.. Many of these mysteries feature as the detective "Bonnie" Dundee, Special Investigator for the District Attorney, including *Murder Backstairs*, *The Avenging Parrot*, *Murder at Bridge*, and *One Drop of Blood*. Several of her mysteries were translated into French, including *Le Pigeon Noir* and *Le Crime Parfume*. Despite her success as a novelist, Anne Austin disappears from the public record after the 1930's.

Greg Fowlkes
Editor-In-Chief
Resurrected Press
www.ResurrectedPress.com
www.Facebook.com/ResurrectedPress

I.

"WELL, my lad, if it's work you're wanting, Lieutenant Strawn here is the man to see that you get your fill of it," Police Commissioner O'Brien, his blue eyes twinkling at the tall young man who sat across the desk from him. "Jawn—" he turned slightly in his swivel chair and drooped a sandy-lashed lid in a significant wink— "this scallawag happens, by the grace of God and a sister—rest her soul!—to be my nephew. Do you think that the taxpayers will rise in their wrath and defeat me at the next election if I give him a job under you at the Homicide Squad? Of course, you're to kick him out if he's no good as a sleuth. But if he's half as clever a snooper as his mother was . . . Why, Nora, bless her heart, knew when I was in love with a girl, before I had tumbled to it myself—"

"And what might his name be, Commissioner?" Lieut. John Strawn of the Hamilton Homicide Squad interrupted, his grey eyes narrowing speculatively upon the smiling young man who had risen and was holding out a hand."

"It might be O'Halloran, if that wilful sister of mine hadn't lost her heart to a Scotchman by the name of Dundee," O'Brien chuckled. "Irish he is, Jawn, as you can see by the black hair and the blue eyes of him, but Scotch he is, too, by the name his father pinned on him. Jimmie Dundee his name is, Jawn, or if you're wanting his alias, you might write him down in your books as 'Bonnie' Dundee. A sorry name for a six-footer like Jimmie here, but Bonnie he's been since a sentimental lass he lost his heart to in high school found a Rab Burns poem called 'Bonnie Dundee' and made him a present of the nickname. So 'Bonnie' he is, and 'Bonnie' he'll be till he dies, I suppose, Jawn. But what do you think? Could you overlook the handicap and give the boy a trial at the detective business?"

"Anything you say goes, Commissioner," Lieut. Strawn agreed grudgingly, at last taking the firm young hand that was still thrust toward him. "Of course, he'll have to take the regular examinations—"

"Of Course!" Bonnie Dundee flashed a wide, disarming smile at the dour man who was to be his chief. "And thanks much, Lieutenant Strawn. I hope you'll forget, after a bit, that I worked pull to get this job—"

"Pull, is it?" his uncle interrupted "I'd have you know, lad, that I've got the interest of Hamilton at heart, not yours! If half this Inspector Jessup of Scotland Yard says about you is true, Jawn Strawn is going to be glad to have you. Just look at this, Jawn!" And Police Commissioner O'Brien drew an official-looking letter from a desk drawer and passed it to the police lieutenant.

"Mmm," Lieut. Strawn remarked non-committally as he read the three or four paragraphs. "So you've worked in Scotland Yard, have you, Dundee?"

"Yes—six months, sir, but only in a very minor capacity. I was under Inspector Jessup in the Department of Records. I did not actually go out on cases, but I did manage to learn something of British police methods," Bonnie Dundee answered, with so much genuine respect for the man addressed that Lieut. Strawn thawed visibly.

"College, I suppose?" he grunted, as if he were prepare to know the worst.

"I'm afraid so," Bonnie grinned "But as l spent most my time reading everything on criminology that I could lay my hands on, I don't think I'm overburdened with an education, sir."

"Hmm! A story-book detective," Lieut. Strawn commented, but there was a glint of not unkindly humour in his grey eyes. "I'm afraid you're going to be disappointed in Hamilton as a crime centre, Dundee. Offhand, I can recall a single case where a rich old man was found dead in his library, a carved dagger in his heart, and doors and windows barred. And so far I knows there's not a single house in all Hamilton with a secret passage–"

O'Brien chuckled. "You're right, Jawn, and it's ashamed of our murderers I am! Not an ounce originality in a gaolful of 'em! Just old-fashioned killers the lot of 'em—shooting off .32's, carving their wives or sweethearts with razors or butcher knives. Sometimes the ladies— God bless 'em—serve arsenic sandwiches at their tea-parties, but on the whole, myboy, they give us a pretty dull time of it, leaving so many clues lying around sometimes Jawn Strawn here is almost ashamed to take the taxpayers' money—"

"Excuse me, Mr. O'Brien," a girl's voice spoke from e doorway, "but here's a special delivery letter for you, marked 'Personal'."

"Eh? . . . Oh, all right . . . No, you needn't wait, Miss Crane," the police commissioner said rather pointedly, as he saw his secretary's intrigued eyes lingering upon the handsome face of his nephew.

As the girl—not a very pretty, one, but striving by make-up arts to appear so—left the room reluctantly, with a long backward glance, the police commissioner slit the envelope, drew out three sheets of cheap, blue-lined tablet paper, and began to read.

"Another nut," he muttered as he finished, and tossed the letter across the desk to Lieut. Strawn. "Poor old lady—bored—trying to kick up a little excitement," he added to Dundee, by way of explanation. "We get hundreds of nut letters in the course of a year. Some of the writers are plain crazy, some trying to cause trouble for their private enemies, some out to kid the police—"

"And which kind is this?" Bonnie Dundee asked.

"The commonest of all," O'Brien chuckled, shaking a leonine head of frost-touched red hair at his eager nephew, "Nothing here to interest a rising young Sherlock Holmes, just an old lady who's got a bug in her bean to the effect that all her fellow-boarders have it in for her and are plotting to kill her. What's that highfaluting name you college boys have for it?"

"Persecution complex," Bonnie grinned. "Pardon— may I see the letter?"

Strawn, who had made no comment on the letter as he read it, beyond a disgusted snort, passed the sheets to the young man.

Dundee's bright blue eyes travelled swiftly down the first page of small, precise handwriting in green ink; then his audience of two saw him frown, as he began to read the sheet, his free hand thoughtfully smoothing the crisp waves of his thick black hair.

O'Brien winked at Strawn, and the police lieutenant returned the pleasantry with great solemnity.

But Dundee's attention was concentrated on the letter:

The Rhodes House,
511, Chestnut Ave.,
June 29, 1929
Police Commissioner Patrick C. O'Brien,
City Hall, Hamilton.

DEAR SIR: —

I read one of your speeches in the paper when you were running for re-election. You said something like this: 'My aim, as police commissioner of Hamilton, has been and will be to decrease crime by sound and logical methods of prevention. In my opinion, crime prevention is of even greater importance that crime detection.' There was lot more to it, of course, but I thought then you were a mighty sensible man.

Well, Mr. Commissioner, I was glad you were re-elected, although I couldn't get out to vote for you because I haven't been able to walk down a flight of stairs for more than two years. I weigh over three hundred pounds, and I have what the doctors call fatty degeneration of the heart.

But now I want to remind you of what you said, in those election speeches, and ask you to prevent my murder, No, I'm not crazy, and I do not know for certian that my life is in danger. It's because of my money though. I haven't got as much as those who would like to get it, by fair means or foul, think I have. Everything I have in the world is in my room, on the second floor of the Rhodes House, which is a boarding-house, as you probably know. First, and last, and by one way or another, I've made a good many enemies during the five years I've lived here, and all because of the money.

There's no use writing me a letter, telling me to put my money in a bank, so I won't be murdered for it. I have good cause to put no faith in banks, and besides my bad heart would keep me from going to the bank to get any of it out when I needed it.

What I want you to do is to send a plain-clothed detective to talk to me, and to protect me from the fate that I am sure is hanging over me. I'll name no name now, but when your detective comes, I'll have plenty to tell him—enough to convince him that I'm not the silly old fool you're thinking me now.

If you want to prevent the robbery and probably the murder of an old woman who has never done anything worse in her life than to arouse in her fellow boarders the passion of greed, you will do as I ask.

Respectfully yours, (Mrs.) Emma Hogarth.

P.S. Please tell your detective not to let on to anyone, even to Mrs. Rhodes, my landlady, that he is a detective. E. H.

"Well, Bonnie," O'Brien challenged, when Dundee had finished reading the letter. "Looks like a big case, doesn't it?" and he winked again at Lieut. Strawn. "What you 'deduce'?"

Bonnie Dundee saw the wink, understood very well it his uncle was "riding" him good-naturedly, but he had no resentment. When a man is only twenty-five years old he does not expect to be taken very seriously by his elders.

"I 'deduce' that Mrs. Emma Hogarth writes a very logical, lucid letter for a 'nut,'" he answered, grinning. "What are you going to do about it, Uncle Pat? She does put it up to you rather strongly, I'd say—'My aim, as police commissioner of Hamilton has been and will be to decrease crime by sound and logical methods of prevention,'" he quoted, his blue eyes sparkling with mirth. "Who wrote that speech for you, Uncle Pat?"

"I wrote it myself, you young whippersnapper!" his uncle retorted. "And just to prove I meant every word of it I'll send somebody around to talk to the old dame—"

"Who seems to be quite an admirer of yours," Dundee interrupted, smiling broadly. "She knows how to get what she wants out of the Irish, doesn't she? . . . Say, Uncle Pat, how about letting me have a powwow with this shrewd old miser?"

"Blithering old nut, you mean," Strawn commented sourly. "As the commissioner told you, Dundee, we've got hundreds of letters like that on file, and not one of the writers has been robbed or murdered yet."

"Somehow," Dundee began slowly, "I feel that this is just a little different from those hundreds of letters. . . . I think I'll see if there's a vacant room at Rhodes House—"

"If you're to believe this letter, it's more likely to be a Rogues' House," O'Brien chuckled. Then his smile faded, as he realised the significance of his nephew's remark. "Listen, boy, you're not going to leave your Aunt Mary and me flat, are you? Isn't our guest-room good enough for you?"

"Too good, since I can't pay for it." his nephew answered seriously. "It's good of you and Aunt Mary to want me, and I've immensely enjoyed this week of being a pampered guest, but now that I've landed a job I'd like to scout around for a good boarding-house. I'm glad Mrs.

Hogarth's letter came while I was here. It may not be an orthodox sort of recommendation, but at least she makes the Rhodes House sound—well, interesting."

Lieut. Strawn rose, knocked the ashes from his pipe into the police commissioner's big brass cuspidor, and reached for his uniform cap.

"Well, I'll be ambling on over to Headquarters. Glad to have met you, Dundee. This being Saturday, guess you won't be ready to report till Monday."

"I may be ready to report this evening Lieutenant," Dundee answered. "That is, if you and Uncle Pat are willing for me to look into this Hogarth letter. It seems to me that I might as well 'protect' the old lady, as she requests, and get a good boarding-house at the same time. It is a decent place, I suppose?"

"One of the best," Strawn admitted "Aside from its fascinating criminal prospects as outlined in that letter, the Rhodes House is convenient to Headquarters and the business district. One of those fine old mansions deserted by their owners when the business district began to spread towards the west. Chestnut Avenue used to be Hamilton's Park Avenue in the good old days. Now the old houses are coming down, and filling stations, garages and apartment houses are going up in their places. If you really want to find a good boarding-house, I suppose you might do worse than the Rhodes House. But I hope you won't be too disappointed when you find that Mrs. Emma Hogarth is just another letter-writing nut."

"I'll try to bear up." Dundee promised, laughing. Then, seriously. "But if I should think her story important enough to pass it on to you, could I reach you to-night?"

Strawn shrugged. "Sure! I seldom leave Headquarters before midnight. Glad to have you drop around any time and tell me all about Scotland Yard".

When the detective left, a slight smile on his big, square face, Police Commissioner O'Brien tilted back in his swivel chair and regarded his nephew with fond, smiling eyes.

"Well, boy, I think we put it over. Strawn's one of the finest, you know, but I had to handle him with kid gloves to keep him from getting sore at me—and you—for slipping a man into his department over his head. He likes you, all right—"

"He conceals it admirably," Dundee laughed. "I may as well add that I like him, too."

"John Strawn has been on the Force for more than twenty-five years," O'Brien went on. "He's a splendid routine detective, thorough-going, tireless, relentless—"

"But unimaginative?" Dundee suggested, rising.

"You'd better park *your* imagination outside Police headquarters Monday morning, young feller-my-lad," his uncle warned him. "Hold on! I'm going to call it a day. We'll go home to lunch and break the news to your Aunt Mary that you prefer a prunes-and-oatmeal boarding-house to her honeydew-melon-and-waffles brand of hospitality. Poor Mary! It's a lonely woman she'll be—"

Bonnie Dundee laid an affectionate arm about his uncle's shoulder. "Suppose you give your brogue a rest when you're talking to me alone, Uncle Pat," he laughed. "I know it goes over swell with the cops and the voters, but—"

"You're an impudent rascal," his uncle charged, but his eyes were twinkling.

As uncle and nephew passed through the outer of the two offices that made up the Police Commissioner's suite in City Hall, a plain girl who hoped she looked pretty, because of the extra layer of make-up she had added to her complexion, carolled a sweet "Good-bye, Mr. O'Brien. Good-bye, Mr. Dundee," her eyes coquetting hopefully with the tall, slender young man.

But Bonnie Dundee was not thinking about her, scarcely heard his own voice answering. He was thinking of a fat, sick old woman who was in terror of her life.

"What's that you're muttering to yourself, Bonnie?" his uncle, asked, when, the wheezy elevator had deposited them on the main floor of city Hall.

"Was I muttering?" Dundee flushed and laughed. "It was just a stanza from one of Burns's poems:

"'I've lived the life of sturt and strife;
I die by treacherie;
It burns my heart I must depart;
And not avenged be.'"

"Have you gone clean daft over the Hogarth Woman?" his uncle demanded in genuine astonishment. "Surely you're not taking that fool letter to heart, my boy."

"Not 'to heart' yet, but 'to head'," Bonnie Dundee retorted. "I can't help thinking about her. If she really has a miser's hoard hidden away in her room, and every one knows it, she's asking for trouble and—well, I'm afraid she's pretty sure it's coming."

"Not with you on the job," his uncle reminded him cheerfully. "By the way, lad; how are you fixed for money? I don't want you to have to rob the old lady to get the money to pay your board—"

"Thanks, Uncle Pat. There's a few hundred left from Dad's estate; enough to see me through if the fair city of Hamilton pays its cub detectives a living wage. By the way, at the Rhodes House I'm going to be a new comer to the city, looking for a job. Which is true enough, isn't it? And even if the Hogarth affair proves to be as trivial as you think it, I'd like to live there incognito—"

"Ashamed of being a dick?" his uncle gibed.

"No. But I rather think life will be pleasanter for my fellow-boarders if they don't know I'm on the detective force—provided I pass my examinations," he added with a grin. "And, of course, if Mrs. Hogarth actually does need protection, I can give it to her much more efficiently if my official connection with her is unsuspected."

"All right, lad. Have your fun," his uncle agreed. "I shan't give you away."

At five o'clock that Saturday afternoon, June 29th, a tall, slim young man, wearing a well-fitting suit of blue serge, whose Bond Street label he had rather regretfully removed, turned up the cement walk leading from Chestnut Avenue to the front porch of the Rhodes House.

Bonnie Dundee's interested blue eyes roved appreciatively on that short journey. The lush green grass of the big lawn needed cutting rather badly, but after the months he had spent in London and, more recently, in New York; even a neglected lawn looked heavenly. Flowers, too, in narrow beds along the walk and below the low porch, which extended the whole width of the house and, apparently, along the entire east side of it. Red rambler roses on a trellis which closed off the west end of the porch. A greenhouse on the west lawn, about fifteen feet from the gravelled driveway which hugged that side of the house. But the greenhouse probably yielded few flowers now, for of its hundreds of little glass panes only a few remained unbroken. A relic of past splendours, when Chestnut Avenue had been Hamilton's Park Avenue, as Strawn had put it.

On the east lawn there was a big garden swing, glistening from a recent coat of green paint. And in the swing a girl sat rocking idly.

"I know I'm going to like this place," Dundee told himself jubilantly. She was a *very* pretty girl, with the afternoon sun slanting golden beams through the brown of her hair—not bobbed, thank God!—with her pale-green organdie skirt fluttering with the motion of the swing.

He flicked his eyes away, for he had stared just a moment too long. The house was a jolly old thing. No, he corrected himself swiftly. He must not lapse into the English phrases he had picked up unconsciously. But it was a fine old place. Three stories, the top one many-gabled, in the fashion of a bygone architecture.

The wide porch, supported by many slender posts, was located on the second floor, and over this double-deck porch extended an abruptly sloping roof from the level the third story. Certainly a gracious, hospitable, comfortable looking house, in spite of the shabbiness of ancient white paint and its general, rather pathetic air decayed gentility

Later, Bonnie Dundee was to feel a curious sympathy and resentment in behalf of the fine old house, when pictured of it appeared in newspapers with the lurid caption: "Murder Mansion."

But now, as he ascended the three steps leading to the porch, he reflected that he would indeed be in luck if he could secure a room here, make this gracious, shabby old house his home, dine at table with that very pretty girl in the lawn swing. . . .

A big, pompous, middle-aged man in a freshly-laundered suit of white duck rose from a porch chair and a friendly greeting:

"How do you do, sir? Do you wish to see the landlady Mrs. Rhodes? I'm Mr. Sharp—Mr. Lawrence Sharp."

Bonnie Dundee set down his heavy suit-case and tended a hand as friendly as the greeting. Nice to these Middle-Westerners!

"Glad to know you, Mr. Sharp. My name is Dundee—a stranger to Hamilton. I'd like very much to get board and room here."

"You picked a good town, Mr. Dundee!" Mr. Sharp boomed heartily. "Fastest-growing city in the Middle-West. Yes, sirree! One hundred thousand by 1930 is our slogan; Mr. Dundee—Oh, here's Mrs. Rhodes. Mrs. Rhodes, I'd like to make you acquainted with a newcomer to our fair city—Mr. Dundee, of—where did say you're from, Mr. Dundee?"

Bonnie hesitated for only a moment. Then: "New York City," he smiled, stating the exact truth, for he come from New York to Hamilton, though he had had no home since his father's death the year before.

Until he saw her smile, Bonnie was afraid that prospective landlady was a formidable one—the kind he particularly detested. Tall, her big bones well covered with flesh which, however, did not give the impression fat; a high, sternly-corseted bosom; an olive-skinned, harassed face, crowned with iron-grey hair in an fashioned, intricate coiffure. He was about to put age tentatively at fifty, when she smiled—a smile drove the anxiety out of her face and made her brown eyes sparkle like a girl's. Bonnie had no glimmering of the fact that it was his own fresh, boyish good looks that had worked the minor miracle.

"Were you looking for a place to board, Mr. Dundee?" Mrs. Rhodes asked hospitably, almost eagerly.

Ten minutes later, the preliminary negotiations concluded, Bonnie Dundee and his landlady stood in a room on the third floor, charming with its sloping ceiling, faded but pretty wallpaper, crisply laundered dotted Swiss curtains in the little gable windows.

"I'm sorry I haven't a room on the second floor you wanted," Mrs. Rhodes worried, stooping to pick thread from the otherwise immaculate green-and-white fibre rug. "But I think you'll find this room very comfortable, Mr. Dundee. Quiet, too, if you like quiet. There are only two other rooms occupied on this floor at present. Miss Jewel Briggs, who has the room across the hall you, is away visiting her family over the week-end, and Tilda, the chambermaid, has the little room at the rear. I'm sorry there's only one bath on this floor—"

"Oh, I'm going to be luxurious up here," Dundee assured her

After a few more remarks, largely concerned with the subject of towels, soap, and bed-linens, Mrs. Rhodes left him, remarking from the doorway:

"Dinners at six, Mr. Dundee. I know that's rather early for summer-time, but my guests are always so hungry after their long days at the office. I'm sure I hope you'll be happy here. If do say it, I have a nice little crowd of guests—more like a family than just boarders."

Freshly tubbed and dressed in his lightest-weight summer suit, because of the brooding, breathless heat, Dundee descended the two flights of stairs at exactly six o'clock. Somewhere below a deep-toned gong was being beaten to summon the boarders—a rather unnecessary formality, the boy thought, for when he entered the dining room the tables were almost filled. Mrs. Rhodes was waiting for him and escorted him to the long table in the centre of the room. "This is the house guests' table, Mr. Dundee. The little tables are for 'mealers'—transients, you know, who come in only for dinner." With her hand on his arm, she performed the introductions: "This is Mr. Dundee, folks. And Mr. Dundee, this is Mrs. Sharp. You've already met Mr. Sharp. And this is Miss Barker; Miss Shepherd; Mr. Styles; Miss Paige; Mr. Magnus, and Mr. Dowd."

There was a chorus of friendly greetings, and as Bonnie Dundee, detective incognito, took his seat directly opposite the very pretty girl who was Miss Paige, he reflected:

"Nice, friendly people. Just folks! I suppose Lieutenant Strawn and Uncle Pat are right and that I'm as big a nut as that poor old woman upstairs."

But just then, in one of those sudden silences that fall in otherwise noisy groups, there came, from above, a raucus screaming of words, in a voice so strangely horrible Dundee's hair rose on his scalp.

"Help! Murder! Police!"

The young detective sprang to his feet, his face paper-white.

II.

BONNIE DUNDEE had knocked over his chair and was half-way to the dining-room doors, that horrible cry for help still ringing in his ears, when Mrs. Rhodes intercepted him, smiling grimly.

"That was just a parrot, Mr. Dundee. Mrs. Hogarth's parrot upstairs . . .Dusty!" she called to a thin, oldish, sullen little man in a crumpled white coat, who was serving plates of food to a table of "mealers". "Just run upstairs and see if old Mrs. Hogarth is all right."

"I'm sure she, is," she turned back to Dundee, "but she made us all promise to come running, night or day, if we heard the parrot scream those words. She's been trying to teach them to him for a week, but he's stubborn sometimes, and pretends not to hear. Then, when you least expect it, he screams out something she hasn't even tried to teach him. A queer bird, Cap'n is. The smartest parrot I ever heard of."

Dundee, feeling very foolish because of the excitement he had betrayed, and more convinced than ever that the old woman upstairs was a "nut," as Lieut. Strawn and Police Commissioner O'Brien had labelled her, laughed apologetically, but lingered on the threshold of the folding doors that led into the hall. He had an uneasy feeling that he himself should have leaped up those stairs at that horrible cry for help, but how could he have done so without betraying his identity as a detective, a secret which Mrs. Hogarth had herself urged him to keep?

"Dusty" Rhodes, the landlady's husband, to whom Dundee had already been introduced, came shuffling down the stairs, a look of disgust and sullen resentment on his weak, unpleasant face.

"Sure she's all right. Settin' up there, laughing her fool head off 'cause Cap'n kicked up a row," he told his wife. "I shut her door and told her she'd have to get shet of that bird if she couldn't keep him quiet."

"Mind your own business, Dusty Rhodes!" Mrs. Rhodes commanded sharply, but in a voice that could not carry to the goggle-eyed "mealers."

Dundee returned to his table and took his seat in the chair which Tilda, chambermaid and waitress for the "house guests," had restored to an upright position. She was placing the cup of jellied tomato bouillon on his plate at the moment, and he smiled up into her plain, stupid face. She smiled back uncertainly, flushed, and almost overturned his glass of ice water.

"Well, Dundee!" Mr. Lawrence Sharp boomed a hearty laugh from the end of the table. "You've had a fine introduction to our prize exhibit! Yes, siree! No dull moments in *this* house—"

"Now, Lawrence!" the plump, complacent motherly-looking little woman who was his wife remonstrated fondly. She smiled around the table. "Isn't he a case?"

"Well, Dolly," her husband chuckled richly, "our new friend might as well hear about old Mrs. Hogarth now as later . . . . Talking about cases, there's one for you, Dundee. Yes, siree! She's a character, if there ever was one."

Bonnie Dundee soft-pedalled his acute interest, and inquired casually: "What sort of character, Mr. Sharp?"

"She's a dear, and l don't think it's nice of you, Mr. Sharp, just to make a funny story out of her!" the very pretty girl protested in an unexpectedly spirited voice.

"That my dear Norma," Mr. Sharp laughed, "is because you happen to be her favourite and heiress for the moment. You'll sing another tune when she cuts you out of her will, as she did Daisy and Cora and Walter—"

"That's not true!" Norma Paige flashed, her lovely eyes seeking those of the young man who sat beside her. "Shall I tell them now, Walter?"

"If you think it's a secret," Walter Styles laughed, his own good-looking face catching the blush from hers.

"Why, how *could* they know, when we only became engaged last night?" Norma asked ingenuously.

"Up with your ice tea glasses, and drink a toast to the bride and groom! " Mr. Sharp boomed.

"Isn't he just terrible?" Dolly Sharp inquired fondly, as she raised her glass obediently.

"She *would* get herself engaged just the night before I come," Bonnie Dundee groaned to himself, but he smiled gallantly at the smiling, blushing girl as he raised his own glass. "May I congratulate you, Miss Paige," he said aloud, "upon being both an heiress and a—very happy girl?"

"Thank you, Mr. Dundee!" she said, with the sweet gravity which he thought must be characteristic of her. "But after to-night I'm afraid you can congratulate me only upon being engaged to Walter—I mean, Mr. Styles. You see," she began to explain, in a little flurry of words, "Mrs Hogarth has—has warned me against getting engaged to Walter. He was her favourite and heir after— after Cora—I mean, Miss Barker—" She hesitated, her blue eyes imploring forgiveness of the thin, dark woman who sat on Mr. Sharp's left.

"Oh, shoot the works!" Cora Barker retorted bitterly, her heavily-rouged mouth twisting unpleasantly. "Or if you're too much of a shrinking violet, I'll put Mr. Dundee wise. I might as well. He'll hear the whole story before dark anyway. . . . You'll think us a funny crowd, I suppose, Mr. Dundee," she added, with a startlingly swift change of manner. Her shadowed, mascaraed black eyes were now bright and arch. A thin, dry-skinned hand, which betrayed her age as near forty, lifted itself to pat a great wheel of black braids over her ear. Those twin wheels of obviously dyed black hair made an exotic frame for her thin, passionate, restless face.

"I think you are all most amazingly friendly to a stranger," Dundee answered sincerely.

"Oh, you won't be a stranger long—not unless you're like Mr. Dowd here—" and she arched her brows at a slight, diffident, very ordinary-looking man of thirty-five or forty seated opposite her. 'Mr. Dowd's been here a week to-day, but he's not what Mr. Sharp would call a good mixer. But that's neither here nor there. I guess what you're interested in is old Mrs. Hogarth. If you're not, you ought to be."

Dundee was startled. Had he betrayed himself in some way? "Why should I be Mrs. Barker? Of course, I am—"

Con Barker's smile was again cynical; "Because you'll be next in line for the great hidden hoard, if I'm not a poor guesser. As Norma has told you, I was our fairy godmother's favourite child before Walter Styles edged me out of the will. That was in May, wasn't it, Walter?"

Norma's young man flushed and lowered his light-brown eyes to his plate. "I—think so, Cora. Lord knows I didn't try to vamp her, but she was looking around for a new heir, and—"

"And *you* got the job of dancing attendance on her!" Con flashed. "As for me, I was sick of it. The hours were too long, and the pay too far in the future—if ever."

"Pretty expensive, too, being her pet, wasn't it, Daisy?"

The big, jolly-looking girl seated next to Cora Barker tore her attention reluctantly from the well-filled plate which had just been set before her.

"I'll say it was expensive!" she chuckled good-naturedly. "You see, Mr. Dundee, old Mrs. Hogarth is a miser. Got a big wad of money hidden away in her room somewhere. Keeps the keys of her trunk and desk on a chain around her neck. She's fatter than I am, by the way—believe it or not!" and Daisy Shepherd laughed wholeheartedly at herself. "Weighs about three hundred, I guess. Can't come downstairs, because she's got a funny heart. I felt sorry for her and spent a lot of time in her room keeping her company. She's a good old scout, but gossipy and mischievous—"

"Mischievous?" Bonnie repeated.

"Sure! Loves excitement. That's the reason she changes her will so much. When she gets tired of one of us, or we get tired of her—as I did, and no hard feelings on my part, either—she picks out another favourite, and as Cora says, I guess you can be the fair-haired boy next, if the idea appeals to you."

"But—why?" Dundee puzzled. His admiring eyes, fixed upon Norma, advertised the fact that he could not conceive of Mrs. Hogarth's getting tired of *her*.

It was Norma's soft voice that answered, for Daisy Shepherd had returned, greedily, to her dinner.

"I thought I explained," she smiled. Her blush deepening under the ardour of his gaze. "Walter and Mrs. Hogarth had a dreadful quarrel, or rather, Mrs. Hogarth acts as if it were dreadful. Walter won't tell me what it was about, but anyway, almost as soon as I came to board here on the third of June, Mrs. Hogarth cut Walter out of her will, and put my name in, instead. But yesterday she told me that if Walter and I became engaged she'd cut me out of the will, too. But we became engaged anyway, and to-night we're going to tell her about it."

"Foolish child!" boomed Mr. Sharp, wagging a playful finger. "Don't tell her till you're married. Maybe she'll be dead by then—"

"Oh! Please don't say it!" Norma begged, suddenly pale. "You know I like Mrs. Hogarth for herself, Mr. Sharp, not for what she might leave me. Besides, I couldn't bear to touch a penny she wouldn't have wanted me to have, if I deceived her—"

Bonnie Dundee could not bear the distress in her lovely face and voice. "I confess my curiosity is consuming me," he interrupted her lightly. "A famous Dundee trait— curiosity. When do I get to meet our lady of mystery?"

Norma smiled upon him. "Would you really like to meet her to-night? She adores meeting new people She's

awfully lonely sometimes, and she's very interesting. You
might be able to get her into such an amiable mood that
she wouldn't be quite so angry with me. I—I—" The soft
little mouth quivered. "I hate terribly to upset her,
because she really is fond of me. I could take you up to
meet her after dinner; then Walter and I could go up
together when you've left her."

Satisfied that the prospective meeting had been
arranged adroitly, the young detective incognito leaned
back in his chair and studied his fellow-boarders keenly,
without appearing to do so.

If by chance, old Mrs. Hogarth was right—not a "nut"
at all—and her life was really in danger, what an
opportunity he now had to observe all of his possible
suspects before the crime was attempted or committed!
But that was a foolish thought, he told himself sharply. If
one of these apparently ordinary, nice people was a
potential robber or murderer, it was his—Dundee's—job
to see that the crime was not committed. Why, that was
what he was here for—not to suffer palpitation of the
heart because a remarkably pretty girl, whom he had
never seen before that evening, smiled at him adorably.
Besides, she was already engaged to that Styles chap.
Though what she could see in him—

Oh, of course. Styles was good-looking enough, with
that smooth, thick brown hair and those candid, light-
brown eyes. But were they candid? Walter Styles didn't
look quite so happy and carefree as a newly-engaged man
is supposed to look. Maybe Styles had got himself
engaged to Norma Paige just to make sure of the old
lady's money, which he had lost when the will had been
changed in the girl's favour. Suppose that was why he
looked so—well, preoccupied now? Had the newly-
engaged pair quarrelled already over Norma's fiercely
upright determination to break the news of the
engagement that very evening, although it meant, in all
probability, her being cut out of the will so recently made
in her favour? If that was so, Dundee told himself with

jubilant hopefulness, maybe Styles would break the engagement.

"Bert, you aren't eating a thing!" If was Cora, Barker's voice, full of mingled anxiety and tenderness, that jerked Bonnie Dundee back from his daydreaming, though the words were not addressed to him, but to the man on his left. Magnus, his name was, wasn't it?

"Too hot to eat, Cora," Bert Magnus answered, with a deep sigh, as he pushed aside the dessert which had just been served him.

Dundee turned to look at him with more attention than he had yet bestowed upon his neighbour. His keen ears had told him that Cora Barker was in love with this man, and he wondered what sort of person her restless, passionate heart had chosen. He saw a rather plump man of medium height; dark-brown, rather oily hair going a little thin on top; light-grey eyes, listless with the heat, behind rimless *pince-nez*; a stubby, reddish moustache, many shades lighter than his hair. Neither handsome nor homely; just another man, say thirty-five years old. What did Cora Barker, who undoubtedly considered herself a charming and fascinating woman, find in him, Dundee wondered?

He was soon to learn.

"Bert, tell me!" she commanded urgently, leaning as far across the table as possible and endeavouring to give a confidential air to the conversation. "Have you heard from your scenario?"

"Hasn't anyone told you yet?" Magnus asked, rather irritably. "I supposed it was common gossip by this time that the story was—returned—to-day. Not even a rejection slip. In fact, the envelope hadn't been opened, or the studio wants to pretend it hadn't. It was stamped, 'Not opened' and sent back to me—postage collect," he added bitterly.

"Oh, Bert!" Cora's voice was heavy with disappointment and sympathy. "And it's such a wonderful scenario too! I bet they did open it, and had it copied, so

they could *steal* your plot! You just wait! I bet I look up
from my piano some day next winter and see *your story*
unwinding on the screen!" She turned her indignant
black eyes upon Bonnie Dundee. "Mr. Magnus writes
scenarios, Mr. Dundee, and you can take my word for it
that this story of his that came back to-day is better than
nine out of ten movies I have to look at. I play the piano
in a movie theatre over on Grand Street, you know."

There was nothing but sympathy in Dundee's
engaging blue eyes as he turned to Bert Magnus "I say—
I'm awfully sorry you got a rotten break on your story, old
man. Have you—er—sold any yet?"

"I had a very encouraging letter from the scenario
school whose course I subscribed," to Magnus evaded,
stiffly. "Well—if you'll excuse me, I'll go up and do some
work. I'm a book-keeper, so I only have my evenings to
write in, and because of this— " and he held out his right
hand, whose thin, unused-looking fingers seemed to be
permanently curled like the petals of a withered flower—
"I can't make much progress on the typewriter, so I have
to keep plugging away pretty steadily. I've got a new
slant on that story, Cora. I'm almost glad they sent, it
back. It'll be better than ever when it goes out again."

"Why, Bert!" It was almost a cry of anguish from Cora
and Dundee was startled "Have you forgotten that you
promised to see the show to-night? You-won't work too
late, will you? The second show starts at nine, you
know—.

"I'm afraid I had forgotten," Magnus confessed,
smiling feebly and mopping the oily sweat from his face.
"This heat—Listen, Cora! Suppose I go to the first show
instead of the second, then maybe it will be cooler and I
can get some good work done on the story—"

"But you promised to take me out to supper after the
theatre closes," Cora reminded him, arch and hurt at the
same time.

The mild, plumpish man seemed to be looking for a
way of escape. Then he brightened. "Tell you what; Cora:

I'll go along with you now and see the first show, then come back here and work on my story till time to meet you at eleven—"

The glow of happiness on Cora's dark, intense face was almost embarrassing to Dundee.

"That will I be fine, Bert!" she cried. "But don't get impatient if you have to wait awhile for me. We have a new violinist, and I'll have to go over the score of the music for the new feature picture with him before it's shown to-morrow. It may be as late as half past eleven when I'm through."

"Then I'll meet you at half-past eleven," Bert assured her. "What happened to Sevier? Fired?"

Cora's nostrils flared and a queer expression crossed her face. "Yes," she answered briefly.

"Then other people besides Mrs. Hogarth must think Emil Sevier's a bad egg," Mr. Sharp, who had been listening unabashed, cut in. "This fiddler, Sevier, had the room next to the old lady," he explained to Dundee, "and she had Mrs. Rhodes, Dundee, kick him out. We never knew the straight of it," he added regretfully, "but it seems that the old lady got it into her head that Cora's boy friend—"

"He's not my 'boy friend'!" Cora Barker denied vehemently, red splotching her cheeks.

"Well, *was* your boyfriend then," Mr. Sharp corrected himself amiably. "Anyway, seems like the old lady got it into her head that Sevier was plotting to rob her of her money. Guess he was behind a week or two with his board anyway, and Mrs. Rhodes told him his room was more welcome than his company. Mr. Henry Dowd, our talkative new boarder, has Sevier's old room, and they do say he nearly talks the old lady to death—"

This was obviously intended to be very humorous, for Henry Dowd had not spoken during the entire meal, except to ask for salt or bread.

He spoke now. "As you know, Mr. Sharp, I've never met Mrs. Hogarth."

Dundee laughed. "Then you're not as curious as I am, Mr. Dowd."

The thin, common-place man took off his glasses and polished the rimless oval lenses very deliberately. "I mind my own business," he said quietly.

"I've never met Mrs. Hogarth either, but after hearing the story all over again this evening, I'm beginning to get curious myself," Bert Magnus admitted. "You're always telling me to put some comedy relief into my scenarios, Cora. Maybe I'll look in on her this evening, if Dundee will give me an introduction—"

To Dundee's relief, but also to his bewilderment, Cora Barker interrupted with passionate vehemence: "Don't call on Mrs. Hogarth this evening, Bert! Promise me you wont—"

Mrs. Rhodes, advancing rather majestically to the table to inquire if her guests had enjoyed their dinner, prevented Cora's getting the promise she had begged for so strangely.

"I was wondering, Mrs. Rhodes," Bert Magnus said tentatively, "if we couldn't hope to have our window screens in soon. I haven't noticed any flies yet, but the light bugs are rather annoying when I'm trying to write."

"Oh dear! That Dusty!" Mrs. Rhodes sighed. "Dusty! Dusty! Come here! How many times have I got to tell you to put those screens up? Here it is almost the first of July, and not a screen—"

"Now Carrie!" her husband protested sullenly. "Am I got other things to do besides put up screens? And on top of all my worries, that old hellion upstairs has to have a special screen, two layers of copper wire and a padlock and the Lord only knows what else! Hope she can't get no air through it and and'll smother!"

"Well, have you finished making her screen yet?" his wife prodded, contempt strong on her face and in the lash of her tongue. Easy to see who wore the trouser here, Dundee thought.

"I told her it'd be up Monday, and up Monday it'll be,'"Dusty Rhodes answered with weak violence."Old fool. Threatenin' to have me arrested for 'misappropriatin funds'! Hunh! Old fool."

It was a relief to Dundee to see Norma's slender, green organdie-clad body weaving through the crowded dining room toward him.

"Mrs. Hogarth doesn't like to have visitors too soon after her meals," she confided, with a delicious air of intimacy. "I'm sure about eight o'clock will be all right. You'll be nice to her, won't you, Mr. Dundee? Not laugh at her, even to yourself? She's really a darling even if she has got queer ideas about—about some of us."

III.

1

IT was nearly half-past eight that fateful Saturday evening when Bonnie Dundee, escorted by Norma Paige, arrived at the closed door of Mrs. Emma Hogarth's room on the second floor of the Rhodes House. Just as Norma lifted a small white hand to knock a throaty voice with a peculiar trill in it could be heard distinctiy:

"Emma, you're an old fool!"

The words were followed by a loud, hair-raising laugh.

"That's Cap'n again—the parrot, you know," Norma whispered, smiling. She knocked, and two voices answered her, almost simultaneously: "Who is it?" It was hard for Dundee to distinguish between the two speakers, woman and almost superhuman bird.

"It's Norma, Mrs. Hogarth," the girl called.

There was a faint sound of a vast grunt or groan, as if a tremendous body was lifting itself slowly. Then came the thudding taps of canes upon the thin summer rug.

"She always keeps her door locked, and asks who it is before she will admit anyone," Norma whispered; her eyes big and round with pity. "Poor dear! It must be terrible to be old and nearly helpless and to be suspicious of everyone, because you have a little money hidden away."

A key turned in the lock, and Norma Paige and Bonnie Dundee entered the room.

It was about ten minutes to eleven when Dundee emerged from that room alone. He hesitated outside the closed door for a moment, in indecision, and was aware that the key was being turned after him. A peculiar old woman, but not "queer"; he was sure of that. But he had a message to deliver. Mrs. Hogarth had told him the location of all his fellow-boarders' rooms. Hers was the centre-front room, with a single large window looking out upon the upstairs porch. On the east, in the corner room, lived Cora Barker. On the west, also in a corner room, with one window opening upon the front upstairs porch and another looking down upon the driveway, lived Henry Dowd, who had occupied the room only one week, taking it when Emil Sevier had been evicted.

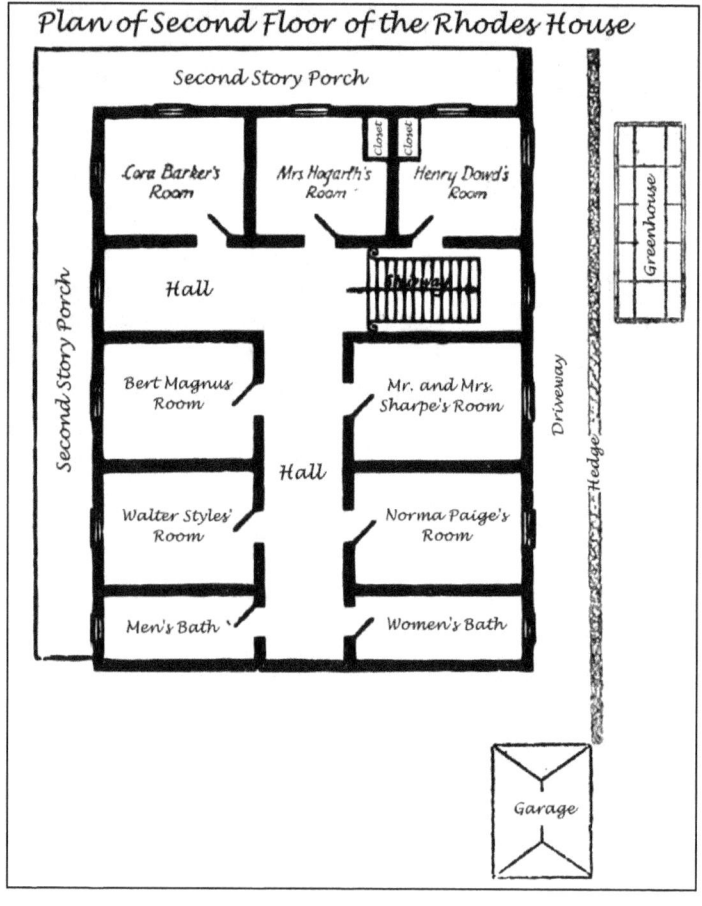

Plan of Second Floor of the Rhodes House

Down the west side of the hall, in the order named, lived Mr. and Mrs. Lawrence Sharp, and Norma Paige, the women's bath being at the end of the hall next to Norma's room. On the east side of the hall, with windows opening upon the side upstairs porch, lived Bert Magnus and Walter Styles, the men's bath being next to Styles's room.

The floor was very quiet, except for the steady slow tapping of a typewriter. His message in mind, Bonnie Dundee stepped quietly to Bert Magnus's door and knocked.

'Who is it?" The answer was decidedly irritable.

"Dundee, Magnus. I have a message for you."

There was a sound of a chair scraping, then footsteps followed by the turning of a key in a lock. Dundee grinned. A nice, trustful house, this!

As if answering the unspoken thought, Bert Magnus, appearing in the doorway in shirt-sleeves, explained with an obvious effort of cordiality.

"Have to keep my door locked or I'd never get any work done. You know what a boarding-house is like—no privacy. Won't you come in?"

Dundee glanced about the small room as Magnus retreated to permit him to enter. A large, old-fashioned roll-top desk, with an ancient typewriter, beside which lay sheets of yellow paper, testified to the fact that Magnus was indeed busy.

"Thanks, no. I see you're busy. Hope the story is going all right," Dundee answered cheerfully, with his engaging smile. "I shouldn't have interrupted, but Mrs. Hogarth asked me to tell you that she'd like to meet you. She seems to be very much interested in your work—"

"Wants to tell me the story of her life and get me to put it into a movie, I suppose," Magnus retorted, grinning wryly.

"I—don't think so," Dundee smiled. "I gathered, from her rather cryptic remarks, that she has a very personal communication to make to you, but naturally I didn't ask questions."

Magnus looked annoyed, and glanced longingly at his work. "God knows I've tried to keep from getting mixed up in boarding-house scandals. Does she want to see me to-night?"

"Or to-morrow, I believe," Dundee answered. "Suit yourself, of course, or don't go at all, if you'd rather not, but I remembered you said you would like to meet her." He also remembered suddenly that Cora Barker had been in a fever of anxiety to prevent the meeting. Why? "Pardon me for interrupting, Magnus. Good luck, and good night."

Before he reached the stairhead, Dundee heard the typewriter going again, very slowly. Poor devil! Packing away with one finger at stories that would never get any nearer the "silver sheet," as he undoubtedly called it, than they were now. But if he enjoyed writing them—

Dundee ran lightly down the stairs, found the big front hall deserted, took his straw hat from the hall tree, and stepped out upon the porch. He was just in time to bump into a Western Union boy.

"Say, Mister. Got a guy named Sharp livin' here? Telegram, collect."

"Lawrence Sharp? Yes. I think he's in his room. Up the stairs, first room to your left, sonny."

The boy entered and Dundee strolled down the walk, whistling "Annie Laurie" very loudly. The lawn swing, which held two shadowy figures very close together, came to an abrupt stop. His signal, previously agreed upon between him and Norma Paige, had been recognised. He waved as the two figures—a man and a slim girl— descended from the swing and started toward the house, Norma slightly in advance, her hand dragging at Walter Styles's—as if she were eager to get it over with and her sweetheart was reluctant.

"If he's marrying her for her money—" Dundee muttered under his breath. Then he laughed at himself, and swung off toward the business district.

The big old brick building which housed Police Headquarters was only eight or ten short blocks away, and it was just a few minutes after eleven when Bonnie Dundee entered the hot, bare cubicle which Lieut. Strawn called his office.

The middle-aged detective in charge of the Homicide Squad was lolling in a creaking swivel chair, drinking from a straw plunged into a bottle of soda water.

"Hotter'n Hades, ain't it?" he growled, by way of greeting. "Want a bottle of pop? I'll send a flat-foot out for one—"

"No thanks . . . Well, I've seen Mrs. Hogarth, but I had mighty little chance to get her story," Dundee told his chief, when he had taken a chair uninvited.

"Because she didn't have anything to tell, more'n likely," Strawn growled

"I think she has," Dundee insisted cheerfully, fanning his heat-flushed face with his straw hat. "The trouble was, no sooner had I been left alone with her and before I could state my official connection—grin, darn you—than people began to drift in to pay the old lady a call. First came Daisy Shepherd—jolly, fat girl, who looks a sylph besides Mrs. Hogarth. Then before Daisy had left Rhodes, our landlady, called to assure Mrs. Hogarth her worthless husband, who goes by the singularly appropriate name of 'Dusty' Rhodes, would surely get the reinforced screen in on Monday. And before she left, in came Mr. and Mrs. Sharp, who insisted on showing snapshots of their adored son, Larry, who is working off a condition or two in State University this summer, so he can play on the Sophomore football team this fall, fondest parents I've run across in lo, these many years—in fact, since my own college days," he grinned, but there was a little quiver of pain about his mouth for the parents who were dead.

"Talk to the old dame alone at all?" Strawn asked economically.

"Only about five minutes. You see, I knew there was a young couple waiting downstairs to break some unpleasant news to her and I didn't want to keep them on the anxious seat any longer."

And then he told Strawn in detail about the old lady's numerous wills, in the last of which Norma Paige was named. He also gave his chief a rapid sketch of the various boarders, including the evicted one, Emil Sevier.

"She hinted dire things about a plot to rob and even murder her," Dundee concluded. "She seems to think Cora Barker, Emil Sevier and Dusty Rhodes are all mixed up in it. Says she woke up one night and saw Sevier in her room, but that he vanished mysteriously, by neither door nor window. She told me to come back to her room about midnight, or a little after, when the house was quiet—late hours on Saturday night, you know—and we could talk undisturbed. Wants me to take away some samples of food she's saved. Says she's sure they're poisoned—by Dusty, who brings her trays."

"Nut!" Strawn dismissed her wearily. "Let's amble down the street and surround a flock of ice-cream sodas. I'll go nuts myself if this heat wave don't break."

Over the ice-cream sodas Strawn became almost flatteringly reminiscent of his twenty-five years on the Force, and it was nearly twenty minutes after twelve when Dundee entered the still unlocked front door of the Rhodes House and tiptoed up the stairs.

A pencil of light under the old woman's door indicated she was still awake. He knocked softly. There was no answer. He knocked again, and listened intently. The second floor was very quiet. The only sound at the moment was the slow, steady tapping of Bert Magnus's typewriter

Dundee knocked again, more loudly. When there was still no answer, a sweat not caused by the heat broke out on his face. Tentatively he tried the knob, sure however that the door was locked. To his surprise it yielded. He entered the room.

Two or three minutes later a white-faced young man staggered out of that room, lurched down the stairs like a drunken man.

"And they sent me to protect her. *Me!*" he groaned.

2

"Sure it's murder?" Lieut. Strawn asked brusquely. Gone was the weary, cynical imbiber of ice-cream sodas, and in his place the keen-eyed manhunter, his nostrils twitching for the scent.

"Strangled—choked to death with her own scarf," Bonnie Dundee answered, grimly. In those eight or ten minutes after his horrible discovery and while he awaited the arrival of his chief, the inexperienced young detective had got hold of his nerves—to a decent extent at least. He had been guilty of a choked voice and tears of rage when he had broken the news to Mrs. Rhodes, who now stood near him in the front hall of the boarding-house.

"You found her, of course? Did you touch anything?" Strawn demanded, motioning for the group of uniformed and plain-clothed policemen to come in from the porch.

"I closed and locked the window, without touching the frame, and locked the door," Dundee answered. "I listened to her heart, too, of course. She's quite dead."

"Will it relieve your feelings any to say 'I told you so'?" Strawn asked gruffly. Then, before his young subordinate could reply, he turned to the landlady. "Mrs. Rhodes, Mr. Dundee is a detective. He came here to investigate Mrs. Hogarth's written claims to the police commissioner that her life and money were in danger. No one but yourself is to know of Mr. Dundee's official status, however. May I depend on you?"

Mrs. Rhodes dabbed at the tears in her eyes, blew her nose, then answered with a dignity that, in other circumstances, might have been comical, because of the fact that her iron-grey hair was rolled on old-fashioned kid curlers and her tall, big-boned body was wrapped in a skimpy kimono of pale blue cotton crêpe, riotous with cherry blossoms.

"I know how to keep a secret," she answered austerely.

"Will you be staying on here then, Mr. Dundee?"

"Certainly. I like my new boarding-house, in spite of what has happened to-night," the young man answered with eager friendliness, which brought fresh tears to the landlady's tragic dark eyes.

"All right, Payne!" Strawn snapped, and a plainclothes detective stepped forward. "I want you to go with Mrs. Rhodes to every boarder's room, arouse them if they are sleeping, and tell them to remain in their rooms until they're called for. If anyone has any information to give about the actual murder—heard or saw anything—bring him or her to me immediately. I'll be in Mrs. Hogarth's room. But leave the examination of the boarders to me . . . Everyone in, Mrs. Rhodes?"

"I'm not sure of Miss Shepherd and Miss Barker," Mrs. Rhodes answered, her voice steadying itself. "My husband is out. He left about eight o'clock and hasn't returned yet. I—don't know where he is. He's nearly always out in the evenings. And Tilda Brown, the chambermaid, who has a room on the third floor, got the evening off to go to a party. She had permission to be out till one o'clock and I'm pretty sure she hasn't come in, yet."

When Detective Payne and Mrs. Rhodes had departed to carry out Strawn's orders, the chief of the homicide squad quickly detailed uniformed men to search the grounds, which occupied nearly half the block, and to watch the house for arrivals or attempted departures from it.

"And keep an eye on the porches and roof." Strawn cautioned, "though whoever did this thing has had ample time to get away, I suppose." He turned to Dundee. "The coroner, Dr. Price, is on his way. Ought to be here any minute now. Better give me the key. We'll go and have a look at the room before Price gets here."

They ascended the stairs, and, paving no attention to the excitement being caused by Payne and Mrs. Rhodes as they aroused boarders on the second floor, Strawn fitted the key in the lock of Mrs. Hogarth's door, taking care not to touch anything but the knob.

"Carraway, our finger-print expert, will be along soon, and we don't want to gum up things for him," Strawn remarked in a low voice, just as the door swung open.

It was a fairly large and very comfortable room, except for the fact that the locked window made it stiflingly hot.

"Afraid the murderer would come back to the scene of his crime?" Strawn asked, as he strode to the window and opened it. A strong breeze, just beginning to blow, eddied the, dotted Swiss curtains.

Dundee flushed, his eyes still averted from the thing in the chair before the desk.

"Partly that, and partly because I didn't want any excited boarder charging in here to see what it was all about," he explained, "but for another reason, too. I—well, I had a queer hunch that the parrot might be murdered, too."

"What?" Strawn ejaculated, incredulous of his young assistant's sanity.

"Well, you see, sir, that's a very remarkable bird. Seems to me to have almost superhuman intelligence. Picks up words more quickly than the average three year-old child. Mrs. Hogarth was awfully proud of Cap'n— showed him off to me with much glee." His voice choked again on the memory.

"And you think the parrot may oblige us with the name and address of her murderer?" Strawn grinned wryly.

"I think," Dundee began slowly, "that Cap'n may repeat the last words the poor old lady ever spoke. If he does, they may be a name or a clue to the identity of the murderer. Of course he has been taught the names of most of the boarders—the old-timers, at least, and if it's one of those names he speaks, it won't help us much. Might mean a lot or nothing, but if he speaks a name or a word she hadn't taught him—"

"Fat chance!" Strawn dismissed the idea, his eyes roving keenly about the room. "Robbery or attempted robbery is pretty evident, isn't it? Trunk open and contents scattered over the floor. Closet door wide and clothes spilling out. Mattress dragged off the bed. Made a pretty thorough job of it, didn't he? Wonder if he found what he was looking for?"

The moment which Dundee had been dreading arrived. With the callousness of long experience, Lieut. Strawn approached the body of the murdered woman. It's great bulk, clad for the sake of coolness, in a thin blue-and-white cotton dress, was slumped in a low-backed armchair. The head, crowned with loosely-pinned, thick white hair, lolled grotesquely to one side, and about the neck, beneath three enormous chins, was tightly tied a black silk scarf, the ends hanging down from the knot at the back.

The body and the chair faced an old-fashioned mahogany desk, the leak of which was lowered. The contents of the pigeon-holes had been scattered widely, some of the pages cluttering the floor about the chair and desk.

"So this is Cap'n, eh?" Strawn asked matter-of-factly, and to Dundee's horror he clucked cheerfully to the bird which cowered on his perch in a low-swung cage not too distant from the dead woman's left arm.

The big green and yellow parrot poked its head through the wire oars of the cage and made an angry effort to reach the detective's wagging finger with its beak.

"Seems pretty much ruffled, doesn't it?" Strawn asked "Several feathers on the floor of the cage. Wonder if he knows his mistress is dead—murdered—and is as sore about it as you are, Dundee?" Without waiting for a reply, Strawn backed away, and stood behind the dead woman's chair, regarding the body intently. "You say that's her own scarf? Pretty hot weather for a scarf, isn't it?"

Dundee joined his superior, glad to put that horrorstricken dead face, with its bulging eyes, out of his sight for awhile. "It's hers, all right. I noticed it this evening, thrown across the back of her chair. By George, Strawn I believe I know what the scarf was used for— before— to-night. As a cover for the parrot's cage, to make it dark for him while the light was still on—"

"Then," Strawn interrupted, "if the cage had already been covered for the night when the murderer entered, and he had snatched it off at the last minute to strangle the old woman with, it's pretty certain Cap'n was asleep when his mistress's last words were uttered—if any. He stood behind her to tie the knot, as you can see. It may be that she never saw her murderer at all, had no intimation that she was not alone until the scarf was thrown around her neck."

"That's right," Dundee admitted, ruefully. "But there's one thing that bothers me, chief. How did the door happen to be unlocked? Norma—Miss Paige—told me Mrs. Hogarth kept it locked, admitted no one until she knew who her visitor was. I myself saw her unlock that door three times this evening, and lock it after each visitor had entered. That rather looks as if her murderer was a member of this household—a person known to her, to whom she unlocked the door . . . Of course," he reasoned aloud, frowning, "the murderer might have wanted us to think just that, and created the impression by unlocking the door before he fled—through the window."

"What's this?" Strawn demanded, returning to the desk and pointing to a thick, green-leather bound book, lying near the edge of the open leaf of the desk.

"Her diary," Dundee answered. "She was just about to write in it this evening when Miss Paige and I came to call on her. She remarked that it had been given her by Cora Barker as a Christmas present—"

There was a knock on the door. Strawn opened it.

"Dr. Price and Mr. Carraway, sir," a uniformed police. man announced.

The coroner and the finger-print expert entered the death chamber.

IV.

1

"OF course, the first thing you're interested in is how long she's been dead," Dr. Price, the coroner, said to Lieut. Strawn. "It's pretty obvious she was strangled. No wound, I suppose?" And he bent over the body of Mrs. Emma Hogarth.

"No sign of one, though we haven't made an examination, of course," Lieut. Strawn answered. "I'd like you to meet Mr. Dundee, doctor. He's a new member of the homicide quad; joined the Force to-day and came here to board."

"Lucky to have him on the scene of the crime. Don't suppose you did it, young feller, to make a good case on which to win promotion?" the coroner chuckled.

Bonnie Dundee flushed, but there was no resentment in his friendly blue eyes. "I feel almost as responsible as if I had killed her, doctor. As a matter of fact, I came here to live to protect her from—just this," and he made a despairing gesture toward the corpse. "I talked with her this evening. Left her alive and as well as usual at about 10:45. When I returned for a private conference at about 12:20—we'd been interrupted by visitors all the evening—I found her dead. So of my own knowledge death took place between 10:45 and 12:10. I say 12:10 instead of 12:20, for it is obvious that the murderer ransacked the room after he had killed her, and it must have taken him at least ten minutes to get the place so completely upset."

"Hmm. You ought to make a good detective, my lad," the doctor remarked, his eyes twinkling. He was an oldish man, about the age of the murdered woman, who must have been between fifty-five and sixty, and his hair was as white as that which crowned the poor, lolling old head. But his dry leanness was in decided contrast to Mrs. Hogarth's vast bulk.

"Heart trouble, high blood pressure, obesity caused by glandular deficiency," Dr. Price diagnosed aloud; "Now, let's see—"

Dundee turned his back while the coroner made further examination of the body. He was thinking of how very much alive the poor woman had been two hours ago, of how her little light-blue eyes had coquetted roguishly with him; of how like a young girl's her face had been—a little smooth face, oddly set in a surrounding of fat, which seemed to have no connection with that face, except as an impertinent frame. And the boy's heart throbbed with pain, and with rage against himself for having let this thing happen to her. She had been so zestful of life, though she had almost lost the use of her great body. What if she had been erratic, a miser, "mischievous" as Daisy Shepherd had expressed it? What if she had created enemies by changing her will so often, had aroused the passion of greed in her fellow-boarders by keeping her money in her room? She had committed no crime, she had meant to reward kindness . . .

And that thought brought Bonnie Dundee crashing against a realisation he had been keeping at bay since he had said so glibly: "Of my own knowledge, death took place between 10:45 and 12:10." The person who would benefit most by Mrs. Hogarth's death, provided she had not been robbed, was Norma Paige. And Norma Paige and Walter Styles had been running to call upon Mrs. Hogarth at ten minutes to eleven. But, of course, Norma knew nothing of this terrible thing! Not lovely, soft, sweet Norma, with her eyes like wood violets.

Unconsciously, Dundee had been watching the swift, efficient work of the finger-print expert, directed by Lieut. Strawn. Now Dr. Price's voice cut into his miserable thoughts and fears:

"Well, Strawn, as near as I can tell you now, she's been dead about an hour. Let's see—" and he consulted his watch—"it's now 12:59. I figure that death took place between 11:45 and 12. Of course, it might have been a bit earlier—say 11:30, but I think not, judging from the—"

Dundee spun on his heel and clapped his hands to his ears. He was still too young and too new at this sort of thing to endure a recital of the pathological findings of the cheerfully interested doctor. If he had not known Mrs. Hogarth, had not seen her laughing and joking and showing off her parrot—

"All right, Dr. Price. And thank you. You can take her away now. By the way, was her death a quick one, or is there any possibility that she lived awhile, seeing her murderer at work robbing her?"

"I'm fairly sure she died almost instantly," Dr. Price answered. "If I'm not badly mistaken, I'll find she had fatty degeneration of the heart—"

"She told us so," Strawn interrupted.

"I thought so. In that case, the fright alone was almost enough to finish her. I doubt that she even screamed, or was capable of doing so. And the knot is a pretty neat affair. Unfortunately for you, it's a perfectly ordinary double knot, the kind any man or woman could tie. Now if it had been a complicated sailor's knot—Well, I'll get the boys. They're waiting below with the morgue ambulance."

It was while the body was being removed by the white-clad ambulance attendants that Dundee, his eyes desperately roving to avoid the horrible event that was taking place, discovered the dead woman's keys. He caught a glimmer of reflected light beside the scattered papers near the desk, stooped and arose with a broken silver chain, to which were fastened, by means of a little ring, three keys of varying sizes and shapes.

"Don't touch them till they can be finger-printed," Strawn cautioned, striding hastily to his side. "That round key is for the desk, I suppose; the flat one for the trunk, and this little gold one for—what?"

"The diary, I imagine. It has a lock clasp on it," Dundee answered.

"Well, if she kept it locked, it isn't locked now," Strawn discovered, lifting the top cover of the green, leather-bound book. "Have you finished with this book, Carraway?"

The finger-print expert came toward them. "That? Oh, it's no use bothering with it! That pebbly leather wouldn't give us a recognisable print. Of course the inside pages would—"

"May I?" Dundee asked, and opened the book, turning the green-ink written pages swiftly, by the very tip-end of them, to the page with the printed date, "Saturday, June 29." He uttered an exclamation: "Look! She was writing it in this evening, after all! Here is the entry—" But he stopped, the words dying away in his throat as his quick eyes took in the damning words which formed the last paragraph of the day's entry.

"Let me see!" Strawn commanded, bending over the

"As hot to-day as my future home will be; that is, if I go where some of my good friends expect me to," Mrs. Hogarth had written, with a grim humour that was now horrible. *"The moths and light midges are a nuisance. If that useless Dusty doesn't put my screen in Monday, I'm going to shake his teeth down his throat. Something very strange about pulling off this job, lazy as he is. I more than half believe E.S. or C.B. has bribed him to leave my window unscreened. It's been five years since I've had such a strong presentiment of disaster as I've had to-day. Wrote the police commissioner to send a plain-clothes detective. I suppose he will laugh at me and let me die like a—"*

The first part of the day's entry ended here, and undoubtedly had been written before the visit of Norma Paige and Bonnie Dundee. But it was the second page, marked "Later," which had made Dundee's heart lunge sickeningly.

"More trouble!" Mrs. Hogarth had written, waveringly as if her hand had been trembling with rage or weariness. *"Norma has defied me and got herself engaged to that fortune-hunter, Walter Styles. Told her I was going to change my will to-morrow. But oh, I don't know! I'm sick of meddling with other people's lives. I've got a lot of fun and excitement out of it, but now I wish I had never started the whole foolish business. The police aren't such fools as I thought them. They sent—"*

The entry stopped abruptly on the incomplete sentence. Had she been interrupted by a knock on her door, or had her murderer entered noiselessly from the porch, the low, unscreened window, and cut short the woman's last communication to her diary and her life, the same time?

"But why should he close the book?" Dundee puzzled aloud. "And here is her fountain-pen, on the desk, not on the floor, where it would probably have dropped if had been startled by an attack."

"Fine points, son," Strawn grinned. "But what I'm interested in is having a chat with Mr. Emil Sevier with Mr. 'Dusty' Rhodes. Step outside and tell Wilkins want him."

Dundee obeyed, finding the detective and Mrs. Rhodes talking together in low voices at the head of the stairs. A uniformed policeman was patrolling the hall to see that no boarder made a bolt for the stairs. All doors were closed, but Dundee could imagine what excitement and terror lurked in each of those rooms.

"Wilkins," Strawn began, "I want you to get a list of all of 'Dusty' Rhodes's usual haunts from his wife, and send a couple of men out to try to round him up. Quick!"

"And Sevier?" Dundee dared question his chief.

"Oh, I set the machinery in motion to drag him in before I left Headquarters," Strawn answered. "As Mrs. Hogarth admitted, the police are not such fools as some people think. The boys ought to be on his trail, by this time. . . . And now, Dundee, I want you to hide yourself behind that screen—" and he pointed to a green burlap screen of three sections that concealed the stationary wash basin—" and listen in on the boarders' stories. Might as well make notes, too. Who has the room next door?" and he pointed toward the west side of the house. "Henry Dowd? All right, we'll have him in first."

2

"Mr. Dowd, sir," a uniformed policeman announced to Lieut. Strawn.

"Just a minute, Boyle. Is Payne around?"

"Talking to Mrs Rhodes in the hall, sir."

"Send him in," Strawn ordered curtly. "I'll see Dowd in a minute."

When Payne, the plain-clothes detective who had notified the boarders of Mrs. Hogarth's death, appeared, Strawn gave him his instructions in a low, rapid voice:

"I'm going to be questioning the boarders, Payne, and I want you to search each room while its occupant is in here with me. I've got a blanket search warrant that will cover the case technically. Do a thorough job— wastebaskets, trunks, desks, closets, everything. Use my bunch of skeleton keys. If you find anything you can't open, let me know and we'll ask the owner to produce the key. The murdered woman was robbed, apparently, and the murderer found what he was looking for. She was supposed to have a pretty big wad of cash hidden in this room, and if she did have, it's gone. Look for it. Did she say anything to you about Liberty bonds, stocks, or any other kind of negotiable paper, Dundee?" he called to the young detective stationed behind the wash basin screen.

"No, chief. She used the word 'money 'several times, but didn't mention any stocks or bonds," Dundee answered.

"All right, Payne. Look for money, and if you find any, besides petty cash, let me know, but don't touch it— Now, tell Boyle to bring Dowd in."

With Mrs. Hogarth's tablet of cheap, lined writing-paper on his knee and a pencil poised, Bonnie Dundee watched through one of the joinings of the three-panel screen as Henry Dowd was ushered into the room. To the diffidence which had characterised this very commonplace-looking man of near middle-age, when Dundee had observed him at the dinner-table that evening, was now added a mild, almost apologetic mixture of apprehension and excitement. He came in dabbing at his forehead with a fresh white handkerchief, and, as Strawn addressed his first question, took off his *pince-nez* and began to polish the lenses nervously.

"Well, Dowd, you know what's happened here to-night. That's your room next door, isn't it? Did you hear or see anything to-night that might throw light on the tragedy?" Strawn asked briskly.

The mild, pale grey eyes blinked twice, before Henry Dowd carefully adjusted the glasses upon his nose. "No, sir," he answered. "That is, nothing to speak of—"

"Then perhaps you'd better speak of it," Strawy snapped.

"Well, sir, I was asleep—"

"When did you go to bed?"

"About ten o'clock, as usual. I'm not much on the social life, not a very good mixer," Henry Dowd explained carefully, and Dundee jotted his words down in hand. "I came up to my room about nine, after sitting on the front porch after supper—dinner, they call it here. I puttered around the room for awhile, then took a bath and went to bed. About ten, that was. I read a magazine, till I fell asleep, with my light burning, and didn't wake up till some time later—"

"And what woke you?" Strawn demanded, impatiently.

"It was that bird squawking, or at least, that's what it sounded like," Dowd answered, painstakingly, his ayes glancing toward the parrot.

"Was the bird talking?"

"No, just squawking, as if it were sore about something." Dowd answered. "I've heard it a good many times, though this is the first time I've ever laid eyes on it. I didn't hear anything else, and didn't think anything of it anyway, so I turned out my light and went right back to sleep. I was hardly what you'd call real awake—just roused up enough to realise I'd left my light on. It hangs over the head of my bed and I just reached up and turned it off. That's all I heard, sir, and I didn't see anything."

"Didn't you hear anything before you went to sleep?" Strawn probed, remembering Dundee's account of Mrs. Hogarth's several visitors that evening.

"In here, you mean?" Dowd asked meticulously. "Well, I heard people laughing and talking, and I heard the parrot talking, too, but I didn't pay any attention. I was reading, and wasn't interested anyway—"

"How well did you know Mrs. Hogarth?" Strawn demanded suddenly.

"Why, I didn't know her at all," Dowd answered. "I'd never met Mrs. Hogarth, and I only happened to see her once, going down the hall toward the bathroom. I didn't see her face then—just her back, but I knew who it was, because I'd heard the folks downstairs describe her as—well, pretty fat, sir."

"You also heard the folks downstairs say that Mrs. Hogarth had a lot of money hidden in her room, didn't you, Dowd?" Strawn asked levelly.

Dowd flushed, took off his glasses again and wiped them nervously before replying: "Yes, I heard something to that effect, though I wasn't interested—"

"So money doesn't interest you, Dowd?" Strawn asked urbanely. "You must be quite flush yourself, then. By the way, what do you do?"

Dundee, watching intently from his hiding-place, saw Henry Dowd's thin, commonplace face go suddenly very pale. The hand which dabbed the handkerchief upon his forehead, higher than nature had intended it to be, because baldness had begun to attack the limp, nondescript straight hair, shook visibly. Dundee dropped his eyes to his notes. He had no relish for the third degree, no matter how mildly it was administered.

"I—the fact is," Henry Dowd confessed haltingly, "I'm—well, looking for an opening. I'm a—salesman."

"What line?" Strawn snapped.

"Well, in my time I've sold a good many things, first and last—vacuum cleaners, aluminum ware, brushes school children's encyclopedia—"

"House to house canvasser, eh?'" There was unveiled contempt in the detective chief's voice "How long you been here—looking for an opening?'

"I arrived in Hamilton a week ago to-day," Dowd answered humbly. "I—haven't yet formed a—connection here—"

"And yet you weren't at all interested in the story Mrs. Hogarth's hoard, hidden in the very room next to yours?" Strawn interrupted;

"No, sir, I wasn't. I had my own troubles to think about—"

"Troubles?" Strawn pounced.

The harassed man went even paler. "Being out of a job in the middle of the summer, and a stranger in town," he explained with a little flash of spirit.

"By the way, Dowd, where did you come from?"

Again the handkerchief dabbed at a moist brow. There was an appreciable pause before Henry Dowd answered.

"Des Moines, Iowa. I—represented a small manufacturing concern, known as The Housewife's Friend Corporation. They made up a little kit of kitchen tools, including at implement that could pare potatoes and apples and cut them in fancy shapes—"

"Where are they located?"

"Nowhere, now," Dowd answered wearily. "The company failed, and I was out of work for several weeks, then I came to Hamilton, because I'd heard times were good here"

"Where did you live in Des Moines?" Strawn interrupted impatiently.

"At—at No. — Mondamin Avenue," Dowd replied; with obvious reluctance.

Strawn regarded the badgered man for a long minute through keen, narrowed grey eyes. Then, abruptly: "You're sure you heard nothing but the squawking the parrot, Dowd? No footsteps, no voices, no sounds objects being thrown about?"

"I didn't hear a thing but the parrot,' 'Dowd replied obstinately.

"Sure it was the parrot?"

"I thought so at the time. I'd heard if squawk before,' Dowd answered.

"Could the noise you heard have been Mrs. Hogarth trying to scream for help?" Strawn suggested.

"It sounded like the parrot to me," Dowd insisted, sullenly.

"What time was this?"

"I don't know. I didn't look at my watch. As I said, I just roused up enough to realise I'd left my light burning, and to reach up and turn it off. I was asleep again almost instantly, I guess, and didn't know anything else till a man knocked at my door and told me to get up, that Mrs. Hogarth had been murdered."

"All right, Dowd. You'll be wanted for the inquest, of course, so don't leave Hamilton to look elsewhere for work. Do you plan to stay on here in this house?"

"Why, yes. My board is paid up for this coming week," Dowd answered unhesitatingly. "I can't afford to lose the money, and since I didn't personally know Mrs. Hogarth—"

"All right, Dowd. You'll be wanted for the inquest."

As Dowd left the room, Detective Payne entered. "Nothing in that bird's room, chief, that looks like a miser's hoard, and judging from his belongings—what there is of them—he's pretty hard up."

"O.K., Payne. Tell Boyle to bring in the Barker woman. And be sure you make a good job of searching her room while she's in here—" There was a knock on the door. "Come in!"

"Telephone for you, sir," Mrs. Rhodes announced.

V.

BONNIE DUNDEE did not have to wait long for the return of his chief. Strawn entered, closed the door, and joined his subordinate behind the screen.

"That was Burlew on the phone—one of the two boys I detailed to check up on Emil Sevier, as soon as I got your message that the old lady was murdered. Burlew says Sevier hung around the Little Queen—that's the movie theatre where he played the fiddle before he was fired Friday, and where Cora Barker plays the piano, you know—until half-past ten or, eleven. The movie manager himself says so. Says he was telling everybody good-bye, and making a nuisance of himself generally. Made a point of telling the manager he was leaving town on the one o'clock train, to look for work in Chicago."

"Natural enough," Dundee commented. "And did he take the train?"

"He took it all right," Strawn assured him triumphantly, "Ran to catch it. Didn't have a hat on. Didn't buy a ticket. Just stopped in the station long enough to get his suit-case from the parcel room, where he had checked it about half-past eight. Burlew had such a good description of Sevier from the theatre manager that he had no trouble striking his trail at the station. Had barely time to make his train. Ran for it, as I said."

"After all, it's not exactly criminal to run for a train," Dundee smiled. "I've been guilty of it myself. Perhaps he bought his ticket from the day ticket agent, since he had been planning to go to Chicago. He would hardly wait till the last minute to get a berth—"

Strawn chuckled. "Right you are, boy. And working on that supposition, I've ordered a wire to be sent to the Pullman and railroad conductors of the train, giving a full description of Sevier. If he's on that train, he'll be yanked off at Greenville, just inside the state line, and brought back here for questioning."

"Not much to go on yet, is there?" Dundee asked pleasantly.

"Look-here, Dundee!" Strawn frowned. "I'm acting on your tip from the old lady, remember! It was you who took her suspicions so seriously. If she saw Sevier prowling around in her room one night, it looks to me that he's our best bet for this particular night. And she had enough on him to have Mrs. Rhodes kick him out of here—"

"Right!" Dundee agreed, his blue eyes smiling brilliantly, disarmingly. "What else did Burlew dig up?"

"He found no trace of our man between half-past ten or a quarter to eleven, when he left the theatre, and one o'clock, when he caught his train by the skin of his teeth. He brushed past the guard at the station gates, by the way, without showing his tickets, if he had any. Swung aboard the day coach after the train was in motion. Burlew talked to his landlady, who runs a cheap boarding-house over on Centre Street, where he lived after Mrs. Rhodes kicked him out of here. The woman says he paid his first week's board; but left owing her for three days. She insisted on keeping his violin, knowing it was his most cherished possession. He didn't seem to mind, she says; told her he'd be flush by Monday, and send her a money order for what he owed her. He was to send his new address then, too. She says he packed his suit-case after supper and left, and that she didn't see or hear from him again. Says he was wearing a straw hat when he left, but he was hatless when he ran for his train—"

Lieut. Strawn was interrupted by a knock on the door. He stepped from behind the screen and called "Come in!"

Patrolman Boyle thrust in his head. "Detective Green, sir, and a Dr. Weeks."

The plain-clothes detective and the doctor, a completely bald, roly poly little man of about fifty, entered the room at Strawn's invitation.

"This is Dr. Weeks, Lieutenant Strawn," Green announced, and waited gravely while the police lieutenant and the doctor shook hands. "Dr. Weeks lives in the first house west of this one. Carrying out your orders to question the residents of the block, I roused Mrs. Weeks at about one o'clock. She said she had not seen anyone leaving these grounds, as she'd been in bed since eleven, but she told me the doctor had had a call from a patient about midnight, and that he might possibly have observed something as he left the house, but that he was still out on the call. When I saw his car drive in a few minutes ago, I asked him a few questions, and—"

"All right, Green. Good work!" Strawn cut him short.

"Now let Dr. Weeks tell me his story. I presume you did observe something out of the ordinary, doctor?"

The Doctor began, carefully accurate as to details "The call came at exactly twelve ten, or rather, it was that time when I looked at my watch after I hung up the receiver. I was still dressed, or half-dressed, as I had not gone to bed—too hot to sleep. I went into the office to get in bag, spent a couple of minutes or so putting in some medicines and instruments I would need on the case, got into my hat and coat, and went out the back way to the garage."

"Just a minute, doctor," Strawn interrupted, glancing significantly toward the screen, as a signal to Dundee to make full notes on the doctor's story—an unnecessary reminder, as his pencil was flying. "Just where is your garage, in relation to the Rhodes place?"

"My garage is on the east corner of my lot, joining the west corner of the Rhodes House grounds, but their garage is about a hundred feet east of mine. There is, as you've perhaps observed, a thick high hedge along the Rhodes driveway, clear to the garage."

"Thank you, doctor. Now will you tell me exactly what you saw?"

The doctor seemed quite willing. "I remember glancing up toward the Rhodes House, for no particular reason, as I hurried down my driveway toward the garage. I didn't see anyone then, but when I reached my back fence, which has wide double gates, through which I often drive my car into the alley, to save a block when my call is on the north side of town, I heard running footsteps pass me on the other side of the fence."

"Then you didn't actually see anyone?" Strawn could not conceal his keen disappointment.

"But I did!" the doctor retorted good-naturedly. "I swung open the gates—I don't keep them locked—and stepped out into the alley, curious to see who was running away from my neighbourhood so fast. Just then a car on Tenth Street—the next north-and-south street to the west of my house, you know—turned into the alley throwing the headlights full on the running man. In a moment the car had backed up and gone on—had either used the alley to make a turn, or the owner had mistaken the alley for a street he was looking for, I don't know, which. At any rate, I saw the big man's figure quite cleary though he ducked and flung up his hat, which he was carrying as if to shield himself from being recognised."

"And did you recognise him?" Strawn asked quickly.

"His back was turned toward me, as I said," the doctor answered, "but I got a vivid impression of thick, longish dark hair before he ducked and shielded his face with the hat."

"A straw hat?" Strawn demanded.

"Why, yes, but in this weather most of us are wearing straw hats," the doctor pointed out. "As for his body, I should say he was of medium height, and of slender build. I think he was wearing a light suit, either light tan or grey, but I confess I paid little attention to his clothes, since I was trying to identify him by other means. I can't be sure that I'd know him again, or that I had ever seen him before, though at the time I thought his back and head seemed vaguely familiar."

"Dr. Weeks, since you're a next-door neighbour, did you personally know any of Mrs. Rhodes's boarders?"

"Yes, to a limited extent. I'm usually called when one of them is ill. In fact, I have attended poor Mrs. Hogarth off and on for the past three or four years for heart attacks. She should have had more frequent attention, and careful supervision of diet, etc., but she protested that she could not afford a doctor. In fact, she was so indignant at Mrs. Rhodes for calling me in the first time that thereafter I never sent Mrs. Hogarth a bill—just charged it up to neighbourly kindness."

"Did you know that Mrs. Hogarth was reputed to be a miser, that she had a hoard of money hidden in her room?" Strawn asked.

"I've heard something of the sort—from my wife," the doctor smiled. "I imagine everyone in the neighbourhood has heard the story. Since it is a characteristic of misers to protest that they can't afford even the necessities of life, I didn't press the matter of my bill, though she did pay the first one. It was only five dollars."

"Did you ever meet a boarder here by the name of Sevier—Emil Sexier?" Strawn asked then.

"Sevier? No, I think not."

"Sevier boarded here for about two months, I believe," Strawn explained. "He was evicted ten days ago, partly on Mrs. Hogarth's complaints that he was trying to rob her, and partly because of an unpaid board bill. Sevier is a rather short, thin young man, very dark-skinned, with a long jaw, pointed chin, and big, aquiline nose. Black eyes, of course. Do you remember seeing him on one your visits, or about the place?"

The doctor shook his head. "Very possibly, but I have no distinct recollection of him. Boarders come and go here, and I really pay little attention. And I am afraid I could not positively identify the man I saw tonight."

"Did you continue to watch the man in the alley doctor?"

"Yes, I watched him until he disappeared," Dr. Week answered. "As soon as the car had backed out of the alley, the man straightened up, and ran faster than ever out of the alley into Tenth Street."

"In the direction the car had taken?" Strawn asked with sudden inspiration. "Perhaps that car, turning briefly into the alley and flashing its headlights, had been prearranged signal—"

"No. The opposite direction—towards Maple Avenue, the street just north of Chestnut, you know. The car turned toward Chestnut."

"Could you distinguish the make of the car or it occupants?"

"No—neither. In fact, I paid no attention to the car. I was watching the man. If I had had my wits about me and had not been in such a hurry to make my call—pretty sick patient, by the way—I suppose I should have challenged the man, or have reported the matter to the police. Or if I had known the man to be a former boarder, an evicted one, I should, of course, have notified Mrs. Rhodes of his strange behaviour. I have a high regard for Mrs. Rhodes—"

"I'm sure you have, doctor," Strawn interrupted, his voice very cordial. "And thank you very much. You've helped us a great deal. You'll be needed for the inquest of course. By the way, doctor, you say you attended Mrs. Hogarth occasionally during the past three or four years. In your opinion, was she—well, mentally normal?"

The doctor chuckled, then remembered he was in room where murder had been committed a very short time before, and looked embarrassed. "One of the shrewder women I've ever met, Lieutenant Strawn. And the most close-mouthed. She never referred in any way to her past life, even refused to give me the name of any doctor who had previously attended her. She had had a serious major operation—abdominal—and I wanted to write her surgeon and ask him a few questions as to what condition he had found, to guide me in treating the old lady. But she absolutely refused to give me any information whatever. A queer woman, but not a crazy woman. I'm sure of that, Lieutenant Strawn."

When the doctor left the room, Strawn spoke briefly to Carraway, the finger-print expert, who was packing his paraphernalia preparatory to leaving.

"Afraid this bunch of prints I've picked up won't help you much, Strawn," Carraway answered. "The murderer was a wise guy—used gloves, or a handkerchief. No prints at all on the window-frame; wiped clean. And none on the trunk lock or the desk drawers. The chambermaid must have dusted in here with an oiled rag sometime Saturday, for the desk was clean even of the old lady's finger-prints—except the top of it, of course. I took her finger-prints first thing, and they match with those found on the desk. No prints on the keys, either. Found a number of prints on the door, inside and out, but since the old lady had a flock of visitors earlier in the evening, I don't think they'll help you much. If the murderer came in by that door, I'll wager he had his wits about him and didn't leave his calling card, since he was so careful everywhere else. But I'll develop the bunch and let you have them for what they're worth."

When Carraway had left, Strawn joined Dundee behind the screen.

"Well, boy, I'm afraid this case is going to be too simple for your tastes," the older detective commiserated, a gleam of triumphant mirth in his grey eyes.

Dundee grinned amiably, then remarked, very casually: "I wonder why it took Sevier—if it was Sevier the doctor saw—so long to *run* from here to the station? He was still running when he caught his train, you know. How far is it from the Rhodes House to the Union Station?"

Strawn scowled. "As a matter of fact, it's only about ten blocks. But that doesn't prove anything, Dundee.

Sevier must have known we'd get on his trail, because of the old lady's complaints against him. He wouldn't board a train with the swag on him. My idea is that he met a fence somewhere, who undertook to take care of the stuff for him until the police were tired of watching him, or released him on insufficient evidence. Either that or he hid it somewhere, and then barely had time to make the train he had advertised he was going to take. No flies on Sevier," he added admiringly. "As a matter of cold fact, unless we get more on him than we now have we shan't be able to get a conviction. If we could find that car— Whoever swung his lights full on a running man in an alley is going to have a pretty good picture of that man fixed in his mind. Guess I'd better get the papers to help me. Mrs. Rhodes is holding some reporters at bay downstairs now."

It was more than fifteen minutes before Lieut. Strawn returned from his session with the reporters. Dundee had begun to feel sorry for his fellow-boarders, all of whom, with the exception of Henry Dowd, were still being held in their rooms to await questioning.

"Well that's that!" Strawn commented with satisfaction. "I gave the newspaper boys the low-down on our suspicions of Sevier, but told them to soft-pedal, just to say that Sevier was wanted for questioning. They ate up the doctor's story of the running man and the car, and are going to ask the driver of the car to come forward, like a good citizen, and tell anything he knows. But by the time the papers are on the streets to-morrow morning I hope to have a confession from Sevier . . . Say young feller-me-lad, what are you grinning about?" he broke, off to demand half-angrily.

"I was just thinking," Dundee confessed, his blue eyes twinkling, "how in my ignorance and inexperience I should have gone about this case."

The careful wording did not deceive Strawn. He flushed, then shrugged. "All right! Spill it! How would you have gone about this case?"

"I'm afraid I should have made an awful lot of work for myself and the police department," Dundee admitted, ruefully. "I should have begun on the supposition that anyone who lived in this house, or who had ever lived in it, or had even taken a meal in it, and had heard the story of a miser with a hidden hoard in her room, was a possible suspect. Greed, you know, is such a universal passion. I believe it is responsible for more crimes than any other motive, isn't it?"

"Well?" Strawn snorted.

"Of course, I realise that things look bad for Sevier—provided anyone comes forward to identify him as the man running down the alley," Dundee went on, with his disarming smile. *"But I can't help remembering, lieutenant, that everyone in this house knew Emil Sevier had been evicted on Mrs. Hogarik's complaints, that Sevier had just been fired and therefore would be leaving town to look elsewhere to work, and that the police would think of him first as the murderer!"*

Strawn looked a little startled at the quiet intensity of his new subordinate's last sentence, but he recovered himself quickly and retorted with amused condescension:

"You didn't think I was through with my investigation, did you, son? But I take things as they come, and Sevier happened to come first. I'll have that Barker woman in now, since she has the room next door—"

"And I also can't help remembering,' Dundee went on, with that same quiet, emphasis, *"that everyone in this house knew that Mrs. Hogarth's reinforced window screen would be installed Monday, making access to her room from the porch impossible.* Unless Cora Barker or someone else has been keeping him informed, Sevier could not have known that the screen was not already in place. Mrs. Hogarth told me she had given Dusty Rhodes the money to buy materials for it nearly a month ago. Also I heard Mrs. Rhodes say, in the presence of all the boarders and 'mealers,' that all screens, including Mrs.

Hogarth's, would be installed Monday. They are the kind that push up and down, like windows. I noticed the grooves for them in my own window."

"Well?" Strawn barked, as Dundee paused.

The boy shrugged slightly. "It just occurred to me that if the murderer was an inmate of the house, he—or she—would want to do this little job of robbing and murdering *before* those screens were installed. As you know, lieutenant, all the rooms on the front and the east side of this floor have windows opening directly upon the upstairs porch. Without screens on those windows, any boarder, on this floor could step out of a window, creep along the porch to Mrs. Hogarth's window, enter noiselessly, since the windows are low, and steal up on the old lady from behind. Once the screens were in, however, the raising of one of the screens might have attracted attention—slight though the noise would be. . . . By the way, I said *all* the roomers on this floor, because those having rooms on the west side of the house, which has no porch, could gain access to the roof merely by walking across the hall, which is T-shaped, you know, with a window opening directly upon the porch. Naturally a roomer on the third floor could have crept down the stairs to this hall, stepped over the hall window-sill, sneaked past Cora Barker's room and on to Mrs. Hogarth's on the front porch. In fact, this house, without screens, is a ideally constructed place, from a robber's viewpoint. If he doesn't care to board here, he can climb the rose trellis on the west end of the front porch, saunter along that porch and enter any room that strikes his fancy."

"Which is exactly what Emil Sevier did," Strawr caught him up stubbornly. "But don't think I'm going to let that 'preconceived idea' of mine, as the lawyer put it, keep me from catching a new one if it comes along. The papers used to call me 'Third Degree' Strawn—not that I deserved such a harsh title, of course," he grinned.

He strode to the door. "Boyle! Bring in Miss Barker and tell Payne to follow orders."

A minute later, Cora Barker, escorted by the patrol man, appeared in the doorway. Through the screen Dundee could see her face, and he almost betrayed his presence by uttering a strangled exclamation of pity.

VI.

1

THE Cora Barker whom Bonnie Dundee had met at dinner that evening had been a woman possessed of a queer sort of beauty, exotic and largely artificial though that beauty was. A woman gallantly holding age at bay, convincing herself and almost convincing her world that she was a charming girl of twenty-five or twenty-eight, instead of a defeated, frustrated, heart-hungry woman of near forty. Then it was only her thin, dry-skinned hands which had betrayed her age, if one were so foolish as to look at them rather than into her great, shining black eyes—eyes like those of a younger girl trembling with first love, when they turned upon Bert Magnus, the amateur scenario-writer.

But the face of the woman who hesitated at the door of the room where murder had been committed was a ravaged thing, incredibly old. The eyes were like burned holes in a yellow blanket. Her right hand was pressed hard against her heart; the left, freshly bandaged, hung at her side. Small wonder that Bonnie Dundee's sympathetic, susceptible young heart was wrenched with pity, so that he almost betrayed his presence behind the screen.

"You're Miss Barker?" Strawn asked briskly, when he had dismissed Patrolman Boyle and had waved the woman to a chair close to the dead woman's desk, at which he himself was seated.

"Cora Barker," she answered, her bluish lips trying to jerk a smile.

"You occupy the room next to this?"

"Yes, sir, the east corner room."

"You know, of course, that Mrs. Hogarth was murdered to-night?" Strawn was brutally direct.

"A man—a detective, I suppose he was—knocked at my, door and told me so," Cora answered unsteadily.

"And that was the first you knew of it?"

Why—of course I—" she gasped, her burned-out eyes dilating to enormous size,

"Where were you this evening, Miss Barker, between eleven and 12:15?"

"I was at the Little Queen Theatre from eleven til twelve, and then—"

"The movie closes at eleven, doesn't it?" Strawn interrupted.

"The last show is over at eleven—yes," Cora answered," her voice growing more steady. "I play the piano there, and I had to stay after the show to go over the score of the music for Sunday's picture with the new violinist, Mr. Frankel. We finished at half-past eleven, and then I waited in the lobby or on the sidewalk in front of the theatre until twelve—"

"'Why?"

"I was waiting for Mr. Magnus—Mr. Herbert S. Magnus, one of the boarders here," Cora replied, her voice quivering on the name. "He had promised to call for me after theatre-closing to take me out to supper and walk home with me."

"And when did he come—twelve o'clock?" Strawn prodded.

The thin shoulders shrugged and then sagged wearily. "He—didn't come," she admitted. "He had promised to be there about half-past eleven, and I waited till twelve. I—I might have waited longer, but the theatre manager, Mr. Hartman, who had been in his office till then, came out and made some joke about—about my being 'stood up,' and I—I came on home. Mr. Hartman and I walked about a block together, to where his car was parked on Fourth and Grand. He offered to drive me home, but since it was only a few blocks I decided to walk."

Dundee, making swift notes on the dead woman's tablet, reflected pityingly that Cora Barker had been in no mood for her employer's joking references to her missing beau.

"What time was it when you got home?" Strawn asked.

"It's only six blocks from here to the theatre, so it couldn't have been later than 12:10," Cora answered. "I didn't look at my, watch after I left the theatre—"

"Coming toward the house and up the front walk, did you see anyone?"

"No, no one at all. I glanced up at the house and saw that Mrs. Hogarth's light was on, but I thought nothing of it. She often sits up—I mean—" and her voice choked. "often *sat* up quite late!"

"Did you notice any other lights on?"

"Upstairs, you mean?" Cora frowned in concentration "No. Mr. Dowd's window was dark, I believe, but I did not particularly notice. Yes, I'm quite sure there was no light in his room. My own window was dark, of course, and I couldn't see any others. The hall light was on downstairs, and the front door was still unlocked. I didn't see anyone downstairs as I came in, or upstairs either. I went straight to my room, and—"

"Did you hear any sounds at all from Mrs. Hogarth's room?"

"No, nothing!"

"Or any sound on the upstairs porch?"

"No, no noise of any kind."

"Did you look out of your windows—either or both of them?"

"No. I just pulled down the shades to undress. When I took off my dress—it's a new one—I saw that the pleats in the skirt had been badly mashed, and I decided to press it, so I put on my kimono and connected up a little electric iron I have—"

"Rather late for a job like that, wasn't it? To-morrow, or rather, to-day, being Sunday?" Strawn suggested, his eyes narrowing upon her.

Dundee saw an ugly dull flush creep over the ghastly pallor of Cora Barker's face. "Yes, it was late, but I—well, you see, Mrs. Rhodes doesn't like us to use electric irons, and if I had waited till Sunday morning she might have— come into my room while I was pressing the dress, and—"

"I see," Strawn permitted himself a brief, twisted smile. "And then?"

"I—burnt my hand, and had to stop and dress it. I keep a tube of salve in my room for burns and sunburn. I was pressing the dress when I heard someone knock on Mrs. Hogarth's door. I didn't look to see who it was, but I do remember thinking it odd that I didn't hear Mrs. Hogarth call out, 'Who is it?' as she always does—did. Then I heard her door open, and a few minutes later whoever it was that had entered came out and went downstairs. The house was still, and I could hear the footsteps. I got the impression somehow that something was wrong, but I didn't investigate, and really knew nothing about it all until the man knocked at my door and told me that—that Mrs. Hogarth was dead and that I was to wait there until I was called for—for questioning."

"I see," Strawn commented thoughtfully, and Dundee, through the joining of the screen panels, saw Cora Barker draw a deep, quivering breath of relief that her ordeal was over. But it wasn't. . . . "Now, Miss Barker, you say you saw no one or heard nothing when you came upstairs—"

"No, I didn't say that exactly," Cora interrupted. " I didn't see anyone, but I heard Bert's—I mean, Mr. Magnus's typewriter. His room is across the hall from mine, you know."

"And you didn't stop to speak to him, to ask him why he had failed to keep his appointment with you?"

The woman's flush deepened to dull crimson. "No, I— well, I was pretty angry with him, and I have my pride—"

"You are in love with Mr. Magnus, Miss Barker?" Strawn asked bluntly.

"You have no right to ask me that! "she flashed, and the dead eyes burned briefly with an angry blaze.

"I see," Strawn drawled. "I take it, then, that you are no longer engaged to Emil Sevier?"

"Engaged to Emil Sevier?" Cora echoed. "I was never engaged to Emil Sevier! And we are no longer even friends—"

"But it was you who suggested that he come here to board, wasn't it, Miss Barker?"

"I worked with him at the Little Queen Theatre. He was violinist and I was pianist. He asked me if I could recommend this as a boarding-place, and I did, of course. We were together a good deal, because of our work and because we both love music, but—"

"You saw Sevier to-night?" Strawn cut in sharply.

Dundee saw that Cora was about to lie, then changed her mind. She flung up her head defiantly, and again her cheeks were yellow. "He stopped at my piano to tell me good-bye. He said he was going to Chicago on the one o'clock train, to look for a new job."

"Isn't it true, Miss Barker, that Sevier asked you to do him a little favour before he left?" Strawn's voice was lazily pleasant, almost coaxing.

"A favour?" Cora echoed, her eyes dilating. "Wha—"

"I mean," Strawn said very slowly and distinctly, "that Sevier asked you to help him rob Mrs. Emma Hogarth; that he gave you your final instructions."

Cora Barker sprang to her feet. "That's not true! That's a lie, I tell you—"

"You don't mean to tell me, Miss Barker, that you didn't know Emil Sevier had planned, even attempted, to rob Mrs. Hogarth?" Strawn smiled.

"I know Mrs. Hogarth made some such crazy charge against him," Cora panted, backing away from the detective, "but—she—she was always getting some crazy idea into her head—"

"And one of those crazy ideas was that she would be murdered for her money," Lieut. Strawn pointed out quietly. "Another of her 'crazy ideas' was to name you in her will, and then later to change that will Miss Barker, cutting you off without a penny. Will you tell me why?"

Again that blaze of anger in Cora Barker's burned-out eyes. "It's none of your business!" she choked, her thin hand at her throat. Then her shoulders sagged. "I'm— sorry. I suppose everything connected with Mrs. Hogarth is your business now," she conceded wearily. "Mrs. Hogarth made a new will just after Christmas, cutting Daisy Shepherd off, and naming me, for no better reason than that I had given her, as a Christmas gift, a rather nicely-bound diary. I—had no ulterior motive. I was not trying to cut Daisy out. But Daisy didn't give Mrs. Hogarth a present, said something about being tired of pampering the old lady. So I was Mrs. Hogarth's heiress until—sometime in May, I believe it was, when she became fond of Walter Styles, a new boarder. She was tired of me by that time, and wanted the fun of having a new heir. She didn't have much excitement in her life, and making wills was her chief indoor sport. Oh, I didn't mean that to sound—ugly. I liked Mrs. Hogarth, even after—"

"After you quarrelled with her?" Strawn suggested, as Cora's words stopped on a gasp.

The yellow pallor deepened. "I—did not have a quarrel with Mrs. Hogarth." She brought out the words with difficulty.

Strawn smiled, and Dundee could have struck his chief. He was very young and very sympathetic.

"But you had come to regard Mrs. Hogarth's hidden hoard as rightfully yours, hadn't you Miss Barker? Felt rather cheated, didn't you, when she changed her will?"

"No! No! I never expected to get it. We all knew how much she enjoyed changing her will. And I didn't need her money. I make a good salary as pianist at the Little Queen, and I also have a number of private pupils to whom I give lessons in the mornings, before the theatre opens at eleven. I make plenty to live on!"

"I congratulate you, Miss Barker!" Strawn interrupted blandly. "Just one other thing, Miss Barker, before I send you to bed, for a good night's sleep, I hope . . . Cap'n, the parrot, is used to your presence in this room, of course. Do you think you could coax him into a talkative mood?"

At that apparently innocent request Cora Barker shrank from her inquisitor as sharply as if he had struck her.

She trembled all over, and the yellow pallor of her cheeks became tinged with a ghastly grey.

"No, no! I—I'm afraid of the parrot. Cap'n has always hated me—never would talk for me—" she gasped.

2

When the completely demoralised woman had been dismissed, Strawn stretched his arms high above his head, yawned, then cocked a quizzical eye towards Dundee behind the screen.

"Well, well!" he commented. "And what do you think of Miss Cora Barker, young sleuth, me lad?"

"I think," Dundee said slowly, "that she has not told all she knows, that she believes Sevier killed Mrs. Hogarth, and is in terror of her life that she will be wrongfully involved—"

"Wrongfully?" Strawn snorted. "I'll wager my badge she was in on it somehow!" He rose and strode to the door. "Payne!" he bawled, and the plain-clothes man came on the run. "What about the Barker woman's room, Payne? Find anything?"

"Not a thing, chief," Payne answered regretfully. "But listen, sir, the Sharps are champing at the bit. It seems that the Sharp dame was packing to catch a train when this rumpus was kicked up. She's missed it, but wants to take the next one. Something about her darling baby boy, I gather."

"All right. Bring them both in," Strawn directed, and Payne left the room to obey.

"I think I told you that a Western Union boy brought a telegram for Sharp as I was leaving just before eleven to go to Headquarters," Dundee reminded his chief, from behind the screen.

"This was a nice, peaceful boarding-house to-night," Strawn commented sarcastically. Then at a knock on the door. "Come in! Mr. and Mrs. Sharp? All right, Payne. Get along with your work," he added significantly, and Payne departed to search the unsuspecting couple's room.

"I'm glad to meet you, Lieutenant Strawn, though I deplore the circumstances," Lawrence Sharp boomed. "The missus and I were great friends of the poor lady who is so tragically dead—"

"So I understand," Strawn interrupted dryly, though he shook hands punctiliously.

"Oh, Lieutenant Strawn, you'll be as brief with us as you can, won't you, sir?" Mrs. Sharp, fully dressed for travelling, even to hat, implored with outstretched hands. "You see, I was going to catch the one o'clock train for the capital, where my son, Larry, or rather, Lawrence Sharp, Jr., is in the State University—"

"Now, now, Dolly!" Mr. Sharp admonished her. "I thought we had agreed—"

"But I know he won't let me go to Larry, if we don't tell him about the telegram, and the terrible trouble my poor boy is in," Mrs. Sharp sobbed. "You won't put it in the papers, or tell the other boarders, will you, Lieutenant Strawn? You look like such a good, kind man, and of course it all has nothing to do with poor Mrs. Hogarth—"

"'Suppose you let me see the telegram you received about eleven o'clock this evening," Strawn suggested.

"You already—knew?" Mrs. Sharp gasped. "You see, Lawrence, I told you the police know everything! Here's the telegram, Mr. Strawn. Lawrence didn't want to show it to you, but as I told him—"

Strawn took the yellow sheet. It was a collect telegram, dated from the state capital. Strawn read it aloud for Dundee's benefit.

IN PECK OF TROUBLE DAD STOP ARRESTED AND GAOLED CHARGE OF DRIVING WHILE INTOXICATED STOP NOT TRUE STOP WAS DRIVING CLASSMATE'S CAR AND WRECKED IT STOP VICKERS THREATENS CHARGE OF STEALING CAR UNLESS I PAY HIM THREE HUNDRED CASH FOR IT MONDAY. STOP FOR GOD'S SAKE DAD RUSH THE CASH AND ALSO ARRANGE TO HAVE ME BAILED OUT STOP TERRIBLY SORRY BUT NOT MY FAULT LARRY

"Larry's a good boy, Mr. Strawn," Mrs. Sharp sobbed. "And I want you to let me go straight to him! There's another train at 3:10, a local, but I won't mind a day coach—"

"Just a minute, Mrs. Sharp," Strawn interrupted, almost gently. "Suppose, Mr. Sharp, you begin with the receipt of this telegram and tell me all that has happened in this house this evening—to your knowledge."

Before her husband could reply, Mrs. Sharp began again, eagerly: "I signed for the telegram, Mr. Strawn. And while I was signing for it Norma Paige and Walter Styles—the young man she's just got engaged to—came upstairs and knocked on Mrs. Hogarth's door. While I was counting the money out of my purse to pay for the telegram—and I know the telegraph company overcharged us!—I heard Mrs. Hogarth call 'Who is it?'. Norma said 'It's Norma, Mrs. Hogarth,' and in a minute Mrs. Hogarth opened the door. When she saw that Walter was with Norma, she seemed to get awful mad. She raised one of the two canes she always used to walk with—because she was so terribly fat and heavy, you know—"

"Did you see her strike Walter Styles?" Strawn interrupted.

"Oh, no!" Mrs. Sharp protested; "She just brandished the cane as if she was going to hit him, and she said something like: 'I've told you to stay away from me, Walter Styles, and I mean it! Now git!'"

"And what did Styles say?"

"Oh, he didn't say anything; he just backed away: and tried to pull Norma with him, but she whispered some thing, and passed on into Mrs. Hogarth's room. I didn't pay any more attention then, because I wanted to see what was in the telegram—"

"Did you see where Styles went?"

"Oh, down the hall toward his room, but as I said I didn't pay much attention. Mr. Sharp was anxious to see the telegram, too, so I closed our door, and we read it, then—" She began to sob again.

"Suppose you take up the story at this point, Sharp," Strawn directed.

"The wife and I talked things over for a while. We were pretty badly shocked, you know, and scarcely knew what to do, but Dolly insisted she was going to him this very night and made me go down to phone about trains and to see if she could get a berth on the one o'clock train, which would get her into the capital at about seven in the morning. It took me about ten minutes, I think, to get the information I wanted and to reserve the berth—I could only get her an upper; it's the Chicago train, you know, and pretty crowded. Coming back up the stairs I saw Norma—Miss Paige—closing Mrs. Hogarth's door. With one hand she was dabbing a handkerchief against her eyes, as if she had been crying—"

"What time was this?" Strawn interrupted sharply, "Be as accurate as possible, Mr. Sharp."

Behind the screen Dundee's pencil faltered in a trembling hand. But not Norma! Not lovely, sweet Norma—

"Why, it must have been about half-past eleven by that time, sir," Sharp answered, hesitatingly. "I hope I haven't—"

"Never mind that!" Strawn commanded brusquely. "This is murder, Mr. Sharp."

The pompous man's florid cheeks blanched; then he remembered something that brightened his eyes. "But it couldn't have been Norma who—" He faltered, could not say the terrible word, "for I heard her call out, 'Good night, Mrs. Hogarth,' and then Mrs. Hogarth's voice answering, 'Goodnight.'"

Strawn's narrowed eyes glanced at the still ruffled parrot. "Are you sure, Mr. Sharp," he asked slowly, portentiously, "that it was Mrs. Hogarth's voice that answered 'Good night'?"

VII.

1

"WHAT do you mean, sir?" Mr. Lawrence Sharp asked blankly.

"I mean—can you swear that it was Mrs. Hogarth's voice that you heard telling Norma Paige good night, and not the voice of the parrot?"

"I—never thought of that," Sharp admitted. "But I feel sure it was Mrs. Hogarth's voice, though now that I think of it, it did sound a little hoarse and queer, as if she had been crying, too—"

"Lawrence Sharp, how dare you encourage this man to think dear little Norma Paige—" Mrs. Sharp began indignantly, but she interrupted herself, while a startled expression banished her generous anger.

Strawn and Dundee, too, from behind the screen missed not a flicker of that new expression. And Dundee's heart sank lower, hurting dreadfully.

"The parrot knows you both, of course," Strawn suggested "Do you think you could coax him to talk?"

Their reception of this suggestion was vastly different from Cora Barker's. Sharp, swelling out his chest a little with importance, stepped up to the bird's cage, readied in fearlessly, and stroked the rumpled red, yellow and green feathers of the parrot's head.

"Hello, Cap'n!" he boomed heartily.

"Hullo, hello!" the bird answered sulkily.

"Good night, Cap'n. Good night!" Sharp continued, while Mrs. Sharp plucked nervously at his sleeve in a futile effort to make him desist.

The parrot turned about on his perch, but cocked one bright eye at his dead mistress's friend. "Goodnight!" Cap'n answered, and to Dundee, behind the screen, the voice seemed to be that of the murdered woman herself. How anyone, hearing this voice, through a closed door, could swear it was not Mrs. Hogarth's, was more than he could tell, and Dundee, in that moment, could gleefully have slain the precocious bird.

"Was it that voice or Mrs. Hogarth's that you heard answering Norma Paige?" Strawn demanded, with slow, terrible emphasis.

"I—" Lawrence Sharp wiped his brow. "I can't swear which voice it was, but I believe it was Mrs. Hogarth's."

"Now, Mr. Sharp, did you hear or see anyone else as you returned to your room, about half-past eleven?"

"No—Yes I heard Bert Magnus's typewriter. His room is directly across the hall from mine, you know."

"Did he see Miss Paige, too?"

"No, he couldn't have. His door was shut when Norma ran down the hall to her room and closed her door—with a bang," he admitted reluctantly, "just as I was closing my own door. Her room is next to ours, you know. I didn't speak to her, or she to me. When I entered our room, I found the wife packing. I told her about the train and the upper berth, and wrote out a cheque for a hundred dollars for bail—"

"Not for the three hundred also, to pay for the car?" Strawn interrupted with lightning quickness.

"Why, no. I shall have to get the 300 from the savings bank, when it opens on Monday morning," Sharp answered. "I don't keep that much in my checking account."

"May I see your savings bank-book, please?" Strawn asked.

Sharp's big, jovial face flushed brick-red. "Sir, I believe you are exceeding your authority—"

"No doubt about it," Strawn admitted cheerfully. "But I'd like to see that savings bank-book. You seem to be one person in this house to-night who had a sudden, unusual, and rather alarming need for money—"

"Sir! Are you intimating that I—I—one of Mrs. Hogarth's closest friends for two years—murdered her for such a ridiculous reason as to get a paltry three hundred dollars for my son?"

Strawn grinned crookedly. "I'm not insinuating anything, Mr. Sharp, but—I'd like to see that bank-book, if you please. . . . Thanks! . . . Hmm! I see that you have a balance of $410.63. Destined to pay the boy's tuition for the fall semester, I suspect?"

"My financial affairs are my own concern, sir," Sharp answered stiffly.

"Just what is your occupation, Mr. Sharp?"

"I am head of one of the house furnishings departments at Marcus-Crane's—the linoleum department," Sharp answered with much dignity. "My salary is—entirely adequate to the needs of myself, my wife and son. Naturally, with my boy in college, I have not been able to save a great deal, but I shall manage nicely, thank you."

"Mrs. Hogarth was such a close friend of yours that she would have admitted you at half-past eleven or even as late as midnight, I suppose?" Strawn asked blandly.

The colour in Mr. Sharp's face became almost apoplectic. "She would have admitted me, sir, if I had knocked! But I did not do so. Neither did my wife. We had no occasion to trouble Mrs. Hogarth with our son's misfortune. In fact, we did not see the poor, dear lady after our call upon her earlier in the evening. Our new boarder, Mr. Dundee, was with her at the time, and Mrs. Rhodes, our landlady, joined the little party before the wife and I had left. Mrs. Hogarth was then in excellent spirits, and had some very complimentary things to say about my son, Larry—"

"Yes, yes," Strawn interrupted impatiently. "Now, Mrs. Sharp, I should like you to tell me why you are afraid that Norma Paige knows something about this bad business."

Mrs. Sharp bridled like an angry hen. "I don't know what you're talking about, sir! I didn't see Norma—that is, I didn't speak to her—"

"I think you'd better tell me exactly what happened, Mrs. Sharp."

"Well, but I can tell you right now, that no matter where Norma was, she didn't have anything to do with this terrible murder!" Mrs. Sharp assured him indignantly. "I did see Norma. After I finished packing, I was awfully hot, and decided to take a cool bath before going to the train. That was about ten minutes after Mr. Sharp came to—"

"About 11:40?"

"Yes. I opened my door, to go to the bathroom, and I saw Norma come out of her room and start down the hall toward the bathroom. I could see she was going to take a bath, for she had her bath towel over her arm, and was wearing bedroom slippers, pyjamas, and a kimono. I started to ask if she'd let me have my bath first, but Mr. Sharp had told me about Norma's crying, and I thought the quicker she got a nice cool bath the better she'd feel, and there was plenty of time before I had to leave for my train.

"I went back into my room, and wrote out a telegram to send to poor Larry from the station, and also one to a lawyer we know at the capital, and then—it was about fifteen minutes, I guess, I thought Norma would be through with her bath, and I took my towel and soap and started for the bathroom again. The door was closed, and I could hear the water running. I thought Norma might just be rinsing out the tub, and I'd call to her to let the water run for me. So I did, but there wasn't any answer. Since that bath is for women only, and there is only Norma and I on this floor to use it now, I tried the door. It wasn't locked. I stepped in and saw Norma's bath towel— she has her own, with her monogram on them —lying with her soap dish on her little stool. The water was running in the tub, but most of it was wasting, for the stopper was half-out, and the tub was only about a third full—"

"Had the towel been used?" Strawn interrupted.

"Oh, no. It was neatly folded and quite dry. I touched it to see. The soap was dry, too—a new cake. So I thought maybe Norma had gone back to her room for something she'd forgotten, and I'd ask her if I could have my bath first, it was getting later all the time. I went to her room—it's next to the bath, you know—and knocked on her door, but she didn't answer, although I could see through the transom that her light was on. I didn't know what to think, but then it occurred to me she might have gone downstairs to telephone, though she wasn't dressed properly, but as it was so late and all, and nobody much around—"

"Then what did you do, Mrs. Sharp?" Strawn asked, to stem the tide of useless words.

"Why, I took my bath. I was going to apologise to Norma if she came and found the bathroom in use, but she didn't come. But when I'd finished and rinsed the tub out, I left the water running for her again, and went back to my room. . . . Oh, yes," she caught herself, up, "I did stop and knock on Norma's door again, to tell her I'd left the water running, but she still didn't answer. I suddenly thought maybe she was in there crying, and I just said: 'Your water's running, Norma dear,' and went on to my room. I intended to go back to the bathroom in a minute or two to see that the tub didn't run over, but when I looked out of my door, I saw Norma going into the bathroom, and I knew it was alright."

"Did you see from which direction Miss Paige came?"

"Oh, no, but from her room, I suppose. She must have been in there crying because Mrs. Hogarth didn't want her to marry Walter, but I just saw her opening the bathroom door."

"Did you see or hear anything else during these trips to the bathroom, Mr. Sharp?"

"No, sir. Yes, I heard Mr. Magnus's typewriter, and I thought to myself that he had a nerve, writing so late at night, though Mrs. Rhodes had told him he could work till twelve last Saturday night, on account of people not going to bed early, and everything, but I do think—"

"Thank you very much, Mrs. Sharp. And you too, Mr. Sharp. I see no reason why you can't take the next train to your boy, Mrs. Sharp."

When they had left the room, Strawn summoned Payne and told him to bring in Norma Paige. Bonnie Dundee's heart, burdened though it was with fear for her, leaped in his breast at the thought of seeing her again.

2

"Well, Miss Paige, I see you're already in mourning for Mrs. Hogarth," Lieut. Strawn greeted the girl who advanced timidly toward the desk where one of the dead woman's last acts had been to record in her diary her intention of disinheriting her latest favourite.

A quick flush tinged the pallor of the lovely little face. Fresh tears welled in the blue eyes, which looked as if they had shed many that night.

I—hardly realised what I was putting on, after—after I was told about poor Mrs. Hogarth," Norma stammered, smoothing the sheenless black of her dress with nervous hands. "But I am—in mourning for her in my heart."

"What was your feeling toward Mrs. Hogarth?" Strawn asked, after he had placed the trembling girl in a chair beside him.

"I loved her very much," Norma answered simply. "My mother and father are both dead, and Mrs. Hogarth seemed more like a mother to me than anyone has since—since—"

"Did you still love her after your interview with her this evening?"

The flush deepened painfully. "I—yes. I knew she was wrong about—about Walter, but I knew she thought she was acting for my own good. Things she said about Walter hurt me terribly, but I didn't quarrel with her or become really angry with her."

"Suppose you begin at the beginning, Miss. Paige—or rather, at about eleven o'clock, and tell me everything you know about this bad business."

"I know nothing about Mrs. Hogarth's—death!" Norma flashed, and Bonnie Dundee, taking notes behind the screen, believed her implicitly, because he so much wanted to believe. His eyes drank in greedily the beauty of her tumbled bronze hair, of her wide blue eyes luminous with tears and anger. "She was as well as usual when I saw her last—"

"And that was when?"

"About half-past eleven. It was nearly eleven when Mr. Dundee—a new boarder here, whom I took to meet Mrs. Hogarth—left the house, and Walter and I came upstairs from the lawn to tell her we were engaged. I knew she wouldn't be pleased, but I couldn't deceive her, and perhaps inherit her money when she wouldn't really have wanted me to, if she'd known the truth."

"Did Mr. Styles, your fiancé, share this noble sentiment?" Strawn asked, and Dundee could have choked his superior officer.

"He came up with me, but Mrs. Hogarth wouldn't let him in.

"Brandished her cane at him and told him never to try to speak to her again, in fact?" Strawn suggested.

The little head flung itself up gallantly. "She said something like that, but I wasn't awfully surprised, for I knew she and Walter had quarrelled, though I didn't know then what it was about."

"And Mrs. Hogarth told you?"

"Yes, but—I don't have to tell you that, do I?" the girl pleaded.

"I think you'd better, Miss Paige," Strawn answered gently. "If you don't, I may think it much worse than it really is, you know."

"It wasn't really bad at all," she protested, tumbling headlong into the trap. "I suppose you've already heard that Mrs. Hogarth changed her will pretty frequently. When Walter came to board here early in May she took a violent fancy to him. He's awfully nice, you know," she added naïvely, not dreaming that she was giving pain to a new admirer concealed behind Mrs. Hogarth's screen.

"It wasn't long before she made a new will, disinheriting Cora Barker and naming Walter as her new heir. Walter has a little haberdashery on Grand Street, but—it isn't doing so very well. He had been head buyer in the haberdashery department of Marcus-Crane's, and he thought he could make a success of a little shop of his own. And he will, too," she added loyally, "if he can pull through the dull summer season."

"And he asked Mrs. Hogarth for a loan?" Strawn suggested.

"Yes, but how did you know?" Norma puzzled. "But it wasn't a terrible thing at all for him to do. He thought that if Mrs. Hogarth liked him enough and believed in him enough to will him her money, she would be glad to help him now, when he needs it so much. But she was awfully angry, and called him a fortune-hunter, and said he cared nothing for her, had been nice to her only for the sake of her money, and—and things like that. She told me herself, to-night, when she said she'd disinherit me if I didn't break my engagement to Walter—"

"And what was your answer?" Strawn interrupted.

The girl's eyes widened incredulously. "Why, of course, I told her I was going to marry Walter anyway!"

"Then what were you crying about when you left this room at half-past eleven?" Strawn demanded.

"I felt terrible because I'd hurt her feelings, after she'd been so kind to me," Norma faltered. "And—and she made me cry, too, by making a wager that Walter would—would jilt me when I told him that she had disinherited me."

"Because you half believed she was right?" Strawn prodded mercilessly.

"No! No! I knew he loved me for myself, not for what Mrs. Hogarth might leave me!"

"But your engagement took place after Mrs. Hogarth had made the will in your favour?"

The flush deepened to scarlet "Please don't be so—so nasty to me!" she begged piteously. "How could Walter and I have become engaged much sooner than we did? I had never seen him before I came to board here on June first."

"Then it took Mrs. Hogarth less time to choose an heiress than for Mr. Styles to fall in love?" Strawn smiled.

"Oh!" She flung out her little hands in a hopeless gesture.

"Very well, Miss Paige. I apologise. Now tell me what happened from half-past eleven on. You left this room in tears—"

"Mrs. Hogarth cried, too," Norma told him. "I bent and kissed her—she was sitting where you are now, at her desk—"

"She didn't get up to unlock the door and lock it after you, as was her custom?" Strawn interrupted quickly.

"I turned the key in the lock myself, but she was rising when I opened the door. I hesitated a moment outside the door, heard her turn the key in the lock, and then I called out good night—"

"And she answered you?"

"Of course! She wasn't angry with me. She was just determined to keep me from marrying Walter—for my own good, she said."

"H'mm! . . . And then, Miss Paige?"

"I went to my own room, then I took a bath and went to bed—" the girl began tremulously.

"Miss Paige, time is precious," Strawn interrupted grimly. "Mrs. Sharp has already told me that you were missing from your room from 11:40 to about 12:10, and that you were not in the bathroom more than a minute or two of that time—just long enough to turn on your bath-water, in fact. I want you to tell me frankly and truthfully just what you were doing from 11:40 to 12:10, when Mrs. Sharp saw you re-enter the bathroom."

Dundee wanted to knock down the screen and rush to the girl, take her in his arms and comfort her. For as the detective spoke, she sank lower and lower into her chair, a white-faced, huddled little heap of terror.

"Miss Paige," Strawn began slowly, portentously, "I believe you spent part or all that time in Mrs. Hogarth's room, and that you know who killed her!"

The girl sprang to her feet. "No, no! I never saw her again, I tell you! I know nothing whatever of her death—"

"Then where were you, Miss Paige? I think you see the necessity for telling the whole truth," Strawn urged gently.

Norma sank back into her chair, her little hands trembling violently against her breast "I—you won't tell on me, will you, Lieutenant Strawn? It was so—innocent, really, but you know how a boarding-house is—"

"What you tell me here is in confidence, Miss Paige," Strawn assured her, "unless, it concerns the death of Mr. Hogarth."

"It doesn't! Oh, please believe I know nothing, and that Walter doesn't either!" she begged, the tears spilling out of her eyes upon her white cheeks. "I went straight to my room after I had told Mrs. Hogarth good night. I—I cried for awhile, then I decided to take a cool bath. I undressed, and put on my pyjamas and a kimono, and took my things to the bathroom—my towel and soap, you know. I turned on the water, and then started back to my room to get my toothbrush. Walter had been watching for me. His room is just across the hall from mine, you know, and as I started back to my room he called to me in a whisper. Of course I knew he wanted to know what Mrs. Hogarth had said to me. I had promised to call him out into the hall when the interview was over, to tell him all about it, but—but—"

"You didn't want him to know how badly Mrs. Hogarth's charges against him had upset you?" Strawn suggested.

Norma bowed her head, then flung it high again defiantly. "But I knew they were untrue, that she was mistaken in him and his motives! As soon as he spoke to me, I began to cry again, and he begged me to fix the stopper in the tub so the water wouldn't overflow, then come into his room to tell him all about it. He thought it was better for Mrs. Sharp or anyone who wanted to talk to me about what Mrs. Hogarth had said—everyone knew all about it, you see, and was interested—to think I was in the bathroom, and—and not in his room."

"Mr. Styles seems to have a talent for plotting," Strawn remarked dryly.

VIII.

1

"You have no right to make such insinuations against Walter Styles!" Norma flamed. He was only thinking of me—of my reputation in a gossipy boarding-house. If anyone had discovered I was in Walter's room, so late at night, dressed as I was—"

"You did enter his room, then?" Strawn interrupted, his voice gentle and placating again.

"Yes, I did! We could hardly talk in the hall, with me crying as I was. But we left the door slightly ajar, and stood near it. We did not even sit down the whole time. I told him, because he urged me to, just what Mrs. Hogarth had said, about his asking her to lend him money for his business, and—and her wager that he wouldn't want to marry me after she had cut me out of her will—"

"And your fiancé was very angry, of course?"

"Of course!" Norma agreed vehemently. Then gasped as she realised the trend of the question. "He was certainly justified in being angry at Mrs. Hogarth's misunderstanding of his motives—"

"And he went on to have a little quiet talk with her, to set her straight on his motives—Wait, Miss Paige! He crawled out of his window and walked along the upstairs porch to Mrs. Hogarth's room, entering by her window—"

"He did no such thing!" the girl almost screamed, her frantic little hands beating her breast. "He didn't leave me for a single minute! We stood right by the door, talking in whispers. I don't know just how long we talked, but we both saw Mrs. Sharp go to the bathroom. She knocked and called my name, but of course I didn't answer, and she opened the door and went in. She must have, seen my towel and soap there, for she went to my room then and knocked. Then, she went back to the bathroom and took her bath, or I suppose she did, for she was in there long enough to bathe. We heard her turn the water on again, and then she came out and knocked at my door.

"We heard her say, 'Your water's running'. Then she went into her room and when her door had closed, I ran across the hall and into the bathroom. I took my bath and had just got into bed when I heard someone knock on Mrs. Hogarth's door, or on some door. I thought it was Mrs. Hogarth's, but I didn't look out to make sure. About ten or fifteen minutes later a man and Mrs. Rhodes came to my door and told me that Mrs. Hogarth was dead. And that's absolutely all I know!"

Strawn regarded the quivering white-faced girl through narrowed lids for a long minute, while Bonnie Dundee, behind the screen, had tremendous difficulty in suppressing an impulse to step out of hiding, go to the girl and tell her that he, at least, believed every word she had said.

But, of course, not even she must know he was not merely the "new boarder," but a new detective as well, as ignorant of the truth of who killed Mrs. Hogarth as she was herself.

"Miss Paige," Strawn began softly, "there is small doubt that Mrs. Hogarth was murdered and robbed during those minutes you say you spent with your fiancé in his room . . . No, wait, please! I am making no accusations. I merely want you to try very hard to remember if you heard or saw anything else while you stood near Mr. Styles's door, which was ajar, you say. I think it is due you to tell you that Mrs. Sharp's story corroborates yours in every way—as far as it goes. Now think! Did you hear or see anyone besides Mrs. Now during those minutes—approximately half an hour?"

The girl seemed pathetically relieved at his implied faith in her word. She drew a deep breath, then knit her pretty bronze brows in an effort to remember. "No," she said at last. "I saw no one at all. Of course, Walter and I were both afraid, and kept looking out of the door, but we saw no one."

"You can vouch for the fact that Mr. Sharp, for instance, did not come out of his room?"

"Oh, yes! I'm sure of that."

Dundee's quick mind took note of the fact that her earnest words had given Lawrence Sharp a perfect alibi. For the Sharps' room did not open upon a convenient upstairs porch, leading to Mrs. Hogarth's room. Their window was set in the west wall of the house, overlooking the driveway. Unless he had jumped from his second floor window to the ground below, and had then climbed the rose trellis at the west end of the porch, he could not possibly have gained access to the old woman's room. And Lawrence Sharp was no slim and agile youth.

"Did you hear anything—anyone?" Strawn persisted.

"No. Oh, yes, we did!" the girl corrected herself hastily.

"One reason we talked in whispers was that we were afraid of Mr. Magnus's hearing us. We knew he was in his room and awake, for he was typing nearly all the time. His room is next to Walter's, you know."

"Nearly all the time?" Strawn repeated. "Just how long a time was his machine silent?"

"Not nearly long enough for him to murder poor Mrs. Hogarth and search her room!" Norma flashed. "If that's what you're wondering! He was typing along steadily, as if he were copying something that had already been written. He said at dinner to-night—or rather, last night—that he was going to revise his story that had just been returned by a studio. Then while Mrs. Sharp was taking her bath, and I was just about to slip across to my own room, to be there in case she came to speak to me, he stopped, and Walter and I were scared to death he had heard us. I—I had become almost hysterical, because of Mrs. Sharp's looking for me, and my not being able to get back to my room, and—and everything, and we were afraid Bert—Mr. Magnus—had heard me crying, for he stopped typing for two or three minutes. We heard him moving about in his room, and for fear he might open his door and look out, I stayed in Walter's room until he began to type again."

"One more question, Miss Paige, please. Have you seen or talked with anyone since you returned to your room after taking your bath? Other than Mrs. Rhodes and Detective Payne, when they came to tell you of Mrs. Hogarth's death?"

"No, sir. No one at all."

The girl, dismissed at last, almost ran from the room, her hands groping before her as if she were blind with tears.

"Boyle!" Strawn bawled. "Tell Payne I want him. And when you see him leave, bring in Walter Styles."

When Payne appeared, he shook his head before Strawn could put a question. "Nothing in the girl's room, chief. Her wardrobe trunk, her closet and her desk were all unlocked. No money anywhere, except about five dollars in her handbag."

"All right, Payne I'm having Styles in now. Go over his room with a fine tooth-comb."

Walter Styles, when he appeared, was wearing a rather handsome silk dressing-gown over shirt and trousers. His brown hair was brushed sleekly smooth, and his light-brown eyes were calm, but there was a betraying tightness about his mouth. Dundee knew that he was alert and anxious, having no idea how much or how little his sweetheart had been forced to tell.

After a few preliminary questions, Strawn asked abruptly: "Where were you between eleven and, say, ten minutes after twelve to-night, Styles?"

A muscle jerked in the young man's cheek, but his voice was steady: "I was in my room."

"Alone?" Strawn asked, with apparent casualness.

Again that spasmodic jerking of a muscle. Then, calmly: "Yes, alone."

Dundee, behind the screen, felt an unwilling admiration for the man he had already looked upon with jealous envy before was engaged to the girl Dundee had himself dreamed of. By betraying Norma's indiscretion, Walter Styles could have clinched the alibi she had given him.

"Spoken like a gentleman, Mr. Styles," Strawn applauded dryly. "But it happens that Miss Paige, your fiancée, has already told me a different story. Now, I'd like your version of that story."

Walter Styles took a quick step toward the detective, his clenched fist upraised. "If you've been badgering and insulting Norma—" he began violently.

"You have a pretty hot temper, haven't you, Mr. Styles?" Strawn drawled. "You must remember that murder has been committed here to-night, and it is my duty to learn every fact that can possibly have any bearing on the case. Sit down and keep your fist to yourself, young man . . . Now tell me exactly what you did between eleven o'clock last night and the time you were informed by Mrs. Rhodes and Detective Payne of Mrs. Hogarth's murder."

Walter Styles obeyed, speaking with a sort of furious calm. He began with Mrs. Hogarth's angry refusal to admit him to her room, along with Norma Paige; told of going to his own room and there awaiting word from Norma as to the result of her interview with Mrs. Hogarth; of Norma's coming into his room, at his request; of Mrs. Sharp's trips to the bathroom and to Norma's room; of Norma's departure to take her own delayed bath after Mrs. Sharp. He told the bare facts, enlarging upon them not at all, and Strawn silently heard him to the end.

"You were very angry with Mrs. Hogarth, for her treatment of Miss Paige and because of the charges she had brought against you, were you not, Mr. Styles?" Strawn asked quietly, when the brief recital had ended.

"I was!"

Strawn stared at the unexpectedness of the admission, then he pounced: "Mr. Styles, did you leave your room at all during the time I have mentioned?"

"Yes—I did!"

2

In the moment of pulsing suspense that followed Walter Styles's defiant, laconic admission, Bonnie Dundee felt sure that his busy pencil would soon be called upon to record a confession of murder.

"As soon as Norma—Miss Paige—was safely in the bathroom," Styles went on, before the astonished Lieut. Strawn could formulate a question, "I stepped out of my window to the porch. Norma and I were both afraid that Bert Magnus, who has the room next to mine, had heard her crying, for he had stopped typing for a minute or two—possibly three. Not until he was at his machine again had the poor girl dared to run across the hall to the bathroom. Knowing how seriously a boarding-house scandal would upset Norma, I determined to find out, if possible, whether or not Magnus had heard anything. I was fairly sure I could judge by his manner, even if he asked no questions."

"Yes?" Strawn prompted, as the young man paused.

"I stepped to Bert's window and called out something to him," Styles went on. "I think I said, 'Beastly hot, isn't it?' or something like that. He was still typing, and I startled him. But he rose and came to the window, remarked about the heat and offered me a cigarette. I felt convinced by his manner that he had not heard anything, and after wishing him luck with the story he was working on, I went back into my room by way of the window, of course. He went back to his typing again, but worked only for a short time longer, I believe, but I didn't pay much attention. I undressed and went to bed then, but was not asleep when Mrs. Rhodes and the detective came to tell me that Mrs. Hogarth was dead."

"Mr. Styles, your business is on the verge of bankruptcy, isn't it?" Strawn asked abruptly.

"It is," Walter Styles answered, with the astounding frankness that had characterised him since the inquisition had started. "And I'll admit, sir, without your asking, that I tried to borrow $2,000 from Mrs. Hogarth, after she had shown her interest in me by naming me in her will. I will further admit that she accused me of being a fortune-hunter, of caring nothing for her except for her money; that we quarrelled, and that she refused to see me, even to permit me to apologise for some hasty things I said to her—"

"Just what had you said to her, Mr. Styles?"

"I told her she was a foolish old woman, who was storing up trouble, even death for herself," Styles said trimly. "She had complained to me about the greed of her fellow-boarders, naming Sevier in particular, and during my quarrel with her, I told her it would not surprise me if she tempted someone to robbery and even murder. I begged her to put her money in the bank, but she told me to mind my own business. I have done so," he added emphatically.

"By becoming engaged to Miss Paige, Mrs. Hogarth's new heiress?" Strawn suggested.

"I asked Norma to marry me because I love her, not because of any money Mrs. Hogarth might leave her."

"But last night. When you learned that Mrs. Hogarth was going to change her will, that you had again lost your chance at her money—?" Strawn began.

Styles's nostrils flared with anger. "If you're insinuating that I stationed Norma as a look-out in my room after hearing the result of her interview with Mrs. Hogarth—"

Strawn grinned crookedly. "You put it very well, Styles. I state—not insinuate—that you heard Miss Paige's story, became violently angry, as well as crazy with disappointment; that you asked Miss Paige to wait in your room while you went by way of the window, to see Mrs. Hogarth—Let me finish, please!" he commanded sharply as the young man sprang to his feet, his hands and lips working convulsively. "I'm not accusing Miss Paige of knowing your intentions. I believe you told her you merely wanted to take Mrs. Hogarth to task for her accusations against you. The cold fact, Styles, is that Mrs. Hogarth was murdered and robbed during the time Miss Paige was in your room. I put it to you now that you went to Mrs. Hogarth, killed her, robbed her, and returned to your room, heard from Miss Paige the full story of Mrs Sharp's trips to the bathroom and of Magnus's typing during the whole time, and were thus able to corroborate her and Mrs. Sharp in every particular."

Dundee, feeling a little sick (for third-degree methods were abhorrent to him), could not bring himself to look at the face of the accused young man. But his pencil mechanically took down Walter's reply:

"If you really believe that, Lieutenant Strawn, you're a fool! If I had murdered Mrs. Hogarth, do you think I'd have been crazy enough to tell you everything damaging to myself that I've admitted so freely? I scorned to lie to you, and now you're proving to me that it does not pay to tell a dumb policeman the truth!"

Oddly, Strawn chuckled. He rose, stretched his powerful arms, and yawned. "We'll have another session tomorrow, Styles. Go to bed now—and sleep, if you can."

When Styles had plunged angrily from the room, Strawn chuckled again.

"What do you think of Norma's sweetie, Dundee?"

Dundee rose, too, came from behind the screen, flexing the cramped fingers of his right hand. "I rather think he was telling the truth, chief."

"Lord! I do, too," Strawn laughed. "But business is business—Come in!"

Detective Payne entered. "Nothing in Styles's room, chief. But a telephone call has just come from headquarters. They've received a wire from the Chicago train, filed at Greenville. Sevier isn't on it!"

"What!" Strawn exclaimed. "Given us the slip, has he? Well, I guess that settles it, Dundee! . . . Did the wire say whether he had been seen on the train at all, Payne?"

"Yes. The day coach conductor noticed him soon after the train pulled out of Hamilton, but when he went to collect his ticket, Sevier had disappeared. The train has been searched thoroughly, from end to end, and it's a sure thing he's not on it now. That's all the wire says, chief."

"Then he's still in the States somewhere, and we'll pick him up!" Strawn prophesied grimly, as he hurried downstairs to telephone further instructions to police headquarters.

"Bring that Magnus chap in, Boyle." Dundee heard him instruct the patrolman from the doorway, a few minutes later. Coming into the room, he growled to Dundee, who had taken his place behind the screen: "We're wasting time here, boy, but I suppose I've got to see the rest of these people, on the off chance they saw or heard something."

"Good night! Good night!" a hoarse voice croaked sleepily.

Strawn whirled, then remembered the parrot and chuckled. You sleepy, too, Cap'n? Well, it won't be long now old top! . . . come in! . . . you're Magnus?"

Bert Magnus, clad in a cheap Terry-cloth bathrobe over cotton pyjamas, stood blinking m the blare of light, as if he had been aroused from sleep.

"Herbert S. Magnus," he answered the detective.

"You board here? Where is your room?" Strawn asked abruptly.

"Across the hall, on the east side, next to Mr. Styles's room," Magnus answered meticulously.

"How did you spend your evening, Magnus, from dinner time until you were told of Mrs. Hogarth's murder?"

"I accompanied Miss Cora Barker to the Little Queen Theatre, where she plays the piano," Magnus answered. "I left the theatre about nine o'clock, and returned to my room. I read over the manuscript of a scenario I am working on, and then began to revise it. I became so absorbed in the work that I neglected to keep an appointment with Miss Barker to meet her after the closing of the theatre. In fact, I did not realise what time it was until too late to keep the appointment, so I kept on with my work."

"How late did you work?"

"Till about 12:20, I believe. Last Saturday night I obtained permission from Mrs. Rhodes to type until 12 o'clock, though, on other nights, she has asked me not to type after eleven, for fear of disturbing others. I presumed on that permission to work late to-night, it being Saturday, and had intended to quit promptly at 12, as she had requested, but when I looked at my watch, a few minutes after Mr. Styles had spoken to me, I found it was a quarter past twelve. I finished the page I had in the machine, and stopped I was just getting into bed when I was told the tragic news."

"Did you hear or see anyone, or anything out of the ordinary, during all that time, Mr. Magnus?"

"Why, no. I was pretty much absorbed in my writing. As I said, Walter Styles, the young man who has the room next to mine, spoke to me from the porch. That must have been a little after twelve, but otherwise I saw and spoke to no one, nor was I conscious of hearing anything unusual. Oh, yes! A new boarder, a Mr. Dundee, interrupted me earlier in the evening—probably about eleven, though I did not notice the time, or realise then that it was so late, or I should have gone to keep my appointment with Miss Barker."

"How long have you boarded here, Mr. Magnus?"

"I came to Hamilton on 5th June, from Philadelphia. I was employed there for a year as a book-keeper, with the

Acme Paper Company. I am originally from Riverside, California—"

A knock on the door interrupted, but before Strawn could call "Come in! " Detective Green, who had earlier brought in Dr. Weeks, plunged into the room.

"A real clue, chief! A hot one!" he exulted, offering a disreputable old tweed cap.

Strawn stretched out a hand for the cap, but Green warned him excitedly: "Careful, chief! Or the green feather will fall out!"

IX.

IT required considerable will power for Bonnie Dundee to remain hidden behind the screen while Lieut. Strawn inspected the soiled old tweed cap which Detective Green had brought in. Dundee was so new to the game of detecting criminals that an actual, tangible clue was the most thrilling thing in the world to him, and here, certainly, was a clue worthy of the name.

"Hmm!" Strawn drew a tiny green feather from the torn silk lining of the cap, stepped to the parrot's cage, swiftly inserted a thumb and forefinger, and withdrew them just as Cap'n's beak made a dart at them. They held a feather retrieved from the bottom of the cage. Comment was unnecessary. The two feathers were almost identical in size and exactly alike in colouring. "Where did you find this cap, Green?"

"Caught in the hedge, sir, that borders the driveway on the west side of the house. I was looking for some evidence that the running man Dr. Weeks saw in the alley had come from the Rhodes House grounds," Green answered proudly.

Bert Magnus, whose story Green had interrupted, uttered an exclamation of surprise or incredulity.

Strawn wheeled to face him. "Did you ever see this cap before, Magnus?"

"I'm not sure, but I believe I have," Magnus answered, with marked hesitation. "Like most of the boarders, I keep my rubbers in the box seat of the hall-tree downstairs, and week before last, when we had quite a rainstorm, I pushed aside a cap like this, looking for my overshoes. I paid no attention at the time, but it looks like the same cap."

"Have you any idea whose it is?"

"Why, no, I have seen no one wear it—hardly the season for a heavy tweed cap like that. And, of course, I did not inquire as to its ownership."

"That rainstorm—was it before or after Emil Sevier was evicted from the house?"

Magnus frowned in concentration. "Let's see . . . The storm was Wednesday a week ago, I remember, because Miss Shepherd, leaving for work as I did, remarked that it would ruin the Wednesday Sale Day at Marcus-Crane's, where she works, in the ladies' dress department. I am not positive, but I believe Mr. Sevier left us that same day."

"Have you seen the cap since then?"

"If I did, I failed to notice it."

"By the way, Magnus, did you know Mrs. Hogarth personally?" Strawn asked abruptly.

"No, I'm sorry to say I never made her acquaintance," Magnus answered. "I was to do so to-morrow, or rather to-day, since it is already Sunday now. She had invited me to call on her, possibly because I had expressed a desire to meet her. Mr. Dundee, the new boarder, dropped into my room last evening as I told you, to give me the message. I was about to pay my call immediately after Mr. Dundee left, but saw Miss Paige and Mr. Styles at her door, and went on with my work."

"Do you know why she wanted so particularly to meet you?

Bert Magnus smiled deprecatingly. "I thought at the time she might want to tell me the story of her life, so I could make a movie out of it. Although I'm only an amateur at this writing business, I find that pretty nearly everybody does want to tell you the story of his life—"

"Well, for once, it might have been worth your while to listen," Strawn commented dryly. "That's all for the present, Magnus . . . You'll be staying on here, I suppose?"

"Certainly. It's an excellent boarding-house, and I may be able to get material for a scenario that will really sell. Good night!"

"Ask Mrs. Rhodes to come in," Strawn instructed Green, when Magnus had left the room. Then, turning toward the screen: "Well, Dundee, what do you think of our clue?"

Dundee stepped eagerly from behind the screen and took the tweed cap from his chief's hands. The silk lining was soiled, frayed and badly torn. He looked closer, then frowned up at Strawn: "Now why should Sevier take the trouble to tear the lining and hide the parrot's feather in it? For I presume you're thinking that Sevier wore this cap in this room this evening?"

"That's exactly what I'm thinking," Strawn retorted. "He was hatless when he ran for his train—"

"But he was carrying a straw hat when Dr. Weeks saw him running down the alley—if we grant that it was Sevier the doctor saw," Dundee pointed out "Of course, he could have hidden his straw hat in the hedge, put on this cap, worn it in this room, then discarded it before leaving the grounds—taking the time to retrieve his straw hat. Rather complicated maneuvers for an amateur murderer, don't you think?" He slowly pulled at two threads ravelled from a tear in the silk. "Whoever wore this cap into this room to-night, chief tore the lining after he had worn it, tore it for the express purpose of tucking one of Cap'n's feathers inside the lining, and—" He paused and cocked a quizzical blue eye at his superior officer.

"Well?" Strawn prompted impatiently. "For the Lord's sake, don't go coy on me. Time's precious and I'm dog-tired!'

Dundee laughed. "Check, chief! Maybe I was trying to give an imitation of a story-book detective. What I was going to add was—our clever friend, the murderer, loved the police so well he couldn't bear to see them without a clue of any kind, so he manufactured a nice, thrilling one. Green, at least, got a great kick out of the parrot's feather in the hedge-hidden tweed cap! The feather, of course, was the surest, proof obtainable that the cap had been in this room to-night, and whoever planted the clue wanted us to believe that the owner of the cap had been here. Or that Sevier, who could have borrowed the cap from the hall-tree, had left it here—"

"Emil Sevier doesn't happen to be an old schoolmate of yours, does he?" Strawn suggested acidly. Then, at a knock on the door: "Come in!

Detective Green announced Mrs. Rhodes, and then, at a signal from Strawn, withdrew. The landlady broke into speech vehemently:

"Excuse me for keeping you waiting, Mr. Strawn, but the Lord knows I've had my hands full! That Dusty! It was a sorry day for me when I married that—"

"You mean your husband has returned?" Strawn interrupted her sharply.

"And how!" she confirmed grimly, the outmoded bit of slang setting oddly on her austere lips. "Dead drunk! Two of your men found him at Dago Pete's and were just lugging him in when you sent Mr. Green down for me. He's passed out cold—was dead to the world when they found him in that dive of a speakeasy. Your men brought two of his low-life pals along with him, and they're waiting downstairs now—"

"With an airtight alibi for your husband, I suppose," Strawn finished her sentence wryly.

"Alibi?" Mrs. Rhodes repeated; then she laughed a snort of angry amusement. "I hope you're not so hard-up for a suspect as to have picked on Dusty, Lieutenant Strawn! He hasn't nerve enough to drown an alley cat's litter of kittens."

"And yet," Strawn told Dusty's wife, with deceptive mildness, "he hated Mrs. Hogarth, and she despised and feared him. In fact. Mrs. Hogarth told Mr. Dundee that she believed Sevier had bribed Dusty to delay putting up her screen until the robbery could be accomplished."

"Bribed him?" Mrs. Rhodes laughed scornfully. "Nobody has to bribe Dusty Rhodes not to do a job of work! If Emma Hogarth said any such thing, everybody else was right and I was wrong—she was crazy!"

Dundee had been holding the tweed cap behind his back. Now, without a word, he extended it to his chief.

"Do you know whose cap this is, Mrs. Rhodes?" Strawn asked offering it to her.

"Of course I do! It's an old one of Dusty's. He hasn't worn it for months. Where did you find it?"

Strawn told her briefly, watching every change of expression on her face, but there was no hint of fear.

"Well, how it got into the hedge is more than I can tell!" she retorted vigorously. "The last time I saw it was a week ago Wednesday, when I was rummaging in the box seat of the hall-tree for a pair of rubbers that Emil Sevier claimed he'd put there. He was packing up to leave, you know, and raising the roof about a measly pair of worn-out rubbers. It was raining, you know, and I guess he did need them—"

"And did you find them for him?"

"No. The phone rang while I was looking for them, and I told him to get them himself, though I knew I was running the risk of his making off with anything else in the hall-tree box that took his fancy."

Toward Dundee, Strawn flashed a grin which plainly said: "I told you so!" To Mrs. Rhodes he addressed an apparently irrelevant question: "I understand that Dusty usually brought Mrs. Hogarth's meals to her?"

"Yes, he did. Nobody but me knew as well what she liked as Dusty."

"What are you trying to do, Dundee?" Strawn whirled to demand sharply of Bonnie Dundee, who had begun to slap at the parrot's cage with the cap he had taken from Mrs. Rhodes.

The young detective was about to reply when Cap'n turned twice on his perch, ruffling his feathers irritably.

Then, in a voice startingly like his dead mistress's, Cap'n
spoke:

"Bad penny! Bad penny!"

X.

1

"GRIN—blast you!" Lieut. Strawn growled at his young assistant on the Hogarth case, but the exultant triumph in Bonnie Dundee's blue eyes was not so easily dampened.

"Mrs. Rhodes, did you ever hear Cap'n say those words before—'Bad Penny'?" Bonnie asked eagerly.

"No. You could have knocked me down with one of Cap'n's littlest feathers," the landlady answered. "That bird does beat all! I never saw a parrot pick up new words like he does—but he never would repeat anything but what he heard poor old Mrs. Hogarth say."

"You're sure those words have never been a part of his vocabulary before?" Dundee persisted, strangely excited.

"Of course I'm sure!" Mrs. Rhodes snapped. "I've set with Mrs. Hogarth every evening of the five years she's been here, and she'd have bragged to me about Cap'n picking up those words if he'd ever said them before. Of course, I wasn't the last one to see her alive this evening. Norma paid her a visit after I left, you know, and it may be that Mrs. Hogarth made some remark with 'Bad Penny', in it while she was talking to Norma."

"Well, I'll soon find out," Strawn said abruptly, starting for the door. "By the way, Mrs. Rhodes, when I first came this evening, you said you weren't sure as to whether Daisy Shepherd was in her room or not."

"Well, that Detective Payne and I found she was, when we went up to tell her that Mrs. Hogarth was dead. But she wasn't in it at five minutes after twelve, or if she was, she was so sound asleep she didn't hear me knocking and calling to her."

"What's that?" Strawn demanded sharply. "Why haven't you mentioned this before?"

"Reckon you haven't give me much chance," Mrs. Rhodes reminded him grimly. "About two minutes after twelve, after I'd gone to bed, the telephone rang. It was long distance for Daisy, and I went up to her room on the third floor by the back stairs, to call her. She didn't answer and I went down and told long distance she was out. I don't know where she was and I didn't see her come in, because I went to bed "

When he had dismissed Mrs. Rhodes, Strawn called in Detective Payne, heard his report that so far no hidden sum of money had been found in any of the rooms, and instructed him to bring in Daisy Shepherd for questioning.

"Back in a minute, Dundee," Strawn called, as he himself was about to leave the room. "I'm going to ask the Paige girl if she knows anything, about this 'Bad penny' business—not that I think it's worth wasting a minute's time on."

Dundee grinned, then again seated himself behind the screen, Mrs. Hogarth's diary in his hands. Before beginning to read it from the first entry he riffled the leaves, to dislodge any memo, letter or card that might have been thrust into the book. In doing so he made a discovery which caused him to purse his lips in a low whistle of surprise. A page from the diary had been torn out—the entry for May . . May. . . May . . . He frowned mightily in an effort to remember. Oh, yes! Cora Barker had said—He turned swiftly to his notes, found Cora Barker's story, located the sentence he was trying to remember: "So I was Mrs. Hogarth's heiress until— sometime in May, I believe it was, when she became very fond of Walter Styles, a new boarder." He was glad now that he had taken such full notes, even to the extent of indicating hesitation between words by dashes. Cora Barker had been disinherited "sometime in May." Could the date have been 10th May? Dundee very carefully examined the fuzzy edge of the remainder of the torn-out sheet There was no doubt that the tear was a recent one. Had the sheet been removed that very night? And had the entry been such that it incriminated the one whom it concerned? Sevier and Cora Barker! After all, why look further for the old woman's murderer, when she herself had believed those two to be in conspiracy to rob her? But Cora Barker had not returned to the house until ten minutes after twelve. Or so she said. And it was scarcely likely that she would have named the theatre manager as a corroborator of her alibi if she had not been sure that he would uphold her story. But Sevier and Cora Barker had talked together at the theatre that evening. Had the final details of the plot been agreed upon then? But if so, how had Cora Barker helped Emil Sevier, without being on the scene of the crime while it was being committed—

"Bad penny," the parrot croaked sleepily.

Dundee was startled for a moment, then he grinned.

"Thanks for reminding me, Cap'n, ' he called softly.

"Have you gone so crazy over this case that you're talking to yourself?" Strawn asked, returning at that moment. "Well boy, you're right—not that I think it amounts to a hill of beans. The Paige girl says she is positive the words 'Bad penny' didn't come up in her conversation with the old lady, and that the parrot had never spoken of them before, or Mrs. Hogarth would have told her. But you've gone nuts from the heat if you think that bird— Come in!"

Daisy Shepherd, escorted by Detective Payne, who immediately withdrew, stifled a very genuine-looking yawn as she took the chair beside Mrs. Hogarth' s desk. Her big, healthy body was clad in nightgown and kimono.

"Excuse me," she smiled at the chief of detectives, "I went to sleep waiting for you to call for me."

"Sorry to disturb you," Strawn apologised brusquely. "Where were you at twelve o'clock this evening, Miss Shepherd? To save time, I may as well tell you that there was a long distance call for you at two minutes after twelve, and that Mrs. Rhodes was not able to find you to answer it."

"A long distance call?" Daisy Shepherd was startled wide awake. "Where was it from? Did Mrs. Rhodes say?"

"No. Were you expecting such a call?"

"I was not! I haven't the least idea who could be calling me long distance."

"Where were you at twelve o'clock and a few minutes afterwards?" Strawn pressed.

"Well," the big young woman laughed ruefully, "I guess this'll teach me a lesson. If you've got to know, Lieutenant Strawn, I was down in the kitchen raiding the ice box. My appetite is something fierce, and I'd been lying in bed since half-past ten reading a book that was simply full of descriptions of swell dinners in Paris. I've been boarding here long enough to make myself pretty much at home, and I knew Mrs. Rhodes wouldn't begrudge me a midnight supper, so I sneaked down the back stairs to the kitchen—"

"Pardon me, Miss Shepherd," Strawn interrupted. He strode to the door, closed it behind him, was gone about five minutes, and returned looking well pleased with himself.

"All right, Miss Shepherd. Please go on. What did you find to eat?"

"You've been down checking the ice box, I guess," Daisy laughed, without rancour. "Well, I helped myself to a few raspberries out of a big bowl on the top shelf, took a slice of boiled ham from an oiled-paper package of it on the bottom shelf, and made a sandwich by splitting a roll I got out of the bread box. Oh, yes, I took a banana, too. There was a dozen in the top of the box, against the ice."

"And after you'd enjoyed your stolen fruits?" Strawn suggested.

"Oh, I only ate the raspberries down there. I brought the sandwich and the banana to my room. The banana skin's in my waste-basket now. I came up the back stairs, straight to my room, and I didn't see or hear anything either trip—up or down," she added positively, but good-humouredly.

"I see. Miss Shepherd, you were at one time named in Mrs. Hogarth's will, were you not?"

"Sure! I guess I held the job longer than anyone else before or since," Daisy chuckled. "I was her heiress for six months—until the day after Christmas this year. Cora Barker got the job, but I was glad to lose it."

Strawn frowned. "Suppose you explain, Miss Shepherd. Did you quarrel with Mrs. Hogarth?"

"If you knew me better, you'd know I never quarrel. I'm one of those good-natured fat people you read about and seldom meet up with," Daisy grinned. "I mean just what I said: It was a hard job being Mrs. Hogarth's favourite. She wanted you to devote most of your time to her, and she expected all sorts of presents. I practically clothed her while I was on the job. I work at Marcus-Crane's, in the ladies' ready-to-wear, you know. Been there three years, and have boarded here for nearly two years. I liked the old lady a lot, and we kept on being good friends even after I told her she ought to pick someone else to leave her money to."

"You told her that?" Strawn was frankly amazed. "Then I gather that you don't care for money—"

"Sure I like money as well as the next one," Daisy retorted. "But I make plenty for myself, without having to lick anybody's boots. I also had a pretty strong hunch that Mrs. Hogarth didn't have any money to leave to anybody—not that I liked her any the less for having her fun with us." She looked interestedly about the disordered room, with its gutted trunk, closet and desk. "You know, Lieutenant Strawn, I'd be willing to bet whoever pulled this job got stung."

2

"Well, Daisy is a daisy, all right," Strawn commented wearily after the big girl had gone and Payne had reported her room innocent of concealed treasure. "How did she strike you, Dundee?"

"Right on the funny bone," Bonnie Dundee chuckled. "I gather that she was telling the truth about the ice box?"

"Went down and had a look at it myself," Strawn admitted. "That part was the truth all right, though there is no proof that she pilfered the ice box when she said she did. Mrs. Rhodes wasn't in the kitchen herself after eleven, when she went to get a drink before going to bed. I asked her when I was checking the contents of the ice box."

"So you think maybe Daisy fortified herself with a little lunch of raspberries, ham sandwich and banana before robbing and murdering her old friend?" Dundee grinned.

"Oh, shut up! You know what I think! Sevier's our baby—"

"'Bad penny,'" Dundee reminded him softly. "'A bad penny always turns up.' Do you really think, chief, that Mrs. Hogarth, hating Sevier and fearing him as she did, would greet him with a merry little quip like that? In my opinion, humble though it is, the poor old lady would have yelled for help, instead of quoting proverbs."

"Oh, you and your blasted parrot!" Strawn retorted with weary anger. "I guess you'll tip off the defence to put the bird on the witness stand in Sevier's favour!

"That wouldn't be such a bad idea— if Sevier ever came to trial," Dundee answered softly.

"Oh, he'll come to trial all right—when we catch him!" Strawn promised. "We've got enough now to go to the grand jury with. I'd bet a month's salary that between them Dr. Weeks and the driver of that car that turned its headlights on the guy running down the alley, will identify Sevier. That places him near the scene of the crime immediately after it was committed. Coupled with that he beats it out of town and disappears off the train without showing a ticket, when he'd said he was going to

Chicago. Those two facts, together with the fact that Mrs. Hogarth saw him in her room one night and warned the police that he was planning to rob her, will bring him to trial all right."

"'Bad penny,'" Dundee repeated, very softly, and "Bad penny!" the parrot echoed sleepily.

"For God's sake, shut up!" Strawn pleaded. "I'll be as loony as you are if I don't get some sleep . . . Who the devil could she have been talking to?" he added unwillingly.

"That," Dundee answered seriously, "is what I'm going to try to find out, if you'll let me keep this diary of hers until morning."

"All right! Have a good time," Strawn conceded sarcastically. "I've got one more job here before I can turn in. The boys are still holding those roughneck pals of Dusty's downstairs. I want to hear them give him an ironclad alibi—I never heard so many iron-clad alibis in my life before! Even Mrs. Rhodes has one—answering long distance at two minutes after twelve, at the very moment when the murderer must have been ransacking this room, or twisting the scarf around the old lady's throat."

"Henry Dowd hasn't an alibi," Dundee reminded him. "He has lived here only one week, had never met Mrs. Hogarth, had never come even face to face with her—"

"So you think he's the 'bad penny' that 'turned up,' do you?" Strawn interrupted. "Well, good luck to you, Sherlock. This plodding old dick will try to find time to visit you in the bughouse—after Emil Sevier gets fitted with his last necktie!"

"Wait a minute, chief. What about those samples of food that the old lady saved to have analysed for poison?" Dundee halted Strawn as the lieutenant was leaving the room.

"Oh, Lord I'd forgot them," Strawn groaned. "Where are they?"

"Here they are," Dundee told him, throwing wide the closet door. She showed them to me last night."

He stooped to the floor of the closet, gathered up three medicine bottles filled with the liquid food—coffee, milk and soup.

"I'll get them analysed," Strawn promised wearily, as he stowed the corked bottles in his coat pocket. "By the way, I wish you'd arrange to get hold of Dowd's and Magnus's finger-prints somehow. Breakfast in the morning might be a good chance. Get Mrs. Rhodes to save, unwashed and otherwise untouched, a glass or a knife or an egg-cup that each of those two uses at breakfast. They both claim they never met Mrs. Hogarth, and if Carraway has a sample of the finger-prints of either one of them in the batch he found in this room to-night, we'll at least know he was lying . . . Well, boy, good night! Watch your chance to sneak to your room unobserved. See you in the morning about eleven, unless you get on a hot trail before then."

"Here?" Dundee asked.

"Sure. I'll have to go through all the junk in this room, then take it down to headquarters for safe keeping. I'm leaving Boyle on guard in the room to-night, and a couple of men on the grounds."

"By the way, chief," Dundee detained Strawn. "Do you think we're going to be able to keep it dark that it was I— the suspiciously interested new boarder—who discovered the murder?"

"We shan't try," Strawn chuckled. "Let the other boarders know all about it. You can tell them that the old lady asked you to buy something at the drug store while you were out, after visiting her, and that you came to her room to give it to her and found her dead. They may or may not believe you. If they don't so much the better, if your hunch that the murderer is an inmate of the house is correct. He—or she—will think you're a prize suspect, and rest easy. Of course, the morning papers will play up Sevier in a big way, but an alternate suspect will help a lot to put the murderer off his guard—provided always, that Sevier isn't our man. Which I think he is!"

It was nearly four o'clock when Bonnie Dundee tested the excellent bed in his third-floor room. But despite its softness and the fresh coolness of its sheets, Hamilton's newest detective did not succumb to sleep. In the light of the electric lamp suspended over the head of his bed he began at the first entry of Mrs. Hogarth's diary and read through it rapidly, pausing now and then, however, to copy an entry upon the cheap little tablet which held his notes on the stories the inmates of the Rhodes House had told to Lieut. Strawn.

And as he read, Daisy Shepherd's amazing statement was never out of his mind—"I had a pretty strong hunch that Mrs. Hogarth didn't have any money to leave to anybody." Before he had finished half of the six months' record of the murdered woman's life, Bonnie Dundee had reached the same conclusion. Not that there was an actual sentence or paragraph upon which he could put his finger and say: "There! She's given herself away!" But there were frequent cryptic references to her "miser's hoard" and to her several wills, and after each reference Dundee fancied he could hear a ghostly chuckle. Was it not entirely possible that the old lady had perpetrated a gigantic hoax on her fellow-boarders? Two good reasons suggested themselves immediately: first, to insure companionship and sycophantic attentions from her temporary "favourites," to alleviate the loneliness of her confinement to her room; second, to gratify her passion for meddling dramatically in the lives of others. Undoubtedly, Mrs. Emma Hogarth had watched with wicked glee her own machinations and the excitement caused by her "last will and testament" changes.

Invariably there was a first-of-the-month reference to "Letter from S. to-day," followed by veiled, cryptic comments on the news in "S.'s" letters. It was when Dundee reached the entry of 1st May that his suspicions were startlingly confirmed:

"Letter from S. to-day. Also the usual. Says she has paid another quarterly premium on her insurance policy. Wish she wouldn't keep it up. I'm sure to die before she does and never need it. S. also writes that she saw in home town paper that our good friend, J. W., is dead. Makes me sadder than I have felt for five years. I'll never forget how good he was to us in our hour of trouble, the last time we ever saw him. I often wonder how S. and I would ever have got away that day if J. W. hadn't helped us pack. S. says the paper gave him a fine obituary. He had risen to cashier of the bank. I'm glad he did so well."

His fingers shaking with excitement, Dundee hastily turned the pages to the entry for 1st June. He caught his breath sharply as he read:

"Letter from S. to-day. The poor girl is lonely and depressed. Wish she could marry again and be happy, but suppose that is impossible. Says she has had no word or news of any kind from D. all these years. For her sake and his, I hope D. is dead, but we may never know it if he is. I've lived for five years in the dread that D. would turn up."

Bonnie Dundee dropped the diary, clasped his hands behind his head and closed his eyes, the better to think clearly. Turn up—turn up—"A bad penny always turns up."

What dreadful secret had old Mrs. Hogarth kept for five years? Who was S.? Certainly someone of whom the old woman was very fond. But why not leave her "miser's hoard" to S. instead of to some temporary favourite in the boarding-house? If there was a hoard to leave! And who was D., of whom old Mrs. Hogarth lived in dread? Obviously he was the husband of S., whom she had not seen for five years, the reason why S. could not marry again. A deserting husband. But why had the old lady lived in dread of S.'s husband's "turning up."?

"At all events, S. must be notified and questioned," Dundee told himself. "If she has written to Mrs. Hogarth once a month all these years, surely Mrs. Rhodes can tell me who she is. Faithful S.! I'm afraid you're in for a terrible shock, my dear!

XI

"GOOD morning, Mrs. Rhodes! Am I the first one down?" Bonnie Dundee greeted his landlady cheerfully, as he entered the dining-room.

Although he had only two hours' sleep, the young detective lived up gloriously to his nickname. He was "bonnie" certainly, with his shining black hair, still damp from the shower, and his brilliant blue eyes, and the fresh colour of youth and health in his cheeks.

Mrs. Rhodes's haggard black eyes brightened at sight of him. "You look as if you'd slept like a baby," she told him, as she poured his coffee and then offered him cream for his raspberries. "I didn't sleep a wink myself, what with waiting on that no-account Dusty—sick as a pup he was, when he finally woke up—and worrying over what happened here last night."

"I'm awfully sorry," the boy sympathised sincerely. "What does the paper say? Have they caught Sevier?"

"No, but I hope to the Lord they do," Mrs. Rhodes. She sighed. "If this thing isn't cleared up in a hurry, my business will be ruined. The reporters have been swarming over the place since daybreak, taking pictures of the house and trying to interview me. Cold comfort I gave them!" she added, with gloomy satisfaction.

"That's right!" Dundee applauded. "Let them get their news from the police."

"Asking me where poor Mrs. Hogarth came from, and who her relatives were, and—"

"I'm afraid I'm going to bother you with just the same questions," Dundee interrupted, apologetically. "You see, Mrs. Rhodes, I read Mrs. Hogarth's diary after I went to bed this morning. And on the first of the month she invariably recorded the receipt of a letter from 'S.' Can you tell me who S. is, Mrs. Rhodes? She must be a daughter or near relative. She must be notified of Mrs. Hogarth's death, of course, but I have no clue to her full name."

Mrs. Rhodes shook her head. "I'm afraid I can't help you, Mr. Dundee. Mrs. Hogarth received a registered letter on the first day of every month for the last five years, unless the first fell on Sunday. But I never saw one of those letters myself. The postman always took it upstairs for Mrs. Hogarth's signature on the return receipt As close friends as we were, she never showed me one of the letters, or mentioned it in any way. I do know, though, that she burned each one after she read it."

"Then I shan't find one among her papers, I suppose," Dundee concluded regretfully. "But what about her outgoing mail? Surely she answered S.'s letters; in fact, she says so in her diary."

"She answered them all right—regular as the clock," Mrs. Rhodes assured him grimly, "but she was just as secretive about the letters she wrote as she was about the ones she received. She always gave the letter to me personally, but it was enclosed in an unstamped envelope, addressed to our postman. We've had the same one on this beat for about eight years. He removed her letter and mailed it for her himself. Of course, I never asked either Mrs. Hogarth or the postman any questions. It was none of my business."

"Hmm." Dundee was very thoughtful. "To-day is the last day of June, and to-morrow, Monday, is July 1st. Since the post-office is closed on Sunday, I suppose there's nothing to do but to wait until he brings the regular first-of-the-month letter . . . By the way, Mrs. Rhodes, did it ever occur to you, knowing Mrs. Hogarth as intimately as you did, that she had no 'miser's hoard' to will to anyone?"

Mrs. Rhodes looked startled, then she nodded slowly.

"To tell you the truth, I always had my doubts. There were a lot of little things, but the most important one was that she always paid her board right after the letter

came. Once—about a year ago, I think it was—her letter
didn't come until the third of the month, and she didn't
pay her board until that afternoon. And she seemed
nearly crazy with worry about the letter."

"How did she pay her board?—the denomination of
the bills, I mean?"

"That was funny, too. Her board and room was only
forty dollars a month. Of course, I lost money on her the
last two or three years, but when I said something to her
once about being obliged to raise the price, the cost of
living being what it is, she carried on something dreadful,
so I dropped it. I was mighty fond of her, peculiar though
she was. But what I started out to tell you was this she
always give me a fifty dollar bill and I gave her the
change in small bills. She spent next to nothing on
herself, outside of the few clothes she needed. Being
confined practically to her room as she was, she didn't
need much.

"So if she received a fifty dollar bill each month from
S., she managed to live on it," Dundee suggested
thoughtfully. "When and where did she get the parrot,
Mrs. Rhodes?"

"I don't know where she got it from, but I do
remember when she got it. It came by express as a
Christmas present the first year she was here. She came
here to live in May, 1924. I was curious about the parrot,
but when I went down cellar to look at the crate it had
come in, I found Dusty had used it for furnace kindling,
without having noticed whether there was a sender's
name and address on it or not."

Dundee was about to ask another question when
Daisy Shepherd entered the dining-room. She was
dressed in a light summer silk ensemble, topped with a
modish little hat that made her broad, pleasant face seem
even larger than it was.

"Going to Sunday School, Daisy?" Mrs. Rhodes
inquired, with an effort to appear her normal, hospitable
self. "I suppose church would do us all good to-day. Here's

an extra big helping of raspberries, honey—though you don't deserve them," and she smiled affectionately.

"Now why bring that up?" Daisy laughed, flushing. "But believe me, Mrs. Rhodes, that was one time when crime was justified. I guess I'm one of the few people in this house last night who had a perfect alibi. . . . No, I'm not going to church. I'm going to a hotel until I can find another boarding-house. Honest, I'd rather be whipped than to tell you that, Mrs. Rhodes, because you've been like a mother to me, but I wouldn't be able to sleep a wink in this house— Oh, hello, Norma! How do you feel, baby? You look as if you'd been crying all night."

"I—have," Norma Paige answered in a low voice, as she slipped into her chair. "Good morning, everybody." She tried to smile, but the childish little mouth quivered, and fresh tears filled the wood-violet eyes. "Thanks, Mrs. Rhodes. May I have the cream, please?"

Bonnie Dundee, eager to be of service to the girl he had lost his heart to, passed the cream pitcher so quickly that their hands touched. To his startled amazement the girl's hands flinched from his, as if—as if he were a murderer!

But as the rest of the boarders drifted into the dining-room; all of them showing the effect of the strain of the tragic night, his keen eyes told him that he was not alone in being a temporary pariah. Every hand that accidentally touched another shrank from the contact. It was then that the full horror of the situation burst upon the boy. In spite of the fact that the morning papers had played up the news that "police throw out drag-net for Emil Sevier," every boarder here—unless, of course, the real murderer was among them—looked with sick suspicion and horror upon every other boarder.

Dundee made a sudden resolution. He had not missed the stricken look in Mrs. Rhodes's eyes as she heard Daisy Shepherd's decision to quit the house of horror. And it was vitally necessary to certain plans of his own that those questioned last night by Lieut. Strawn remain in this house. He rose to his feet, smiling his friendly, disarming smile:

"I know you will all think it's none of my business, and that this speech, if made by anyone, should come from one of the older inhabitants of the Rhodes House. . . . I'll be brief, folks; I realise it will not be very pleasant for any of us to go on living in this house of tragedy, but I, personally, intend to stay. I've paid two weeks' board in advance, and I can't afford to lose it, and I wouldn't have the nerve to ask Mrs. Rhodes to refund any part of it. I imagine most of you have paid in advance—" He paused, noted the reluctant nods of his fellow-boarders, then went on: "But there is another angle to be considered. I hate like the devil to point it out, but I'm including myself, too, you know. The fact is, that every inmate of this house is bound to be more or less under suspicion, since the police have undoubtedly decided upon greed as the motive for the murder of poor old Mrs. Hogarth—and every one of us could use more money. In view of these circumstances, I move that we all stick by Mrs. Rhodes, and show the police that we have nothing to run away from."

Mrs. Rhodes gasped, then dropped her quivering face into her hands. Dundee sat down, and over the edge of his coffee-cup observed the effect of his speech upon his fellow-boarders. They eyed each other furtively, suspiciously, but slowly came their assent, led pompously by Mr. Lawrence Sharp, "speaking for myself and the wife." Walter Styles and Norma Paige said, "All right," in unison, and Cora Barker, whose haggard face was the colour of old linen, nodded mutely Henry Dowd and Bert Magnus agreed promptly and cheerfully. But Daisy Shepherd shook her head vigorously

"I'm sorry, Mrs. Rhodes, but honest, I'd go nuts if I stayed here. I've got a perfect alibi, and the police can suspect me all they want to—"

Her defiance was interrupted by the ringing of the doorbell. Mrs. Rhodes excused herself to answer it, then re-appeared almost immediately in the doorway.

"You're wanted, Mr. Dundee."

Bonnie Dundee sprang to his feet, grinning cheerfully at his startled table-mates. He found Lieut. Strawn in the hall, and, after asking Mrs. Rhodes, in a low voice, to set aside the dishes used by both Dowd and Magnus, for examination by the finger-print expert, followed his chief upstairs to the murdered woman's room.

"Any news, chief?" Dundee asked.

"Nothing new," Strawn admitted wearily. Then, to Boyle, the uniformed policeman who had kept watch in the room and who looked sadly in need of sleep, 'Anything happen after we left, Boyle?"

"Quiet as the grave," Boyle answered callously. "The parrot squawked once or twice, but I shut his trap by covering up his cage with one of the old dame's skirts."

As Strawn dismissed the policeman, Dundee stepped to the cage and removed the smothering skirt. "Poor Cap'n," he sympathised. "Nearly dead, old top? I'll fill your water dish."

And he did, reaching fearlessly into the cage while Straw looked on in amazement, for the drooping, disspirited bird made no attempt to nip his fingers. Dundee filled the little dish from the tap of the basin behind the green burlap screen, returned it to the cage, and, with the door still open, stroked the bird's feathers with a gentle hand. Suddenly he uttered a startled exclamation.

"What is it?" Strawn asked sharply, striding to the cage.

"Look!" And Dundee drew out something between thumb and forefinger and offered it for his chief's inspection. "What would you say this is, Strawn?"

Lieut. Strawn took the thing, rolled it on his palm. Looks like a bit of skin, doesn't it? How did that get into the parrot's cage?"

"Cora Barker burned her hand last night, chief," Dundee reminded him softly. "Rather an odd time— a quarter past twelve—for a tired working woman to decide to press a dress she would not wear till Sunday, Wasn't it?"

"You think she burned her hand to cover up the evidence that she'd been bitten by the parrot?" Strawn demanded, in amazement. "Well, if that's so, I guess we've got her dead to rights as Sevier's accomplice! I'll have a look at that hand—"

"Just a minute, chief," Dundee begged. "I found two or three rather important items in Mrs. Hogarth's diary, and this morning in talking with Mrs. Rhodes before the others came down, I learned a few other things that seem pretty important to me."

In spite of his chief's impatience, Dundee quietly read the noteworthy excepts from the diary, then told in detail his conversation with Mrs. Rhodes.

"Don't you agree with me, lieutenant," he concluded eagerly, "that there may be another motive for the crime that we haven't discovered yet? It seems absolutely clear to me that the old lady had no hidden miser's hoard in this room—"

"Makes no difference, if Sevier and Cora Barker thought she did," Strawn interrupted almost angrily.

"Bad penny," Dundee reminded him stubbornly.

"Bosh!" Strawn dismissed the idea contemptuously.

"I'm afraid it isn't bosh," Dundee insisted quietly.

"For five years, by her own written admission, Mrs. Hogarth lived in 'dread'—not fear, mind you, but dread that P., S.'s husband, would 'turn up.' It seems pretty clear to me that S. and Mrs. Hogarth fled from their hometown. I don't know whether they deserted D. or whether he had already deserted them, but the two women, Mrs. Hogarth here, and S. in some other city, dreaded his 'turning up.' Suppose he did 'turn up' in Hamilton with the express purpose of seeing Mrs. Hogarth. She dreaded his 'turning up,' but she has recorded no fear of consequence to herself if he did appear. What if D. came through that window last night, and Mrs. Hogarth saw him? She would not cry out to alarm the house, if she recognised him, but she might very well greet him with the old proverb, sarcastically: "So the bad penny has turned up at last.' I can imagine, chief, that those words, 'bad penny,' were repeated two or even three times, between Mrs. Hogarth and D.—"

"You can imagine a lot of tommy-rot," Srawn interrupted irritably. "This isn't a detective story, Dundee. It's an everyday police case in the ordinary little old town of Hamilton, in these prosaic old United States. No, boy, you're having a swell time, and I hate to ruin your day, but Mrs. Hogarth was murdered for the money she either had or was supposed to have hidden in the room, and when we find Sevier— Why, look, boy! Your own story is full of holes! If this mysterious D., whoever he is, actually did come to see the old lady, he would have known that she had no money and that S. was supporting her. And if Mrs. Hogarth 'dreaded' him but did not fear him, why did he kill her and ransack this room?"

"I'm not clairvoyant," Dundee grinned, "but isn't there a chance that Mrs. Hogarth had something else that he wanted, and which she refused to give him? Remember, chief, Mrs. Hogarth was a mighty mysterious character herself. She was in hiding from something in her past. In all the five years she lived here she never referred to her previous place of residence, or to any person in her past. And she wrote to and received letters from only one person—S., guarding the address so expertly that not even Mrs. Rhodes knows it. Even if you aren't interested I'll watch for that postman to-morrow more eagerly than any girl ever waylaid him for a letter from her sweetie, and—"

"What's that?" Srawn interrupted him. He hurried to the door, flung it open.

Norma Paige was at the head of the stairs, calling frantically. "Dusty! Oh, Dusty! Quick! Mrs. Rhodes! Dusty!"

"What's wrong, Miss Paige?" Strawn called from Mrs. Hogarth's door.

"Oh!" She was startled, then smiled uncertainly. "It's just Cora's wash-basin, sir. It's stopped up and the water's running out on the floor. I was helping her wash her hair, on account of her burned hand, you know, and—"

"Oh, Dusty! Please hurry and get your tools to unstop Cora's basin!"

"Maybe I can help," Strawn suggested, and by a jerk of the head invited Bonnie Dundee to accompany him.

They found Cora Barker in her room, rubbing her long wet hair with a bath-towel. At the unwarrantable intrusion of the lieutenant of detectives, and of the young man she knew only as the new boarder, the woman's haggard face flushed an angry scarlet. "Give me an extra bath-towel. I'll try to keep more water from spilling," Strawn directed, ignoring her anger.

Dundee and Strawn were mopping at the pool of water on the floor when Dusty Rhodes, much the worse for his last night's debauch, came slouching into the room, followed by his anxious wife.

"If you females wouldn't break the rules and wash your hair in the basin, things like this wouldn't happen," Dusty complained disgustedly as he knelt to ply his wrench.

A minute later, as Dusty pulled out the upper section of the drain-pipe, its little cross bars matted with long black hair, Dundee risked exposure of his connection with the police by staying the hand of the landlady's husband.

And over Dusty's protest he took the short section of drain-pipe, and walked to the window with it. Strawn followed, bending curiously over his subordinate as Dundee's fingers began to untangle the mass of hair.

"Look!" he urged in a whisper, though the others had not drawn near. "Pellets of paper caught in among the hairs. Paper stained with green ink!"

"Well?" Strawn puzzled.

"A page was torn from Mrs. Hogarth's diary last night—the entry of 19th May," Dundee answered in so low a voice that it could not carry to the group around the basin. "Here it is—or what is left of it! And last night the parrot nipped a piece of flesh from Cora Barker's hand!"

Strawn grunted incredulously, but quickly removed all the tiny pellets of water-soaked paper from the tangled mass of hair.

"Go and take your place behind the screen in Mrs. Hogarth's room," Strawn directed, his lips scarcely moving. Then, turning toward the group about the basin, he said in a normal voice: "That'll be all now, Dundee. Don't leave the house. I may want to question you again."

"Say, can I go on with this here job?" Dusty whined. "I got other work to do—"

"Here you are, Rhodes," Strawn conceded cheerfully, as Dundee hurried out of the room, striving to give a perfect imitation of a man incensed by the unjust suspicions of the police. But Norma's eyes, wide with suspicion, hurt him intolerably. . .

Two or three minutes later, Dundee from behind the screen saw Strawn enter the room, followed by a terrified woman, her head wrapped in the damp bath-towel, her bandaged hand instinctively hidden in the bids of her kimono.

"I don't know what you want of me!" Cora protested angrily. "If it's a crime to wash your hair on Sunday—"

"For the moment, I'm not interested in the blue laws," Strewn said with terrible humour. "I'm merely interested in the laws relating to robbery and—murder."

"Oh!" Cora gasped, and swayed as if she were about to faint.

"Here! Take this chair, Miss Barker. And don't faint. I'll simply have to use valuable time to revive you, and you'll be questioned anyway. Now—suppose you tell me the truth about last night, not the nice little fairy story you fed me at two o'clock this morning. . . . No, wait a minute. I know you didn't get home until about ten minutes after twelve. I checked your alibi—that far. Now suppose you begin at the moment you turned into the

Rhodes House grounds. I want to know everything—including just why and when you entered Mrs. Hogarth's room, and what you did here!"

Cora cowered in her chair. The bandaged hand fluttered to her heart "You—you know—I was in here?" she gasped.

XII.

1

"YES, Miss Barker," Strawn answered sternly. "I now that you were in this room last night after you returned from the theatre. I know that you tore a page from Mrs. Hogarth's diary—the entry for May 19th. I know further that that diary entry told the true story of why you were disinherited by Mrs. Hogarth. I know that before you burned your hand it had been severely bitten by this parrot here, that—"

"Oh, stop!" Cora moaned. "I'll tell! I was crazy to think I could keep you from knowing!"

"Knowing that you helped Emil Sevier rob Mrs. Hogarth after he had killed her?" Strawn interrupted grimly.

"No, no! That's not true!" Cora cried despairingly. "I know you must think that, but it's not true—not true!"

"All right. Spill your story," Strawn ordered sternly; glancing toward the screen where Bonnie Dundee was waiting to take down every word of Cora Barker's revised story of the murder night.

"It was just as I told you—all the beginning," Cora said wearily. "I did wait at the theatre until twelve o'clock for Bert—Mr. Magnus. When I got home about ten minutes after twelve I saw no one on the grounds or on the porch—either the upstairs porch or the downstairs porch. Not that I looked closely. I wasn't expecting to see anyone—"

"Not Emil Sevier, with whom you'd been whispering earlier in the evening at the theatre?" Strawn reminded her implacably.

"No! I didn't think he'd have the nerve to do it—rob her, I mean—after I'd told him for the third time that I'd see him in hell before I'd help him do it."

"You admit, then, that Sevier did try to get your help in robbing Mrs. Hogarth?"

"Oh, I'm not trying to lie to you now," Cora assured him with tragic hopelessness. "But please let me tell it in my own way—just as it happened. Emil said he was going to make another try at it to-night, before he left for Chicago. He was dead broke and deeply in debt. The first time he talked to me about the—the job, as he called it, was on the, night of 18th May, or rather it was after midnight that Saturday night. About one o'clock, I think it was, when he sneaked into my room from his, by way of the porch and the windows. I hadn't dreamed he was that kind of man, and at first I thought he was joking.

He'd been—making love to me, and we—we had talked some about getting married, but we weren't actually engaged. I—I never was really in love with him, but when a girl gets to be—nearly thirty—Oh, I won't lie about that either! I'm—thirty-nine years old, but I'll— I'll—oh, I don't know what I'll do if you tell the reporters—"

"The secret of your age is safe with me," Strawn assured her, the slight emphasis on the last word indicating that her secret would undoubtedly come out before the grand jury. Dundee, listening hard as he took down her words in rapid shorthand, felt his heart twist with pity. . . .

"Well, I managed to make him leave my room at last. It was nearly two o'clock," Cora went on, with the quietness of despair. "We thought Mrs. Hogarth would surely be asleep and not hear or see him when he crawled past her window, but—she did see him—was standing in the dark at her window., She said something sarcastic to Emil. She thought, of course, that Emil and I were lovers, but—we weren't! Please believe that!"

"All right!" Strawn grinned in a way that made Dundee clench his free fist. He wanted to shout to his chief: "For God's sake, ease up on her! She's telling you the truth now! Be decent to her!"

"The next day—Sunday, 19th May—Mrs. Hogarth sent for me and taunted me with having a lover. She'd always disliked Emil anyway. She told me she was going to cut me out of her will, and I told her to do so, and welcome. I couldn't explain what Emil was really in my room for—Well, I knew it would all go into her diary. Everything that happened there, that interested her, got into the diary I myself gave her. She changed her will, and named Walter Styles as her new heir, and Emil stopped pretending to be in love with me. I—hated him then."

Strawn nodded understandingly. "And when was the second time he asked you to help him rob Mrs. Hogarth?"

"I can't remember exactly. It must have been around the first of June," Cora went on dully. "I refused again, and threatened to tell Mrs. Rhodes if he didn't give up the idea."

"Why didn't you?" Strawn snapped.

"Isn't that—obvious?" Cora asked, with a shrug of her thin shoulders. "He would have told Mrs. Rhodes that he had been my lover, that Mrs. Hogarth herself had seen him coming out of my room at two o'clock in the morning, and that I was just sore at him for not wanting to marry me."

"I see. Go on."

"Well, it was about two weeks ago that Mrs. Hogarth woke up suddenly in the night—toward morning—and saw a man in her room. He had a flashlight turned on and it made just enough light for her to see that it was Emil. She turned over in bed to reach the light switch near the head of the bed, and when the light went on Emil was gone. She didn't know how he got out, because he didn't leave by either the door or the window—"

"But you know how he managed it, don't you?" Strawn pounced.

"Yes," Cora admitted unhesitatingly. "It was part of his plan. I'll show you," and she rose from her chair and stepped to the clothes closet.

Strawn followed, watching curiously as the woman entered the closet, knelt, and pointed to a wide board which formed part of the back wall of the closet.

"The nails have been pulled out of that board from the other side. Mrs. Hogarth's closet has the same back as Emil's—or rather, Mr. Dowd's. But Emil had that room then, and fixed this board so he could push it inward into Mrs. Hogarth's closet and crawl through. All he had to do to be in Mrs. Hogarth's room then was to turn the inside knob of the door. He vanished that night by stepping into the closet, whose door he had left ajar. Not that he told me, but, of course, since I knew about the closet, I knew how he had worked his disappearance."

She emerged from the closet, and quietly took her seat again beside Mrs. Hogarth's desk.

"It was soon after this informal visit, then, that Mrs. Rhodes evicted Sevier?" Strawn asked.

"Yes. I was glad when he left. I never wanted to see him again, but I had to—every day, for he played violin beside me at the theatre. Mr. Hartman, the manager, fired him last Friday, and Saturday night, as I told you, he made one more attempt to get me to help him rob Mrs. Hogarth. I refused, and I was sure he wouldn't have the nerve to go through with it alone. He wasn't a regular crook, you know, but Mrs. Hogarth's money had tempted him terribly. Well, I came home, and as I passed by Mrs. Hogarth's door on the way to my mom, I saw that her light was still on. I'd noticed it as I came up the front walk, too. I—I was terribly worried—"

"About Sevier? You intended to warn her?" Strawn asked sarcastically.

Cora flushed darkly. "No. I was worried sick over Bert's not having met me at the theatre as he'd promised to. All the way home I'd been almost crazy for fear Bert had called on Mrs. Hogarth, as he'd said he had a good notion to do, and that she'd told him that story about Emil—about his crawling out of my window at two o'clock in the morning. It would have been just like Mrs. Hogarth to think it was her duty to warn Bert against me. She must have heard the gossip about Bert and me— Everyone teased us—" Her voice broke, but soon she mastered her emotion and went on:

"I suddenly decided that, since she was awake, l'd simply ask her if she had told on me. And if she hadn't, I was going to plead with her not to—for God's sake, for the sake of the affection she had once had for me.

"Well, I knocked. There wasn't any answer. I knocked again, very low, and when she still didn't answer, I got terribly frightened. I thought maybe she had had one of her heart attacks and needed help, or that Emil had— had—" Again her voice broke. "Though he never said one word to me about killing her if she caught him trying to rob her!" Cora protested passionately.

"So you opened the door and entered?"

"Yes, I thought the door would be locked, as it always was, but it wasn't. The light was on. At first I thought she had fallen asleep, writing at her desk, then—then I saw she was—dead." Cora hid her face in her trembling hands for a moment, while the room pulsed with suspense. Then she dropped them heavily, and went on:

"I started to run out and call Mrs. Rhodes, but—I've read so many stories about the person discovering the body being suspected of the crime that I—I didn't have the courage. And then it came over me in a flash that she was dead, that she could never tell on me, but that it was all written down in her diary about Emil and me. I don't know now how I did it but I turned the pages of the diary to 19th May, tore the page out, and as I was tearing it my hand brushed against the parrot's cage. He pecked me so hard that it bled, and I knew I could never explain how my hand had got bitten like that. I was nearly crazy—"

"But you had presence of mind enough to heat your electric iron and burn your hand to cover up the bite," Strawn reminded her grimly. "Miss Barker, it is my duty to arrest you and hold you as a material witness against Emil Sevier, who will be charged for the murder of Mrs. Emma Hogarth."

"Arrest me," Cora gasped. She rose slowly, swayed, then fell in a faint at the detective's feet.

2

It was two o'clock—just after the big Sunday dinner for which few of the Rhodes House boarders had any appetite—when Lieut. Strawn sought out Bonnie Dundee in his little third-floor room.

"Well, boy," he greeted his newest associate cheerfully. "She's locked up. She'll get a hearing in the morning, and I suppose they'll grant her bail. I'll make a plea in her behalf myself, if it's necessary, but I've already had a talk with Sherwood, the district attorney, and I think it'll be all right, if she can get anyone to go on her bail."

"It seems ghastly unjust to me," Bonnie Dundee began violently, "that a woman who has done everything in her power to speed justice should be clapped into gaol as a material witness."

"Oh, she'll get out on bail. When I left the gaol, she was having the warden telephone to Hartman, manager of the Little Queen," Strawn assured him easily. "So you think she was telling the truth, the whole truth, and nothing but the truth, boy?"

"I certainly do!" Dundee answered vehemently. "Any woman who would tell her right age, when it hurt as badly as it hurt Cora Barker, would not stick at telling the whole truth about anything else under the sun. By the way, chief, have you heard anything on those food analyses?"

"No poison in 'em," Strawn grunted, as he sat down heavily on Bonnie's bed. "Didn't think there would be. And Carraway says none of the finger-prints he found in the room match up with Dowd's or Magnus's. So you see the trail keeps leading right back to Sevier."

"Of whom we have no finger-prints," Dundee reminded him softly. "Oh, maybe you're right, chief, and Sevier is our man, but—"

"If you croak 'Bad penny' at me again, I'll brain you," Strawn threatened with a grin. "By the way, in my car going down to headquarters, Cora told me how she got out of the room. She didn't leave by the door—crawled out of Mrs. Hogarth's window, then through her own window. But before she left she took her handkerchief and wiped off any finger-prints she might have made on the window-sill. Quick thinker, that dame! Of course, she destroyed Sevier's finger-prints at the same time, if he left any. Carraway is sure, though, that he used gloves. She told me something else, too. Said that, while she was on the porch going to her room, she heard a slight noise at the west end of the porch, by the rose trellis."

"I'm not surprised," Dundee admitted, with queer reluctance. "I had a look at the rose trellis while you were gone, and someone has been climbing it, all right. One of the little green slats was freshly broken, and a branch of the climbing roses was torn off the trellis."

"Good work!" Strawn commended him heartily. "I guess all we need now to convict little Emil is—Emil himself! Wonder where the devil he's hiding? Looks like he simply melted away in last night's confounded heat."

"Have you checked Dusty's alibi?" Dundee remembered to ask.

"Oh, yes. Of course, that whole lousy outfit down at Dago Pete's could be lying, but they've given him an ironclad alibi all right. He was playing pool there, behind the speakeasy bar until eleven-thirty. Then he started in to drink in a serious way, and never left the joint till my men found him and brought him in—dead to the world."

"And what did you find out about Tilda Brown, the housemaid?"

"She came in at two o'clock this morning, in a Ford, with three other whoopee-makers," Dundee answered. "Wilkens, who's on duty again, told me he talked with the whole bunch, then let Tilda go to her room. They'd been together all evening at a dance at some cheap little roadhouse twenty miles out in the country."

"Well, I guess that clears us up," Strawn yawned. "Sorry for your sake, boy, but there's not a 'bad penny' among the whole lot. Maybe he'll turn up yet, and make a claim for the old lady's estate. Fat lot of good it will, do him, eh?" he chuckled. "She sure put it over this bunch, didn't she? Leading the boarders a dance for three or four years—"

"But for once it was the piper who paid," Dundee reminded him gravely. "She has certainly paid for her fun. . . . And now what, chief?"

"I'm going to chuck everything belonging to the old lady into her trunk, lock it, and take it down to head quarters for safe keeping. Down there I can take my time looking over her papers and things, for any clues to her past—relatives who ought to be notified, and so on. Her will must he among them somewhere, and your little Miss Paige will inherit—a bunch of old clothes about ten times too big for her."

Dundee flushed at that "your little Miss Paige," but said nothing.

"You can stick around here, if you like, Bonnie," Strawn went on, addressing the boy affectionately by his nickname, for the first time. "Keep your eyes peeled and your ears open, but personally I think the case is about closed."

"Well—I don't," Dundee retorted, but the words were spoken to himself alone, after the door had closed behind his complacent chief.

Suddenly he remembered something, and sprang to the door, in time to hail Strawn before he reached the stairway. When the detective lieutenant was back in the room Dundee asked:

"Sorry, chief, but it's my insatiable curiosity: did you check up on Daisy Shepherd's midnight long distance call?"

"Oh, sure! Matter of routine. The call came from a drug store coin box in Chicago, so we don't know who was calling our Daisy. Why?"

"Well, Daisy insisted on leaving here to-day. Said she'd 'go nuts' if she stayed on here. I thought that was a little queer, in view of the fact that she claimed she'd fallen asleep while waiting to be questioned this morning," Dundee answered.

"Where did she go? I'll have a dick trail her for a couple of days, until the inquest is over—not that there's any real need,' Strawn answered good-humouredly.

"She said she was going to the Curtis Hotel until she can find another good boarding-house. By the way, when will the inquest be held?"

"I talked with Sherwood about that to-day. He's in favour of holding it off till Wednesday, unless we can catch Sevier before then. Otherwise—that is, if we drag him in to-day or to-morrow, the inquest will be held Tuesday. I'm depending on you to keep this bunch in the corral here until after the inquest, anyway."

With a grin, Dundee told him of the successful speech he had made at the breakfast-table that morning: successful in holding all boarders except Daisy Shepherd. "Which makes you the fair-headed boy with Mrs. Rhodes, I guess," Strawn chuckled "She'll be offering you board free if you don't watch out. Well, so long again. You're a good boy, Bonnie, even if you have got fancy ideas."

When he felt sure that Strawn had finished his work in Mrs. Hogarth's room and had departed with her trunk, Dundee wandered down to the second floor, rather aimlessly. What he really wanted to do was to take a long, cooling drive with Norma Paige, but he had no car, and no claims at all upon another man's sweetheart's time.

"Hello, Dundee. Feel like paying a call?" a cheerful voice hailed him as he turned towards the stairs.

It was Walter Styles, standing in the door of his own room near the end of the hall.

"Thanks. I am feeling rather at loose ends," Dundee replied gratefully, as he joined Styles. And he wondered what Styles could want with him. . . .

Nothing, apparently, for the young haberdashery-proprietor seemed to have no deeper designs upon the new boarder than to engage him in conversation They talked about the murder, of course, and of Cora Barker's arrest as a material witness, Dundee guarding his own speech carefully so as not to betray his official connection with the case. And as they talked, Styles went on with the work on which he had been engaged before he hailed Dundee.

"I'm afraid I'm worse than any girl in the house— about breaking the rule which says 'Positively no washing in rooms or bathrooms,'" Styles laughed, as he soused a pair of grey silk socks in his stationary basin. "But I have the same excuse as the girls. I actually haven't the money to spare to get all my laundry done outside. Believe me, Dundee, I've become an expert on cleaning, pressing, and light laundry. About the only things I can't manage myself, are my shirts and pyjamas."

"What do you use for taking out spots?" Dundee asked, with idle interest, his eyes roving about the pleasant little bedroom. On a chair-back, protected by a towel, hung three pairs of socks. On a line strung between the dresser and the bedpost hung other garments—washable ties, handkerchiefs, even a pair of white duck trousers, and at the very end, a pair of grey suede gloves.

"This!" Styles held up a bottle of cleaning fluid triumphantly. "It really works! Well, if you'll excuse me, I'll dress, now that my womanish work is over for the day.

I'm going to take Norma for a walk, and to a movie, too, if she'll consent to go. Poor girl! This terrible business has hit her harder than any of us. She was really crazy about that queer old woman. I liked her myself, in spite of— well, a lot of things," he added evasively, not having the slightest suspicion that Dundee had overheard both his and Norma Paige's story to Strawn.

As Dundee closed Styles's door behind him, he became aware of the slow tapping of Bert Magnus's typewriter.

"Well," he grinned, as he knocked, "he can't do more than kick me out . . . Gloves . . . Gloves! In this kind of weather!" he added to himself very thoughtfully, but the words did not refer to Bert Magnus, who was opening the door to him grudgingly.

XIII.

1

"OH, hello, Dundee! I'm glad to see you," Bert Magnus greeted his Sunday afternoon caller with surprising cordiality.

"I'm afraid I'm interrupting you again, old man," Dundee apologised, as he took the comfortable, shabby arm-chair beside Magnus's desk. "But I believe I'd never get to pay you a visit if I didn't have the nerve to butt in. You're certainly an industrious chap!"

"Industrious—yes!" Magnus agreed with a bitter twist of his mouth. "And a fat lot it's got me. If I hadn't been so industrious last night, poor Cora wouldn't be in gaol now. I'll never forgive myself for not meeting her after the theatre as I promised. The truth is, I forget everything when I'm absorbed in tinkering with this fool yarn of mine. But all the success in the world wouldn't make up to me, for causing that poor girl one hour's stay in a dirty gaol."

"I wish Cora could have heard him say that," Dundee thought, as Magnus took off his nose glasses and polished them very hard to remove the moisture which had suddenly misted the lenses. Aloud, he remarked: "She's charged only with being a material witness, you know, Magnus, I'm sure she can arrange bail the first thing to-morrow after court opens."

"I wish to heaven I had the money to go on her bail myself," Magnus worried, running his left hand distractedly through his dark-brown, oily hair. "She wouldn't have been a material witness if I had kept my promise to her. Did she actually see Sevier crawling out of Mrs. Hogarth's window? That's the rumour about the house, I believe."

"I'm sorry, but I can't tell you," Dundee answered truthfully. "But let's try to forget the whole miserable business. We can't catch the murderer or do poor Cora Barker any good by mulling it over. How's the story coming on?" And he glanced toward the battered old typewriter on the open roll-top desk.

"That's not the story," Magnus told, him, glancing toward the sheet of paper rolled into the machine. "I was trying to frame a letter to my family in Riverside, California. They're likely to see newspaper accounts of the murder at the Rhodes House, and be worried about me. Finest family a chap ever had, Dundee. I was a fool to wander, I guess, but I got the idea I'd do better absolutely on my own, not tied to mother's apron-strings. Well, she—died less than a year after I began my travels, and—" He coughed, then suddenly reached into the desk for an envelope.

"Like to see some snapshots of my folks?" he asked, his voice slightly husky. "This is my kid sister, Gertrude. Trudy, we call her. I can hardly believe she's got to be such a big girl. She was only thirteen when I left home five and a half years ago . . . Here's Dad—one of the grand old men of the fruit industry out there. He's president of a Fruit Growers' Association now, and when I go home, I guess I'll be content to take a job under him. Here's a picture of my older brother—known as 'Red.' He's dead, too, now. Wish I could have seen him again. My funny little red moustache looks as if it had wandered from his face to mine. I know I look queer with a red moustache with this dark hair of mine, but—my mother had red hair—"

He rambled on, showing more snapshots of the pleasant Spanish type of home, the "folks" in the family car, a police dog—

"I'm homesick as the devil," he acknowledged with a sigh, "but I've got a stubborn streak in me. I talked so big before I left home, and I hate to go back with empty pockets and—this." He held out the crippled right hand, with a curious gesture of contempt and self-loathing.

"Your hand was—hurt after you left home?" Dundee asked sympathetically, his eyes veering from the curled, withered fingers.

"Yes, and I've never had the nerve to write the family just how much damage I suffered in the accident. I feel like half a man, especially when I look at these pictures of Dad and Red. Splendid types, aren't they? It happened four years ago in Florida. I was travelling in a motor-bus between Miami and Hialeah, on a real estate company's sightseeing tour. The bus collided with a heavy truck and it was badly wrecked—turned over and the top caved in on us. Two of the passengers and the driver were killed outright. I thought I was lucky to get off with nothing worse than an injured hand—cut straight across the palm with a piece of the windshield glass," and he exhibited the scar.

"Rotten luck anyway," Dundee sympathised.

"Yes, the ligaments of the fingers were cut clear through, though I didn't realise it immediately. The fact is when I came out of the ether at the hospital, the nurse told me my folks were wiring frantically, and I dictated an answering wire to her—assured them I was only slightly injured. I wish now I'd had the nerve to tell them the truth later. I played the fool, too, on compensation—signed a release to the motor-bus company for a paltry five hundred, when I might have got twenty or thirty thousand out of them, if I'd known how completely my hand was ruined."

"Can't you use it at all?" Dundee asked.

"Oh, some. The thumb is all right, and I use it to space with when I am typewriting. But the fingers are useless. I learned to write with my left hand, or my career as a book-keeper would have been ended forever . . . by the way, would you like to see the story I'm working on?" he asked with engaging eagerness.

Dundee shuddered inwardly, but his affirmative was cordial.

"I'm afraid my typing is rotten," Magnus apologised ruefully. "I'm copying it over, thinking perhaps the bad typing was one reason the movie company turned it down. People are so prone to judge by appearances, you know.

"Here it is. What do you think of the title, *'More To Be Pitied'*?"

"Fine!" Dundee applauded, but inwardly groaned. Was he going to have to read through this bulky manuscript?

"I don't want to bore you," Magnus apologised, but the grey eyes behind the oval lenses were shyly eager, and Dundee could never bear to hurt anyone's feelings.

He made a pretence of skimming through the terrible, amateurish scenario, remarking, lest Magnus think he was turning the pages too fast: "I'm a quick reader. Ought to get me a job as a reader in a publishing house."

The story was so absurd, so, hackneyed, so badly written, even as a scenario, that Dundee pitied with all his heart the man who so eagerly awaited the verdict. Ashamed of his insincerity, but because those shy, eager eyes were pleading with him, Dundee read aloud, with apparent relish, the last paragraph of "More To Be Pitied":

"'And so here, with the setting sun turning the windowpanes of the old homestead into squares of pure gold, the long hard trail ended. Little Madge was at home again, but not alone now. No longer could the fierce temper of her grandfather terrify her, for she had Big Buck of the Lonesome Hills to protect her, to shield her against every storm of life, to be the father of the new little lives which would one day make the old homestead ring with happy laughter.'" He laid the script down upon the desk.

"That's a swell conclusion you have, Magnus. The fans will eat it up."

"Cora thought maybe I ought to have Madge and Big Buck walking hand in hand up the hill into the setting sun, with apple blossoms drifting down about them," Magnus worried. "What do you think? Seems to me like that's been done before—"

"I think your own conclusion is fine," Dundee assured him mendaciously. "Oh, sorry!" he exclaimed, as his elbow knocked a book off the edge of the desk. He stooped to retrieve it, saw that the front cover had flown back, revealing the flyleaf, on which was inscribed: "Herbert S. Magnus, Riverside, Calif., 10th January, 1924." He closed the book and returned it to the desk, noting that it was a text-book on scenario writing.

"You've been working at this game quite a while, I see," he remarked, hoping that the pity he felt did not show in his voice.

"Off and on. I subscribed for this course in 1924, but I've just lately got down to serious work. You see, I want to make some quick money, so I shan't be too ashamed to go home. And—well, maybe I'll take someone with me . . . Is there usually much disgrace attached to a—a woman if she's held as a material witness in a murder trial, or do you know, Dundee?"

"I wouldn't worry about that," Dundee reassured him, extending a hand which the other gripped awkwardly with his left. "Cora needs you to stand by her now, and if you feel that way about her—"

"I'll stand by, no matter what they say she did," Manus said earnestly, his grey eyes blinking rapidly behind his glasses.

"Poor devil!" Dundee groaned to himself as he made his escape. "This is the worst of the business I've elected. I'll be seeing innocent lives wrecked all the time—the flotsam and jetsam that washes ashore after every murder trial . . . But he's going to have his girl, and Cora's going to get off with as clean skirts as possible, or my name's not Bonnie Dundee."

This resolve buoyed him up temporarily, but the new detective found it hard to wait with any degree of patience for the next scene in the drama. He had ideas of his own about searching every boarder's room for possible clues, but he could do nothing on Sunday. With his fellow-guests at work on Monday, and with Mrs. Rhodes's connivance, he would have a free hand. Monday, too, would bring the postman, and he in turn should bring old Mrs. Hogarth's regular monthly letter from "S."

Sunday evening Dundee strolled down to Police Headquarters, endured a good deal of affectionate kidding from his uncle, Police Commissioner O'Brien, learned from Strawn that nothing new had developed, and that Sevier was still most emphatically missing. Dundee was discouraged. If he was right about the importance of the "bad penny" clue, then why was Emil Sevier a fugitive from justice?

Fortunately the first mail delivery was not until half-past nine on Monday, and Dundee was the only boarder who was watching for its arrival, as the stooped, grey little man plodded up the Rhodes House walk.

2

"Good morning, sir," Dundee greeted the postman deferentially. "You've probably heard that Mrs. Emma Hogarth is dead. I'm a detective," and he showed a badge which Strawn had brought him on Sunday, to be used in emergency. "I understand that you have been delivering a registered letter to Mrs. Hogarth on or about the first of the month for the past five years."

"That's right," the postman nodded. "And I was saying to myself just as I come up the walk that this is the first time that letter ain't come, regular as the calendar itself."

"What!" Dundee ejaculated."You're sure the letter didn't arrive? I'm afraid this is serious—"

"No, sir. It ain't here. You can see for yourself," the postman insisted. "First time—no, it ain't the first time either. I recollect now that one month it didn't come till the third, and the old lady was in an awful stew over it. But it did show up finally, and I reckon it will this time."

"Probably, but the letter is important," Dundee interrupted. "Mrs. Hogarth's correspondent is undoubtedly a close relative, and we sorely need the name, in order to notify her of what has happened here."

"Well, if that's all that's worryin' you," the postman brightened, "I can help you out, my boy. Fact is. I know that lady's name as well as my own. Reckon I ought to, after five years—"

"What is it?" Dundee was sorry to be so impatient, but the old man might ramble indefinitely.

"Name of Graves—Miss Sally Graves." the postman replied deliberately. "Address—No.— West 53 St., New York City."

"Graves?" Dundee repeated. "Sally Graves? That name sounds sounds familiar—"

"It's a common sort of name," the postman told him mildly. "A funny thing—The poor old lady never got letters from anybody else and never wrote to anybody but to this Miss Sally Graves. Always put her letters to Miss Graves in an envelope addressed to me, and I had to take 'em out and mail 'em for her myself. A queer character, that poor Mrs. Hogarth—"

"Yes," Dundee agreed absently, his brow knotted with an effort to remember why that name rang a bell in his memory.

"Yes, sir. A funny character," the postman went on, with almost ghoulish relish. "I've seen many a funny thing in my time—husbands and wives gettin' secret letters and usin' false names at the general delivery, but in all my experience I never did know of a woman being afraid for it to get out that she was writin' to another woman . . . Well, sir, I'll be moving on. Want to take this mail into the house for me, young feller? Save these old legs o' mine a few steps. And don't you worry. That letter'll come along on the next delivery, more'n likely—"

"No!" Dundee almost shouted. "No, it will never come!"

And pausing only to snatch the bundle of Rhodes House mail from the astonished postman's hand, Bonnie Dundee plunged up the steps and into the hall. As he tossed the mail into the hall table and reached for the phone he was half-sobbing under his breath "My God! My God". Into the transmitter he breathed urgently "Police Headquarters, and make it snappy, for heaven's sake— Dundee speaking. Put Lieutenant Strawn on the wire, please," he panted.

"Hello, boy! What's up? Have you caught the murderer?" the welcome voice of his chief came banteringly to the excited new detective.

"Listen, chief! I've got to see you right away. Wait for me there, won't you? Something big's broke. Something that puts an entirely new light on the whole terrible business!"

Ten minutes later a breathless, hatless young man catapulted into Lieut. Strawn's small office at Police Headquarters.

"What's up, Bonnie? Take it easy, boy, or you'll be passing out with the heat," Strawn urged, as he rope and swung up a chair for his subordinate.

"S. is dead! Murdered!" Dundee panted.

"Who the devil is S.?" Strawn puzzled. "Oh, yes, that dame in the old lady's diary. How do you know she's dead? Nothing in the diary about it   "

"Remember I told you as I was going to watch for the postman and get the regular first-of-the-month letter from S.?" Dundee tried to get control of himself. "Well, it didn't come, but the postman was able to tell me who S.. is—or was! Sally Graves! Sally Graves, of New York City!"

"Graves?" Strawn puzzled. "Does sound familiar—"

"Such is fame, even when you get murdered," Dundee cut in bitterly. "Sally Graves was murdered while I was in New York. Let me think—it was—yes, it was on 2nd June. A Sunday, I remember, because my boat from England docked on Saturday and one of the first things I read in a New York newspaper was the mysterious murder of an equally mysterious young woman—one Sally Graves, living, in an old brown-stone front house on W. 53rd Street. She—"

"Have they caught her murderer?" Strawn asked, almost as excited as Dundee "I remember it dimly now, but didn't keep up with it—"

"No, unless they've caught him since I arrived in Hamilton," Dundee assured him eagerly. "But let me tell you all about it, as I remember it from the newspaper accounts."

"Sally Graves was the head milliner in a smart West Fifty-Seventh Street hat shop. Had been with the shop for three years, coming to them from the millinery department of a big store. I remember that the papers commented on the fact that she had been extremely reticent about her past; in fact, none of her business associates knew the slightest thing about her, except that she was an excellent designer and apparently had no friends outside the shop."

"How was she murdered?" Strawn interrupted impatiently. "Strangled, I suppose—just to make it more hair-raising—"

"No," Dundee retorted reluctantly, but with a grin at his own expense. "Her head was bashed in with a heavy desk lamp, but there were no finger-prints on it—just blood and a few hairs. And there were no finger-prints on anything, except the dead woman's, although the murderer ransacked her one room and kitchenette apartment. She had the rear half of the second floor in one of those old brown-stone fronts, converted into light housekeeping apartments. The police found fresh ashes in the grate, indicating that the murderer had burned all of Sally Graves's papers, for none were found—not even a letter or an advertising circular."

"Any clues as to the murderer?" Strawn demanded.

"Practically none at all. The tenant of the front apartment on the second floor told the police that he heard the faint ringing of a doorbell in the rear apartment about 8:30 that Sunday morning. The medical examiner placed the time of death between eight and nine of that morning, the tenant told of hearing a man's voice call out, 'Special delivery for Miss Graves,' but paid no attention. Did not even open his door to look out; no reason why he should spy on his neighbour, of course. When he went out for breakfast about ten minutes later, he says, he heard and saw no one. As a matter of fact, the murderer could not have picked a better time to enter and escape unobserved. New York is still asleep at nine o'clock on Sundays. The Graves girl—police placed her age at about 28—was dressed in nightgown and kimono. Evidently she had risen from bed to answer the doorbell, rung by the fake special delivery postman. Post-office records showed no such letter had been received for her."

"Who discovered the crime?" Strawn asked.

"Miss Graves's first assistant designer at the hat shop. It seems that Sally had asked her friend—using the word in a loose sense, since she did not make a real friend of anyone, apparently—to have Sunday breakfast with her at eleven o'clock. The two girls were going to make new summer hats for themselves—a sort of busman's holiday—and the young assistant brought some of the materials with her. When she could not arouse Miss Graves, she became alarmed, and asked the janitor to open the door with his passkey. It was a ghostly sight. One of the tabloids carried those atrocious faked pictures showing just how the crime was committed . . . Well, the last I read of the case the poor thing was still lying in the morgue, waiting to be claimed by some close friend or relative. And the police were no nearer a solution than they had been one hour after the discovery of the body."

"I wonder why Mrs. Hogarth didn't happen to read of it in the local papers?" Strawn mused questioningly.

"Wait a minute! We've got a file of the three local newspapers. I'll look it up."

He returned very shortly. "No wonder she didn't see it. June 3 was the day that passenger plane crashed at our local airport, killing eleven people. Everything else was crowded out of the paper that day, and since they hadn't printed the lead story, the papers here practically ignored it. An obscure New York murder doesn't mean a whale of a lot in Hamilton, you know . . . Well, boy?"

"Well!" Dundee smiled, but without triumph. "'D.' turned up, didn't he? I wonder what he was looking for. Evidently he failed to find it in his wife's apartment in New York, found her mother's address instead, and came on here to look further. My God! No wonder Mrs. Hogarth 'dreaded' that he would 'turn up'!"

"Aren't you jumping to conclusions?" Strawn frowned. "In the first place, you don't know that Sally Graves was Mrs. Hogarth's daughter; in the second, you have absolutely no evidence of a connection between the two murders."

"Good Lord!" Bonnie Dundee ejaculated, in honest amazement. "I'll lay you two bets: first, that Sally was Mrs. Hogarth's daughter, and second that the 'bad penny turned up'! Let's have a look at that trunk of hers. I'll lay you a third wager that we find something in it on which to win at least one of my bets!"

XIV:

"AHA! This looks promising!" Dundee exclaimed triumphantly, as he bent over the trunk, which held all of Mrs. Hogarth's possessions. "See, Strawn? The lining of this trunk lid is loose," and he tugged at the stiff, cretonne-covered pasteboard. "A good hiding place for documents—and here they are!"

"If that's the great hidden hoard—" Strawn began, grinning cynically as Dundee straightened, two thin envelopes in his hand.

"It is—all the hoard that the poor old lady had to hide, I'm afraid," Dundee agreed solemnly. "The life insurance policy referred to in the diary. In spite of Mrs. Hogarth's prophecy, she did outlive her daughter, though she never suspected it."

"Let me see!" Strawn took the crackling green-and-white document. "You were right, boy. This policy for $2,000 was taken out by Sarah Harkness Griffin, 'also known as Sally Graves,' aged 27 years, and is made payable to 'Mrs. Emma Harkness, also known as Mrs. Emma Hogarth—Mother.' So both our murdered women were living under assumed names, and Mrs. Hogarth was really Mrs. Harkness. I wonder why—"

"So that 'D.' could not find them, of course," Dundee answered impatiently. "But he was cleverer than they were—"

"Remember, Bonnie, there's still not a shred of evidence to connect the two murders, let alone any basis for the assumption that both were committed by the same person," Strawn reminded his subordinate stubbornly. "Stranger coincidences than this are common in every police department."

"Yeah?" Dundee grinned. "Well, let's have a look at this other envelope. By the way," he interrupted himself, his blue eyes shining with sudden joy, "that will the old lady left isn't just a scrap of paper any longer! Since Mrs. Hogarth—and I'm going to call her that till the end of the chapter, if you don't mind—died without having collected the $2,000 for which her daughter's life was insured, it will automatically fall to her heiress—Norma Paige!"

"And that will be nice for Walter Styles," Strawn grinned "I believe he figured it would require just $2,000 to save his little shop from bankruptcy."

"That's right," Dundee agreed moodily,, as he slit the plain, unaddressed envelope he had found along with the insurance policy. "Hooray, chief! Look what's here!" And he excitedly waved the official-looking document under Strawn's nose.

"What is it? Looks like a marriage certificate—"

"Exactly what it is!" Dundee exulted. "Obliging us with the name of the murderer! This priceless paper certifies that on June 2, 1922, in the town of Belton, Mo., one Sarah Jane Harkness and one Daniel Thomas Griffin were united in marriage. So D. was Daniel Thomas Griffin—a very bad penny!"

"I wish you wouldn't keep harping on a conclusion for which we have no supporting evidence," Strawn complained, as he scanned the precious marriage certificate.

"By George! Sally Graves, or Griffin, was murdered on her seventh wedding anniversary!"

"Another nice little coincidence?" Dundee taunted his Chief good-humouredly. "Listen, Strawn! I'm not leaping to conclusions nearly so wildly as you think I am. Sally Graves was murdered on June 2, and all her papers were burned by her murderer! Can't you agree with me that, in all likelihood, there were letters among them from her mother, Emma Hogarth—letters which carried the return address of the Rhodes House?"

"Perhaps," Strawn agreed grudgingly. "But not if Sally was as careful about destroying letters as her mother was. Mrs. Rhodes told you that Mrs. Hogarth burned each letter from Sally as soon as she had read it."

"Why should Sally have been so careful?" Dundee countered. "She had her own apartment, did not live in a boarding-house, had no reason to fear a robbery, as had Mrs. Hogarth. If Sally Graves was the devoted daughter her monthly letters, containing fifty dollar bills, indicate, it's pretty likely that she kept her mother's letters to read over and over. It's possible that Mrs. Hogarth mentioned, in one of those letters, her pranks with will-making and hidden hoards, without making it clear to anyone but Sally that the hoard was mythical. She may even have deplored her own folly, remarking on her fears that she would be murdered for her money."

"Not likely she'd confess to her daughter that she was making such a fool of herself," Strawn objected.

"Well, what if his mother-in-law's address was the only thing that interested Daniel Griffin?" Dundee conceded. "I'll wager anything you like that he found the address, and memorised it before destroying any and every paper that could connect Sally Graves with Mrs. Emma Hogarth of Hamilton. But there was some reason why he killed Sally Graves, or Griffin, still his legal wife. What that reason was I don't know. It could hardly have been robbery since she was living cheaply and had only a moderate salary as a head milliner. The natural supposition would be that he killed her when she refused to take him back as her husband, if it were not for the fact that he came on to Hamilton and killed her mother too. That would be carrying revenge a little too far—"

"Well!" Strawn sighed. "I'm glad you admit that."

"Yes, I admit he thought Sally had what he very much wanted, that he killed her to get it, and that when he failed to find it in her possession, he believed her mother had it, and came to get it. The bad penny turned up."

"He wasn't in any hurry, was he?" Strawn gibed. "But probably he felt that a month's vacation between murders was no more than he was entitled to."

"You can't make me sore," Dundee assured him cheerfully. "I think Griffin would naturally have lain low for a while after killing his wife. And murdering Mrs. Hogarth presented slightly greater difficulties, you must remember. Not so easy to gain access, unnoticed, to a boarding-house room, as to walk-up apartment houses in New York, where everyone minds his own business. This murder required careful planning; the other was immensely, successful, although impromptu. Or it may have been carefully planned for weeks, to occur on that fateful wedding anniversary."

"I'm afraid Emil Sevier would resent the calm way you ignore him," Strawn grinned.

"But I'm not ignoring him," Dundee protested. "I think he was the keystone of Griffin's plans. Let's imagine that Griffin arrived in Hamilton on or before the date of Sevier's eviction from the boarding-house, as an undesirable tenant, and as a possible menace to Mrs. Hogarth's life and money. The dining-room is a hotbed of gossip. Probably every 'mealer' who ever dropped into the Rhodes House for dinner has been treated to a more or less complete account of Mrs. Hogarth's eccentricities and her hidden hoard. And lately, of course, has heard all about her suspicions of Emil Sevier. I can imagine Daniel Griffin dropped in for a meal, his head already teeming with plans for murdering his mother in law, and was regaled with a full account of Sevier's eviction in disgrace. To him Sevier must have seemed made to order as the perfect suspect—"

"And a most obliging one," Strawn interrupted sarcastically. "How could he have guessed that Sevier would so conveniently disappear after the murder?"

"That I don't know," Dundee conceded frankly. "But Griffin may have scraped an acquaintance with Sevier, learned, from him something that we don't know—

something that made Griffin sure that Sevier was going to be a very hard man to find after one o'clock on Saturday night. But there are at least two other reasons why it was necessary for Griffin to do the job not later than Saturday or Sunday night. As you already know, the screens to all windows, including a heavy, reinforced one for Mrs. Hogarth's window, were to be installed on Monday."

"And the other reason?" Strawn prompted, interested in spite of himself.

"That is fairly obvious," Dundee replied, but so pleasantly that his words did not carry a sting. "Always granting, of course, that I am right, and that Griffin committed both murders. If he had very much of a conversation with Sally before he killed her, he probably learned that she was supporting her mother, sending a fifty dollar bill in a registered letter, to arrive on the first of each month. To-day is the first of July. Griffin knew that if he delayed his job longer than the first, Mrs. Hogarth would not receive that regular first-of-the-month letter, and that very soon she might wire or write her daughter to learn the cause of the extremely unusual delay. If she had done so, she would inevitably have learned from the police, who are undoubtedly watching for mail addressed to Sally Graves, that her daughter had been murdered. And she would have put the police on the trail of Daniel Thomas Griffin!"

"I don't see how he could figure on the police not learning the connection between the two women," Strāwn objected.

"I believe he thought he was fairly safe on that score, after rummaging through Mrs. Hogarth's things and finding not a scrap of paper bearing Sally Graves's or Sally Griffin's name," Dundee answered. "Remember, he had already destroyed all evidence of that connection at the other end—documentary evidence, I mean. And probably Sally assured him that no living person besides her mother knew her real name. If she did not, the newspapers reporting the murder performed that service for him, by failing to unearth a single clue as to her past or to find a single intimate friend of the dead milliner. But—as usually happens—Griffin made one big mistake. He failed to notice that the lining of the trunk lid was loose at one corner."

"Well!" Strawn drew a deep breath, a mingling of incredulity and hope, as he reached for the telephone on his desk. "We'll see what your uncle, the police commissioner, has to say. This thing's too complicated for me. I'd rather take orders for a while." And he called a number.

Ten minutes later Police Commissioner O'Brien strode into-the chief of detectives' office, clapped his nephew on the back affectionately, then settled down in the only comfortable chair to hear Strawn' s story of the, latest developments in the Hogarth case.

Dundee listened respectfully, but as Strawn conscientiously repeated all of the amazing and unsupported deductions which his newest assistant had made the boy felt a genuine affection for the older, detective growing rapidly in his susceptible young heart. None of Strawn's own incredulity crept into the tale, nor did he minimise the fact that it was Dundee who had unearthed most of the new facts and made all of the deductions from them.

When he had finished, O'Brien's blue eyes were twinkling. "Didn't I tell you to park your imagination before taking your new job, Bonnie?" he reproved his nephew fondly. "Well, Strawn, I suppose we'll have to humour this lad. Get New York on the wire. And ask for Inspector Holloway. He's a friend of mine and he'll know, all about the Sally Graves case. I'll talk."

While they were waiting for the long distance call to be put through, Commissioner O'Brien took time off from his affectionate riding of his nephew to impress upon Lieut. Strawn the fact that the search for Emil Sevier must be pursued relentlessly, and that the newspapers within another twenty-four hours would be howling, editorially, for an arrest.

"I'm not letting up on Sevier," Strawn growled. "As far as I'm concerned, he's still the man we're looking for."

The call came through then, Commissioner O'Brien being fortunate enough to have caught Inspector Holloway at Headquarters.

After an exchange of cordial greetings, O'Brien rumbled into the mouthpiece: "Listen, Holloway: Have you anything new on that Sally Graves murder? . . . Well, I've got some news for you, but I'll have to ask you to keep it quiet. Not a word in the newspapers until we give the word, or you may gum up a little party we've got on here . . . Thanks, Holloway, I knew I could count on you. Now, listen! "

With an astonishing economy of words O'Brien informed the New York detective of all that had been learned from the documents hidden under the trunk lid lining—that Sally Graves was really Mrs. Daniel Thomas Griffin, formerly of Belton, Mo., and that her mother, Mrs. Emma Harkness, known as Mrs. Emma Hogarth, had been murdered. He answered questions with the precision and rapidity of a machine-gun spitting out bullets.

When at last he hung up the receiver he mopped his florid brow and beamed on his subordinates. "Guess I gave Holloway a jolt, all right. He says they haven't made the slightest headway on the Graves case, but can go ahead now on the tip I have given him. They're sending a man to Belton to-night, and I guess you'd better hop down there and make it a pleasant little twosome, Strawn. First, though, I want you to get the Belton chief of police on the wire for me. It may not even be necessary for you to make the trip."

"The telephone company must be trying to make a record for service," the commissioner chuckled, when, after an astonishingly short interval, the Hamilton operator announced, "Ready with Belton."

"Hello, Chief!" he shouted into the mouthpiece. "Police Commissioner O'Brien of Hamilton, speaking. I'd like any information you can give me on Daniel Thomas Griffin, a former resident of your town. That's right. Griffin! G-r-i-f-f-i-n . . . What's that? Good Lord! . . . May, 1924, you say? Yes, yes, go on! I can hear you! . . . No trace of him since then? . . . Can you give me a description of him now? . . . No, don't bother to call back. I'm sending one of my men down to Belton to-day. He'll explain when he gets there. . . . Thanks, old scout! Hope I can return the favour sometime. Good-bye!"

"Don't keep us in suspense," Strawn growled, as the police commissioner rocked back and forth in his chair, smiling significantly at his nephew.

"Well, Bonnie! Score one for imagination!" his uncle chuckled. "There's little doubt, lad, that Dan Griffin was a bad penny, but so far we have no proof that he turned up in Hamilton . . . All right, Strawn! Keep your, shirt on! Here's the dope: Dan Griffin, his wife Sally, and his mother-in-law, Mrs. Harkness, lived in Belton, Mo., until May, 1924. On May 10, 1924, Dan Griffin, who was a teller in the First National Bank of Belton, relieved the bank of $10,000 in unidentifiable bills of varying denominations—"

"What!" Strawn's tilted chair-legs crashed to the floor. "Mrs. Hogarth's hidden hoard!"

Dundee grinned at his chief's excitement, but said nothing, though his blue eyes were glittering with triumph and, excitement.

"Maybe," the police commissioner agreed. "Anyway, Mrs. Harkness and Mrs. Griffin left town hurriedly a few hours before the embezzlement was discovered by the bank examiner, but Dan Griffin was not with them. He was trailed to his deserted home, which he visited shortly after his wife and mother-in-law had taken a train. But there his trail ended. He has so far never been arrested for his crime, and the police also failed to trace the movements of Mrs. Harkness and Mrs. Griffin."

"Did you get a description of Griffin?" Dundee asked.

"No. The Belton chief was talking from memory. Said their files had been destroyed in a fire two years ago, before he became chief of police, but that he could secure a description for me from bank officials. I told him not to bother, that I was sending you down to-day, Strawn. But I want that description as soon as u can wire it back—in code, of course . . . And Bonnie, you're in charge of the case from this end until Strawn gets back. I'll rescind that order about parking your imagination, but—keep your head, lad."

XV.

1

IT was nearly noon when Bonnie Dundee left Police Headquarters, after a short session with Sergeant Turner of the Homicide Squad, who was to be his nominal chief during Strawn's absence in Belton. Because it was still considered of vital importance that Dundee remain in the Rhodes House incognito, it was Sergeant Turner who would receive the newspaper reporters, and Sergeant Turner who would relay Dundee's orders to uniformed policemen and plain-clothes men, whenever he required their services. The telephone company had been given a rush order for a direct line to be installed from Dundee's third floor room in the Rhodes House to Police Headquarters. And Turner had given his promise that nothing at all should be given out to the Press without Dundee's sanction. Not a syllable concerning Dan Griffin or the Sally Graves murder was to get into the papers, lest the murderer, if he was still in Hamilton and possibly in the Rhodes House itself, be frightened away.

As Bonnie ran lightly down the stone steps of the old. building which housed Police Headquarters, a camera was aimed at him, and a reporter sprinted to join him.

"You live at the Rhodes House, don't you?" the reporter asked. "Can you tell me why Strawn has had you up on the carpet so long this morning? We know that he called in Police Commissioner O'Brien, too, to help question you!"

"Do you?" Dundee grinned. "Sorry, but I'm afraid I can't tell you anything."

"Just a minute!" the reporter pleaded. "What's the attitude of the other boarders at the Rhodes House toward Cora Barker? I suppose you know she has been released on bail, furnished by Hartman, manager of the Little Queen?"

"I'm glad to hear it," Dundee said heartily."All of us feel sincere sympathy for Miss Barker, and a complete belief in her innocence of any connection whatever with the case . . . Is that an extra you have there? Thanks!" he added, as the reporter presented him with the paper.

Bonnie scanned the front page with intense interest as he strolled down Chestnut Avenue toward the boardinghouse. "HOGARTH WITNESS OUT ON BAIL" was the streamer headline. According to the newspaper account the preliminary hearing had been extremely brief, sufficient only to justify Cora's being granted bail as a material witness against Emil Sevier, still regarded by the Press as the favourite suspect. But if there was little news, the staff photographers had not been idle. There were snapshots of all the boarders taken separately, except in the case of Norma Paige and Walter Styles, as they left for work that morning. Mr. Lawrence Sharp had posed smilingly for the camera, as if he enjoyed the limelight, but if it had not been for the caption Dundee could not have recognised the picture of Henry Dowd, for that particular inmate of the Rhodes House apparently had so little relish for publicity that he had used his straw hat to screen his face from the camera. On Magnus's face there was a deprecating smile as he had hurried past the camera, but the likeness was very good.

Daisy Shepherd, as the only boarder who had fled from the house of tragedy, had rated an interview and a flattering "studio portrait," but the story she had obligingly given to the Press told Dundee nothing more than he already knew. There, too, were Dusty Rhodes, Mrs. Rhodes, and stolid Tilda Brown, the combination waitress and chambermaid. In the very centre of the picture layout was a pen drawing of Cap'n, the murdered woman's parrot, the only eye-witness to the atrocious crime. But to Dundee's vast relief there was not a word concerning Cap'n's startling revelation—the cryptic "bad penny," which, the young detective believed, would eventually bring Dan Griffin to the death house.

As he folded the paper and thrust it into his pocket Bonnie Dundee again quoted softly:

> "I've lived a life of sturt and strife;
> I die by treacherie:
> It burns my heart, I must depart,
> And not avenged be."

He drew a deep breath, realising his new responsibility for the first time. "We shan't let her go unavenged, shall we, Cap'n?"

When he entered the dining-room, a few minutes after twelve, Dundee found it crowded with "mealers," among them a half-dozen young men and two girls who, by their professionally probing questions, betrayed themselves as reporters taking this method of getting news and "human interest" angles on the sensational case.

At the long table in the centre of the room, devoted to inmates of the house, he found Mr. Sharp, booming away cheerfully to the delight of the nearby reporters; Walter Styles and Norma Paige, both very silent; Bert Magnus, whose cheerfulness could be accounted for by the fact that Cora Barker was no longer in gaol; and Henry Dowd, whose eyes were gloomily fixed upon his plate. He was not surprised at Cora's absence from the meal, nor at the explanation which Mr. Sharp immediately volunteered:

"Greetings, Dundee! Is it hot enough for you? Sorry you weren't here to welcome Cora home. She came in not ten minutes ago, after having a long talk with her lawyer. She's all in, poor girl. Having a tray in her room."

Dundee was murmuring a sympathetic commonplace when a very much made-up and overdressed little blonde dashed into the room and flung herself, panting, into a vacant chair at the boarders' table.

"Hello, Jewel!" Mr. Sharp boomed. "You've been missing things! . . . Meet our new boarder, Mr. Dundee, Jewel . . . Miss Jewel Briggs, Hamilton's most beautiful stenographer, Mr. Dundee!"

The diminutive blonde propped her elbows on the table and rested her little pointed chin on her clasped hands as she gazed with exaggerated soulfulness upon Bonnie Dundee. "I'll tell the cock-eyed world I've been missing things!" she agreed, her voice an arch drawl. "Where have you been all my life, Precious?"

"Looking for you," Dundee laughed, though he coloured to the roots of his hair.

"Then we must make up for lost time," the audacious little manufactured beauty took him up promptly. "Now —tell me everything, people! Simply everything! Isn't it just my rotten luck to have been away when all this gorgeous excitement was going on? But I didn't miss it all! You know I went straight from the train to the hotel—I'm a public stenographer at the Grandview Hotel, Precious," she explained to Dundee. "Well, there was a grand big flat-foot waiting to ask me all sorts of thrilling questions. I tried to make him believe I sneaked home from Coreyville to rob Mrs. Hogarth Saturday night, but he wouldn't so much as arrest me—and me simply dying for some good publicity so I can get in the movies or in vaudeville, at least! . . . Bert's going to write a scenario especially for me—aren't you, darling?"

"No," Bert Magnus answered unsmilingly.

"He don't love me no mo'," Jewel mourned, her rouged lips pouting. "But what do I care—now?" and she gave Dundee another soulful glance out of her yellow-green eyes. "But hurry, hurry! Tell me everything!"

Mr. Lawrence Sharp was still endeavouring to obey her, down to the minutest detail, when Dundee made an excuse to leave the table before dessert was served. He had heard a boy's soprano piping: "Western Union," and had seen Mrs. Rhodes leave the dining-room to receive the telegram. It might be for him—

"No, sir. It's for Mr. Sharp. From Mrs. Sharp, I suppose," Mrs. Rhodes told him.

He detained her for a moment to ask her, in a low voice, if she kept a register of her guests.

"Only of the house guests, Mr. Dundee. There are so many 'mealers' coming and going that I don't try to keep up with them. But I do take down the name and the last address of every house boarder. I would have asked you to sign in on Sunday, if things hadn't got so upset. Here it is, sir, and I hope you can read the different handwritings in it. Some of 'em you'd think never went to school—"

"Thanks, Mrs. Rhodes. May I take charge of this for the present? . . . That's fine; I certainly appreciate your co-operation."

He took the register to his room on the third floor, and found that his telephone had already been installed. He tested it, and was answered immediately by a voice at Police Headquarters.

"If any wires come for me, have them sent here immediately," he instructed, and then devoted himself to a perusal of the rather soiled, inky pages of the Rhodes House register. For the moment he was interested only in men who had come to board here since 2nd June, the date of Sally Graves's murder in New York. The first name he encountered after that date was Herbert S. Magnus, who registered on 5th June, from Philadelphia. That was no more, however, than Dundee already knew, for Magnus had willingly volunteered the information. Philadelphia was only two hours from New York, and New York only nineteen hours from Hamilton, Dundee reflected. Certainly a check-up on Herbert S. Magnus's past and upon his movements since 2nd June was indicated, but until he had a description of Dan Griffin there was no sense in jumping to conclusions, in suspecting everyone helter-skelter—

As if drawn by a magnet the young detective's eyes returned to a demure little signature under the date of 1st June—Norma Elizabeth Paige. Styles called her

Norma, of course, but now in his own heart Dundee could murmur that stately middle name of hers—Elizabeth. Betty? No, a Betty should be jolly and roly-poly . . . Elizabeth. And how like her that signature was—small, neat, entrancingly pretty handwriting, not scrawly and half-legible and inky like some of these others.

And then his eyes, making comparisons so wholly favourable to Norma Paige's handwriting, as they ran down the remainder of the column, widened with surprise, then slowly narrowed to gleaming slits.

2

The words themselves conveyed no information not already in Dundee's possession—"Henry Dowd, Des Moines, Iowa, 22nd June." It was the manner in which the line was written into the Rhodes House guest register which caused the young detective's heart to beat fast with excitement. For the words were printed, not written in the usual sense of the word. Each letter stood alone, as unshapely and clumsy as the first attempts at printing of a child who has not yet been introduced to the art of handwriting.

In college Bonnie Dundee had known two men who used the printing type of handwriting, but in both cases the script was almost as perfect as if the letters had been cast in metal, and yet so distinctive that a forger would have found it a hard task to imitate it. Nothing at all like this sprawly, childish "printing".

"Henry Dowd screens his face from the newspaper camera, so that his likeness cannot be published. Mr. Henry Dowd disguises his handwriting. Mr. Henry Dowd occupies the room next door to Mrs. Hogarth. Sally Graves is murdered in New York on 2nd June. On 22nd June Mr. Henry Dowd comes to board at the Rhodes House. On 29th June Mrs. Emma Hogarth is murdered," Dundee mused, telling the points off on the fingers and thumb of his left hand. "Ergo, I think Mr. Henry Dowd is asking for my earliest consideration."

He closed the register, placed it in a drawer of his chiffonier, pocketed the key, and was about to leave the room when a sudden thought occurred to him. From his coat pocket he drew the little cheap blue-lined tablet which had belonged to the murdered woman and upon which he had written in shorthand the stories of the inmates of the house as they had been told to Lieut. Strawn. Turning the pages quickly he found what he was looking for—a vital part of Henry Dowd's story:

Q. (Strawn.) By the way, Dowd, where did you come from?
A. Des Moines, Iowa., I represented a small manufacturing concern, known as The Housewife's Friend Corporation. They made up a little kit of kitchen tools, including an implement that could pare potatoes and apples and cut them in fancy shapes—
Q. Where are they located?
A. Nowhere, now. The company failed, and I was out of work several weeks, then I came to Hamilton, because I'd heard times were good here—'

Dundee slapped the tablet exultantly. "Clever Mr. Henry Dowd! 'Out of work several weeks,' were you?' And where did you spend those several weeks? In Des Moines, or—New York City?"

He was again on the point of leaving his room when the telephone rang. Eagerly he snatched the receiver from the hook. "Dundee speaking."

"Sergeant Turner, Dundee. A couple of wires for you, received within five minutes of each other. Shall I read them to you or send them by messenger?"

"Read them, please . . . Just a minute till I get a pencil . . . All right."

"This one is from the Des Moines police department," Turner told him. "Ready? 'Receiver for Housewife's

Friend Corporation says no such name as Henry Dowd appears on company's books as salesman or, other employee. Stop. Dowd also unknown at No. – Mondamin Avenue.' . . . Got that?"

"Yes!" and Bonnie Dundee's voice rang with triumph. "What's the other wire, Sergeant? I'm ready!"

"From Philadelphia," Turner answered. "Here goes:

'Hebert S. Manus employee of Acme Paper Company as bookkeeper from 1st May to 4th June, 1929. Recomiendations excellent. Resigned as of 1st June, but worked Monday and Tuesday, 3rd and 4th June, to turn over books to the bookkeeper. Purchased ticket for berth for Hamilton 4th June, leaving on 4:20 train. Roomed in private home, No. — Spruce Street. Landlady, Mrs. Christine Starrett, not at home Sunday, 2nd June, until late afternoon, having spent Saturday and Sunday in Atlantic City, but Magnus had supper with family and bed has been slept in Saturday night. Signed, Inspector Garnett, Police Department.' Got it?"

"Every word," Dundee answered. "Thanks, Sergeant."

"Wait a minute!" Sergeant Turner protested at the finality in the young detective's voice. "Since Strawn's out of town, and you're on the job incognito, don't you want me to grill this Dowd bird for you? He sounds mighty fishy to me—"

"Not just yet, thanks. I don't want to make any move until I get Strawn's description of Griffin, but I'd appreciate it if you'll detail a plain-clothes man to keep an eye on Dowd. He's out of the house most of the day, looking for work—or so he says. If he makes any move to leave town, of course I'll take you up on your offer to give him the works."

"Suit yourself," Sergeant Turner answered stiffly, as he hung up the receiver.

"I don't believe I'm very popular with Sergeant Turner," Dundee mused ruefully. "Not that I blame him —having to take orders from a cub detective."

For a long minute he stared at his shorthand notes, then returned the precious tablet to his pocket.

"I'm afraid you're rather a clumsy liar, as well as a clumsy printer, Mr. Henry Dowd," he murmured, almost regretfully, "and just now I was calling you clever. At any rate, you know your Des Moines, don't you? I'd like to have a look at the ledgers of the Housewife's Friend Corporation, for I have a hunch that you did honour that unfortunate concern with your humble services, even if the name Henry Dowd does not appear on the payroll."

There was still another telegram which should arrive at any time now, but Dundee had no intention of idly awaiting it in his room. While talking with Sergeant Turner on the telephone he had heard a door across the hall open and close, and now he locked his own door, crossed the hall and knocked.

Tilda Brown, half-undressed and with a confession magazine in her hand, opened to him, then a blush suffused her broad, stolid face. She dropped the magazine and clutched at the open front of her, cotton kimono.

"Oh!" she gasped. "I thought it was Mrs. Rhodes!"

"I'm sorry I startled you, Tilda," Dundee smiled. "But I want your help, unless you're trying to take a nap. I had a private telephone installed to-day, as you probably know—and mustn't mention to anyone else! —and I'd like you to listen and call me if it rings. I'll be either in the house or on the grounds somewhere."

"I'll be awful glad to, Mr. Dundee," Tilda assured il him eagerly. "You're a detective, ain't you, sir? I just been readin' about a detective that raided a poor, innocent girl's apartment and framed her so her husband could get a divorce to marry a blonde—"

Dundee laughed. "I'm sure you don't think I'm that sort of a person, Tilda. And you must not tell a soul just what kind of a person you do think I am."

He left the chambermaid-waitress staring stupidly at the five-dollar bill he had tucked into her hand, and descended to the main floor, where he found Mrs. Rhodes in the large, room behind the parlour—a pleasant chamber which served her as bedroom, private sitting-room and office. She was seated at a handsome new mahogany secretaire, frowning over a sheaf of bills.

"Why the heavy scowl, Mother Rhodes?" he asked lightly but sympathetically.

At the honorary title which her new boarder had bestowed upon her, Mrs. Rhodes's austere mouth quivered and her dark eyes misted with tears. "Goodness knows I try to be a mother to my young people, but sometimes I think I'm nothing but an easy mark. Just look at this light bill! Women in a house are always smuggling in electric irons and curling tongues and fans. And on top of that, somebody's been trying to use a fan or something that's got too high a voltage or whatever you call it, because the fuses have burned out three times this last month. Running a boarding-house is enough to try the patience of a saint—"

"I'll try to find the culprit for you, Mother Rhodes," Dundee promised, "for I'm afraid it's my unpleasant duty to make another search of the boarders' rooms. I presume you have a passkey?"

Mrs. Rhodes drew her, bows together. "Of course I have, but—" She sighed deeply, resignedly, then took the key from one of the drawers of the secretaire. "I suppose, being a detective, you've got a right to go poking about as much as you please, but I do hope, Mr. Dundee, that you'll try to leave everything as you find it, so my boarders won't get on their highhorses and leave me flat. This is the only way I've got to make a living—"

"I'll be very careful," Bonnie assured her gently, his blue eyes smiling at her with genuine affection. "I don't know what I'd do without your help. And now—one more thing. Can you tell me whether Emil Sevier was in Hamilton the week-end of June first and second?"

"He was right here every week-end after he came to board at my house early in May," Mrs. Rhodes said positively. "He was always grouching about having to

work on Sundays. Friday was his day off at the theatre,
and Tuesdays is Cora's."

"You're sure that Sevier was here both Saturday and
Sunday, June first and second?" Dundee persisted.

"As sure as I'm sitting here this minute," Mrs. Rhodes
retorted. "And here's proof of it."

She reached into a pigeonhole of the desk and drew
out a small notebook. "I always set down in this book the
date each boarder pays me," she told me. "Let me find
it—Here it is! 'E. Sevier—$15-2nd June.' He usually paid
on Sunday, instead of Saturday—when he paid at all. He
owed me two weeks' board when I asked him for his
room—the thieving murderer!"

Dundee grinned. Emil Sevier was undoubtedly a very
objectionable person and a defrauder of landladies, but
unless he—Dundee—was very far off the right track
Sevier was not a murderer. But it was as well not to
deprive Mrs. Rhodes of the pleasure of thinking he was.

"That's a handsome desk," he remarked admiringly,
as Mrs. Rhodes returned the notebook to its place.

"It's the first new piece of furniture I've treated myself
to in years," Mrs. Rhodes answered, her work-worn
fingers caressing the satiny wood. "I let Mr. Magnus have
my old desk—"

"Any secret drawers in it?" Dundee asked quickly.

Mrs. Rhoades snorted. "Hunh! Now you're talking
like a story book detective! Get along with you now, and
let me worry over these bills."

But, belying her brusqueness, her great dark eyes
followed him fondly as he left the room, swinging the
passkey on its loop of soiled twine.

The first door he opened with it permitted him
entrance into the room of Mr. Henry Dowd.

XVI.

1

THE securing of the passkey from Mrs. Rhodes was an act of courtesy rather than of necessity, for Bonnie Dundee had borrowed Strawn's very complete collection of skeleton keys before the detective chief had departed for Belton, Mo., on the trail of Dan Griffin.

In asking for the keys Dundee had said to Strawn: "I want to make another search for that money—and for other things, as well."

"I thought you'd made up your mind that the old lady had no hidden hoard," Strawn had reminded him.

"And so I had—before I knew about Dan Griffin's theft from the bank," Dundee had replied. "The fact that the mother was murdered after the daughter proves that if either of the women had the stolen money, it was the old lady. Isn't it fairly probable that Griffin had entrusted his stolen money to his wife, that she and her mother became panicky and fled with the money just before the theft became known to the bank? Griffin, according to the Belton chief of police, risked arrest to return to his house with the police on the trail. He would scarcely have done that for any other reason than to get his stolen money. But he found that his wife and mother-in-law had flown, in the nick of time. If he found that his money was gone, too, can't you see him searching for them for five years, with hatred and revenge in his heart? Yes, it most decidedly seems to me what Dan Griffin was after was that $10,000! If Mrs. Hogarth did have the money it must have been a sore burden to her. She could not return it to the bank without laying herself and her daughter open to arrest, and she could not use a penny of it, with a clear conscience—and I firmly believe in Mrs. Hogarth's own honesty. But she may have felt justified in willing it to a favourite fellow-boarder. Her daughter probably felt the same way about the money as did old Mrs. Hogarth—regarded it with fear and loathing. That would certainly account for the fact that Mrs. Hogarth never made a will in her daughter's favour."

And now Bonnie Dundee was going to make a serious effort to find that much-discussed "hidden hoard." He realised, fully as well as the sceptical Strawn, that the chances were about fifty to one against its being concealed in this house, but in the profession he had chosen, not even such a long chance as that could be overlooked. And as Dundee had told himself a short time before, Mr. Henry Dowd had certainly invited his earnest consideration.

The room was singularly bare of evidence of Mr. Dowd's occupancy. With the exception of a cheap black comb and a pair of cheap new military brushes on the chiffonier, and two magazines devoted to adventure stories which lay on a small bedside table, there was absolutely nothing in sight to indicate that the room was rented.

Mindful of his promise to Mrs. Rhodes to leave every thing as he found it, Dundee turned rapidly through the meagre pile of garments in the chiffonier. On shirts, soft collars and underwear, all rather badly worn, he found the laundry mark, "H. D.," and when he used one of his skeleton keys to unlock the closet he found the same initials on an imitation leather suit-case, which was empty. But his suspicion that Mr. Henry Dowd—or whatever his real name was—had something to conceal was confirmed by the fact that clothiers' labels had been ripped from the topcoat and the coat to Dowd's "other suit," which was neatly disposed on hangers in the closet.

But there was nothing else—not even a scrap of paper bearing a sample of Dowd's handwriting. If the man had received any letters since his arrival in Hamilton he was carrying them or had destroyed them. Satisfied upon this point, Dundee entered the closet and pressed upon the wide board to which Cora Barker had called Lieut. Strawn's attention. It yielded easily, with only a faint whining of the nails at the top. Yes, it made a wide enough hole to permit a slim man's entry into Mrs. Hogarth's closet.

Emil Sevier had contrived that illegal entry into Mrs. Hogarth's room, but—he had kindly left it available to the next tenant of his room! Was it not entirely possible that Henry Dowd, whether or not he was Dan Griffin, had discovered that ready-made passage and had made use of it on the night of 29th June? Henry Dowd had no alibi for the time of the murder, beyond his own statement that he was in bed in his own room. And, with that loose board between the two closets, he could have committed the murder and robbery without having once stepped out of his own door or window. And since Dundee had proved that Henry Dowd had lied, either as to his name or as to his business and home addresses in Des Moines, not much faith could be placed in any statement he had made.

"But of actual evidence against him I have none," Dundee reminded himself ruefully, "unless Dan Griffin's description happens to fit. If it does then we can add motive to opportunity—" He broke off to listen, then hastily scrambled out of the closet, having replaced the loose board, and ran from the room, closing the self-locking door softly behind him.

"Coming, Tilda!" he shouted up the stairs, and took them two at a time. "Thanks awfully, Tilda," he said a minute later, as he closed his door upon the girl who embarrassed him by the unmistakable devotion in her popping, stupid eyes.

"Sergeant Turner again, Dundee," came a voice over the wire from Headquarters. "An answer has come to your wire to the Riverside chief of police. Ready? 'Herbert S. Magnus, son of Benjamin H. Magnus, prominent fruit-grower, lived in Riverside until February, 1924. Profession, bookkeeper. Age 34. Weight about 170, height 5 feet 9 inches. Dark-brown hair, grey eyes, red moustache. Wears glasses. Family in regular correspondence with him. Father, questioned, has read newspaper account of Hogarth murder and is worried lest son involved. If so, wants to go to him. Get all that, Dundee?"

"Every word," Dundee assured the man who was now technically in charge of the case. "Please wire the Riverside chief of police our thanks and tell him Magnus is not in the least involved, and that there is no necessity of his father's making the trip, since our inquiry was merely routine. . . . Anything new on Sevier, Sergeant?"

"Half a dozen false leads," Sergeant Turner replied. "You know how it is when you set the newspapers and the public on a man's trail. Any number of helpful citizens think they have seen him, all the way from here to Chicago, and from here to Cleveland."

"Has the motorist who turned his lights on the running man in the alley come forward yet?"

"Not a peep of him. Looks to me like them lights musta been a signal," the sergeant growled, then added, "though I guess my opinion ain't asked for—"

It required five precious minutes for Dundee to soothe and cajole the disgruntled sergeant into something approaching good humour, but he counted the time well spent. New to the detective force himself he could not afford to antagonise the humblest man on the Homicide Squad, and much less so a man of Sergeant Turner's rank and real value.

Back on the second floor and, ready, to resume his unpleasant duty of snooping in his fellow-boarders' rooms, Dundee was about to pass by Bert Magnus's door when a sudden thought made him pause. He had become so enamoured of his hunch that the Hogarth murder had been a direct outcome of the Sally Graves murder, and that Dan Griffin must eventually answer for both, that he had almost overlooked a possibility which thorough-going Lieut. Strawn would undoubtedly have pointed out to him.

It was certain now that Bert Magnus was not Dan Griffin, for in February, 1924, Dan Griffin had been a teller in the First National Bank of Belton, Mo. And on 2nd June, 1922, Dan Griffin had certainly been 'a resident' of Belton, since he had married Sally Harkness on that date. But— what if the two murders had not been committed by the same man, after all? What if Dan Griffin had found what he was looking for in his wife's apartment, and had had no reason to journey to Hamilton to kill and rob his mother-in-law. Certainly this possibility existed, and was strong enough so that every inmate of the Rhodes House on the night of Saturday, 29th June, was still open to suspicion, since greed is the commonest of all murder motives.

"Even so, Bert Magnus has an alibi," Dundee argued with himself against his distaste for searching the room of a man he both liked and pitied. "Four people heard him typing in his room at the very time Mrs. Hogarth was being murdered and robbed. But there still remain two very faint possibilities: first, that he had an accomplice typing in his room while he himself slipped out of his window and did the job; second, that, knowing he had an ironclad alibi for himself, he could take a chance on acting as an accomplice for someone else, in the capacity of receiver of stolen goods. Which is tommy-rot and I know it, but—here goes!" And he used Mrs. Rhodes's passkey to unlock Bert's door.

The big roll-top desk, the chiffonier and the clothes closet were all unlocked. Dundee turned his attention first to the closet. Bert's clothes were very good but not expensive, and the clothier's labels were intact. Indeed, a well-worn winter overcoat still bore the label of a River-Side, California, haberdashery. A pocket of the coat held a pair of soiled brown leather gloves, but Dundee's common-sense was not so submerged in suspicion that he could fail to realise than an overcoat pocket was the most natural place in the world for a pair of winter gloves.

After satisfying himself that the closet afforded no hiding-place for a large sum of money, Dundee turned to the desk. Its numerous drawers and pigeon-holes were practically empty, but the young detective conscientiously accounted for every inch of space before he abandoned his search for the stolen money. Scattered upon the desk-top were pages of the manuscript, "*More To Be Pitied,*" the scenario for which the gullible amateur himself was more to be pitied than censured; a stack of cheap yellow copy paper, and three letters. The return addresses told Dundee that Bert's correspondents were his father, his sister and his Philadelphia landlady, Mrs. Christine Starrett. A romance there, possibly?

Memoranda and notes on the scenario also afforded several specimens of Bert's rather cramped handwriting—the awkward script of a man who had been forced to change from right hand to left. Out of curiosity, Dundee compared the left-handed writing with the only available sample of Bert's right-handed script—the signature on the flyleaf of the textbook on scenario-writing which he had briefly examined on his visit to Magnus' s room the day before. The two samples matched as well as could be expected.

The young detective was about to leave the room, glad to be finished with that part of his ugly duty, when his eyes caught sight of a small army trunk pushed far back beneath the desk, against the wall. He stooped, dragged it forward, and opened it, for it was not locked. At what he saw he uttered a sharp exclamation of surprise—and then he grinned broadly.

2

"I think I've found the culprit who has been blowing out your fuses, Mother Rhodes!"

Mrs. Rhodes looked up from the cheque she was writing.

Her black eyes snapped. "Then I'll give you a recommendation as a detective," she promised grimly. "What did you find?—a fan with a D.C. current? We have A. C. here—"

"Bert Magnus has enough electrical junk in his room to blow out a dozen fuses," Dundee laughed. "I never suspected he was mechanically inclined."

"He's not, and I'll have to take back that promise to give you a recommendation," Mrs. Rhodes retorted. "That box of junk was left behind by a boarder who sneaked out in the night with nothing but a suit-case, leaving me to whistle for the three weeks' board he owed me. I rented his room the very next day to Bert Magnus, before that worthless husband of mine had got around to storing the box in the basement."

Dundee grinned. "And Dusty still hasn't got around to taking the box away?"

"I did manage to push him up the stairs one night to do the job, but then he and Bert got to talking radio, and between them they thought they could construct a radio set out of some of the junk. It seems that most of the parts for a small set are there, but I could have told Bert then that it'd be a cold day in August when he got Dusty to do anything that looks much like work. If the Rhodes House ever has a radio, I'll have to buy it. But since Bert didn't seem to mind having the box in his room, I thought I'd just leave it there till the thirty days are up. The law requires me to hold a boarder's trunk for thirty days before selling-it to satisfy his unpaid board bill. Not that there's a chance that that electrical junk is worth $48, the amount Wheeler owed me. If he'd paid more attention to his job and less to that silly invention of his, he could have kept his job and paid his board bill—"

"Invention?" Dundee inquired.

"Oh, some silly gadget to be applied to a sewing machine," Mrs. Rhodes answered vaguely. "I never did get the straight of it, but he used my machine to try it out on. Well, have you found anything else to get all het up over?

Dundee flushed and laughed. "Nothing much," he evaded. "By the way, what's happened to Cap'n?"

"Norma took him, though it's more out of a sense of duty than anything else. Poor girl! I suppose that's all she'll get out of being Mrs. Hogarth's heiress, and she's afraid of the bird."

"I'm rather fond of Cap'n myself," Dundee smiled "Believe I'll run up and take a look at him—"

"If that means you're going to search Norma's room," Mrs. Rhodes began, frowning, "you'd better make quick work of it, for Norma comes home around half-past three."

"Where does she work, by the way? Those sound like bankers' hours—"

"She's not working now. She's going to a business college, to learn to be a stenographer and bookkeeper. I reckon she'll be ready for work in Walter Styles's shop by fall, though personally I don't hold with a husband and wife seeing too much of each other—"

"When do they plan to be married?" Dundee asked, and hoped that Mrs. Rhodes's keen eyes would not discover his secret.

"In September, I think, unless Walter's business goes bankrupt before then. But I guess Norma would be a big enough fool to marry him anyway, and pay for the honeymoon out of her own savings. Sho was a kindergarten teacher for three years, but decided there wasn't enough chance for advancement."

Dundee hoped for more crumbs of information about the girl whose very name had the power to make his heart beat faster, but Mrs. Rhodes abruptly changed the subject.

"I'm going to depend on you, Mr. Dundee, to help make things as pleasant as possible for poor Cora. I'm giving you credit for enough sense to know she didn't have a thing to do with murdering and robbing Mrs. Hogarth."

"Thanks," Dundee grinned. "Of course, I agree with you, and I'll do my best—"

"You don't have to go so far as to make Bert jealous," Mrs. Rhodes interrupted grimly with one of her grim smiles. "Looks like the Rhodes House will have two weddings in the near future. I'm glad for Cora; she's a fine woman, even if she did let Emil Sevier make a fool of her."

"Then you think that Cora and Sevier were—well— lovers?" Dundee probed diffidently.

"If I'd thought so, I wouldn't have let it go on in my house," Mrs. Rhodes retorted. "But there was certainly a good deal of what the kids these days call 'heavy petting'. By the way, Daisy Shepherd is coming back here to board. I thought she would—"

"What! She's changed be mind already?" Dundee exclaimed.

"Daisy always was sort of flighty, but I'm mighty fond of her, so when she phoned at noon to-day and asked for her old room back, I told her to come right ahead. She'll be here in time for dinner to-night. I told her Sunday morning, when she came out into the kitchen and began to cry on my shoulder, that she'd want to come back to Mother Rhodes. She seemed to hate to leave as much as I hated to have her go. Hung around in the kitchen all morning, first crying and then laughing at herself for a big baby, but—you'd have died laughing at the sight, munching at something nearly all the time. I never saw such a girl for eating in all my born days. Why, when I came back down after they'd arrested poor Cora and taken her away, there was Daisy— Oh, drat that phone! I guess it's another reporter—"

But whoever it was and whatever further confidence in regard to Daisy's greediness had been interrupted, Dundee did not wait to find out. Very slowly, very thoughtfully, he ascended the stairs on his way to Norma Paige's room.

"There are so many possible angles to this fiendish case that I'll go dippy if I don't find a solution soon," the young detective told himself disgustedly.

"Hullo! Hullo!" the parrot greeted him cheerily as he entered the girl's room.

"Hello, Cap'n!" Dundee went to the cage and fearlessly reached in to stroke the green-and-yellow head. "I'm thinking of turning this pesky case over to you, old sport. How about it?"

The parrot turned gravely on his perch and cocked a bright eye at the detective. "Bad penny! Bad penny!" he croaked, proud of the new addition to his extensive vocabulary.

"Right you are!" Dundee laughed. "Between us," we'll avenge your dead mistress yet, Cap'n. Thanks for reminding me."

He was more cheerful as he set about the disagreeable task of searching Norma Paige's room, for the parrot's words seemed like a good omen. The room, unlike Henry Dowd's, was redolent of its owner's personality. Dainty curtains of white voile, splashed with yellow daffodils, fluttered at the double windows, and the same material—immaculate, ruffled—was used for bedspread and dressing-table cover. Dundee had a strong suspicion that the girl's own exquisite taste and competent, little hands were responsible for this expensive daintiness, unusual even in so good a hoarding place as the Rhodes House. Big, fleecy towels and absurdly pretty little face towels of line linen, all embroidered with a monogrammed "P," hung on the rack above the stationary basin, and upon the green burlap screen were tacked a score of water-colour sketches —undoubtedly the girl's own handiwork, which she had once used in her kindergarten classes, for the subjects were the sort to appeal to small children.

Against the wall near the door was a small table, bearing an old typewriter of the same make and vintage as the one used by Bert Magnus. He was later to learn that both machines had been rented from the same agency.

Beside the machine was a stack of yellow second-sheet paper, also identical with that which Magnus used. In the little drawer of the table were a great many letters, some of them addressed in a bold, masculine handwriting, but most of them obviously from girls. Dundee glanced at them enviously. So many people knew her better than he did, but no one could think her dearer, sweeter, prettier.

Fighting with the distaste he felt at the thought of rummaging among her intimate belongings, the young detective paused before the dresser. In neat little silver frames there were three enlarged snapshots: one of Norma and Walter sitting very close together in the lawn swing; another of Bert, Cora and Norma on the front porch; the third a group of small children, with Norma a laughing nucleus for the charming picture. For the moment Bonnie Dundee was tempted to commit a small burglary of his own, but he had promised Mrs. Rhodes to leave everything as he had found it.

Sighing, he forced himself to go on with his ugly duty, which he performed as thoroughly as if his heart were in no way involved. But in dresser drawers, bookcase and clothes closet he found absolutely nothing to cast the slightest shadow of suspicion upon the girl he believed in so implicitly.

He had scarcely closed her door after his unchivalrous visit when he heard light, swift steps upon the stairs.

"Oh, hello, Mr. Dundee." Norma Paige greeted him with a tiny but cordial smile. She was swinging her broad-brimmed Leghorn hat, and as she spoke she pushed the moist bronze curls from her white forehead. "Did you find a position to-day?"

"I'm afraid I was too lazy to hunt very hard for a job," he grinned, and hated the necessity for lying to her. "But I've got a little scheme for work I can do in my own room. Had a private phone installed to-day," he explained, on the spur of the minute, for he knew his telephone would excite comment and speculation. Then, sounding more bold than he felt: "Won't you be a Good Samaritan and come down to sit on the porch with me? I believe it's a little cooler now and I'm aching for some cheerful conversation—"

"I'm awfully sorry," Norma interrupted hastily. A little stiffly she justified herself: "I've got to practise on the typewriter till dinner-time. My first speed-test to-morrow, and I'm simply terrible on typing!"

"You have your own machine?" he asked, to make conversation, so that he might hold her a little longer.

"Oh, no! I rented it; or rather Mr. Magnus rented it for me, since he was getting one for himself. It's a fearful old rattle-trap, but it's good enough for practice work. I can use the machine at school only an hour a day and that's not enough for a slow-coach like me."

More disappointed than he would admit to himself, Dundee had no choice but to idle until dinner. With Norma at home there was no chance for more room searching that day. But scarcely had the six o'clock meal started than Bonnie Dundee realised that a detective does not keep union hours—that his day's work was not yet over. . . .

XVII.

1

DINNER that Monday evening began as a rather ghastly affair, due largely to Cora's first appearance in the bosom of the boarding-house family since her arrest the day before as a material witness against Emil Sevier, charged with the murder of Mrs. Emma Hogarth, but still a fugitive from justice. Much as Dundee admired her courage there was no question that Cora Barker was like a death's head at the feast. And feast it was, for Mrs. Rhodes, whether from fear of losing her boarders or out of the very real kindness of her heart, had outdone herself on the menu.

Making a brave effort to ignore the unusually large crowd of "mealers" at the little tables scattered throughout the dining-room, the regular boarders tried to chat normally with Cora, expressing their sympathy only with their eyes. But it was no go. Cora's tragic, suddenly old face brooded somberly over the food she scarcely touched, and the only answers she gave were monosyllables—until Bert Magnus entered the room, a little late.

Dundee wished that the two could have had that first moment of meeting after the tragedy alone, unwatched by the curious though sympathetic eyes of all their fellow boarders. By accident or design, the chair next to Cora's had been left vacant, and now Bert Magnus slipped into it. Without actually seeing the clasp, Dundee was sure that their hands—Berts uncrippled left and Cora's right—met and clasped beneath the table-cloth, and there was no doubt at all of the fond, faithful light in Bert's eyes as they clung to the woman's tragic dark ones.

It was Jewel Briggs who broke the tension. "I tell you, folks! Let's all walk down to the Little Queen with Cora and see the movie, just to show everybody that we're her friends. Bert, you walk with Cora, Walter with Norma, and I'll let Mr. Dundee escort me, if he's very good—"

Dundee's impulse was to refuse, tactfully, but as he was about to speak he caught a strange expression on Cora Barker's face. Her eyes were blazing upon Jewel Briggs and her nostrils were flaming ominously, but she said nothing, and Jewel seemed to be blissfully unaware of the searing glance. But Cora's enmity toward Jewel Briggs required investigating. Besides, he could do little sleuthing until the next day, when the boarders would again be out of the house.

"Am I going to be left out of this little pleasure jaunt?" Mr. Lawrence Sharp boomed.

"Remember you're a married man, you old sheikh," Jewel laughed. "But since, Mrs. Sharp is still out of town, suppose you beau Daisy—if she'll take a chance—"

Daisy Shepherd, whose broad, jolly face was entirely free of any embarrassment, although she had been unmercifully teased about her speedy return to "Mother" Rhodes' good meals, seconded Jewel's suggestion heartily and so the party was arranged.

At a quarter to seven the four couples sallied forth from the Rhodes House, rather self-conscious of their championship of a woman under arrest, but talking and laughing at a great rate to hide their embarrassment. Before they had walked a block the pairing off had taken place, and Dundee found Jewel Biggs clinging to his arm, her small, over rouged face dimpling and coquetting with him. A few paces ahead of them Walter and Norma strolled together slowly, the man's head bent worshipfully toward the hatless, bronze-curl crowned head of the girl.

But that would not bear thinking of and Dundee resolutely turned his attention to Jewel's chatter.

"Of course, I'm terribly sorry for her, but isn't it lovely how this awful murder has brought them so close together?" Jewel was saying eagerly.

"Miss Paige and Mr. Styles?" Dundee asked, slightly puzzled.

"Oh, dear. You weren't listening," Jewel cried reproachfully. "Of course I don't mean Norma and Walter. They were engaged before the murder. I do believe you're half in love with Norma already, you bad boy. Is my heart going to be broken all over again?"

"Not by me!" Dundee laughed, and hugged her arm close to his side. He might as well play up. "Whom did you mean then, Jewel?"

"Cora and Bert, of course, stupid! I'm going to ask Cora to let me be maid of honour at her wedding—if you'll be Bert's best man."

"Are they engaged?"

"I don't suppose he's asked her yet, but a blind man could see that he will. I've always heard that sympathy is love's first cousin. Now if only I could get into some terrible trouble—"

"I rather imagine you will if you ask Cora to let you be her bridesmaid," Dundee chuckled. "You don't seem to be her favourite girl friend at the moment—"

"Oh, as soon as she and Bert are really engaged she'll get over that," Jewel retorted happily. "You see, Precious, I used to have a crush on Bert myself, and Cora's still just a little mite jealous. I wasn't really in love with him, but I was sorta thrilled over him being a writer and—all that. He's written the grandest scenario! Cora heard me offer to copy it for him, or let him dictate it to me, straight to the machine, you know, because I'm an awfully fast stenographer, and it made her wild. Not that she had the least cause to be really jealous! Bert's not the type of man I could love in a big way, not tall and handsome—like you! And he is sort of—well—"

"Boring?" Dundee suggested, laughing delightedly.

"Well, yes, because I'm not a bit literary myself, and a girl does want to talk about something besides stories and travelling. Do you blame me, Precious?"

Bonnie Dundee reassured her with great gravity, and proceeded to talk on the subject most interesting to Miss Jewel Briggs—herself. But at the entrance to the Little Queen Theatre Jewel hung back, to revert to the topic of Cora's jealousy.

"You really believe me when I say Cora had no cause to be jealous of me with Bert, don't you, Bonnie?" she coaxed, for she had managed very skilfully to extract the secret of the young detective's nickname.

"Of course, Jewel," Dundee assured her gravely.

"Besides," she rushed on eagerly, "when I was flirting with Bert—oh, in a nice way, you understand!—Emil Sevier was still at the Rhodes house, and we all thought Cora had no eyes for anyone but him! Goodness knows she let him make love to her enough! I thought Bert would be too slow for Cora. Honest, Bonnie, I don't believe that flat-tyre ever kissed a girl in his life! And how Cora could fall for him, after Emil's ninety-horse-power kisses—"

But at that interesting moment the rest of the party gaily demanded that the two loiterers join them. There was only time for Jewel to whisper urgently:

"Promise me you won't let Cora tell you any jealous old fibs on me, won't you, Bonnie Dundee?"

He gave the promise readily enough, but he knew he had no intention of keeping it, if Cora Barker had any real information which she might feel impelled to give the new boarder. For—Jewel Briggs was really worried. Why? Why?

Although he and Jewel walked home together after the first show, leaving Bert to see the picture twice and then escort Cora home when her work as pianist was finished, Dundee was no nearer to finding the answer to that question than when they had entered the theatre.

He was still tantalised by this new and probably trivial mystery when he set about his work upon the major mystery the next morning—a mystery still very little nearer a solution than it had been two hours after Mrs. Hogarth's murder. A cold chill of fear settled upon the young detective's characteristic optimism. He who had been so sure of a penchant for criminology that he had stubbornly blasted his father's hopes of making a surgeon of him! Still, he told himself miserably, he had not been altogether useless. It was he who had hit the trail of Dan Griffin, he, really, who had sent Lieut. Strawn to Belton, Mo. But what if, as Strawn stubbornly insisted, that was a wild goose chase?

Well—he shrugged, as he hung up the receiver of his private telephone to Police Headquarters—if he was failing, he was in good company. The police system of the entire state had as yet failed to turn up the slightest clue to their whereabouts of their own pet suspect—the elusive Sevier. But that reflection, instead of raising Dundee's spirits, depressed them the more. Where the devil was Sevier—and why? If Sevier were as innocent of the actual murder as Dundee believed him to be, why in the name of all that was sane and reasonable was Sewer in hiding? Certainly no other crime had been unearthed against him; therefore his extreme invisibility must have some connection with the Hogarth case. But what? *What?*

These questions nagged at the young detective's brain like buzzing mosquitoes which one slaps at but never hits, as he doggedly followed his programme of searching every room in the Rhodes House. To make matters worse, Bonnie felt like a meddlesome busybody as he pawed through the highly innocent and uninteresting possessions of Mr. and Mrs. Lawrence Sharp. For one breathless moment he thought the treasure hunt was ended when he found a thick package of what he felt like greenbacks tucked away between Mrs. Sharp's decorous nightgowns. But the greenbacks proved to be cigar coupons.

"Now what?" Dundee asked himself, after he had made a very thorough job of the big, pleasant room. "Guess I'd better tackle the fair Tilda's domicile next. Poor Tilda's so dumb she wouldn't have got wise to it yet if the murderer had tucked his stolen fortune into one of her apron pockets."

But if Tilda could have overlooked such a dubious present, Dundee's keen young eyes would have discovered it—and it was certainly not to be found in that cheerless little room. The chambermaid's cheap finery—ten-cent store perfume, face powder, lipstick, glass beads— touched the too susceptible young detective's heart. And when he found a pathetic little ten-cent-store wrist-watch, whose painted hands were destined for ever to record the time as 6:10, Bonnie Dundee registered a mental vow to replace the heart-wrenching imitation with a real watch of white gold—when the troublesome case was solved. . .

There was no use wasting time in Daisy Shepherd's room, he told himself, since Daisy had returned to it the night before after a thirty-hour sojourn in an hotel since the murder. But he might as well have a look, on general principles.

Daisy had unpacked her wardrobe trunk the night before, he discovered, but the lazy Dusty had not yet removed it to the basement storeroom. The two halves stood slightly ajar, and Dundee was about to turn away from its obvious emptiness when he caught sight of an envelope lying face downward in the shoe compartment. There was no letter inside, but the address was: "Miss Daisy Shepherd, care of Marcus-Crane's Department Store, Hamilton—" Odd that this letter should not have come to the boarding-house, where Daisy's other mail was delivered, as he had already observed. The postmarks were Chicago, 27th June, and Hamilton, 28th June. In the upper left-hand corner was the picture and name of a Chicago hotel, and below the name of the hotel was inscribed in ink the name of the writer, "A. B. Wheeler."

Wheeler. Wheeler. Dundee frowned. He had heard that name very recently, but when, where, in what connection?

2

"No, nothing from Lieutenant Strawn yet," Sergeant Turner answered Dundee's telephone inquiry at noon that Tuesday. "But we could hardly expect anything before the middle of the afternoon; he didn't arrive in Belton until this morning. But as soon as that description of Griffin comes in, I'll phone you. . . Anything from your end?"

"Nothing of importance," Dundee confessed. "I've been going over the house with a fine tooth-comb, but haven't found a trace of the $10,000 yet."

"Why should you?" Sergeant Turner chuckled maliciously. "Sevier's got it—wherever he is!

"Probably you're right," Dundee conceded without resentment.

After luncheon, the most cheerful meal since the murder, the young detective followed Mrs. Rhodes into her own bed-sitting-room.

"Well, Mother Rhodes, I'm nearly through with my snooping," he greeted his landlady, with the wide, disarming smile which always brought an answering smile to her austere face. "There's only the basement left—"

"Well, if you're expecting to find whatever it is that you're looking for down there, I'm afraid you're going to be disappointed," Mrs. Rhodes answered flatly. "The basement's used as a storeroom and it's one place I make sure is locked all the time. There's only one door—at the foot of the kitchen stairs; and the two little windows are barred. The door was locked on the night of the murder— same as it always is. I gave one of your detectives the key that night and when he'd got through searching the basement he gave it back to me."

"Does anyone besides yourself ever use the key?" Dundee asked.

"Dusty, of course. Once a day he takes all the waste papers down and stuffs them into burlap sacks, to be used for starting fires in the furnace in the winter. But I make him give the key right back to me—"

"Then all the trash from every boarder's room since the furnace was last used is down there now?" Dundee asked, his blue eyes glinting with excitement.

"Reckon it is," Mrs. Rhodes conceded. "But there won't be any way to tell whose rooms a lot of the stuff came from. Mamie, the chambermaid who had been with me for nearly two years, got married last week and Tilda has only been here since Thursday."

"Could I get in touch with Mamie, if necessary?"

"If you want to make a trip to New Mexico I guess you could," Mrs. Rhodes retorted.

Five minutes later the landlady was pointing to two big sacks, the second of which was only half-full of trash.

"Those are the last two sacks Dusty has filled," she said, in answer to his question.

"When did he begin to use that one?" Dundee asked, pointing to the one which was overflowing.

"Let's see—must have been about the first of June. Yes, those are two of the new bags that I bought the last week in May."

"Thanks awfully, Mother Rhodes. You're wonderful! If everyone had as good memory as you have, a detective's work would be a cinch," the boy assured her gratefully

"Yes, I've got a good memory—too good for my own good, maybe," Mrs. Rhodes retorted, as she turned toward the stairs leading to the kitchen.

"Now what did she mean by that?" Dundee puzzled. Then he suddenly remembered another matter that had been nagging unsuccessfully at his own memory. "Just a minute, Mother Rhodes!" he called, and the landlady paused on the top step. "Didn't you mention a man named Wheeler yesterday?"

"You're a fine detective, I must say!" she gibed at him fondly. "Wheeler is the man who skipped out, owing me three weeks' board, and leaving nothing to pay it with but that trunk of electrical junk in Bert's room."

"Of course!" Dundee cried, deep chagrin on his handsome face. "You said he sneaked out the night before Magnus came here to board, didn't you? That was on June fourth then . . . By the way, Mrs. Rhodes, were Wheeler and Daisy Shepherd particularly interested in each other?"

"They paired off a lot, but I wouldn't say they were dead in love with each other," Mrs. Rhodes answered grudgingly. "Daisy's a mighty popular girl, even if she is big and no raving beauty, but she's got too much sense to marry a no-account chap like Arthur Wheeler."

Tilda's voice called her urgently then, and there was no opportunity for Dundee to question her further. But he was whistling cheerfully as he set to work, in spite of the unpleasantness of his task. Sometimes his fingers flinched fastidiously, but gradually, as the little pile of promising finds increased, his squeamishness was forgotten.

It was in the first sack—the half-filled one—that Dundee made his first important discovery. It was a Pennsylvania railroad envelope, on the face of which had been jotted by the ticket seller:

"Lv. N.Y. 6.15 P.M. June 3 Ar. Chi. 2.05 P.M. June 4."

To the left of these two lines was a pencilled memorandum of the amount of the fare and the cost of the Pullman upper berth. Stubs for both the railroad and Pullman tickets were in the pocket-soiled and crumpled envelope, but it was not this discovery which made Bonnie Dundee whistle long and low.

"How very careless of you, dear Henry—or whatever your name really is," Dundee murmured reproachfully. "And you really ought to learn to print more neatly if you're going to adopt that method of disguising your penmanship."

For on the back of the railroad company's envelope were three samples of Henry Dowd's amateurish printing, and the samples were three names: Henry Dobbs, Herman Dodd, Henry Dowd. The first two had been crossed out, showing that the man who was now known as Henry Dowd had, for reasons known only to himself, hit upon the last of the three as his choice of an alias, to fit the initials of his real name, whatever it might be.

That "Henry Dowd" was an alias was no surprise to Dundee, for he had suspected as much after receiving the wire from the Des Moines chief of police. But that "Henry Dowd" had left New York on 3rd June, one day after Sally Graves had been murdered—

For the first time since he had taken up his profession Bonnie Dundee felt the itch to apply the third degree. With all his heart, right then, he longed to belabour the meek, diffident little Mr. Henry Dowd with a machine-gun fire of questions. But since he was under orders to remain incognito, so far as his official connection with the case was concerned, the savage joys of the third degree were not for Bonnie Dundee—yet. And he had no relish for the idea, of turning this new, information and Henry Dowd over to Sergeant Turner And after all—he consoled and excused himself at the same time—nothing could really be done until Strawn had wired his description of Dan Griffin Strawn should bring back Griffin's finger-prints, too, and samples of his handwriting. If Dowd's finger-prints matched those of the bank embezzler—

"Whoa, Bonnie, my lad!" the young detective checked himself ruefully. "Even if we proved that Henry Dowd is Dan Griffin, we'd still be pretty far from a conviction on either the Sally Graves or the Hogarth murder. If Sally's murderer or Mrs. Hogarth's murderer left a single clue on the scene of the crime we've still to find it. Except—" and he grinned broadly, "'Bad penny.' Good old Cap'n! But I'm afraid Strawn's right—and that our one eye-witness could never be allowed to take the stand. Too bad, Cap'n. You have more sense than a lot of morons who raise their right hands and swear to tell the truth, the whole truth and nothing but the truth—and then tell anything but the—Heigh-ho! Now what's *this*?"

This was a wad of yellow typewriter paper—four sheets folded together six times, so that the result was a small tight oblong. But what made it puzzling was the fact that the wad was frayed and oil-stained. After frowning over it a bit Dundee tossed it aside, but when, farther down the sack, he came upon an almost exactly similar wad he decided to add it to his collection of things that should be pondered over.

Toward the bottom of the big bag he found three or four sheets of what seemed to be one of the discarded versions of Bert Magnus's scenario, "*More To Be Pitied*"— torn across twice. Poor devils. He could revise that drivel until he was a grey-haired old man, and still it would be fit only for the waste-basket, Dundee reflected.

"Believe I'll help him make a scenario out of this case, if I ever solve it," he grinned. "It ought to make a swell talkie—with Cap'n in the title role."

On the very bottom of the bag he found half a dozen crumpled sheets of the yellow tying paper. As he smoothed one his heart leaped, and involuntarily he raised the paper to his lips. For it was her slim, white little fingers which had blunderingly hit the keys to record the lines with which the sheet was half-filled. There was her lovely name, comically misspelled, so that she became Noram Elizbaeht Paige." With the fourth line of practice, however, Norma had become quite proficient. Three times she got it beautifully correct—Norma Elizabeth Paige. And then she had essayed a new practice line, not quite so successfully, for she had written: "Mrs. Watler Havrefrod Styles." Possibly it was her disgust at having so mutilated her future name that made the girl tear the sheet from the machine and discard it. Dundee took care not to kiss *that* line! Of the remaining crumpled sheets, two were doubtless Norma's, two Bert's, for Dundee recognised badly typed paragraphs from the scenario. But the ownership of the last sheet was problematical. There was nothing on it but a string of q's, then, half-way down the sheet and several spaces toward, the centre, a q struck over so many times that the paper had been almost cut through.

"Machine out of order," Dundee diagnosed, and made vague plans of hinting to Norma that he was awfully good at fixing things. If it was her typewriter that was acting up he might have the inestimable pleasure of repairing it for her.

He was about to stuff the mass of trash back into the bag when his exploring fingers touched something hard and cold, and he brought out into the light a broken *pince-nez* lens. The glass had snapped at the edge where the nose-piece had gripped it. Without thinking much about it, Dundee added the broken lens to his small collection.

Stuffing the trash back into the bag the detective caught sight of a crumpled sheet of pale-blue notepaper. Funny he hadn't noticed it before. He smoothed it over his knee, saw that the handwriting was a woman's, that it was dated "The Rhodes House, Sunday, 22nd June"— just one week before Mrs. Hogarth was murdered. A girl's unfinished letter—and certainly none of his business, Dundee told himself. Then his eyes involuntarily, swept over the short, incomplete message, and he discovered, with a startled exclamation, that it was most decidedly his business . . .

XVIII.

BONNIE DUNDEE sprang to his feet and held the crumpled sheet of pale-blue notepaper close to the unshaded bulb which swung from the ceiling of the basement. But his eyes, in the dimmer light of the corner where the trash bags were kept, had not deceived him. He read it again:

The Rhodes House,
Sunday, 22nd June.
I have asked you repeatedly not to bother me. I have no intention of doing what you ask and it will be useless to call me or write me again—

"Now who—?" he frowned, and then so simple an explanation occurred to him that he could have kicked himself for his stupidity. "Cora, of course! Warning Emil Sevier to lay off, that she wouldn't have anything to do with his plan to rob Mrs. Hogarth."

He added the note to his little pile of possibly important "clues" to he knew not exactly what, and was rummaging in the other trash bag when his self-respect reared its bruised head and demanded audience with his brain.

"Why should Cora Barker have to write to Emil Sevier, when they worked side by side at the movie theatre? Why couldn't she simply tell him to let her alone? And somehow I can't see Cora using baby-blue stationery. Orchid or cream or grey—yes; but, baby-blue No!"

Then he temporarily dismissed the unfinished letter from his mind, for he had made another discovery. Not much of a find, certainly, but at least it gave him an excellent specimen of Emil Sevier's handwriting, if such a thing should ever be needed. The thing Dundee held in his hand was a Little Queen Theatre programme, for the week of 9th—15th June. The double sheet had been folded back and forth, time and again, in "accordion pleating," but before nervous or absent-minded fingers had done the pleating, they had written all over the white margins: "Emil Sevier, Emil Sylvester Sevier, E. S. Sevier." It was a dashing signature, one ornamented with many fancy curlicues. It was easy for Dundee to picture the man who now was a fugitive from justice, brooding in his room, and absent-mindedly scribbling his name upon the programme of the theatre which he had honoured with his services as violinist.

"Join your little friends, Emil, but don't contaminate them," Dundee, chuckled, as he laid the pleated theatre programme besides his other finds.

And back to the messy task he went. Lord, what a lot of junk accumulated in a boarding-house! Empty face-powder and candy boxes; silk stockings hopelessly "laddered"; wrapping paper and twine; advertising circulars; cigarette stubbs—ugh! And then he found still another sheet of paper which made him pause and speculate with narrowed eyes.

It was a billhead of "The Gentleman's Shop," owned by Walter Styles. There was one long column of figures, which added to a four-figure total, and another column whose sum was considerably smaller. The liabilities and the assets of "The Gentleman's Shop"? More than likely, Dundee concluded. Scrawled across the two columns were the words: "Oh, God! What's the use?" And helter-skelter across the bottom of the sheet he found:

"$20,000? $15,000? $10,000?"

"My dear Walter, I do believe you were speculating upon the amount of money poor old Mrs. Hogarth had cached away in her room, and which you were temporarily an heir to! Or were these interesting calculations and speculations made after you were disinherited, and just before you proposed to Norma Paige, the new heiress?

"At any rate, my dear Walter, one might say, off-hand, that you were a fairly desperate young man when you did this bit of figuring."

That betraying evidence of Walter Styles's urgent need for money was the last find Dundee was able to add to his little collection, however. Bundling the lot into his handkerchief and stuffing it into his coat pocket, he trudged upstairs to the kitchen, where he found Mrs. Rhodes temporarily alone, engaged in dicing apples and celery for the dinner salad.

"One more favour, Mother Rhodes," he coaxed, as he returned the key to the basement door. "Do you recognise this handwriting?" and he showed her the sheet of pale-blue stationery, taking care, however, that only the first words of it—" The Rhodes House, Sunday, 22nd June" — were exposed.

"Of course I do! I seen it often enough," she retorted. "That's Daisy's handwriting, and the very stationery I gave her for a Christmas present, if you must know. A Fine detective you are—fishing girls' love letters out of the trash—"

"Then I don't deserve an apple, do I?" he sighed regretfully.

"Oh, take it and run along," she scolded, but she polished the little red apple until its cheeks shone. "I suppose you've got to earn your living somehow, but it does seem to me—"

"Me, too!" he laughed, as he strolled out of the kitchen, munching his apple.

"But he was not laughing when he returned Daisy Shepherd's unfinished letter to his coat pocket. To whom did that letter, in its final form, go. And what did the person want Daisy Shepherd to do? How easy it would be to leap to conclusions! So easy to connect the board-beating A. B. Wheeler, who had written Daisy from Chicago, with the long distance call which had come on

Saturday night at twelve o'clock, and which Daisy could not be found to answer. So easy to put two and two together and make it add up to five! For he had no proof at all that this peculiar message in his pocket had ever been intended for A. B. Wheeler, or that even remotely concerned Mrs. Emma Hogarth's "hidden hoard."

"Why the devil doesn't Strawn wire that description of Griffin?" he asked himself angrily, and then charged up two flights of stairs to make the same demand, but more tactfully worded, of Sergeant Turner.

"I've been ringing you, but you didn't answer," came the detective sergeant's retort. "Just got a wire from Lieutenant Strawn. Says he's leaving Belton to-night, but prefers to wait till he gets here to give you his news. Trip not very successful, he adds."

"What does he mean—not very successful?" Dundee cried. "If Griffin lived and worked in a bank in Belton, I guess he can at least get a description of the bird, can't he?"

"Lieutenant Strawn is my superior and yours," Sergeant Turner answered brusquely, and hung up the receiver without the formality of good-byes.

"Damn!" Lieut. Strawn's new subordinate was near to unmanly tears of rage, as he slammed the receiver upon the hook "Nothing to do but mark time for another twenty-four hours—"

Deeply discouraged, he transferred his little collection of "clue" to his suit-case and locked them up contemptuously. "Maybe Mrs. Rhodes is right in her estimate of me—just a kid having a lot of fun at playing story-book detective! Clues! Hunh! Bet there's not a real honest to-God clue in the whole lot!"

But he felt better when he had had a cool shower, washing away all traces of his trash burrowing, and had arrayed himself handsomely in his best summer suit. Maybe Norma would join him for a stroll about the grounds this afternoon before dinner . . . .

But though he strolled most conspicuously, taking care to keep in sight within her window, in the hope that she might look out, see him, find the prospect not unpleasing and join him, he was again doomed to disappointment.

It was nearly five o'clock when the sight of Dusty Rhodes shambling toward the abandoned hothouse on the west lawn reminded the young detective that he had neglected to search that particular place.

"She says I gotta mow the lawn for an hour before dinner," Dusty replied to Dundee's idle question. "Lawnmower's in the hothouse. Allus got somep'n for me so do. If it ain't this it's that; and if it ain't one durn thing it's two."

"Life's like that, Dusty," Bonnie sympathised hypocritically. "Mind if I have a look at this old greenhouse of yours? . . . Hmm! Pretty sad, isn't it?"

"I'm aimin' to get around to settin' out some plants, but she's allus got somep'n for me to-do," Dusty sighed, as he trundled the squeaking lawn-mower out into the sunshine, leaving the young detective to stare about at the desolation within.

At least half of the glass panes which formed the walls and the sharply peaked roof were broken, and those that remained were opaque with dust. Scattered about the dirt floor and upon sagging shelves were ancient flower-pots, the burying places of long-dead plants. But in one of the pots, half-hidden under the sere leaves of a dead geranium, Dundee made a discovery. It was a cigarette butt, showing half the name of a brand which Dundee recognised as a Cuban import—a cheap cigarette, but not very popular because of its biting strength. He was about to leave the hothouse, elated over his find, when he caught sight of a piece of paper blown against the underside of one of the lower shelves. He retrieved it, and then his heart sank. So Strawn was right after all, and Sevier had been on these grounds as late as last Saturday!

For the thing which Dundee held in his hands was a programme of the Little Queen Theatre, folded in accordion pleating, exactly like the programme he had found that afternoon in the trash bag. And while this programme was not lavishly autographed by Emil Sevier, there could be no little doubt that the same nervous hands had folded both.

Twenty minutes later Dundee was making Sergeant Turner, his nominal chief during Lieut. Strawn's absence, a present of his two finds.

"I've checked them both," he admitted, with admirable grace, for he was keenly disappointed to find that he had apparently been on the wrong track all along. "This is the brand of cigarette that Sevier smoked, according to Mrs. Rhodes. None of the other smokers in the house could stand them, always refused when Sevier offered them. The flower-pot in which I found it is directly under a broken pane in the roof. It rained early Saturday morning, and hasn't rained a drop since. If the stub had been there before Saturday, it would have been soaked. You can see that it hasn't been rained on."

"And the theatre programme? What does that prove, beyond the fact that Sevier probably folded it?" Sergeant Turner asked.

"The programme is for the current week at the Little Queen, that is, for the week beginning last Sunday. But I telephoned the manager and he told me that the new programmes are distributed in the theatre on Saturday. Sevier was at the Little Queen Saturday night, as we know. Undoubtedly he picked up one then, and while waiting his chance in the hothouse, absent-mindedly pleated it in his characteristic fashion, then carelessly dropped it."

"They always leave some clue," Sergeant Turner commented tritely. "Well, congratulations, my boy! We've got Sevier sewed up—if we ever find him!"

But Dundee was not quite so happy as Sergeant Turner. It is hard to give up a pet theory.

XIX.

1

"HELLO, folks! How's tricks?" Jewel Briggs demanded gaily, as she took her place at the dinner-table that evening. "Everybody happy? I am! Made $13 to-day! Big beauty-and-leg man from the east. Press agent for a musical show that's going to make us hicks sit up and take notice. You never saw such a flock of letters and wires, and I charged him double the usual rates without batting an eye—"

"By winking an eye, you mean, don't you?" Daisy Shepherd chuckled.

"Now, Daisy!" Jewel pretended to be not angry, but just very, very hurt. "At that, he did tell me he could get me a job in the first row of the chorus, but I told him I could make more as a public stenographer, so long as nice old suckers like him stopped at the hotel. Oo-oh, look! Our Henry is actually smiling! What's happened to you, Henry? Land yourself a swell job?"

Henry Dowd cleared his throat and stuck out his chest a hit. "I was fortunate enough to make an advantageous connection—yes," he admitted.

"He means he got a job," Jewel elucidated to Bonnie Dundee, on her right. "And say, what about you, boy friend? I warn you I'm an expensive sweetie, so if you want me to be true to you, you'd better make an advantageous connection yourself."

"Don't let Jewel fuss you," Daisy advised comfortably. "If a man walks down the street with her once she makes him stop at the jeweller's to pick out a wedding ring. But if you're really up against it for a job, Mr. Dundee, I can speak a word for you at Marcus-Crane's. There might be an opening for a floor-walker—"

"Can't you just see him in a morning coat and striped trousers, and a gardenia in his buttonhole?" Jewel cried, clasping her hands ecstatically. "They'd need a traffic cop in his department."

"Thanks, Miss Shepherd," Dundee responded gratefully, ignoring Jewel. "I've been lining up what I thought was going to be a good job, but it doesn't look so good right now."

"That being the case, you need cheering up," Jewel decided. "Can't have my sweetie sad! This is your night off at the theatre, isn't it, Cora? What say you play the piano for us so we can dance?"

"That would be rather a bus-man's holiday for Miss Barker, wouldn't it?" Dundee suggested, after a keen glance at poor Cora's tired, ravaged face. "I'm sure she'd rather rest—"

"No. I'll be glad to play for all of you. I—I don't want to be alone," Cora answered huskily. And across the table her tragic black eyes sought Bert Magnus's, with such wistful appeal that Dundee felt his throat constrict painfully.

"Don't you worry, Cora!" Jewel sung out brightly. "The worst of this awful business will be over after the inquest to-morrow. Won't it be thrilling to attend a real inquest? I'm going to be there, too, though I really don't have to be, since I wasn't here Saturday night. But I wouldn't miss it for world—Why, Norma! What's the matter, honey? We haven't had dessert yet—"

"—I don't feel well," Norma Paige gasped, as she rose hurriedly from the table, her lovely little face as pale as the ivory-silk dress she was wearing.

"Aren't you and Walter going to dance?" Jewel persued incredulously.

"I hardly think dancing is in very good taste—just yet." Walter Styles said sternly, as he rose to follow his fiancée from the dining-room.

"A slap on the wrist for you, Jewel!" the little stenographer addressed herself pertly, but her yellowish-green eyes snapped angrily. "This is a boarding-house, and none of us is kin to old Mrs. Hogarth, so far as I know!"

And although the others seemed a little self-conscious they gathered around Cora Barker at the piano. Jewel seemed to have voiced the majority opinion.

"Play something snappy, Cora," Jewel urged, and as the first notes of a new fox-trot followed the swift play of Cora's slim fingers she held out her arms to Bonnie Dundee.

Jewel danced as audaciously as she talked, and there was a faint flush on the detective's check before the fox-trot was finished. As they danced past a window he saw Norma and Walter seating themselves in the lawn swing.

There was a spatter of applause, led by Mr. Lawrence Sharp, who had been pompously propelling Daisy Shepherd up and down the long parlour.

"Splendid, Cora! How about a waltz next? The wife and I took prizes for our waltzing, before we were married," he boomed.

But Cora, to the surprise and consternation of everyone, swung into "The Prisoner's Song." With chin raised and nostrils flaring, she played on and on, with Bert Magnus bending protectively over her as he turned the sheets of music.

"Telephone, Jewel!" Mrs. Rhodes called in a loud whisper from the doorway, and Dundee grateful made his escape to the front porch.

He wandered up and down the porch for awhile, frowning, his hands thrust deep into his pockets. Poor Cora! She was at the breaking point—

Suddenly a rather good tenor voice was lifted in song:

> "Please meet me to-night in the moonlight,
> Please meet me to-night all alone;
> For I have a sad story to tell you—

It's a story that's never been told."

Dundee strolled to the french-window nearest the piano and peeped in. It was Bert Magnus singing.

"He's playing up magnificently," Dundee reflected, and felt a strong desire to shake Bert's hand.

Cora Barker must have felt some such impulse, though much stronger, for Dundee saw her turn and lift her face to Bert's—her great dark eyes swimming with tears.

When the dismal chant was finished there was a chorus of shivers and protests from the small audience, with an urgent request from Jewel, who had returned.

"Pity sake, Cora! Play something livelier for Bert to sing. And what a Rudy Vallee he turned out to be! Come on now; something real sweet and drippy."

Cora, flashing a defiant, hate-charged glance at the vivacious girl, softly struck the first notes of "Drink to me only with thine eyes," and Bert, after a whispered word with the pianist, the while his hand lay gently on her shoulder, began to sing, his voice vibrating with sincerity.

When the song was finished, Dundee, who still lounged against the window, saw Cora drop her face into her thing hands, heard Bert say in a low, shaken voice:

"Thank you, dear. Won't you play another of the old ones?"

But Cora shook her head as her hand groped for his. Rather hating himself for prying, Dundee listened as she gasped in a choked voice:

"Oh, Bert! You do like me a little, don't you? I've been so unhappy—"

"More than a little, Cora," Bert Magnus answered earnestly. "When all this trouble is over, and you are free to go where you like—"

Dundee was about to slip away then, but Cora's eager interruption held him:

"Oh Bert! . . . Then you didn't mean what you said to Jewel?"

"Jewel? I don't know what you mean, dear," Bert answered, in a puzzled voice.

From the front end of the porch there came a glad cry: "Oh, there you are, Bonnie Dundee! Can't escape Mama!"

It was Jewel, of course, and there was nothing for Dundee to do but to join her, with as good grace as possible.

"Listening in on the love birds, you bad boy?" Jewel chided him gaily as she clasped his arm with both hands. "Are they engaged yet?

"Not quite," Dundee grinned, as he followed Jewel into the parlour.

"I do wonder what Cora's got such a hate on me about—now that she's got Bert just where she wants him," Jewel whispered, apparently much puzzled.

Dundee forbore to tell her that he might have been able to enlighten her if she had not called him away, and when he saw Bert and Cora, now seated side by side on the piano bench, in earnest conversation, he wished the more profoundly that Jewel had not so arbitrarily fixed upon him as her new "boy friend."

"Though it probably hasn't the remotest connection with the case, and I'm excusing my insatiable curiosity on the grounds that a detective must find out everything," he told himself ruefully.

At last Cora raised her head and, after dabbing at her eyes, flashed a completely happy and oddly triumphant glance about the parlour.

'What shall I play next?" she cried.

For a long time to come, Bonnie Dundee was to remember that proud, triumphant look on Cora Barker's face; and thank God that it had been granted to her to be wholly happy that Tuesday evening.

2

Down into slumber fathoms deep the shrill clamour of a telephone reached and pulled Bonnie Dundee up into startled wakefulness. But he had been dreaming that Norma Paige had broken her engagement to Walter Styles and was whispering to him: "I only thought I loved Walter, because after I met you—" so his voice was none too cordial as he snapped:

"Dundee speaking."

"Sergeant Turner," came the familiar voice. "We've got Sevier. Better come down."

"So that's that," Dundee told himself lugubriously, as he jerked on his trousers. "I suppose they'll get a full confession from him by morning and me and my 'bad penny' will be the joke of the police department."

He looked at his watch. It was twenty minutes past two. As he tip-toed into the third floor hall he hoped the clamour of his telephone had awakened no one, but even if it had, and his connection with the Hogarth case became known, it could make little difference now, probably. He was relieved, however, when not a door opened, either on the third floor or on the second, as he stole downstairs. The house was utterly still, and dark except for the weak little bulb shining dimly in the front downstairs hall. He let himself out as noiselessly as possible, feeling in his pocket to make sure the front door key which Mrs. Rhodes had given him was there, to insure an equally noiseless return.

Ten minutes later a uniformed policeman, who looked as triumphant as if he had effected the capture himself, single-handed, was ushering Dundee into a small room at Police Headquarters.

"Says he was on his way here to give himself up for questioning," the policeman whispered, chuckling. "That's what they always say—when they get nabbed within a mile of Headquarters. There he is, sir. Looks like a tough baby, all right, don't he?"

And Dundee, after his first glance at Emil Sevier, wanted for the murder of Mrs. Emma Hogarth, was forced to agree.

Sevier was crouching in an uncomfortable straight chair in the centre of the small room, his handcuffed hand tightly clasped, and the knuckles pressed against his bared teeth, so that he seemed more like a snarling dog worrying at a bone than a man. Thin, rather short, olive-skinned, black-eyed, with longish black hair in tortured disorder, as if the manacled hands had been tearing at it in helpless rage. Directly above his head hung an unshaded, high-powered light in an eye-searing blue bulb. The lids of his eyes were already red-rimmed, either from sleeplessness or from that pitiless glare of electricity. It was hard to imagine this tormented wretch as Cora Barker's lover, whose "ninety-horse-power kisses," as Jewel had described them, had been the talk of the boarding-house, His light-tan suit needed pressing rather badly, but his shirt was immaculate.

Around the captured suspect were clustered nearly a, dozen plain-clothes detectives and three uniformed patrolmen, and planted wide-legged, truculent, menacing, before him was Sergeant Turner.

"I'm asking you again, Sevier, and I've got means of making you sorry if you don't answer—where have you been hiding yourself since you killed and robbed Mrs. Hogarth?"

Sevier's teeth closed sharply over his knuckles before he lifted his head to answer, his eyes glaring hatred at his tormenter and accuser:

"I've told you I didn't kill Mrs. Hogarth, and I'll see you all in hell before I tell you where I've been since Saturday night. This is what a guy gets," he added bitterly, "for coming forward like a man to give himself up for questioning—"

Sergeant Turner's short laugh was like a bark. Then he thrust his head almost into Sevier's face. "Yeah, you gave yourself up! That's good for a laugh with me any time, that is! My men nabbed you five blocks away from Headquarters—and you were headed in the other direction!"

"I was going to give myself up," Sevier insisted doggedly. Then he flared up: "What the 'hell do you think I'd be hanging around Hamilton for, if I hadn't come back here of my own accord to give myself up? You cops were looking for me for three days and you didn't find met And you'd never have laid a hand on me if I hadn't come back of my own accord—"

"All right then, all right!" Sergeant Turner snarled. "You come back here to give, yourself up for questioning—" and he mimicked Sevier's fear-cracked voice—"so suppose you loosen up and do a little answering. You ready to take down his confession, Brede?"

A sallow-faced boy seated at a small pine table, in a corner of the room looked up from his notebook and nodded.

"He'll sit here till hell freezes over if he waits for me to confess to a murder I didn't do!" Sevier promised violently, his voice breaking on a sob. "'And you can keep me here till you starve me to death before I'll tell where I've been these last three days!"

"And you're the nice young man who was strolling over to Police Headquarters to give himself up for questioning!" Sergeant Turner taunted him. "just oblige me by telling me the kind of questions you intended to answer, Sevier! Was I to say, 'Hello, Emil! How's the boy?' and 'Is it hot enough for you?'"

At that, Dundee stepped into the room from the threshold, where he had been a silent, slightly nauseated spectator.

"Good evening, Sergeant Turner," he greeted his superior quietly. "I believe Lieutenant Strawn might prefer to have me question Sevier, since I have been actively at work on the case, and have all the threads in hand."

For the moment Dundee was afraid that Sergeant Turner's vitriolic tongue would be turned upon him with a contemptuous refusal, but just as the outraged sergeant was opening his mouth to speak a familiar voice boomed heartily from the doorway.

"Well, well! This looks quite like a party. Glad you remembered to invite me, Turner!" It was Police Commissioner O'Brien, and when he had joined the group around, the prisoner he clapped an affectionate hand upon his nephew's shoulder. "Am I in time to hear you strut your stuff, boy? Going to teach us old fogies some new tricks, eh?"

"I have not had time to question Sevier yet, sir," Dundee answered with his wide, boyish grin, "and I'm afraid I'm an awful cub at the third degree. Mind if I handle it in my own way?" The last words were tactfully addressed to the glowering police sergeant.

"It's up to you," Sergeant Turner muttered.

"Thank you. Will you let me have that small package I brought you this afternoon, Sergeant? Yes, that's right. Thanks," and Dundee confronted the somewhat neglected and puzzled suspect, balancing a large envelope thoughtfully on his left palm.

He did not speak for a long minute, but held Sevier's eyes with his own until some of the wild fear and anger had faded out of them.

"Your name is Emil Sevier?" he asked at last, as cordially and easily as if he were addressing a fellow-guest at Mrs. Rhodes's table.

"You know it is!" Sevier retorted sullenly, but without violence.

"Your full name is Emil Sylvester Sevier, I believe?"

"How the devil do you know that?" the prisoner demanded, startled, "Sylvester is my middle name, all right, but I don't like it, so I don't use it—sign my name Emil Sevier, or E. S. Sevier."

"I got the information from this," Bonnie Dundee told him, and drew from the envelope the accordion-pleated theatre programme on which Sevier had scribbled his name in all its variations. "This is your signature, isn't it?"

The manacled hands reached for the programme, which Dundee politely permitted the prisoner to examine.

"Yeah, that's my writing—but what of it?" Sevier still held the programme, and, as Dundee watched, the nervous brown fingers began to re-pleat the double sheet, as if from force of habit, while his trap-fearing eyes stared at this strangely friendly young man.

"Sevier," Dundee began quietly, "I see no use in wasting time. I know you want to get this business over with as badly as we do. . . . Now listen to me courteously, please, without interrupting, and I promise you courtesy in return."

There was a snort of contempt from Sergeant Turner and an answering chuckle from one of the uniformed policemen. But Dundee went on as calmly as if he had not heard:

"I am not going to ask you, Sevier, if you were at the Rhodes House last Saturday night, for I know you were and as I said, I don't want to waste time. . . . No, please! There's no use trying to protest, Sevier, for I have proof and I am willing to show you the proof when the time comes. For several weeks you planned to rob Mrs. Emma Hogarth of the money she had, or was supposed to have, hidden in her room. By the way, Sergeant Turner, was any large sum of money found in this man's possession when he was arrested?"

"He was too smart to be carrying it around with him," the detective-sergeant answered, with poorly-veiled contempt for the questioner.

"I never— "

"All right, Sevier," Dundee interrupted. "As I said, you planned for weeks to rob Mrs. Hogarth and you tried to get Cora Barker to help you do the job. She refused several times, the last occasion being Saturday night, at the Little Queen Theatre. Once you tried alone—entering Mrs. Hogarth's room from your own room by means of a loosened board in the clothes closet. Mrs. Hogarth saw you and later warned the police that you were trying to rob her, and that her life as well as her money was in danger."

As Dundee spoke, very quietly, almost soothingly, the prisoner appeared to be shrivelling up, turning into a wrinkled, dried little old monkey of a man before their very eyes. But he obeyed Dundee; he did not speak. Only his eyes—held as if hypnotised—alternately denied, agreed, or pleaded.

"On Saturday you announced your intention of going to Chicago to look for a new job, having been fired as violinist for the Little Queen. Early in the evening you checked your bag at the parcel room of the station, and shortly before eleven o'clock you told everyone good-bye at the theatre. Then you went to the Rhodes House, bent on carrying out alone the scheme which you had planned for weeks. It was still too early for safety, however, so you managed to gain the shelter of the old greenhouse on the lawn, there to bide your time. As you waited you pleated the new programme for the Little Queen, which you had picked up in the lobby that evening—just as you are pleating that one now—"

The prisoner drew a shuddering breath and dropped the programme with a gesture of fear and loathing. But before his trembling lips could form a lie, Dundee went on quietly, but relentlessly:

"While you were waiting, Sevier, you smoked one of your favourite cigarettes, and put the stub in a flower-pot. Here it is. I see you recognise it," he added, but without triumph, as the stricken man's eyes widened and then set in a stare of horror.

"A few minutes before twelve o'clock, Sevier, you believed the coast was clear. You crept out of the green-house, crossed the driveway and climbed to the second story of the house by means of the rose trellis on the west side of the porch, and although you are not a heavy man your weight broke one of the little slats in the trellis, and—I see by your hand—the thorns of the climbing rose scratched you rather badly."

The prisoner's eyes wrenched themselves away from the hypnotising stare in which Dundee's gleaming blue eyes held them, and fell to gaze stupidly upon the ragged but almost healed scratch which zig-zagged across the back of his right hand. But still he did not speak.

"You had already possessed yourself of Dusty Rhodes's old tweed cap and you were wearing it when you entered. Mrs. Hogarth's room and killed her. . . . No, wait!" he commanded sharply, as Sevier gasped for words. "When you left that room by the window you were still wearing the cap, but you had removed it once to insert one of the parrot's green feathers beneath the lining, so that Dusty Rhodes might be accused of your crime. . . . Keep your seat, Sevier!" he commanded sharply, as the prisoner struggled to his feet. Then, as Sevier sank back into his chair with strange docility, Dundee continued: "Dr. Weeks saw you running away from the Rhodes grounds, down the alley, at about a quarter, after twelve. Mrs. Hogarth was murdered between 11:45 and 12 o'clock, Sevier, and—well, I think that's all," he concluded quietly.

"All!" Sevier tried to shout, but the word was a strangled sob in his throat. His manacled hands tore at his collar, as if to help the words come out. "All lies! Think you got me framed pretty, don't you? Well, I didn't do it! See? It's a pack of lies—"

"Then why did you run away and hide for three days?" Dundee asked quietly.

XX.

DUNDEE'S quiet question made Sevier's jaw drop and a momentarily blank look take the place of frenzy in his eyes. Then he made a superb effort at recovery:

"I hadn't done anything wrong. I had a right to go where I pleased. And I came back here as—as soon as I knew the police were looking for me."

"You don't really expect me to believe that, do you, Sevier?" Dundee asked reasonably. "You had a ticket for Chicago. You ran to catch the train. But you left that train at the first stop, before the conductor had had time to collect your ticket. You were so broke that you could not even pay a three days' board bill, were compelled to leave your violin with your landlady as security. And yet you wasted a ticket to Chicago, made no effort to cash it in at any ticket-office in the state, although you could have done so if you had no fear of showing your face. . . . Now, Sevier, I suggest that you tell me the truth about last Saturday night. If some of my conclusions are wrong, you can undoubtedly set me straight— by telling the whole truth. You fled from the Rhodes House grounds that night because you knew Mrs. Hogarth was dead—murdered!"

"But l didn't kill her!" Sevier screamed. "And I don't know who did! But I know who was in on it!"

"Whom are you accusing, Sevier?"

"Who do you think?" Sevier leaned back in his hard, straight chair, his chest heaving, a flame of hate and triumph in his red-rimmed eyes. "Cora Barker! That's whom I'm accusing," he mimicked Dundee's perfect grammar. "I wouldn't have told on her if she hadn't tried to pin it on me. She wouldn't help me, after all that had been between us, and after promising once to help me get hold of the money if I'd marry her, but she'd do the job for somebody else—some new sweetie, I guess—"

For the first time since he had begun the inquisition ' of Emil Sevier, Bonnie Dundee felt a thrill of hope that his cherished theory of the murder was not yet wholly blasted by the capture of this suspect. He had been willing to acknowledge himself in the wrong, but now hope reared its bruised head. For, at his insistence, not all of Cora Barker's second story of the murder night had been given to the Press or revealed in her preliminary hearing for bail after her arrest as a material witness. The public—and therefore Sevier, too, unless he had been in communication with Cora—knew only that Sevier had importuned Cora to help him rob Mrs. Hogarth. Not even Cora's fellow boarders knew she had admitted to being in the old woman's room after the murder and before the discovery of the body by Dundee.

"You say that Cora once agreed to help you rob Mrs. Hogarth? Dundee interrupted. "When was that?"

"May it was, when I first got all het up over the idea," Sevier answered readily enough. "Cora was named in the old lady's will anyway, and I put it up to Cora that there wasn't any use us waiting around for her to die. The money wasn't doing Mrs. Hogarth any good—"

"I see. You were making plans to rob Mrs. Hogarth the night—18th May—when she saw you crawling out of Cora's window."

"Yeah, but I don't know how you know so damned much!" Sevier agreed sullenly.

"What caused Cora to change her mind about helping you?"

"The old lady seeing me come out of Cora's room, of course. Cora tried to rush me into getting married to her right off, so the old lady wouldn't tell tales on her to the other boarders. But I said we'd get our hands on the money first, beat it, and then get married, when it was safe. Cora thought I was planning to stand her up after the job was done, and she wouldn't go ahead with it, unless I married her first."

"Of course you had no intention of marrying Cora if she did help you," Dundee suggested casually.

Almost as if he were hypnotised, Sevier fell in with the suggestion. "Guess I wouldn't have married her, but I'd have split with her all right. Cora was too crazy about love-making to suit me—always wanting ten-minute kisses—"

There was a snicker from a policeman, and Sevier whirled toward the sound with a snarl. Dundee spoke quickly to divert him: "I can understand your objection if you were not in love with Cora. . . . But now, Sevier, I'd like you to tell me exactly what you did and saw last Saturday night after eleven o'clock," he added, so cheerfully that the prisoner was incensed.

"You don't need to grin at me like that!" Sevier cried futilely. "I'll tell the truth all right, whether you believe me or not! I did go to the Rhodes House Saturday night, but it wasn't till half-past eleven. Right up to the last minute I didn't have any intention of going, but —well, I was broke and I'd been fired, and I knew it might be a long time before I got a job, what with the talking movies having their own musical accompaniment, and all that. I had a notion I might still persuade Cora to help me—"

"I can't quite understand why you needed Cora's help so badly," Dundee interrupted. "It seems rather a one-man job to me, simply searching a helpless, sleeping old woman's room for hidden money—"

"The plan was for Cora to give her just a tiny bit of chloroform, not enough to hurt her but enough to keep her asleep while we searched the room," Sevier explained. "Cora used to be a trained nurse when she was a young girl, and she knew how to do it. I was afraid to try it by myself, because I didn't want to take any chance on killing the old lady with an overdose. Cora said the smell would blow out of the room by morning, with the window open, and we thought Mrs. Hogarth wouldn't even know she'd been drugged. We sort of counted, too, on Mrs. Hogarth not looking for her money, for several days—long enough to give us—me—a chance to get clear away. And she wouldn't have been able to say just when it was stolen either."

"A very clever scheme," Dundee commented without malice. "You had the chloroform, I suppose."

"Yes. I had some for a long time—got it for a toothache," Sevier answered. "I threw it away—out of the train window—"

"Suppose you begin again, Sevier, at half-past eleven, that night," Dundee interrupted.

"Well, I came up the alley and crawled along the driveway hedge till I got to the greenhouse. I wasn't going to try anything till Cora came home, because I thought maybe if I'd make love to her a little she'd still come across. A lot of the glass panes are broken in the greenhouse and I could see the house and the front walk clear to the street I had to wait so long for Cora to come home that I finally took a chance and smoked a cigarette, and I guess I folded that theatre programme, just like you said," Sevier conceded, with a gleam of something like admiration for the detective. "Cora was so late that I was about to give up and go on to the station, and I was nervous anyway, because the light was on in the corner room—that room I had when I boarded at the Rhodes House—and I knew I'd have to pass by Dowd's windows if I went to Cora's or Mrs. Hogarth's room by way of the upstairs porch. But the light went off finally—"

"When?" Dundee interrupted sharply.

"About ten minutes to twelve. I got a radium dial wrist-watch and I kept looking at it because Cora was so late. And then something else made me nervous—"

"What?" a strange exultation in his voice.

"I didn't know then what it was, but now I guess it must have been that cap of Dusty's because I didn't have it—never had the thing in my hands or on my head in my life. Anyway, somebody threw something from off the upstairs porch or out of a window, for it came sailing down into the hedge not far from the greenhouse. I was so nervous about what I was planning to do that I didn't sneak out to investigate—thought at the time it didn't amount to anything anyway—just one of the boarders throwing something away. Dowd had just turned his light off and I thought it was him—"

"It appeared to come from that part of the upstairs porch?" Dundee pressed.

"Yeah but I didn't see it coming I just heard it hit the hedge, and I doped it out that it came from Dowd's window."

Dundee considered for a moment, his eyes narrowed to blue slits, as he pictured the west side of the Rhodes House.

If Sevier was telling the truth—and Dundee believed he was—the cap could have been thrown, so that it would strike the hedge, from any one of three windows—Henry Dowd's, Lawrence Sharp's, or Norma Paige's.

"The something—whether the cap or not—was thrown soon after Dowd's light went off, you say?" Dundee asked.

"Not very, soon—maybe ten minutes afterwards. About twelve o'clock, I'd say," Sevier, almost at ease now, replied eagerly. "And it was exactly ten minutes after twelve when Cora at last came up the walk. The greenhouse isn't near enough to the front porch for me to have attracted her attention, and I didn't try. I just waited till I was sure she'd had time to get to her room, and then I climbed the rose trellis. I left my straw hat on the ground by the trellis, and when I came back down I stepped on it and smashed it. But that's getting ahead of my story," Sevier caught himself up almost cheerfully, for there was nothing alarming or incredulous in Bonnie Dundee's intent blue eyes.

"I climbed up as noiselessly as I could—I broke the trellis coming down, not going up—and when I got on to the porch I saw that Mrs. Hogarth's light was on. If I'd known that before I climbed up, I'd never have done it, but I couldn't see her light from the greenhouse. I started to turn back then, but I listened and didn't hear a sound, except Dowd snoring—"

"You're sure of that?" Dundee interrupted sharply.

"Sure! He'd had plenty of time to get to sleep, because he'd turned out his light more'n twenty minutes before I got up there," Sevier answered. "He was sawing wood, all right, and that was the only sound there was. I figured that maybe the old lady had gone to sleep with her light on, or that she wouldn't hear me if I crawled on my hands and knees to Cora's window. When I got to Mrs. Hogarth's window I raised up on my knees and looked in. And there was Cora doing something at the old lady's desk—seemed to me later like she was looking for something in an awful hurry, but I didn't look at Cora much then, because I could see that Mrs. Hogarth had been—was—dead—" And a sudden ague seized the prisoner's limbs.

"How could you tell?" Dundee prodded. "Her back was toward the window—"

"Yeah, but she was in a low-hacked arm-chair and I could see something black—that scarf she used to throw over the parrot's cage, the papers said it was—tied in a knot at the back of her neck, it was, and her head all rolled over like her neck was broken." Sevier shivered again and raised his manacled hands to press them against his trembling mouth.

"And then—you spoke to Cora, of course?" Dundee suggested quietly.

"Who—me? Speak to Cora?" Sevier echoed scornfully "All I could think of was getting away from there! I didn't want to be mixed up in no murder! Cora knew I'd always drawn the line at that, and if she hadn't been so busy trying to keep out of trouble herself, she would have told you that."

"She did say you never planned to murder Mrs. Hogarth in order to rob her," Dundee assured him. "And she did not tell us that you appeared at the window. She said she never saw you again after you told her good-bye at the theatre."

"She didn't try to frame me? You're—you're not kidding me?" Sevier asked, so strangely that Dundee was at a loss to read his tone or expression.

"Cora admitted only that she was afraid it was you because you had asked her to help you rob Mrs. Hogarth. And she told us about being in that room herself. She said she knocked on Mrs. Hogarth's door, after seeing her light was on, and when she received no answer, became afraid that the old lady had had a heart attack, opened the door and found her dead. Cora was looking for a page Mrs. Hogarth's diary—the entry in which Mrs. Hogarth had recorded your visit to Cora's room the night of 18th of May."

Sevier stared stupidly for a moment, then he became oddly violent. "Say! Don't let her kid you! She's in on this, or I'm—I'm—" He caught himself up sharp, gasped, then mopped his wet forehead on his coat sleeve.

"Did Cora see you?" Dundee interrupted.

"I didn't know then whether she did or not, because I ducked when I saw her lift her head and turn her face toward the window. Guess I must have made some little noise, like taking a sharp breath when I saw that the old lady was dead. But when I saw in the papers Monday that she'd been arrested as a material witness against me, I thought she must have seen me and would be doing her best to put the rope around my neck, instead of her own."

"And what is your opinion, Sevier?" Dundee asked. "Do you think Cora Barker murdered Mrs. Hogarth?"

"I don't think she'd hardly had time, because I came up the trellis the minute I thought she'd got to her room." Secier answered slowly.

"Did you yourself have time to notice whether the room was in disorder or not?"

"I didn't realise then I was noticing, but by the time I got back down the trellis it came to me that it couldn't

have been Cora because the room was all in a mess—
things thrown out of the trunk and desk and clothes
closet, but what I thought she was doing was covering up
the tracks of the man who did it. I figured it out later that
she wouldn't help me, because I wouldn't marry her, but
she'd help the guy that would. She was going around with
a silly-looking little bird—Magnus—"

"Go on with your story, Sevier," Dundee interrupted.

"Well, I was so scared I didn't give a hoot about the
money then. If I'd seen Cora with it in her hands, I'd have
beat it just like I did. I didn't want to be mixed up in
murder! So I ducked when she looked up, and crawled on
my hands and knees to the trellis. I was in such a hurry
going down that I broke one of the slats and scratched my
hand on the thorns. I nearly forgot to get my hat, but I
heard it crackle when I stepped down into it, so I picked it
up and run as fast as I could, which wasn't very fast
because I had to run all humped over so the hedge would
hide me from the house. I got to the alley, and like Dr.
Weeks said, that fool car turned its lights on me from the
entrance of the alley on Tenth Street. I threw my hat
away in a trash-can somewhere on my way to the train—"

"Just a minute, Sevier. According to your story, you
must have left the Rhodes House grounds not later than
twenty minutes past twelve, and yet you had to run to
catch the one o'clock train. Where were you in the
meantime?"

Sevier started to speak, then locked his lips
stubbornly.

Dundee did not press the point then. "You caught the
train and left it—where? And where have you spent these
three days?"

"None of your damned business!" the prisoner snarled.

"I conclude then, Sevier, that you somehow managed
to put in a long distance call from a coin-box before
leaving Hamilton, and that you arranged a refuge for
yourself not very far away. I also feel quite sure that your
protector was a girl whom you care for a great deal, and

that she finally persuaded you to come back to Hamilton and give yourself up. That is true, isn't it?"

"You think you're smart, don't you?" the man snarled. "Well, think what you damned please, but I'll see you in hell before I'll tell you anything else. I've told you the truth about Saturday night, up to one o'clock, and that's as far as I'm going to tell. . . . And I want a drink of cold water!" he added defiantly.

Sergeant Turner could restrain himself no longer. "You'll get a drink when you've come through with a confession, you cold-blooded murderer! Wilkins, bring that electric heater and turn it on this miserable liar. Maybe he'll get hot enough and thirsty enough to tell the truth—"

"May I speak with you a moment outside, Sergeant?" Dundee interrupted respectfully. "And you, too, Uncle Pat?" he added to the Police Commissioner.

When the three stood together in the hall outside the. closed door into the inquisition chamber, Dundee began earnestly:

"I have a request to make, Uncle Pat. I know both of you will think I'm just a credulous young idiot, but I believe Sevier is telling a pretty straight story—as nearly a truthful one as any man could tell when it reflects against him as much as his story does. There is only one point in it that I seriously doubt—and that is that Cora Barker ever agreed to help him rob Mrs. Hogarth, on his promise of marriage or for any other reason. I believe he put that in to make things a little less black for himself."

"Shall I go in and apologise to him for arresting him?" Sergeant Turner interrupted him sarcastically.

"That was not exactly the request I had in mind," Dundee answered, with his wide, disarming smile. "Please bear with me a little longer, Sergeant."

"What do you want to do, boy?" Police Commissioner O'Brien asked, laying a hand on the young detective's shoulder. "I think you've done a good job so far. Being polite is a new kind of third degree, but I'm a son of a gun if it don't work! What do you want now? Going to take his pulse on one of those lie detectors, like a story-book detective?"

Bonnie laughed, but he flushed with gratitude at his uncle's praises and faith in his ability. "Maybe I'll get around to that later, Uncle Pat, but right now I want to do nothing more absurd than to bring Cora Barker down here to face Sevier. I have a hunch that if Sevier is lying the truth will come out when those two come face to face."

"Good idea, Bonnie!" O'Brien applauded. "Go get her yourself, and in the meantime I think you can count on your little playmate's having his drink of water. Eh, Sergeant?"

The disgruntled sergeant stamped away without replying, and O'Brien winked broadly as he clapped his nephew upon the shoulder. "Don't let Turner get your goat, Bonnie. He always was an old sorehead, but he's a damned good man—for routine work."

"I can't blame him for resenting me," Dundee answered gravely. "Now, Uncle Pat—about my going personally for Cora Barker. That will let her into the secret that I'm working on the case, and may hamper my work at the boarding-house, if she talks."

"We'll see that she doesn't talk," O'Brien promised. "She would get wise anyway, if you questioned her and Sevier together. Better take one of the boys along with you, to help convince her of your authority."

Dundee agreed, choosing Detective Payne, who had been most active in assisting Lieut. Strawn and himself immediately after Mrs. Hogarth's murder.

"Seems rather a shame to drag Cora out of bed at this time of night—or rather morning," Dundee remarked to Payne, as the two young men swung down the quiet, deserted streets together. "It's nearly four o'clock."

"Well, if ladies will go around getting themselves mixed up in a murder, they gotta expect to lose a little sleep," Payne retorted cheerfully. "Say, Dundee, mind if I tell you that you did a swell job with Sevier? By being smooth and polite and dead sure of your facts, you got more out of that bird than Sergeant Turner could a-jerked out of him in ten hours of third-degree."

"Thanks, Payne. What did you think of Sevier's story?"

"Had sort of a hunch he was pret-near telling the truth," Payne answered thoughtfully. "Never can tell though. I was at Headquarters when the boys brought him in, and he sure was in a state. Nerves shot to hell. Funny way for a man to act if he was really coming to give himself up for questioning. Reckon, though, you were right about that dame of his. A man'll do a lot for a girl he's nutty about. I'm engaged myself, and Betty could make me jump through hoops if she wanted to."

"Where was he picked up?"

"Near here. On Eighth and Main—five blocks from Headquarters. As soon as he saw the cops coming toward him he began to run up Eighth, but when Patrolman Callahan shouted to him to stop, calling his name, he stopped, and came along without any fuss. But the boys said he was white as death and sort of doubled up, as if he was sick at his stomach. Funny, ain't it?"

"Very!" Dundee agreed, and the two men walked the remainder of the short distance to the Rhodes House in silence.

Dundee glanced up at the second story front windows. There was no light showing. Not a sound except the soft pad of their rubber-heeled shoes disturbed the brooding peace. He sniffed gratefully the cool, sweet odour of new-cut grass, mingled with the fainter fragrance of sleeping flowers. Suddenly he realised that he was very tired, and that he had little heart for the task he had set himself. Cora Barker had suffered enough already. It seemed inhuman to waken her now and drag her down to face the man who had pretended to love her, in order to insure her aid in a sordid crime. Perhaps even now she was dreaming of the cleaner, sweeter, less tempestuous love which had come to her—a love she valued so dearly that, to protect it, she had unwittingly involved herself in a murder.

Dundee sighed deeply, as he inserted his key in the lock. The low-powered hall light gave scarcely more illumination than a candle. Tiptoeing, the two detectives ascended the stairs.

"Dowd's snoring," he whispered, grinning in the dark. "At least Sevier didn't lie about that. Hope we don't arouse the house, knocking on Cora's door."

He knocked softly at first, then, as there was no answer, more loudly. Odd. He would have sworn Cora was a light sleeper. When there was still no answer he placed his lips against the crack between door and frame and called softly, wishing that the rooms were equipped with old-fashioned locks having big keyholes, rather than with Yale locks.

There was no answer. Dundee's hands began to shake violently as he selected a master key. Even before he found and snapped the light switch he was sure of what that deep sinister silence portended.

XXI.

"STEADY, boy!" Police Commissioner O'Brien warned, as his white-faced nephew opened the door to him and Sergeant Turner ten minutes later, then stood clinging to the knob, his tall, lean, young body swaying drunkenly. "Can't have you keeling over before Dr. Price gets here. He's on the way. This is tough on you, I know—but all in a day's work for a detective."

"I know." Dundee wiped a string of icy sweat beads from his forehead and stood aside, to let the new-comers see the ghastly sight upon which his own eyes had rested when he had forced his way into Cora Barker's room.

"Have you touched the body?" Sergeant Turner demanded briskly.

"No." Dundee pressed his knuckles against his mouth to still the quivering of his lips. "I wanted to lift her back into her bed, but—Payne reminded me. She's—just as we found her."

"Good!" Sergeant Turner, followed by O'Brien, stepped to the east window of the room and knelt beside the huddled body on the floor. "Good Lord! Strangled with her own braids! That's a new one on me. Pretty clever! There'll be no finger-prints on her throat. Sevier's a handy bird, isn't he? Doesn't take the trouble to provide a weapon in advance; just uses anything that will serve the purpose . . . Poor old girl!"

Sergeant Turner's casual sympathy made Bonnie Dundee clench his fist in boyish rage. Poor old girl! Indeed! Why, that was Cora Barker there on the floor—Cora whom he had eaten with, to whose playing he had danced, Cora whose face a few hours before he had seen light up with the glory of triumphant love. Poor, passionate, love-greedy Cora. And poor Bert Magnus. A new wave of nausea swept over Dundee when he thought of Bert's being told. The one beautiful thing that had come out of the Hogarth tragedy—the drawing together of Bert and Cora in a love founded on sympathy and faith—was murdered now, too.

Sergeant Turner rose and stepped aside and again Dundee's eyes took in the whole horrible picture before he could wrench them away. Cora had gone to the window—and to her death—clad only in a thin yellow silk nightgown. Undoubtedly her murderer had called her to the window, and she had sprung from her bed—which had been slept in—without taking time to drape herself in the kimono which hung on a chair. Had gone to that window with her long braids of black hair swinging over her shoulders. Had her murderer counted on that very thing? Had he known that Cora would come to him, unconsciously offering perfect means of strangulation? Or had the murder, been unpremeditated?

At any event the long braids had been crossed in the back, drawn around and tied beneath her chin in a single knot. The wiriness of the hair had loosened the knot now, but the hands of the murderer had held fast to the ends of the braids until life had been extinguished in that thin, proud, passionate body.

Dundee drew a shuddering breath. He was glad the poor, discoloured face was bowed down upon the grotesquely sprawled knees, so that he could not see it in all its horror.

"She's been dead for hours," he heard Sergeant Turner saying to Commissioner O'Brien. "Rigor mortis has already set in. I think it will be better for us to get the body to the morgue before we rouse the whole house, don't you, Commissioner?"

"Yes, by all means. Warn the boys to keep a sharp watch over the boarders' rooms, but not to answer any questions. You've got three men on the grounds, haven't you?"

"Four," Turner answered. "Routine precaution. They won't find anything, unless it's another Cuban cigarette stub. We've got our man already. I guess Patrolman Callahan will rate a promotion out of this night's work, Commissioner."

He left the room, carefully and noiselessly closing the door behind him, to give the necessary instructions to the silent men posted in the downstairs and upstairs halls. In the brief moment while the door was open there was no sound of any disturbance. Apparently none of the sleeping boarders had been aroused by the quiet entry of the police upon the scene of the new tragedy.

When he returned, Dr. Price, the coroner, was with him.

"Nobody's awake yet but Mrs. Rhodes, and I aroused her myself to break the news," Sergeant Turner announced in a low voice. "You came on the ambulance, didn't you, Doctor?"

"Yes. You want to get the body away a soon as possible, I suppose," the coroner answered, as he knelt before the thing which had been Cora Barker.

As if through a deafening fog Dundee heard the doctor's brisk comments as he made his examination: "Death due to strangulation . . . No finger-prints on the throat . . . Marks where the braids cut into the skin . . . It was no weakling that tied this knot, Commissioner."

"How long has she been dead?" Turner asked.

"Hmm. A little hard to tell. Rigor mortis has set in but in some cases that happens more quickly than in others. But—at least three or four hours, I should say. I'll try to give you a more exact answer after I perform the autopsy—condition of stomach contents, etc. I'll call the boys now. I've arranged a signal, to keep things as quiet as possible," and he went to the front window, stepped out upon the porch, and waved, his handkerchief to the waiting ambulance below.

"This seems to be a pretty decent bunch of people, and since it's your home, temporarily at least, I want to spare the house as much of the horror as I can," O'Brien explained to his nephew.

"That's white of you, Uncle Pat," Bonnie thanked him, a lump in his throat.

As silently as if they were paying tribute to the dead the ambulance attendants came up the stairs and entered the room, carrying the stretcher on which Cora's body would be borne away. Sergeant Turner listened anxiously at the door, but the house was still sleeping apparently.

"Let me help!" Dundee begged, as the white-jacketed men bent over the dead woman. For suddenly he could not bear the thought that only uncaring, alien hands should touch her. He sprang to the chair across which her kimono hung, then rejected the garment when he saw that it was an old, slightly soiled one. Cora would have a better one, he knew—and he found it in her closet. There were tears in his eyes as he draped the pretty negligee of orchid chiffon and ostrich feathers about the poor, rigid shoulders. And regardless of onlookers he stooped and laid his lips lightly against the stiffening, thin, dry-skinned hand which had aroused his compassion when Cora Barker was alive. He stood aside then as the body was lifted to the stretcher, and was about to turn his face away when his eyes telegraphed an amazing message to his brain.

"Look, Dr. Price?" he called urgently. "Did you notice this? Her mouth is bruised . . . Please, may I?" and he gently lifted the discoloured upper lip, turned it back till it touched the nose. "Dr. Price, her lips have been pressed so hard against her teeth that the print shows plainly. See?"

"You're right," Dr. Price said slowly, as he bent to examine both lips. "But I don't quite understand—"

"I do!" Dundee cried in a choking voice. "Don't you see—Uncle Pat, Sergeant Turner? Cora Barker was killed with a kiss!"

"What do you mean?" Sergeant Turner demanded incredulously.

"Oh, can't you see? I thought it was odd that she could be strangled to death without making sufficient outcry to awaken anyone. Bert Magnus's room is the nearest, and yet he evidently heard nothing, or he would have investigated, and—and found her like this. I'm glad he didn't. Thank God for that, at least. He was in love with her—was going to marry her, I think, when the Hogarth case was settled."

"Steady, boy!" O'Brien warned. "You're getting as hysterical as a woman. Tell us quietly just what you mean."

"I mean," Dundee forced himself to speak in a calmer, lower voice, "that whoever murdered Cora Barker strangled her while she was being kissed. The man pressed his mouth so tightly against hers that she could not cry out when he tied the braids of her hair . . . Can't you see it all? He was so well known to Cora that when he called to her from the porch in a low voice she came instantly, recognising him, of course. Maybe they talked a bit first —I don't know, but he certainly made love to her, played with her hair. Maybe he remarked on how long the braids were. I can hear him saying: 'Why, they come clear to your waist, even when they're crossed in the back,' and he crossed them in the back to prove it. Crossed them to make strangulation possible. Then he brought the crossed braids over her shoulders, and, while kissing her, suddenly tied them and drew the ends so tightly that she was strangled—his lips still on hers."

"My God!" Commissioner O'Brien breathed, and turned sharply away.

"What a newspaper story this is going to make!" Sergeant Turner commented with morbid satisfaction. "Emil Sevier will sure go down in history as the most cold-blooded murderer this state has ever had. Still want him to have plenty of ice water and an electric fan, Dundee—instead of the bad old third degree?" he added tauntingly.

The boy whitened to the lips, then he flung up his head. "I suppose you're right, and I was a credulous fool, Sergeant Turner. But if Sevier did this I'd like to put the thumb-screws on him myself."

"Good boy!" Turner applauded heartily. "Run along and do it. I'll handle the case from this end—nothing much to do anyway, I suppose, but listen to how sound asleep everybody was when Cora was being strangled. What a fiend that fiddler turned out to be. Croaked her because he thought she'd told us a lot more than she had—"

"Or possibly because he got cold feet and beat it before the money was found. Maybe she'd promised to send his share to him—" Commissioner O'Brien began to speculate, then shrugged. "Get the truth out of him this time, Bonnie, lad. You've got plenty of work on fortunately. According to Dr. Price, the woman has been dead three or four hours, which means that Sevier probably killed her just before he was picked up. He was nabbed between here and Police Headquarters, you know, a few minutes after two."

"I know," Dundee agreed grimly.

"So this was the solution of the Hogarth case. And Cora had to die to convince me that I was on the wrong trail," he told himself bitterly. "Me and my 'bad penny'. Well, Sevier is certainly a bad enough penny . . . But why, why did Mrs. Hogarth greet a fiend like Emil Sevier in that joking way? Why didn't she scream? She wasn't killed with a kiss—"

He preceded the slow-moving stretcher through the door and was half-way down the stairs when he heard a door open, then Bert Magnus's voice: "Is anything wrong? What's that? Not—oh, my God! Not Cora! Wait! For God's sake, tell me—let me see her!"

Almost in a frenzy himself, Bonnie Dundee tore on down the stairs, jerked open the door and plunged out into the grey of the dawn.

XXII

1

AT half-past eight that Wednesday morning an exhausted young detective was hauled back to consciousness by an urgent but kindly hand upon his shoulder. He sat up, dazed, to find himself not in his bed but in a creaking swivel chair, and that his pillow had been his own arms crossed upon an untidy desk.

"Wake up, boy!" Lieut. Strawn greeted him with brusque sympathy. "Better go grab a bite of breakfast and get into bed. You'll need some rest before the double inquest this afternoon."

"You're back?" Bonnie Dundee ran a shaking hand through his disordered black hair and blinked dazed blue eyes at his chief.

"Sure! Just got in. Got a morning paper at the station. I'm damned sorry about Cora Barker. Have you got a confession out of that swine, Sevier, yet? The paper says he's been on the grill since he was nabbed at two o'clock this morning."

Dundee shook his head gloomily as he rubbed his aching arms. "No. I was at him hammer and tongs for more than two hours after we discovered Cora's murder, but he stuck to his story. Fainted when I broke the news to him, but in between being sick as a poisoned pup he kept denying he'd been any nearer the Rhodes house than the spot where Patrolmen Callahan and Lunt picked him up."

"And what was his story?" Strawn demanded. Dundee told him briefly, wearily, what Sevier had admitted.

"Rot!" Strawn spat contemptuously into the big brass cuspidor beside his desk. "He's guilty as hell. Smart, too.

Frankly admitted everything he was sure you already had against him, what you told him you had on him. And he killed Cora Barker because he was sure she'd told the police the whole truth against him, or to keep her from doing so. He knew he couldn't stay under cover for ever— probably his girl forced him out—and he figured he could only swing once anyway, and he might as well get even with Cora before he got his rope necktie. Remember, he knew she'd been arrested as a material witness, and he had no way of knowing just how much she had already told."

"But why would Cora let him kiss her?" Dundee asked wearily.

"Maybe he stole the kiss—then kept on kissing till the braids were tied so tight she could never object again to anybody's kisses," Strawn surmised callously.

"Don't!" the boy shuddered.

"You're all shot, Bonnie," Strawn was brusquely contrite. "Better get back to the Rhodes House, to breakfast and to bed . . . By the way, see if you can work that speech stunt again, to keep the boarders where they are until the inquest to-day, anyway. There's just a chance of course, that something may develop this afternoon that will make us want to keep them all together. Or maybe I'd better drop in and make it an official order."

"I wish you would," Dundee admitted. "I don't feel up to pleading with anyone to stay in that house any longer."

"'Murder Mansion' the paper calls it," Strawn grinned. "See?"

"Thanks—I'd rather not," Dundee repudiated the newspaper with a gesture of distaste. "By the way, we're holding Sevier as a material witness, not on a charge of murder yet. The district attorney advised it, so we could get Sevier's testimony at the inquest this afternoon. Well. I believe I'll go now—"

"Good idea." Strawn agreed. "Just one other thing. Who had charge of the investigation this morning at the Rhodes House?"

"Sergeant Turner. I suppose he's snatching a nap now, but I can tell you anything you want to know. He came back to Headquarters about six. Said his questioning of the boarders, Mrs. Rhodes, Dusty and the maid, Tilda Brown, brought out absolutely nothing. According to their stones, they were all asleep when the murder must have been committed. Heard nothing, saw nothing. Blanks all along the line."

"What does Dr. Price say?"

"That Cora was strangled between one and two o'clock, judging by the extent of rigor mortis, and the stage to which digestion had progressed. He got busy immediately on the autopsy."

"Good man—Price . . . And what else has Turner been able to dig up? Any residents on the block who saw or heard anything?"

"Absolutely nothing, so far, to prove Sevier or any other prowler was on the scene of the crime," Dundee replied heavily.

"Hmm. Eighth and Main—that's where they nabbed him, isn't, it?—is near enough for any jury. Just four blocks from the Rhodes House," Strawn exulted. "Well, get along with you, Bonnie. The case is solved, whether Sevier confesses or not. Get some sleep now. You've earned it."

The nerve-shattered young detective was lurching unsteadily toward the door when he remembered something that had once seemed of vast importance.

"I forgot to ask you about your trip, chief," he confessed, his tired eyes brightening a bit. "Turner says you wired that you hadn't been very successful, but I suppose you got a description of Dan Griffin?"

"Why worry about Griffin now, kid?" Strawn chuckled indulgently. "It was a swell theory, but Emil Sevier's thrown the monkey wrench into it. The detective from

New York arrived in Belton just before I left, and I turned over all the information I'd been able to collect, which wasn't much."

"I believe I'll sleep better if my curiosity is satisfied," Dundee persisted, with his disarming grin, as he again slumped his weary body into Strawn's swivel chair.

"All right, boy. It's your sleep you're losing!" Stawn conceded, leaning back in the straight chair and hooking his thumbs in his braces. "Remember, the Belton chief told us over the 'phone that their Police Headquarters had been destroyed by fire two years ago? . . . Well, Griffin's fingerprints went up in smoke, as well as the description of him they had on file. So I had to paddle around and pick up what I could at the bank and from neighbours who had known the Harknesses and Griffin."

"And what was he like?" Dundee urged, his fatigue almost forgotten.

"Ask me another!" Strawn grinned ruefully. "It was funny, but everybody I questioned had a slightly different picture of Dan Griffin in mind. That frequently happens, of course, after a crime has been committed, and the criminal has skipped. Some folks'll say he looked like a fiend incarnate, others that 'you'd never have guessed to look at him,' etc. Same way in Belton. I finally doped it out that Dan Griffin must have been so ordinary looking a young man that his face made no deep impression on anyone. For instance, one chap at the bank said he had blue eyes; another that he had pale grey eyes; another that they were hazel; another vowed they were light brown. And some said he had sort of sandy hair; others that it was a kind of darkish blond. He didn't wear a moustache or glasses—that much they all agree on. And he was neither tall nor short, but their estimates of his height varied from five feet seven to five feet ten. I gathered, too, that he was of average weight, inclined to be slender rather than heavy; that he had regular features—nothing odd about them, but that he was neither handsome or homely. Just an ordinary-looking young man of about thirty when he robbed the bank and beat it—very successfully."

"Any doctor or dentist who might help to identify him?" Dundee persisted.

"It's a small town, and I canvassed every doctor and dentist who lived there when Griffin did. By the absence of evidence, he must have been a healthy guy, with teeth that didn't need tinkering on."

"Handwriting?"

"Sure!" Strawn was mildly triumphant as he pulled out his wallet. "Got some old deposit slips from the bank, bearing, his signature, or rather his initials, and some notations he made on scratch paper. They had other samples of his handwriting, but had turned them over to the police, along with the card he'd filled out when he went to work for the bank. They were burned, too, of course, but you've got his 'John Henry' there all right. Keep 'em as a souvenir of the 'bad penny' that didn't turn up!"

"Thanks!" Dundee replied quietly, as he placed the papers in his own pocket.

"Don't think I'm trying to ride you, Dundee," Strawn apologised awkwardly. "You've done mighty good work on this case, and I want you with me on the next one."

"Thanks," Dundee replied again, and thrust out his hand. There was no use in arguing. It would only sound foolish for him to persist: But why, why did Mrs. Hogarth call Sevier a 'bad penny,' when she hated and feared him? Why didn't she scream? But until those questions were answered to his own satisfaction, the Hogarth case and the Barker case would not be closed, in his eyes, at least.

"Say! I nearly forgot it, but here's something you may be interested in. The newspapers will love this." Strawn halted the boy at the door. "A picture of the old lady and her daughter, when they were Mrs. Emma Harkness and Miss Sally Harkness."

Dundee almost snatched the cabinet photograph from his chief's hand. The picture was dated by the

photograph—1921, the year before Sally Harkness's
marriage to Dan Griffin. The mother, dressed in black
silk, overflowed the ornate chair in which the
photographer had seated her, but her bulk had been
many pounds less then than it was at the time of her
death. Her little, light-blue eyes gazed out upon Dundee
with the puzzled innocence of a child who could not
believe that the big body was really hers. The girl
standing to one side and, slightly behind her mother's
chair was so very pretty and slender . . . and so young
that the boy's throat constricted painfully . . . Dark,
curling hair cut in a long, fluffy bob; wide, dark eyes, wise
and sweet and somehow more mature than the mother's.
Both dead now—murdered within the same month.
Coincidence? Puzzled, childish blue eyes and wise, sweet
dark ones stared at him steadily . . .

"Chief, I've got a request to make!" Dundee spoke
suddenly, tensely. "Let me keep this picture awhile,
please! Don't turn it over to the papers yet! Don't tell
them anything at all about Mrs. Hogarth's really being
Mrs. Harkness, whose daughter has been murdered, too.
If Sevier' confesses, all right! But if he doesn't, will you let
me have until Monday to work on the case in my own
way?"

Strawn started to refuse, then shrugged. "All right,
kid! You're not asking much, and I expect a confession
from Sevier any minute now, anyway. I'll wire the New
York police to keep mum, too, until we give the word.
Now, shut up, go home and get some sleep. See you at the
inquest at three o'clock at the morgue."

2

The inquest into the death of Mrs. Emma Hogarth
and of Cora Barker was being held in the small funeral
parlour of the city morgue. Chairs had been placed upon
every available foot of space, but only a fraction of the
mob which had been milling about the doors of the

morgue since early morning had been able to obtain seats.

Around one large table sat Coroner Price and his jury of six citizens. Around another sat representatives of the Hamilton newspapers—four men and three women feature-writers. At one end of the Press table was a well-known staff writer from the most sensational Chicago paper—looking aloof and slightly bored. His published account of the proceedings, however, bore not the faintest trace of ennui.

Side by side, behind the coroner's table, were two sheeted stretchers, one bearing a mountainous bulk, the other a burden so slight that the sheet was scarcely raised from the thin mattress.

In spite of the real grief which lay like a hot stone in his breast, Bonnie Dundee, novice detective, found himself becoming weary and even bored. He had been able to snatch less than two hours of fitful sleep after his interview with Lieut. Strawn, but that brief nap had deprived him of luncheon. And he had not had the temerity to intrude his needs upon his stricken hostess when he descended the stairs an hour before it was time to leave for the inquest.

He had found Mrs. Rhodes in her bed-sitting-room at her desk, her fine figure stiffly upright in its confining corsets, but the hard-wrung tears of grief and despair ploughing down her cheeks.

At Dundee's sympathetic question she had answered dully, heavily: "I never thought to see the day when my guests would be forced by fear of arrest to stay in a house of mine."

"Arrest?" Dundee had echoed incredulously.

"Yes, arrest!" Mrs. Rhodes retorted bitterly. "That Lieutenant Strawn of yours called all the folks together in the parlour after lunch and told them they were to stay here until he gave them the word they could leave. Said if anybody tried to leave he'd put him or her under arrest as a material witness. Nearly scared them to death, he did!

Everybody knows if poor Cora hadn't been arrested as a material witness she wouldn't be dead now."

But even as Dundee sympathised and mentally deplored his chief's methods of keeping all possible witnesses under one roof, he was grateful for the result. For he still had a stubborn conviction that the Hogarth case and the Cora Barker case would not be solved to-day.

For an hour and a half now he had listened to the taking of testimony. Mrs. Rhodes had been called upon to identify both bodies, a shiver of ecstatic horror running through the morbid audience as the landlady, bent first over one stretcher and then the other as Coroner Price lifted the sheet to disclose the dead face beneath.

Witness after witness had been briefly but thoroughly questioned by Dr. Price, after he himself had given his own testimony as to the cause of death and the approximate time at which life had been snuffed out. Dundee had long since made a complete transcription of his own notes, taken from behind the screen in Mrs. Hogarth's room as the inmates of the Rhodes House had been questioned in the small hours of the morning following the first murder; With these notes in hand, supplemented by the record of the investigation made from young Brede's notes of Wednesday morning's inquiry by Sergeant Turner into Cora Barker's death, Coroner Price questioned his witnesses with a swiftness and precision which won Dundee's admiration. As Lieut. Strawn had said: "Good man, Price!"

The young detective, still incognito, sat among the witnesses—all inmates of the Rhodes House except Dr. Weeks. The stories now told tallied remarkably well with the stories told originally. Not even Henry Dowd varied his meagre testimony, for at Dundee's urgent request the coroner had not been taken into the confidence of the Vice on the subject of Dowd's alias. And none but Sergeant Turner and Lieut. Strawn knew that Henry Dowd had purchased a ticket in New York on 2nd June for Chicago. For the murder of Sally Graves, and the relationship between the New York girl and the Hamilton woman who had been murdered were not to be touched upon at the inquest.

Dundee himself had been one of the first to be called before the coroner's jury, for it was he who had discovered Mrs. Hogarth's body. The fact that he, together with Detective Payne, had also discovered Cora Barker's murder was skilfully omitted from Dr. Price's questioning of the young detective.

"And where were you between one and two o'clock this morning?" Dr. Price asked.

"Asleep in my room on the third floor of the Rhodes Dundee answered.

"And of your own knowledge can you throw any light whatever on the death of Cora Barker?" the coroner asked.

"I cannot."

Dismissed, with his official connection still a secret, Dundee had returned to his seat between Norma Paige and Daisy Shepherd, and had listened to witness after witness with apparently no more acute interest than that of any other boarder in the Rhodes House.

One thing Dundee had confided to Coroner Price just before the inquest, however, and his weary boredom lifted when Daisy Shepherd was called to the witness chair.

When she had admitted, flushing deeply, that she had raided Mrs. Rhodes's kitchen on Saturday night, at the very time that Mrs. Hogarth was being strangled to death, Dr. Price asked suddenly: "Are you acquainted with a man named Arthur B. Wheeler, Miss Shepherd?"

Daisy's broad, pleasant face went pale, and her lips jerked oddly as she retorted: "Of course I am! He was a boarder at the Rhodes House. All of us knew him—that is, all who were boarding there before he left."

"And that was on what date, Miss Shepherd?"

"I don't know!" she blazed. Then, reconsidering: "I think it was early in June—about the third or fourth."

"Have you any reason, Miss Shepherd, to believe that the long distance call which came for you shortly after twelve o'clock last Saturday night was from Mr. Wheeler?"

"I don't know who was calling!" Daisy retorted sullenly.

"The call was from Chicago," the coroner reminded her. "You knew Mr. Wheeler was in Chicago, didn't you?"

"I—yes, I did! But I can't see what Arthur Wheeler—"

"Just a minute, Miss Shepherd!" Dr. Price interrupted peremptorily, as he shuffled among the mass of papers before him. He selected a blue-tinted sheet of notepaper and an empty envelope, both of which Dundee had given him. Presenting the note to the witness he asked courteously: "Do you recognise this, Miss Shepherd?"

Daisy's hands trembled as she stared at the sheet of blue notepaper. "I don't know where you got this and how anybody had the nerve to go poking about in my things, but—sure I recognise it! It's a letter I started to write to Arthur Wheeler and didn't finish."

"Will you kindly read to the jury what you had written, Miss Shepherd?"

"I don't see why I should!" Daisy cried angrily. "It has nothing to do with the murders—Oh, all right. It says: 'The Rhodes House Sunday, 22nd June. I have asked you repeatedly not to bother me. I have no intention of doing what you ask and it, will be useless to call me or write me again—"

"Thank you, Miss Shepherd. Now will you please tell this jury why you wrote as you did, and what requestMr, Wheeler had made to you?"

Daisy obviously fought with an impulse to tell him that it was none of his business or the jury's, but she finally answered, defiantly: "Arthur Wheeler had been pestering me for weeks to put my savings into an invention he was all worked up over. Said he would, give me a half-interest in it if I would, but I worked too hard for my money to waste it on some silly invention I couldn't even understand—"

"What was this invention, Miss Shepherd.?" the coroner interrupted.

"Some gadget to go on a sewing-machine," Daisy answered sullenly. "I didn't pay enough attention to his harping on it to understand just what it was supposed to do. All I know is he made up a model of it and tried it out on Mrs. Rhodes's machine, and he needed more money to get it patented and to try to market it."

"Do you know what became of this model, Miss Shepherd?"

"He took it away with him, the night he sneaked off without paying his board bill, but he left the rest of his junk, in his room."

"And did your hear from Mr. Wheeler again, after 22nd June?"

"Yes, I did. I didn't send this letter, but I wrote another one, not quite so snippy, but I told him pretty much the same thing. But he wrote me again anyway and I suppose it was him calling me from Chicago—I don't know."

"This is the envelope in which he mailed you a letter from Chicago on 27th June, is it not?" Dr. Price asked, and handed her the envelope which Dundee had found in her wardrobe trunk.

"Well, of all the nerve!" Daisy ejaculated, with righteous indignation. "Yes, it is, if you must know, but I tore the letter up. He wrote me that he was down to his last dollar, and begged me to change my mind about putting my savings into his invention. I didn't take the trouble to answer it."

"Mr. Wheeler, of course, knew that Mrs. Hogarth was supposed to be a miser—to have a large sum of money hidden in her room?" Coroner Price asked.

"He wasn't deaf!" Daisy retorted. "Everybody that ever boarded at the Rhodes House knew that story, but if you're thinking that Arthur was so hard up for money that he killed and robbed Mrs. Hogarth, then I don't see how you can think he was calling me from Chicago that same identical time!"

"Do you know anyone else in Chicago, Miss Shepherd, who might have been calling you long distance?"

"Not a single, solitary soul!" Daisy retorted emphatically.

"Now, Miss Shepherd, may I ask if you were—well, romantically interested in Mr. Wheeler?"

"Hunh!" Daisy snorted contemptuously. "If you'd ever seen him you wouldn't ask me that! And say, does this letter sound like I was 'romantically interested' in that sap?"

During the gust of laughter with which the delighted audience greeted Daisy's retort, the big girl was dismissed. She returned to her seat, muttering indignantly, but obviously pleased at the showing she had made.

Mrs. Sharp, who had returned to the Rhodes House from the state capital the night before, leaned forward from her chair directly behind Daisy's and patted the girl encouragingly upon the shoulder.

"Mr. Herbert S. Magnus!" Dr. Price called.

There was a buzz of excited comment, for the newspapers had carried the rumour of Bert's engagement, on the very eve of her murder, to Cora Barker.

XXIII.

1

CORONER PRICE'S first half-dozen questions brought out Bert Magnus's story of Saturday night. As Dundee listened to the familiar tale he averted his eyes from the heart-wrenching sight of Bert's suddenly old and ravaged face. The amateur scenario writer looked as if he had passed through some terrible and blighting illness during the few hours since he had stood beside Cora Barker, singing in his surprisingly good tenor, "Drink to me only with thine eyes!" Occasionally, as he answered the coroner's, questions, his voice wavered, and he pressed the fingers of his uncrippled left hand into his temples as if trying desperately to remember things which had now, in comparison with the terrible tragedy of the night before, lost much of their meaning and importance.

When he told how he had become so absorbed in the revision of his scenario, "*More To Be Pitied*" that he had neglected to keep his appointment with Cora Barker, his voice broke, and tremblingly he took off his glasses to wipe them, holding them awkwardly in his right hand, between the withered fingers and the thumb which had escaped injury.

"I realise," he said unsteadily, "that, if I had kept my appointment to meet Miss Barker at the theatre last Saturday night, to take her to supper after the last show, she would not have had occasion to go into Mrs. Hogarth's room and would not have become involved in the case, as a material witness."

There was a rising murmur of excitement, punctuated by sharp exclamations from reporters, witnesses, and the audience of morbidly curious. For this was the first news the public had had that Cora Barker had been in the murdered woman's room after the crime was committed.

Dr. Price looked somewhat nonplussed at the unsolicited revelation, but asked his next question quietly: "Did Miss Barker confide in you concerning her visit to Mrs. Hogarth's room after the murder?"

"She did—as we were walking together to the Little Queen Theatre on Monday night," Magnus answered, huskily. "I believe she told me the whole truth about her connection with Emil Sevier. It was a relationship of which I believe she was unnecessarily ashamed."

"Please tell the jury as nearly as you can remember just what Miss Barker told you," Dr. Price directed, after pounding with his gavel for order in the excited audience.

Bert Magnus restored his pince-nez to his nose, touched his little reddish moustache with trembling fingers, then answered in a low voice that was frequently shaken with emotion: "Cora—Miss Barker—told me she wanted me to know exactly why she had been held as a material witness. She said she had been engaged, in May, to Emil Sevier, and that she had broken the engagement when Sevier had importuned her to help him rob Mrs. Hogarth. She had once been a trained nurse and Sevier wanted her to administer a small dose of chloroform to Mrs. Hogarth, to insure her being deeply asleep while the two of them searched her room for the hidden money. As I said, Cora refused, and broke the engagement, but, she admitted frankly, Mrs. Hogarth had seen Sevier leaving Cora's room by the window on the night of 18th May—or rather, at two o'clock in the morning of 18th May. When I failed to meet her last Saturday night, she became obsessed with the fear that I had met Mrs. Hogarth and that she had told me this bit of scandal against Cora."

"And had you met Mrs. Hogarth?" Dr. Price interrupted.

" I have already told you that I never met or spoke to Mrs. Hogarth in my life," Bert answered with quiet emphasis.

"Very well, Mr. Magnus . . . Now, why was Miss Barker so concerned over the possibility of your having heard this scandal from Mrs. Hogarth?"

Magnus flushed, but raised his head proudly. "She—valued my good opinion of her."

"Go on!" Dr. Price directed curtly, but not unkindly.

"As I said, it was fear that Mrs. Hogarth had gossiped against her to me which made Cora decide to question Mrs. Hogarth when she returned from the theatre at ten minutes after twelve Saturday night. She told me that she knocked on Mrs. Hogarth's door, after having seen that the light was still on, and that when she received no answer she tried the knob and found the door unlocked. She entered, and found Mrs. Hogarth dead. Knowing that Mrs. Hogarth kept a diary and feeling sure that the diary would contain an account of Sevier's visit to her room on the night of 18th May, Cora, as she told me, tore the page from the diary before leaving the room. Fear of being implicated caused her not to give the alarm, she said—and I quite understood and sympathised with her decision."

"Did Miss Barker tell you, in confidence, anything to implicate Sevier or anyone else, beyond the fact that Sevier had asked her help in robbing Mrs. Hogarth?"

"No, except that he again asked her that Saturday night, and she again refused."

"She did not tell you that she saw Sevier in the room or at the window on the porch?"

"She did not. I feel sure she did not know any more than she told me," Magnus answered, with a note of pride and faith in his shaken voice.

"Now, Mr. Magnus, you were in private conversation with Miss Barker again on Tuesday evening," Dr. Price continued, and the audience held its breath. "Will you tell the jury the gist of that conversation?"

"I—it was of an extremely private nature," Magnus protested.

"I am afraid it can be private no longer, and I must ask you to answer the question fully and frankly," Dr. Price replied with firm but kindly emphasis.

Dundee, who had been an eavesdropping and unsuspected witness to part of that conversation, leaned forward and listened intently as Magnus answered, hesitatingly: "Cora played the piano—we were all in the Rhodes House parlour—and I sang, and—and then we talked, Cora and I. She told me she had been very unhappy—"

He was floundering hopelessly, and Dundee sympathised with his dilemma. How could any man be expected to repeat the intimacies which he had overheard between Cora and Bert—the shy half-promises, made more by eyes than by lips?

The coroner cleared his throat harshly, and took off his own spectacles to wipe the moisture from the lenses "I will ask you, Mr. Magnus, if you and Miss Barker became engaged to be married, during that conversation yesterday evening?"

A dull red spread over Bert Magnus's chubby, plain face, but his eyes were steady and his voice unfaltering as he answered: "Not exactly, in so many words, but I intimated very plainly to Cora that when this bad business—meaning the Hogarth case, of course—was cleared up, and she was free to go where she pleased, I would have something to ask of her. As a matter of fact, I believe I did not even complete the sentence, but Cora understood, and—and we were very happy, looking forward to a future of which we could not even talk until—until—"

"I understand," the coroner cut in hastily. "Now, Mr. Magnus, did Miss Barker tell you why she had been so unhappy."

Dundee leaned forward tensely. Was Magnus going to introduce Jewel Briggs's name? He remembered very clearly that Cora had cried: "Then you didn't mean what you said to Jewel?"

Then he settled back in his chair, undecided whether to be disappointed that the small mystery concerning Jewel was not to be cleared up, or to admire Bert's chivalry in leaving the girl's name out of the record. For Bert was saying, haltingly: "I think it was—well, obvious that Cora was sad and humiliated over her arrest as a material witness, and over the gossip connecting her with Emil Sevier."

"Did she mention Sevier's name that evening?" the coroner prodded.

"Yes!" and Bert's voice rang with sorrowing rage. "She said she would sleep more easily if she knew Emil Sevier was safe behind bars—that her dreams were haunted by fears of his coming to avenge himself upon her for the little she had told the police against him."

The close-packed audience was suddenly as still as if the wings of death had swept over it. Dundee, sitting between Norma Paige and Daisy Shepherd, saw both girls shiver and huddle lower into their seats.

"Did she definitely say that she had cause to believe that Sevier would kill her?" Dr. Price asked at last.

"Not in so many words. I have repeated what she said as nearly as I can remember," Bert answered, his voice breaking. Then: "I begged her to tell her fears to the police, to ask for protection until Sevier was caught. But she refused. She said the police might think she had cause to fear Sevier—believe that she had helped him kill and rob Mrs. Hogarth."

"Did Miss Barker tell you that she believed Sevier to be guilty?"

"She did not express such a belief, but I know she was afraid it was true. She was a—loyal friend, even to a man like Sevier," Bert answered huskily.

After a few questions concerning Magnus's movements after the breaking up of the impromptu party the night before, Dr. Price said: "I understand then, Mr. Magnus, that you heard nothing, saw nothing until you opened your door about half-past four this morning and saw the stretcher, being carried out of Miss Barker's room."

"That is correct," Magnus answered, his face so white and drawn that Daisy Shepherd involuntarily moaned: "Oh, the poor little man!"

"Will you tell the jury what you said then—the words you addressed to the dead woman when you knew it was her body on the stretcher?

"I—" Magnus began, then bowed his head in his hands, his shoulders heaving.

"I will ask if these are the words you spoke, Mr. Magnus," and the coroner selected a sheet of young Brede's notes and read aloud: "My poor darling! If you had only let me watch outside your windows, as I wanted to—"

"Yes, that is what I said," Magnus spoke from behind his shielding hands. "I had told Cora, as we came upstairs together, that if she were really afraid of Sevier, I would stand guard over her. She refused, said there must be no more scandal against her in that house."

"Now, Mr. Magnus, can you tell what awakened you at half-past four this morning?"

"No—I—I really have no idea," Bert stammered. "I dislike the word 'premonition,' but I woke, terrified, sure that something dreadful had happened. It is possible, of course, that I was subconsciously aware of the entry of the police and of the low-spoken conversation of the officers. But I can now recall no definite noise that awakened me. As I have told you, I went to sleep about midnight, and did not awaken at all until half-past four."

"That is all, Mr. Magnus—and may I extend to you the sympathy of myself and this jury? . . . Bring in Emil Sevier," Dr. Price directed, turning brusquely to a patrolman stationed at a door leading into another room of the morgue.

2

The creaking of chairs, the gusty sound of sharply indrawn breaths, awed exclamations, marked the entrance of Emil Sevier, suspected slayer of two women. The handcuffs had been removed, but two huge policemen guarded the man who was as yet booked only as a material witness. He had not yet retained a lawyer, and as he slumped wearily into the witness chair his hunted eyes glared about an audience containing not one friendly face.

The hours of grilling—and Dundee now knew that that was not merely a sensational newspaper term—had reduced Emil Sevier, erstwhile violinist for the Little Queen Theatre, to a cowering, quivering wreck. Dundee knew he had neither slept nor eaten since he had been arrested at two o'clock that morning. Nearly fifteen hours of torture! The young detective felt a sharp twinge of pity, then, remembering the kiss with which Cora Barker's lips had been gagged as her own braids were drawn tight about her throat, his heart hardened and his eyes were as hostile as any that gazed upon Emil Sevier.

Norma Paige covered her lovely, pale little face with her trembling hands and Dundee envied Walter Styles the privilege of slipping a comforting arm about her shoulders.

"What is your name?" asked Dr. Price briskly.

"Emil Sevier—Emil Sylvester Sewer," the prisoner answered dully, without raising his eyes.

"You were acquainted with Mrs. Emma Hogarth and Miss Cora Barker?"

"Yes."

The examination was on. Dundee, suddenly almost as weary as the prisoner himself, leaned back in his uncomfortable chair and closed his eyes. Question and answer—all nauseatingly familiar to him now—followed each other in swift succession, until Dr. Price demanded:

"I will ask you, Sevier, if it is not true that you planned to rob Mrs. Hogarth of the money she was reputed to have hidden in her room?"

Sevier, who had too frankly admitted as much to Dundee early that morning, now stirred and straightened in his chair. He frowned, closed his eyes a moment, then glared them defiantly at the coroner.

"I refuse to answer, on—on the grounds that it—it might tend to incriminate or degrade me," he jerked out.

"So Sevier has had time to think, during these fifteen hours." Dundee reflected, "and he is not the fool I thought him. "

"Give an account of your movements on Saturday evening, 29th June, from approximately eleven o'clock on," Dr. Price directed sternly.

Haltingly, conscious that every word he said wound a loop of the hangman's rope about his neck, Sevier told the story which he knew Dundee could prove against him. Again he told of going into the Rhodes House grounds, of waiting in the greenhouse until Cora Barker returned home, of climbing up the rose trellis to the upstairs porch, of looking into Mrs. Hogarth's room from her window, of seeing the dead woman in her chair and Cora Barker searching for something at the desk; of scuttling away down the rose trellis, of sprinting down the alley, his crushed straw hat in his hand.

But as before, Sevier refused to tell anything else after that moment when Dr. Weeks had seen him, raising his hat to shield his face from the glare of the headlights of the car which had turned at the entrance to the alley.

"I ask you again, Sevier, where you kept yourself from that night until this morning at two o'clock," Dr. Price reiterated sternly.

"I refuse to answer," Sewer retorted wearily, for the third time.

"Is it not true, Sevier, that you returned to Hamilton last night, climbed to the upstairs porch of the Rhodes

House, called Cora Barker to the window, and strangled her?"

"No, no! That's a lie!" Sevier screamed. "I tell you, I never laid eyes on Cora Barker after I saw her in Mrs. Hogarth's room last Saturday night! I never went near the Rhodes House last night—"

"Where and at what time were you apprehended by the police this morning, Sevier?" Dr. Price interrupted.

"About two o'clock, at Eighth and Main. I was going to Police Headquarters to give myself up for questioning. I saw by the papers that I was wanted," Sevier answered sullenly, subsiding into his chair after his outbreak.

"Do you know where the Rhodes House is, in relation to the corner, Eighth and Main?" Dr. Price asked.

"Sure I do. It's four blocks, but I wasn't any nearer to the Rhodes House than that," Sevier retorted, with weak violence.

And a dozen more questions elicited not another atom of information from Emil Sevier.

Finally, Dr. Price asked: "Just what was your relationship with the dead woman, Cora Barker?"

"I refuse to answer," Sevier replied sullenly.

"Is it not true that you were once engaged to be married, that you made love to her frequently?"

"I refuse to answer."

"Is it not true that you were so incensed against Cora Barker for having informed the police of your previous plans to rob Mrs. Hogarth that you came back here, at the risk of arrest, to kill her?"

"No, I tell you! No! I never saw Cora Barker last night. I never spoke to her or touched her, and you and your damned third-degree cops can—"

"Order, order, please!" Dr. Price rapped sharply on the table with his gavel. "What is the matter there, officer?"

Dundee turned and saw a young girl struggling with the uniformed policeman who guarded the entrance to the room.

"A lady—says she's got something to tell," the officer panted.

"Then bring her forward," Dr. Price commanded sternly.

In the deep hush, a girl, followed by a grim-faced man of middle-age, ran down the aisle between the two sections of seats. She was very young, and her pretty face was swollen and blotched from crying. Before she reached the coroner's table, Emil Sevier half-rose in his seat, cried out something inarticulate, then sank back, turning his head sharply away and shielding it with his crooked elbow.

"That is all for the moment, Sevier," Dr. Price snapped. "Take him away, officers—"

"Please let him stay. I want him to know—to hear—" the girl panted, her hands stretched toward the coroner.

"Who are you, young lady?" Dr. Price asked sternly.

The middle-aged man stepped forward before the girl could answer. "This is my daughter, Miss Myra Cannon. I am George H. Cannon, of Mercyville—"

"Please let me talk first, sir!" the girl appealed to the coroner. "Father is so angry with me for coming here; he didn't want me mixed up in it—"

"Just a minute, Miss Cannon. Officers, guard your prisoner. He may remain here until I instruct you to remove him. . . . Now, Miss Cannon—"

A minute or two later, the girl, duly sworn in, was pouring out her story in a flood of words and tears, only occasionally interrupted by a question from Dr. Price.

"I first met Emil—Mr. Sevier—last winter when I was studying music in Hamilton. I thought he was a wonderful violinist. I met him at my teacher's studio, where he sometimes took a lesson. He used to come and see me at my boarding place, and we'd practice together for hours. We—we got engaged to each other—"

"When?"

"In April—12th April, it was. I remember so well—" and the girl's voice broke down completely for a minute.

Then, dabbing fiercely at her drowned grey eyes, she went on: "I told Daddy the very next Sunday, when I went home for the week-end, and he wouldn't let me come back. The next Friday Emil came out to see me—Friday was his day off at the theatre, and he and Daddy quarrelled terribly. Daddy made me promise I wouldn't see Emil again, but—but we wrote to each other. I sent his letters to the theatre and Emil sent his letters to me to a girl friend of mine. We were planning all the time to get married and go far away. But Emil didn't have any money, and neither did I, except my allowance from Daddy. And—and I never dreamed Emil would plan such an awful way to get it as that—that woman says he did."

Dundee flinched at the way she designated poor dead Cora.

"You didn't know anything of his plans then?" Dr. Price interrupted.

"Of course not! He told me he was going to come into some money when his father's estate was settled, but I know now—Anyway, last Saturday night, at about half-past twelve or a quarter to one, the phone rang, and it was Emil, calling me from Hamilton. It was lucky I answered the phone and that Daddy didn't wake up. I— my mother is dead, and there's nobody but Daddy and me and the cook. Emil said he was in trouble, but that he hadn't done anything wrong. He asked me to drive to Greenpoint, and wait for him there a piece down the road from the station. He said he would drop off the train there when it slowed up. It doesn't stop at Greenpoint, you know, but it slows up to go through the village. So I did, and nobody saw me, and Emil told me just exactly what the trouble was—"

"Kindly tell the jury what Mr. Sevier told you that night," Dr. Price directed.

Rapidly the girl told the same story that Sevier had repeated so many times to the police and, that afternoon, to the coroner's jury.

"He said he was terribly sorry he'd ever planned to get money in that awful way," the girl sobbed, "but I knew he was telling the truth when he said he didn't kill the poor old lady, or rob her either. So I said I'd take him home with me and hide him in the rooms over the garage, because the cook lives in the house since—since my mother died and Daddy is away from home so much. Daddy was nearly crazy when he read the papers and saw that Emil was wanted by the police, but it wasn't till last night that he caught me taking food to the garage for Emil. He was so mad I thought he'd kill Emil, but pretty soon he got out the car and made Emil get into it and said he was going to take him to Hamilton to the police-station. I made him let me go, too, and, of course, with me along, Daddy couldn't drive right up to the station with Emil, because he didn't want my name mixed up in Emil's trial. Emil promised him he'd cut his tongue out before he'd tell where he'd been hiding, and he wouldn't have told! I know he wouldn't!"

In the deep silence from the audience the sobs of the girl were cut across by two groans, one from the girl's father, the other from the man she still loved and believed in—in spite of everything.

The coroner cleared his throat, then asked gently: "Where, and at just what time, did your father put Sevier out of the car?"

"It was about a quarter to one," the girl answered, "on the corner of First and Chestnut, but he didn't kill Cora Barker! That's why I came here to-day. I told Daddy I'd kill myself, if he wouldn't come with me to help me prove Emil didn't kill her. Daddy would like to see Emil hanged, he's so mad at him, but he'll have to tell the truth! Because he knows as well as I do that Emil didn't kill Cora Barker!"

XXIV.

"PLEASE tell the jury, Miss Cannon how you know Emil Sevier did not kill Cora Barker," Dr. Price instructed the weeping girl quietly.

Above the scratch of pencils and the frantic shuffling of papers at the Press table, the girl's voice rose triumphantly:

"Because Daddy and I followed him in the car until he was picked up by two policemen!"

"You kept him in sight all the time?" Dr. Price asked.

"Every single minute!" Myra Cannon cried. "He'd promised Daddy to go straight to Police Headquarters, and Daddy told me he was going to make sure he gave himself up that night. Emil didn't know we were following him, and he just walked around and leaned against buildings and lamp-posts, as he was awful sick. I knew he was scared to death that the police wouldn't believe him, and I wouldn't let Daddy get out of the car and jerk him along to Police Headquarters, like he kept threatening to do. Finally—it seemed like hours, and Daddy was getting madder all the time—a policeman saw Emil, and Emil started to run, then the policeman yelled out: 'Stop, Sevier, or I'll shoot!' and Emil stopped and let himself be arrested, and Daddy drove back to Mercyville just as fast as he could. And then—then this morning the papers said Cora Barker had been strangled, too, and that poor Emil was being 'grilled' by the police, and—and I couldn't stand it and made Daddy bring me here."

"And so," Dundee said to himself, "that's that!"

But there was no such dejection in his face as that which had settled upon Lieut. Strawn and Sergeant Turner.

Five minutes later George H. Cannon, rich and highly respected citizen of Mercyville, was testifying: "What my daughter say is true. God knows I have no love for that—that man," and he jerked his head contemptuously toward Sevier, who sat with his face bowed upon his hands. "But I cannot withhold evidence. I discovered Sevier upon my premises at half-past eleven last night. I drove him and my daughter in my car to Hamilton, putting Sevier out at the corner of First and Chestnut, at a quarter to one. If you wish, I can draw you an approximate diagram of the course Sevier took as he wandered about the streets, and as, my daughter and I followed him in the car."

"That will not be necessary at this time, Mr. Cannon," Dr. Price replied. "You are ready to swear, however, that from quarter to one, when you discharged your passenger, until a few minutes after two, when he was picked up by police, he was not out of your sight?"

"I can—and do," Cannon answered grimly. "He could not have murdered the Barker woman, since he was no nearer the Rhodes House than Eighth and Main."

"You are familiar with the streets in Hamilton?"

"I lived here until five years ago, and I am in the city frequently on business."

"Thank you . . . Now, Mr. Cannon, did Mr. Sevier make any confession to you regarding the murder of Mrs. Hogarth?"

"He did not. On the contrary, he denied it a great many times, for I myself accused him," the witness answered positively. "However, I believe—"

"I am afraid a statement of your belief cannot be admitted into the inquest record," Dr. Price interrupted courteously. "Excused—with the thanks of the jury, Mr. Cannon."

Half an hour later—it was nearly six o'clock—Bonnie Dundee entered Lieut. Strawn's office at Police Headquarters. His chief and Sergeant Turner were slumped in chairs at the lieutenant's desk—each a study in profound dejection.

"Grin, damn you!" Strawn growled, as his newest detective greeted him. "Go on—say it—'I told you so'!" He spat gloomily, then sat more erectly. "Well, anyway, we got one verdict against Sevier. He'll be indicted by the grand jury on Monday—"

"Do you really think, chief, that the grand jury will be so stupid as the coroner's jury?" Dundee asked pleasantly, as he seated himself in the open window. "I see you haven't any screens, either, chief. Still, your windows are nicely barred. Now if the Rhodes House screens had been put up on Monday, as Dusty promised they would be—"

"What do you mean—the grand jury stupid?" Strawn growled angrily.

"Why, surely, unless the grand jury is stupid, or unless our district attorney is, it will be quite plain to them, after mature deliberation, that if Emil Sevier didn't kill Cora Barker he likewise didn't kill Mrs. Hogarth. In fact, the grand jury will think the coroner's jury incredibly stupid not to have rendered the same verdict on the Hogarth murder as upon Cora Barker's death at the hand of person or persons unknown. For the same hands that strangled Mrs. Hogarth tied Cora's braids about her throat. One crime grew out of the other."

"Hunh!" Sergeant Turner snorted. "Thought you said Cora was 'killed with a kiss'! How many sweeties did that dame have, anyway? She'd been carrying on with Sevier, she'd just got herself half-way engaged to this Magnus chap last night—"

"And Magnus has an alibi for last Saturday night. He could no more have killed Mrs. Hogarth than Sevier could have killed Cora," Strawn cut in disgustedly.

"Women have been known to kiss other women—and Cora didn't take trouble to put on a kimono," Dundee contributed, very thoughtfully.

"What do you mean?" Strawn crashed his tilted chair to the floor. "I thought you'd come in here crowing about your 'bad penny,' and now you've switched around to a woman!"

"I haven't forgotten my 'bad penny,' but—I'm trying to consider every possibility," Dundee answered soberly. "And I'm not so sure that what I said just now was true —that the same hands strangled both women, but I do believe that the second crime grew out of the first."

"And me—I'm not so sure of that," Strawn retorted stubbornly "Was any of the other girls at the Rhodes House jealous of Bert Magnus's attentions to Cora? If all that love-talk took place at the piano last night, I guess everybody in the room got wise to what was going on."

A half-dozen little, unexplained things that Jewel Briggs had said flashed into Dundee's mind. For a tantalising moment he felt that the solution of both murders was on the very threshold of his mind, knocking for admission. Then the conviction was lost. He shook his head hopelessly.

"Jewel Briggs was watching the progress of Bert's affair with Cora with much interest," he admitted slowly, "but she didn't act jealous. Seemed to be glad Cora and Bert were going to be happy, but—Cora hated Jewel, and—Jewel warned me that Cora might try to tell me some jealous old fibs on her—to use Jewel's very words."

"And Jewel Briggs was spending the week-end with her folks when Mrs. Hogarth was murdered," Strawn pointed out wearily. "I'm stumped, Dundee. I'm still convinced that Sevier killed Mrs. Hogarth, but I'll be damned if I've got an idea as to who murdered Cora Barker.

"Look, Dundee!" he added suddenly, as if struck with an inspiration. "Every detective knows that one crime breeds another—and that the two are not necessarily connected. Three torch murders in or around New York in one year! Here we have an old lady strangled. No clues. No arrests. Looks like a good way to bump off somebody you don't like—don't it? And there's murder in the air. Everybody's thinking about murder, got murder on the brain. Suppose somebody—a woman or a man—either in the Rhodes House or living somewhere else—had it in for Cora Barker, and was smart enough to figure that the police would lay the blame on Sevier, since he was at large and wanted for the other murder. See?"

"It's possible," Dundee admitted reluctantly.

"Look!" Strawn urged. "You say Cora was murdered by the same person that killed Mrs. Hogarth. Why?"

"Because the two crimes must be connected," Dundee retorted.

"Yeah? Well, the only person Cora suspected or had said one word against was Emil Sevier. Far as I can see, Sevier was the only person connected with Mrs. Hogarth's murder that had any cause to bump off Cora—and he didn't do it!"

"I know!" Dundee agreed, shrugging. "But look, chief! Here we have three murders, all committed within a month of each other, and you expect me to agree with you that they are coincidences—that Sally Graves, as she called herself, was murdered by one person, her mother by another, and poor Cora by still another!"

"And what do you think?" Strawn taunted him wearily. "You think that 'bad penny' turned up once more, do you?"

"Yes, I do!" Dundee jumped to his feet, an almost fanatic light in his blue eyes. "I believe Dan Griffin murdered his wife and his mother-in-law and that he killed Cora Barker because he was sure she knew something against him, or—Wait! Suppose Dan Griffin sneaked back to the Rhodes House last night to make another search of Mrs. Hogarth's room. Trust him to know it was no longer guarded by the police! Suppose Cora Barker heard a step on the porch and ran to her window in her night-gown to investigate. Suppose she looked out, he seized her and kissed her against her will, tying her braids as he did so. If she did see him; he would have no choice but to kill her to keep her from giving the alarm."

"And why should he be coming back to Mrs. Hogarth's room?" Sergeant Turner demanded sarcastically.

"To look for the money he failed to find that night!" Dundee retorted triumphantly. "Suppose a little more! Suppose he fled from Mrs. Hogarth's room Saturday night before he succeeded in finding the money, because he heard Cora knocking. The papers have made no secret of the fact that any money the old lady had in that room was not found by the police after her murder. If Dan Griffin had reason to believe that she had the money he stole from the bank, he might risk anything to go back and look for it—with some hunch of his own as to where it was hidden."

"There's just one little flaw in that pretty yarn," Strawn interrupted. "Sevier didn't see anybody else while he was hanging around waiting for Cora, and he was climbing up the rose trellis himself just about the time Cora was knocking on the old lady's door—that is, if he and Cora are telling the truth. Believe me, if Sevier had seen or heard anyone he'd have been hollering about it by this time!"

"He would!" Dundee agreed triumphantly. "Oh, he would, all right! That's why I think Dan Griffin gave him no chance to see him, for he did not leave the Rhodes House that night!"

"What's that?" Strawn ejaculated, daredly.

"I mean I am convinced that Dan Griffin murdered three women and that he is still living at the Rhodes House!"

"And who might Danny be?" Sergeant Turner gibed nastily.

"That is what I'm going to find out!" Dundee shouted, as he strode to the door. "Remember, chief, you promised to give me till Monday, and to let me work in my own way! As pay, I promise to give you a 'bad penny' by Monday night!"

XXV.

BONNIE DUNDEE'S rushing out of Lieut. Strawn's office at Police Headquarters on the heels of his promise was due not so much to a boyish love of a dramatic exit as to an almost panicky desire to evade questioning by his astute chief.

For Strawn would inevitably have demanded: "If you believe Dan Griffin is a boarder at the Rhodes House, who else could he be but Henry Dowd? He is the only member of the household who has given a false name and false address. Better let me put him on the grill. I'll soon find out if he's Dan Griffin!"

And Dundee did not want Strawn or anyone else to "grill" Henry Dowd just yet. For he sincerely believed that such tactics would get them nowhere, at least for a long and tedious time. For if Henry Dowd was indeed Dan Griffin, murderer of three women, he was a consummately clever villain. For five years Dan Griffin had lived under some alias or other, in perhaps a score of cities.

And if Henry Dowd was Dan Griffin, he had undoubtedly covered his tracks well, had built up a story of his "past" which would necessitate endless police investigations before its falsity could be proved, and his real identity pinned upon him. Not tamely would a man who had the brains and the cold-blooded courage to kill three women confess that he was not only a bank absconder but a murderer.

Moreover, Dan Griffin, whoever he was, had been amply assured by the newspapers both in Hamilton and New York that he had not left a single clue upon the actual scene of any of his three crimes. With this assurance, Henry Dowd, if he was really Dan Griffin, could simply deny all knowledge of the three crimes, as, before the coroner's jury and upon first being questioned, he had denied all knowledge of or complicity in the Hogarth and Barker murders. As for his alias, if it was challenged, he could stick to his story or present the police with an intricate new one which would keep them busy for days or weeks before they could prove its falsity.

And even if its falsity was proved, where would the police be then? In five years Dan Griffin had had ample opportunity to change his appearance and personality so that an identification by a Belton acquaintance would be practically an impossibility. But granted that Henry Dowd could be proved to be Dan Griffin, just how near a conviction would the police be then? The district attorney could prove opportunity, and motive, but of actual evidence connecting Henry Dowd with the crimes there was none. The fact that Dowd had left New York the very evening of the day that Sally Graves or Griffin had been murdered would be strong circumstantial evidence, but it alone could not secure a conviction of murder against him.

As for the two murders at the Rhodes House, a clever defence attorney could convince any jury that, no matter if Dan Griffin was an inmate of the house when the two crimes were committed, others beside Griffin had had both motive and opportunity to kill Mrs. Hogarth—the motive being agreed.

No, his case was not complete by any means, would not be complete even if he proved that Henry Dowd was Dan Griffin, Dundee told himself ruefully as he took his seat at the dinner-table. But he liked a hard job.

He was late. The soup plates had been removed and Tilda, red eyed and nervous, was serving the well-filled plates of roast and vegetables.

The dining-room was crowded with "mealers"—many of them the sensation-seekers who had filled to overflowing the inquest room at the morgue. These transients, shuddering delightfully over their daring in actually coming to the "Murder Mansion" for a meal, exchanged theories in thrilled whispers, and quite openly studied the group of regular boarders with speculative eyes.

But upon that large table in the centre of the room a blight had fallen. Mrs. Rhodes had considerably rearranged the chairs and removed one so that the horror of gazing upon Cora Barker's empty chair was spared the remaining boarders. There was almost no conversation. On every face were the marks of strain and terror. As clearly as if it were spoken aloud a dread question made itself heard above the faint tinkle of silver and glass and china—"Who's next?"

Dundee, taking his place with only a nod to his fellow guests, knew that that table would have been deserted if Lieut. Strawn had not brutally commanded them to remain as guests of the house, on pain of arrest as material witnesses if they dared flee to less sinister quarters.

"Have you heard the news, Mr. Dundee?" Lawrence Sharp broke the heavy silence at last.

"No. I hope it's good news this time," Dundee answered quietly.

"Poor Cora's mother arrived from Quincy, Illinois, just before dinner," Mr. Sharp answered, pleased in spite of his depression at having news to impart. "She's having a tray in her room, poor old soul . . . Cora's room, that is. She asked to be permitted to stay there until her train leaves after midnight. Getting Cora's things together, I understand."

"Are the police permitting her to remove Cora's belongings?" Dundee asked innocently.

"I believe so. Mrs. Barker has just telephoned Police Headquarters and Lieutenant Strawn is coming over shortly to be here while she packs. But I understand that nothing has been found in the poor girl's room to aid the Police in any way. It was the sad privilege of the wife and

I to have a short talk with Mrs. Barker, and to tell her how much all of us had loved her daughter."

"I wish I hadn't come back last night," Mrs. Sharp broke in tearfully. "I wish I'd stayed out the week with Larry. He wanted me to—"

"I presume Mrs. Barker will take Cora home with her for—for burial?" Dundee asked, with a fleeting glance of sympathy for Bert Magnus, who was not eating but whose eyes had not left his untouched food since Dundee had entered the room.

"On the one o'clock train," Mr. Sharp replied heavily. "Will you pass me the catsup, please Mr. Dowd? Not that I have the slightest appetite, but we must all try to keep up our strength—"

As Henry Dowd complied silently with the request, Dundee studied him covertly but keenly. With Lieut. Strawn's meagre description of the Dan Griffin of five years ago in mind, the young detective noted and catalogued every feature and characteristic of the man seated opposite him.

"I finally doped it out that Dan Griffin must have been so ordinary-looking a young man that his face made no deep impression on anyone," Strawn had said. And that characterisation could aptly be applied to Henry Dowd.

If—before this moment—Dundee had been called upon to describe Henry Dowd for a police dossier, he would have been hard put to it to achieve even a fair degree of accuracy. For Dowd's was one of those faces you simply cannot recall vividly to mind.

"What colour are his eyes anyway?" Dundee puzzled. "I would have sworn they were blue-grey and now, in this light, and behind those glasses of his, they look grey-green. Hair—thin, light-brown mixed with grey. Forehead very high, but that may be because he's growing bald. Age? Say 34 to 38, and I'd defy anyone to hit it closer than that. Griffin would be about 35, so that checks. A gold eye-tooth on the right side, but that dental job could

have been done any time during the last five years as a
tiny item towards creating a subtle disguise. But I'll be
eternally confounded if Henry Dowd or whoever he is
looks subtle!"

No, there was nothing in Henry Dowd's face or
manner to suggest cleverness or subtlety. The only two
words which adequately described him were "meek" and
"diffident." But of Dan Griffin his acquaintances in Belton
had said, "You'd never have guessed, to look at him, that
he'd rob a bank."

Mentally, Dundee ticked off other items of Strawn's
description of Dan Griffin: "Neither tall nor short—
between five feet seven and five feet ten. Average weight,
inclined to be slender rather than heavy. Regular
features—nothing odd about them, neither handsome nor
homely."

So far so good! The meek little man across the table
fitted those qualifications exactly. "But Dan Griffin did
not wear glasses," he reminded himself. "Glasses are,
however, the first thought of the amateur criminal trying
to disguise himself. Effective, too, for glasses have been
known not only to change the facial appearance of a man
but his personality as well. But if Henry Dowd is Dan
Griffin, he was clever enough not to adopt any of the
other obvious methods of disguising his looks—dyeing his
hair or wearing a wig, growing a beard, affecting a limp,
scarring his cheek. For two years Dan Griffin has known
that there are no records of his finger-prints in existence.
Trust him to know that the Belton police station, with all
its records, was burned to the ground! But there is a
sample of your handwriting in my pocket, Mr. Daniel
Thomas Griffin, and I rather think my next step is to
obtain a specimen of the real handwriting of Mr. Henry
Dowd—not that clumsy printing with which he signed the
register and scribbled aliases."

The young detective was jerked out of his reverie by a
soft, hesitant voice at his elbow. Possibly Mrs. Rhodes
had guessed that Bonnie Dundee would appreciate the

honour, but at any rate his chair was now on Norma
Paige's left. On her right sat Walter Styles—of course!

"Are you going to Mrs. Hogarth's funeral to-morrow,
Mr. Dundee?" Norma asked. "Mrs. Rhodes thought to-
morrow was the best day, since it is the Fourth, and none
of us will be working—"

Dundee hesitated. He had forgotten that the next day
would be a holiday and that his operations as a detective
would be hampered by the presence of the boarders. But
if they were all going to the funeral—

"I'm afraid not, Miss Paige," he answered regretfully.
"As I told you, I'm trying to do some work in my room,
and having lost to-day on account of the inquests I think
I'd better buckle down to it to-morrow, even if it is a
holiday—"

"Everyone in the house is going except you," Norma
answered with faint reproach. "Even Mr. Dowd and Mr.
Magnus, who never met her . . . I've been taking up a
little collection for flowers, but, of course, since you
hardly knew Mrs. Hogarth—"

"Please let me have the pleasure," Bonnie interrupted
hastily, and slipped a five-dollar bill along the edge of the
table. "I've been wondering about the funeral. Since Mrs.
Hogarth was robbed of all her money—"

"Mrs. Rhodes's church volunteered to-day to pay the
funeral expenses," the girl whispered, tears springing
into her dark blue eyes. "Mrs. Rhodes was going to pay
everything herself, but her pastor said it wasn't fair—
Oh!" she broke off, with a little cry of pain and grief. "It's
horrible to think of poor Mrs. Hogarth having to be buried
on charity, when she was so proud, and counted so on
helping others with her money when she died—"

Dundee wanted to tell her then of the $2,000 life
insurance which Mrs. Hogarth had died without knowing
she had a claim to. But no one, not even Norma Paige,
must know yet that there had been a daughter who was
murdered. Later, when the three murder mysteries had
been solved, and Norma had come into her small

inheritance under the terms of Mrs. Hogarth's will, the girl could reimburse the church for the old, lady's funeral expenses.

But to-morrow, while others were paying tribute to the dead woman, Dundee would be serving her in another way. For he still believed that the key to both the Hogarth and the Barker murders was concealed in the Rhodes House . . .

Bonnie Dundee fully intended to devote at least two hours of hard thinking that Wednesday night to the murder mysteries which he had so rashly promised Lieut. Strawn to solve by Monday evening, or confess failure. But when his telephone rang at eight o'clock it startled him out of a sound sleep and interrupted a gorgeously satisfactory dream—a beautifully intricate solution of the triple murder mystery, a solution bristling with fantastic clues, secret passages, disguises—

"Hello! Who is it? . . . Oh, hello, Uncle Pat!" he cried, sleepy irritation changing into affection.

"Lieutenant Strawn's just been here, Bonnie," the Police Commissioner told his nephew, "and I've asked him to give you a free hand, since you've got some sort of wild theory and it seems he has none, at least about the Barker murder. I told him I'd pull you off the case and let him handle it any way he saw fit, but he confesses himself stumped, and seems to be willing to give you a chance. Maybe he thinks you'll make a fool of yourself, and that the 'old man' won't interfere with his department again. You've got to uphold the honour of the family, boy!"

"I'll do my best," Dundee assured his uncle gratefully. "It's awfully decent of both of you—"

"You realise, of course, that you're working under Strawn, and that credit for anything you may discover goes to him, as chief of the Homicide Squad. I can't have him resigning and accusing me of nepotism."

"I don't care anything about the credit," Dundee retorted. "All I want is a chance to play my hunch. And if

Strawn or Turner or anyone else gets hold of a better theory I'll be tickled to death to do anything I can to help him prove it."

"Good boy!" his uncle applauded. "Just one warning, Bonnie. Don't get so crazy about this hunch of yours that you'll be blind to other possibilities. I'd rather not speak more plainly over the phone, but I think you know what I mean. Don't twist and bend facts simply to make them fit your theory, and don't let any apparently insignificant facts slip past you because they don't fit your theory."

"Right!" Dundee agreed heartily.

"One more thing," his uncle went on. "Strawn has detailed two men to guard the Rhodes House night and days, as unobtrusively as possible, and has detailed one of our best men to shadow Dowd. It seems that Dowd has a job soliciting subscriptions for *The Morning News*."

"Good! That makes it easy to get a specimen of his real handwriting," Dundee replied. "He 'printed' his name in the Rhodes House register—and very amateurishly; an obvious attempt to disguise his penmanship."

"Well, boy, if you get anything definite on him, don't give him too much rope. He might use it on you," his uncle advised with a laugh which was not exactly mirthful.

Dundee hung up the receiver. "Good old Uncle Pat! He's certainly giving me the breaks . . . Now what the devil was that dream? Oh, yes, secret passage!" He grinned. "That loosened board in Dowd's closet has been clapping hard against my subconscious, all right. But it was a swell dream. Wish I could remember all of it. Had a great kick in it— Let's see; Daisy Shepherd was Dan Griffin, disguised as a woman, and she or rather he had hidden the loot in the flour bin! But where did that secret passage come in?"

Suddenly he struck his rumpled black hair with a disgusted fist. "Lord! What a fool I've been! No wonder my subconscious had to step in and help!

For the belated brain wave was simply this: If Henry Dowd was Dan Griffin, and he had used the loose board of his clothes closet to effect an entry into Mrs. Hogarth's room, why in the name of all that was reasonable would he not have used the same means of entry to make a further search of Mrs. Hogarth's room on Tuesday night, instead of prowling about on the upstairs porch so that Cora had heard him and had made it necessary for the prowler to murder her to protect himself? And what other possible explanation of Cora's murder could there be, provided, of course, his theory of Dan Griffin's being responsible for both murders was the correct one? Certainly Cora Barker had finally told the police all she knew about the first murder. Dundee would stake his hope of eternal happiness on that.

"Well, I'm glad I thought of it before Strawn did," the chagrined young detective, told himself. "Of course, there's just a chance that Mrs. Rhodes sicked Dusty on to the job of nailing the loose board back into place before Cora was murdered. In that event, Friend Henry—if he is Dan Griffin—would have had to use the windows Tuesday night. But—oh, damn!—why should Cora have gone to her east window instead of her south window, which is the nearer to Mrs. Hogarth's room? If it was Dan Griffin, alias Henry Dowd, that Cora saw trying to get into Mrs. Hogarth's room, he would have had no-business at all on the east side of the porch . . . Guess I'd better get me a job of soliciting newspaper subscriptions, same as good old Henry. I seem to be a perfect dub this game.

His tangled reverie was broken by a knock upon his door. Jerking on a dressing gown he padded across his little room barefoot to answer it. It was Mrs. Rhodes, fresh towels on her arm, her austere face dark with trouble and anxiety.

"Just the person I most want to see!" Dundee, cried heartily. "Come in!"

"There's a dozen things I ought to be doing," the landlady reproached herself and him as she sank into the

only arm-chair the room boasted. "Lord! What a day this
has, been! New locks on all the doors, screens put up after
it's too late to help poor Cora! Any other time I'd have got
a sight of pleasure out of seeing Dusty run around like
he's done to-day. Lieutenant Strawn said there wasn't
any call to change the locks, but I think the folks might
feel better—safer—" She sighed heavily, as she handed
towels and key to her new boarder.

"Thanks, Mother Rhodes! It was kind of you to go to
all that trouble and expense," the boy said sincerely. "By
the way, I suppose that loose board in Dowd's closet has
been nailed down?"

"I made Dusty 'get around' to that yesterday," Mrs.
Rhodes said, smiling wryly as she quoted her husband's
favourite expression.

"So that's that," Dundee said cryptically. He did not
explain that half the mystery which had been tormenting
him had been solved. Granted that Dowd was Dan Griffin
and the murderer, he would have been forced to leave his
room and enter Mrs. Hogarth's through windows. But
there still remained the puzzle of why Cora had been
murdered at her east window, instead of at the south one.

"I ought to be getting back downstairs," the landlady
sighed again. "Mrs. Barker, poor soul, is resting in my
room now. She's all worn out, what with reporters
pestering her, and that Lieutenant Strawn pawing over
Cora's things before he'd let her pack 'em. I guess he
didn't find any clues, because he said it would be all right
for her to take them away with her. She's taken a great
shine to Bert Magnus. Says Cora wrote her how much she
thought of Bert, and poor Mrs. Barker was counting on
Cora being happy at last. . . . Oh, dear!" she sighed again,
as she started to rise.

"Just a minute, please, Mother Rhodes!" Dundee
detained her apologetically. "I can't ask anyone else, and
I must know just what sort of man Arthur B. Wheeler is.
What he looks like, I mean."

"You are hard up for somebody to suspect, aren't you?" Mrs. Rhodes gibed, as she sank back into the arm-chair. "Well, I guess you know your own business. Arthur Wheeler is about 27 years old, more'n six feet tall, skinny as a snake, and so light-complected he just misses being an albino. His eyes are so blue they look like a new-born baby's, and I guess they're about as strong as a baby's too, because he wears glasses with lenses nearly half an inch thick. They make him look like a scared rabbit—"

"Then it wasn't Wheeler who broke his glasses not long ago," Dundee interrupted, memory flashing back to that broken lens he had found in the trash bag in the basement.

"It was Bert Magnus that broke his glasses," Mrs. Rhodes informed him, "though it beats me how you know. Jewel was frolicking around him at breakfast one morning about two weeks ago, and knocked his nose-pinchers of. Mr. Sharp recommended him to his own oculist and Bert had a new lens by dinner-time."

"Thanks, Mother Rhodes," Dundee said cheerfully, but mentally he chalked up another disappointment. "Tell me more about Arthur Wheeler, like the lamb you are!"

"Lamb!" Mrs. Rhodes snorted, but she was not displeased. "He's got a funny little pug nose, and a moustache about the size and colour of a toothbrush. All the girls laughed at him, he was so comical-looking, and I guess Daisy was the only one that ever spoke a kind word to him."

"And Daisy is probably wishing now that she had been as hard-hearted as the other girls," Dundee smiled. "I can understand why she so resented the coroner's asking her if she was'"romantically interested' in Arthur Wheeler. Well, again—that's that!" he added, dismissing the inventor as a possible Dan Griffin.

He expected Mrs. Rhodes to hurry away then, but unaccountably she lingered, her fingers nervously pleating the lace ruffle of her jabot. Finally she flung up her head and demanded defiantly: "Listen here, young man! Have you got sense enough to go off half-cocked if I tell you something I ought to have told at the inquest this afternoon and didn't?"

Dundee's heart leaped, but he answered quietly: "I think I have."

"Well, I don't suppose it amounts to a row of pins, and to tell you the truth I forgot all about it last night when Sergeant Turner was putting us all through the third-degree, trying to find out what we knew about poor Cora's death."

"Yes?" The boy was trying hard not to appear impatient.

"Well, last night while all you folks were in the parlour, with Cora playing and Bert singing, I called Jewel to the phone, and then I stood in the doorway for awhile, listening to the music. Then Cora stopped playing, and she and Bert talked real low, and it looked to me like they were getting engaged, or at least coming to an understanding. I haven't kept a boarding-house fifteen years for nothing."

"And you were right, as Bert admitted at the inquest this afternoon."

"But I wasn't sure then, and I thought if I dropped into Cora's room after she'd gone upstairs she might tell me all about it, if there was anything to tell. I was mighty fond of Cora, and I wanted her to be happy. . . . Well, it must have been about eleven o'clock when I went up, but I didn't knock on Cora's door for I heard her and Jewel quarrelling, and since I didn't want to have anything to do with it, I went back downstairs."

"Quarrelling?" Dundee echoed, startled. "You're sure you recognised Jewel's voice?"

"Of course I am. You know how shrill her voice is! Besides, the door was ajar, and I could see her as well as hear her, though neither of them saw me. She was sitting on the edge of Cora's bed and Cora was standing at her dresser, braiding her hair." The landlady shuddered a she recalled to what horrible use those braids had been put just two hours later.

"Did you catch any of the actual words spoken?" Dundee urged.

XXVI.

1

"I JUST hesitated at the door long enough to make sure they were quarrelling, and that it was no place for me," Mrs. Rhodes answered. "But I did hear Jewel say 'You're crazy, Cora! If Bert Magnus said anything like that to any girl, it wasn't to me! I've never been in Bert's room in my life, much less at midnight last Thursday!' And then Cora said: 'You're lying! You've been running after Bert Magnus ever since he came here to board, and I myself heard you offer to help him type his scenario.' Then Cora whirled around and shook her comb at Jewel and said, 'If it wasn't you he was talking to on Thursday night at midnight, I'd like to know who it, was! There's no other "perfect stenographer" in this house that I know of, and I heard him with my own ears,' Cora says. She says, 'Bert was standing by his dresser with his back turned to the window, and I heard him say, plain as I hear my own voice this minute, "Go to it, Sweetheart! The perfect stenographer!" That's what he said, and if he wasn't talking to you, I'd like to know who it was. '" Mrs. Rhodes paused for breath, and Dundee whistled softly.

"Did you hear anything else, Mother Rhodes?"

"Well, I did listen a second longer, because I thought if Cora was right and Jewel was cutting monkey-shines in my house, she'd hear from me in a double-quick hurry! But Jewel brazened it out. She says to Cora: 'I'll face Bert with you! He'll tell you it wasn't me!' And Cora said "Oh, don't bother! He's already told me it wasn't you, but any fool would know he was just trying to be a gentleman.' And then says: 'Listen, Jewel! I'm not blaming Bert! I blame you, and I'm warning you to leave him alone!' I tiptoed away then, because I didn't want to get mixed up in their quarrel," Mrs. Rhodes concluded.

"I see," Dundee said, frowning, but he did not see at all. "'Why didn't you tell this at the inquest, Mother Rhodes?"

"Because I didn't want to make trouble for Jewel, of course," Mrs. Rhodes answered defiantly. "She was called before I was, and she swore she didn't see Cora after the party broke up downstairs. If I'd told what I heard last night, like as not they'd have arrested Jewel for murdering Cora, and you know as well as I do, Bonnie Dundee, that that flighty, silly little pint-size stenographer wouldn't have the nerve to kill a woman just because that woman was jealous of her, or even because she might tell tales on her. Jewel hasn't been so almighty careful of her reputation, anyway, though I don't think there's a grain of real harm in the girl. So l kept my mouth shut, and I'd not have told you if I hadn't thought you had sense enough to know it didn't amount to anything."

"You're a darling, Mother Rhodes!" the boy cried, putting his arm about her broad, stern shoulders as he followed her to the door. "By the way, Bert didn't overhear them quarrelling over him, I suppose?"

"I told you that was just about eleven o'clock," Mrs. Rhodes reminded him severely. "And I guess you heard Bert tell at the inquest that he went for a long walk right after the party broke up downstairs. He didn't get back till after twelve, and according to his story, he was asleep almost as soon as he hit the bed."

"I wonder if Jewel has told Bert yet that she and Cora quarrelled over him," Dundee speculated, his eyes narrowing.

"Hunh! Jewel ain't a fool! She's not going to tell anybody! Why should she? She thinks Bert stood up for her anyway, whether he was lying or not, and she hasn't any ideal heard a word. Goodness knows, I didn't tell on the poor, flighty kid to get her into trouble—"

"Please don't worry, Mother Rhodes!" Dundee begged. "You did exactly right to tell me, and I give you my word I'm not going to cook up any wild theory about Jewel's murdering Cora."

"You're a nice boy, as boys go," Mrs. Rhodes admitted. "Now tumble back into bed and get some sleep. You need it."

Dundee obeyed her as to the tumbling, but he intended to do some heavy thinking, once his light was off and he could concentrate. The next thing he knew he was starting up to answer a loud knock at his door. Couldn't he be let in peace for a minute? But it was broad daylight and Tilda was calling through the door: "It's way after nine o'clock, Mr. Dundee, and Mrs. Rhodes says if you want any breakfast you'd better come down right away."

"Upholding the best traditions of the force—sleeping on the job!" he grinned ruefully, as he padded down the hall for his shower.

When he entered the dining-room, only Mr. Lawrence Sharp sat at the big centre table, the morning paper propped against the sugar-bowl.

"Hullo! Where's everybody? I suppose I'm the last one down," Dundee greeted the head of Marcus-Crane's linoleum department cheerfully.

"Good morning!" Mr. Sharp answered with rebuking solemnity. "Although this is the Fourth of July, it is a sad day for this household, Mr. Dundee. The wife had her breakfast in bed. The poor girl is sadly upset over the tragedies. It is an outrage that the police won't let us move to more pleasant quarters, where we could try to forget."

"It is too bad," Dundee agreed, peppering his cantaloupe. "Everybody taking a holiday, I suppose, and going to the funeral this afternoon?"

"Jewel elected to work until funeral time," Mr. Sharp answered. "You know she's a public stenographer—her own boss. And Mr. Dowd is taking advantage of the holiday to find prospective subscribers to *The Morning*

News at home this A.M., I understand. I take it that the
whole household except yourself will attend the funeral,
sir. Mrs. Rhodes made rather a point of it."

Dundee grinned. He knew where that idea had
originated. What would he do without her help?

Mr. Lawrence Sharp caught the grin and rose in
pompous disapproval. "Here is the morning paper, sir. It
seems odd to see one's own and one's friends' photographs
so prominently displayed in the Press."

Alone, Dundee studied the picture layout. As the
paper proudly assured its readers, these were brand new
pictures, snapped by alert photographers before and after
the inquest on Wednesday.

"Good heavens! They caught me squinting, and I
thought I was cured of that habit when a mere infant!
Swell picture of Jewel—'Miss Jewel Briggs, beautiful
blonde stenographer, quizzed at double inquest.' But I
fancy I detect a gleam of fear in your eyes, my Jewel! . . .
Caught you this time I see, Mr. Dowd," he went on
cheerfully "Full face—looking right into the camera, and
not bald at all. Quite a clear likeness. Mother Rhodes, you
really ought to learn to smile pretty at the birdie! And
dear Walter, what's your grouch about?' he silently
addressed the snapshot of the scowling young proprietor
of the financially crippled 'Gentlemen's Shop.' "Oh,
Norma, Norma, why do you have to be so exactly what
I've dreamed of and inexcusably engaged to another
man?"

But he was not half so sorrow-stricken as he
pretended to be, or he could not have devoted himself so
ardently to the plate of bacon and eggs which Tilda set
before him.

"My hat was on crooked," Tilda mourned, looking over
his shoulder at the propped paper.

"So it was, Tilda, but your face was never more
charming," he assured her ambiguously but truthfully.

Tilda, blushing furiously, rewarded him with a whole
pot of piping hot coffee, and it was an extremely well-fed

young man who shortly left the Rhodes House, bound for the offices of *The Morning News*. He paused briefly on the front steps and addressed Mr. Sharp as if all were harmony between them.

"I've been having a little trouble with my eyes. Thought I ought to have an oculist give them the once-over," he said mendaciously. "Can you recommend a good man, Mr. Sharp?"

"Certainly, certainly!" Nothing pleased Mr. Sharp so much as having his opinion asked. "My man is Dr. Edmund Bolger; offices in the Gaylord Building, on Main Street, you know. Fifth and Main. Closed to-day, of course. . . . What seems to be the trouble, Dundee?"

"Spots, and—er—floating specks," Dundee replied vaguely, and, after thanking Mr. Sharp heartily, continued on his way.

About an hour later Dundee was admitted to the study of Hamilton's leading handwriting expert, Mr. Norman Brooks, to whom he had been sent by his uncle, Police Commissioner O'Brien.

"I'd like a snap judgment, Mr. Brooks," Dundee explained, "not a detailed analysis—yet. Could you tell me, offhand, whether in your opinion the same man wrote these—and he laid before the expert the specimens of Dan Griffin's handwriting procured by Lieut. Strawn from the bank in Belton—'and these," and he added three receipts for subscriptions to *The Morning News*.

The expert studied the exhibits for a long minute in silence. Then he looked up and shook his head. "I do not believe any handwriting expert could say, with confidence, that they were or were not the work of the same hand. You have, of course, observed that these receipts are signed in what is popularly called 'printing.'"

"Yes, that seems to be Henry Dowd's line now and he intends to stick to it," Dundee agreed "He signed the Rhodes House register the same way, and also made this notation in the same clumsy fashion," and he showed the expert the envelope on which had been "printed" the three names—Henry Dobbs, Herman Dodd, Henry Dowd.

"As you see, Mr. Brooks, our amateur printer was torn between three aliases, and finally chose 'Henry Dowd'— heaven only knows why. Then the same man may have written both?"

"Or may not. A microscopic analysis might betray some definite points of similarity, but I doubt if there would be sufficient evidence to hold up in court, which is undoubtedly what you have in mind."

"So that, too, is that," Dundee told himself as he left Mr. Brook's house. "And friend Henry is exactly as clever as I knew he must be, provided he is Dan Griffin. And I am as far from being able to prove he is Griffin as I was before Strawn went to Belton. But if he isn't Griffin, who the deuce is he? And why does he sneak around under an alias and disguise his handwriting? Damn it all, he's got to be Dan Griffin! There's nobody else that comes anywhere near filling the bill! Oh, Lord! What a washout as a Sherlock I've turned out to be. Maybe what I need is a Watson," he concluded his gloomy reflections with a grin.

That last foolish idea recurred to him as a big-time inspiration when he encountered, Norma Paige in the second floor hall just before two o'clock—the hour set for Mrs. Hogarth's funeral services at the undertaker's parlours. The girl was dressed all in white, except for a band of black velvet ribbon about her Leghorn hat. She wore no rouge, and her lovely little face, even to the lips, was pathetically pale.

"I wonder if you'd let Cap'n keep me company this afternoon?" he asked eagerly.

Her dark-blue eyes stared at him with incredulity and she reproved. "I thought you said you were going to work this afternoon, which was why you couldn't attend the funeral," she said stiffly. "I should think the parrot would be quite distracting. He chatters a lot. How ever—"

"Thanks awfully!" Dundee interrupted contritely. "I am going to be busy, but—funny as it may sound—I'm counting on Cap'n to help me."

2

"Now, Cap'n!" Bonnie Dundee finished laying out his small collection of what he hoped were clues, retrieved from the Rhodes House trash bags, and addressed the parrot briskly. The wrought-iron stand for the cage was so low that he could, sitting at ease in his armchair, look the bird in the eye—when he could catch that tiny, bright bead. "We're all set to make pow-wow, Cap'n, or rather, 'my dear Watson.'"

The parrot turned on his perch, cocked his head, and slowly drooped a white lid. "Make whoopee!" he croaked, in a startling imitation of his dead mistress's voice.

"Fie, fie, Cap'n!" Dundee reproved him. "I beg you to be serious. No whoopee till you and I have finished our little job of avenging Emma."

The name struck a chord in Cap'n's memory. He spread his wings and croaked angrily: "Emma, you old fool!" How many times the foolish old lady must have apostrophised herself thus, and how it must have amused her to hear her parrot echo the charge!

"I quite agree with you, Cap'n," Dundee said gravely. "Emma Hogarth was certainly an old fool in many respects, but she was rather a dear, too, and I'm sure you are mourning her more sincerely than anyone who is attending her funeral this afternoon . . . But, Cap'n, the point is that she is dead, and you and I haven't done anything much about it yet."

The bird seemed to glare at him reproachfully, and Dundee hastened to apologise: "Oh, I know you've done your part, old man! You've harped away on 'Bad penny,' but to tell you the truth, Capn, I haven't been able to turn him up yet."

"Bad penny! Bad penny!" Cap'n croaked and turned twice, excitedly, on his perch. Did he remember that those were the last words he had ever heard his mistress speak, and did he wonder why she spoke no more, why alien, fearful hands fed him?

"I agree with you, Cap'n, and I wish I could oblige," Dundee assured the bird gravely. "But the only bad penny I happen to have at present looks suspiciously like a counterfeit bad penny, if there can be such a thing—but I'm sure you know what I mean. Let me explain, my dear Watson: You have probably guessed that the only bad penny I have so far turned up is the meek and diffident little Mr. Henry Dowd. Not to bore you with too many details, these are the facts I have against Friend Henry: First, he fairly well fits the description of Dan Griffin— Dan Griffin—" he repeated the words slowly, hopefully, forcefully, but the apparently attentive parrot gave no sign that he had ever heard the name before.

Dundee went on, only mildly disappointed: "Yes, Cap'n, allowing for the ravages of time—five years— Henry Dowd fits our rather faulty description of your mistress's thief of a son-in-law. Second, he assumed an alias when he came to this house. Third, he came here from New York, and not directly from Des Moines, as he gave the police to understand. Fourth, he is 'unknown,' at least as Henry Dowd, at the Des Moines address he gave. Fifth, he disguises his handwriting. Sixth, he hides his face from newspaper photographers . . . Yes, I know that a full-face snapshot of him was in this morning's paper, but I'd have given a raisin cooky to see his expression when he made the discovery. I am convinced he was unaware of the honour which the Press was conferring upon him . . . Seventh, he did not meet your mistress, though I've been told she had invited him to call, as she did each new boarder. Eighth, he occupied the room next to Mrs. Hogarth's and may very well have discovered that Emil Sevier had prised the closet board loose. Ninth, his light was on at the actual time of Mrs. Hogarth's murder.

He admits that, and Sevier confirms it. But whether or not he was really asleep, and was aroused by your charming voice, Cap'n, just sufficiently to realise the economic waste and turn it off, who can say? Tenth and last, but no means least, Cap'n Watson, Friend Henry left New York the very evening of the very day on which Dan Griffin's wife, Sally Graves, as she called herself, was brutally and mysteriously murdered . . . Well what about it, my dear Watson? Ten nice, big, juicy facts. What do you deduce from them?"

The parrot, as if infinitely wearied, turned his back upon the loquacious young detective. Dundee shrugged, and laughed.

"Right you are, my dear Watson! Ten facts, and not one shred of actual proof that Henry Dowd is either Dan Griffin or that he was ever in Mrs. Hogarth's room! Am I barking up the wrong tree, Cap'n? In your honest opinion, am I all wet?"

Cap'n turned slowly about, cocked his head and drooped that paperish white lid again, giving an effect of sly mirth.

"I'm afraid you're right, old man," Dundee agreed. "All wet. I simply can't get steamed up about Henry. Just can't bring myself to the point of clapping him on the shoulder and saying: 'The jig is up, Dan Griffin! I charge you with the murder of Sally Griffin, Mrs. Emma Harkness, known as Mrs. Emma Hogarth, and Cora Barker.' On the other hand, facts are facts, and I wish you'd quit winking at them."

"Help! Murder! Police!" Cap'n shrieked suddenly.

"Yes, Cap'n," Dundee said soberly, "both you and your mistress warned us, and we let it happen. I'll never forgive myself—But let's get on, my dear Watson!" He cleared his throat huskily. "If Henry Dowd isn't Dan Griffin, who is? I confess I've toyed with the happy theory that Arthur B. Wheeler, no longer with us, might be the villain, and Daisy Shepherd his tool, the actual strangler. Now that is your cue for a deep, throaty chuckle, Cap'n!"

But the parrot did not laugh.

"No?" Dundee raised his eyebrows. "Sorry you have a deficient sense of humour, my dear Watson. You see, neither Daisy nor Wheeler was in New York on 2nd June. Wheeler is undoubtedly as little like Dan Griffin as a man could well be, and, granted that Wheeler could so badly desire Mrs. Hogarth's money that he would return here to rob her, or that he would have the power to enlist Daisy's aid to rob her, there is no earthly reason Mrs. Hogarth should have uttered the now historic words, 'bad penny,' upon sight of either of them. And furthermore, if Cora Barker had known one atom of evidence against either, of them she would not have hesitated to tell it. And still furthermore, Arthur Wheeler is to-day, and has been continuously for the last two weeks, a guest of an extremely low-rate hotel in Chicago, as Lieutenant Strawn took pains to learn by wire—"

Again the parrot turned his back on the detective.

"Bored, Cap'n? Or simply disgusted with my stupidity?" Dundee asked solicitously. "The fact is, Cap'n, I don't know where to look for that ' bad penny;' and yet, unless my whole theory is cock-eyed, he must be living in the house. Lawrence Sharp? Far too old to be Dan Griffin, and not conceivably the 'bad penny to whom Mrs. Hogarth addressed her last remarks. Walter Styles? Far too young, and, besides, he's practically a native of Hamilton. Forgetting the Dan Griffin theory, for the moment, is it possible that Mrs. Hogarth, who, just an hour before, had driven him away from her door with her cane, would have hailed him jovially or even, sarcastically as a bed penny, when he hove over her window-sill? Furthermore, Norma Paige has given him an alibi, and that's enough for me."

Again the parrot cocked his green-and-yellow head, and drooped an eyelid.

"So you're on to the fact that I'm heartbroken, are you?" Dundee demanded. "Well, to make a shameful confession, Cap'n, my heart has been broken several

times before, and will probably mend to be broken again.
I seem to have fallen into the habit of adoring girls who
are already engaged or married . . . All of which is beside
the point, and I don't blame you for turning your back on
me . . . Well, we've only got Bert Magnus left, haven't we,
old man? I do seem to bump into Bert every time I turn a
corner in this case, but I think you'll agree that there's
only one thing to chalk up against him: he is the only one
man in the house, besides Henry Dowd, that had never
met Mrs. Hogarth . . . No, I'm forgetting! There's one
other thing: Bert was in Philadelphia, on 2nd June, and
Philadelphia is only two hours from New York. But wait!
It's worse than that!" and he scrabbled among his small
collection for a copy of the telegram with which the
Philadelphia police department had replied to his request
for information regarding Herbert S Magnus. "Hah! My
memory is still clear, Cap'n! Listen: 'Landlady, Mrs.
Christine Starrett, not at home Sunday, 2nd June, until
late afternoon, having spent Saturday and Sunday in
Atlantic City, but Magnus had supper with family and
bed had been slept in Saturday night' . . . Philadelphia—
New York, two hours! Landlady away!"

He returned the telegram to the table and sighed as
he fingered the small collection of trash bag "clues." "See
how hard up I am for a Dan Griffin, Cap'n? Bert Magnus
can't be Dan Griffin, because he's indisputably Herbert.
S. Magnus, formerly of Riverside, California. Didn't leave
Riverside until February, 1924, and Dan Griffin was at
that very time working in the Belton bank, which he
neglected to rob until May of that year. And during these
more than five years Bert has been in regular
correspondence with his family. Not only does his family
so assure me, through the Riverside chief of police, but
I've seen some of the letters with my own eyes. Of course
I didn't read them through, Cap'n—just glanced at them
to make sure—" He stopped short, then, uttering a sharp
exclamation, he dashed from the room, not taking the
trouble to excuse himself of his strange audience.

Five minutes later he was back in his room, his handsome young face pale with excitement, an open letter in his hand. The new lock on Bert Magnus's door had of course yielded to his skeleton key.

"What do you make of this, Cap'n?" he asked huskily. "Am I a fool, or—Well, listen: 'Father is heartbroken because you won't come home, even for a visit, Bert darling. You know he's getting old, and he hasn't been himself at all since our dear Red's death. I think he's afraid he'll die without seeing you again, and as for me, I'm sometimes frightened at the thought that I might not even know my own dear brother if I met him on the street. You know I was only thirteen when you left, and five years is a long time. You haven't even sent us a picture of yourself, and I'm always sending you snapshots. Your letters are wonderful, though, and I'm so glad you're working at your scenario-writing again. I'm so thrilled! I remember how excited I was over that first story of yours. It was called "*More To Be Pitied*," wasn't it? But I'm sure you have much grander plots now—"

Dundee dropped the letter. "Well, I'll be—Cap'n. won't you please nip me good and hard on the ear?" But without waiting for the favour, he plunged out of the room again. It was half an hour, before he was back, in one hand a sheaf of torn manuscript typed on white bond paper, the other gripping the latest version of "*More To Be Pitied*," the very script upon which Magnus had been engaged on the night of Mrs. Hogarth's murder.

"And there it was in the trash bag all this time, Cap'n," he enlightened the bird, as he fitted torn fragments of the white-paper manuscript together. For ten minutes there was silence in the room, except for the rustling of paper. Then he read, his eyes darting from the perfectly typed white sheets to the badly typed yellow, ones.

"Almost word for word the same!" he cried, and made a grab for the telephone. "Hello, hello! Police Headquarters? . . . Dundee speaking. Connect me with Western Union, please! . . . Hello! Western Union?

Detective Dundee, Homicide Squad, Police Headquarters, speaking . . . Right! Take a telegram, please, to Chauncey Smith, Optician, Riverside, California."

XXVII.

1

THE answer to the telegram to Mr. Chauncey Smith, Optician, Riverside, California, came at ten o'clock on Friday morning, bringing a new lustre to eyes heavy with doubt and sleeplessness. And thereafter, for twelve hours, no one could have accused Bonnie Dundee, novice detective, of being a lazy man, or one incapable of moving his long legs swiftly.

Among his activities was the filing in person of long telegrams at his own expense, so that their contents and the information they elicited would not become the property of any curious mind at Police Headquarters.

Four times that busy day a Western Union messenger rang the Rhodes House bell, and three times Dundee was awaiting him to snatch the yellow envelope with avid fingers. When a telegram came about three, however, it was Mrs. Rhodes who accepted the message, having been warned to guard it with her life until the addressee returned from a momentous interview.

He came back accompanied by a keen-eyed, sharp-faced young man, who had been getting his daily dozen during a heated hour with Dundee, by alternate nodding and shaking his head with great vigour. A most opinionated young man, but one who undoubtedly knew his stuff. One, too, who asked no annoying questions when he saw an excited detective committing unlawful entry by means of a most efficient skeleton key.

"Look at this!" Dundee cried exultantly, when the door of another man's room had closed upon the two. And he handed over the message which Mrs. Rhodes had signed for. "I guess that clinches it, doesn't it? You said if he'd that training, he could do it!"

"Hmm," said the head-shaker-and-nodder, but nodding this time. And then he got busy, uttering "Hmms" interlarded with occasional sharp exclamations of admiration. Finally he arose, dusted his hands and conceded: "You were right! But there's one thing missing," and he proceeded to describe it minutely.

"I'll find it!" Dundee promised rashly, exuberantly. "Can't fail now. Well, what do you say? If I do find it — and I will, somehow—what do you want to do, so that I can pull off my party?"

"Work here most of the day to-morrow, if the coast is clear," the keen-eyed, sharp-faced young man answered.

"The coast will be clear, all right," Dundee promised.

The first thing Dundee did when he was alone again in his own room on the third floor of the Rhodes House was to call Police Headquarters. Two minutes later Sergeant Turner's voice vibrated harshly against his eardrum.

"Dundee speaking, Sergeant. Yeah, pretty busy. Listen, Sergeant, and this is more important than I can possibly tell you. I want you to detail one of your best men to shadow Miss Jewel Briggs. He's not to let her out of his sight a minute during the day, and to-night I want him stationed in the vacant room directly across from Jewel's. Furthermore, please instruct one of the men patrolling the Rhodes House grounds to keep an eye on Jewel's window."

"That makes three men you've got tied up, besides the two on the grounds," Sergeant Turner grumbled. "What—"

After skilfully evading the curious but scoffing sergeant's questions, Dundee hung up the receiver, cast a loving eye upon some apparently uninteresting items from the Rhodes House trash bags, then locked them up and went down to the basement again to see if he could add to them.

As he borrowed the old-fashioned padlock key from Mrs. Rhodes, who was alone in her bed-sitting-room at the time, he noticed that she was studying an extremely legal-looking document.

"Thanks, Mother Rhodes . . . What's the heavy literature?"

"A deed. I'm selling the Rhodes House," she informed him stiffly "Getting a good price, too. They're going to use the site, for an apartment house. In a few weeks there won't be any 'Murder Mansion,'" she added bitterly.

"But what am I and the rest of us pampered boarders going to do?"

"I'm thinking of buying a house four blocks further down to Chestnut, and opening again about the first of September, if you really want to stay with me," the landlady answered brusquely, but there were tears in her eyes.

"Want to? Just try, to get rid of me," Dundee retorted and hugged her close for a moment before dashing down to the basement.

He knew that what he was looking for could not be far down in the unfilled trash bag, if it was there at all, which he doubted. His pessimism was justified. Empty-handed, he plodded slowly upstairs; then, seized with a sudden inspiration he halted in the second floor hall, took out his skeleton key, and again effected unlawful entry.

Ten minutes later he had the keen-eyed, sharp-faced young man on the phone, was exulting: "Found it! And you'd never guess where. See you in the morning about half-past nine."

And once more he made a demand upon Mrs. Rhodes: "Have you got such a thing as a small-size phonograph record? The kind they make nursery rhymes on?"

"I know where I can get one. Dr. Weeks has a whole book of them for his grandchild."

"Great!" Dundee hugged her again. "Send Tilda up with it as soon as possible, and you might lend me a needle and some white thread, too."

"If you've got any mending to do, I guess I can do it for you," she assured him brusquely.

"Your stitches would be far too neat!" he refused gaily, "but I'll remember your offer when I cast a button!"

2

"Well, how are you coming on?" Lieut. Strawn greeted his newest recruit rather sourly at eleven o'clock on Saturday.

"You'd be surprised!" Dundee grinned. "Is it all fixed up with the district attorney to keep the boarders tied up all afternoon in his office? It'll wreck my plans if they buzz around the house this half-holiday."

"He'll keep 'em busy, quizzing 'em about Sevier and the Hogarth case, all right," Strawn promised. "But I'd like to know what the devil you're up to anyway. Seems to me you're either lying down on the job or being damned mysterious."

"The latter, chief, though I'm not being mysterious just for the fun of the thing," Dundee assured him. "There really isn't much to tell yet, though I haven't been lazy. The truth I've got a pot on the fire which I'd like you to bring to a boil for me to-night."

"How?"

For ten minutes Dundee explained, without, however, giving away to his chief the contents of the pot which he hoped would boil over that evening. It was not an easy task, but he left Police Headquarters with Lieut. Strawn's unwilling and puzzled promise of assistance.

At five minutes to eight that Saturday evening Bonnie Dundee was pretending as much surprise and indignation as any other boarder when Lieut. Strawn, assisted by Detectives Payne and Wilkins, brusquely ordered all inmates of the Rhodes House to the second floor.

"Where is he going to hold the meeting?" Dundee heard Norma Paige quaver. "In—in Mrs. Hogarth's room?"

Strawn himself answered the question by commanding curtly: "Open your door, Styles. . . . Oh, it's not locked. . . Come in, everybody, and make yourselves comfortable."

"I fail to see why my room was chosen if you want us to make ourselves comfortable," Walter Styles retorted angrily. "It's too small—"

"Bring some chairs, boys," Strawn ordered the two plain-clothes men. "Five or six. The others can sit on the bed."

When his order had been carried out and the Rhodes House residents had seated themselves, he looked about the small room sternly. "Everyone here? Answer to your names, please." He consulted a slip of paper: "Mrs. Caroline Rhodes . . . Mr. Rhodes . . . Mr. and Mrs. Lawrence Sharp. . . Miss Norma Paige . . . Mr. Walter Styles . . . Mr. Henry Dowd . . . Mr. Herbert S. Magnus . . . Mr. James Dundee . . . Miss Jewel Briggs . . . Miss Daisy Shepherd . . . Miss Matilda Brown. Is that everyone who belongs in the house, Mrs. Rhodes?"

"All but the cook, and you said she could go home," Mrs. Rhodes answered.

Dowd, Magnus and Dundee had seated themselves on the bed, which was along the wall in which the door was set. The door was open. The others occupied chairs, Walter sitting with his arm about Norma's shoulders.

"I shall not keep you long, folks," Lieut. Strawn began, from his position beside the open window."The truth is I want you to help me. First, I must tell you about some new evidence that has just come to light. Five years ago a Mrs. Emma Harkness and her daughter, Mrs. Daniel Thomas Griffin, fled from their home in Belton, Mo., a few hours before the police were notified that Griffin, the son-in-law and husband, had robbed the bank in which he worked of $10,000. Griffin was never caught, and for five years young Mrs. Griffin lived in New York under the name of Sally Graves, and Mrs. Harkness lived in this house as Mrs. Emma Hogarth. On 2nd June Sally Graves, or Griffin, was murdered. On 29th June Mrs. Harkness, or Hogarth, was strangled to death in this house. In the early morning of 3rd July Cora Barker was also murdered by strangulation."

Lieut. Strawn paused, his face stoical, as exclamations, shudders and half-uttered questions filled the room. Dundee glanced at the two men sitting beside him. Neither face betrayed anything but horrified surprise.

Lieut. Strawn went on: "I have reason to believe that Dan Griffin committed all three of these fiendish crimes, and that he is or has been a boarder in this house! Wait!" he commanded sharply. "Let me describe him. Five years ago Dan Griffin was 30 years old, of medium height and build, with light brown or reddish blonde hair, light eyes of hazel or grey; was neither handsome nor ugly but of extremely ordinary appearance. I'm asking you now, and I want you to consider carefully before answering: Is such a man known to any of you, either as a present boarder, a former boarder, or as a transient 'mealer' in this house?"

The question was such a bombshell that it was greeted with profound silence. Mr. and Mrs. Sharp, Walter Styles and Daisy Shepherd craned their heads to cast fearful, speculative glances at Henry Dowd. But no one spoke.

As the horror-laden silence throbbed on, Dundee raised his handkerchief to his brow, as if to wipe away cold beads of perspiration. A shadow which had lain across the floor outside the open door wavered, disappeared.

A few seconds later, when that silence was becoming too terrible a thing to be borne, it was broken by the tap, tap, tap of a typewriter.

With a hoarse oath Bert Magnus sprang from the bed, and inched toward the door. "Who the hell is using my typewriter—" he snarled thickly.

The shadow of a man again lay across the open door, as Dundee followed the enraged scenario-writer who was plunging toward the door of the next room. The tap, tap, tap went steadily on.

As Bert Magnus tore the knob, Dundee laid his had upon his shoulder.

"Griffin, there is no one in your room now, just as there was no one in there last Saturday night when your mother-in-law was being murdered. No one but—'the perfect stenographer'!"

XXVIII.

"WHAT do you mean, 'the perfect stenographer'?" Lieut. Strawn demanded, as Detectives Payne and Wilkins devoted their entire attention to subduing and handcuffing the raging creature who had been known as Bert Magnus. "Is there a girl in there?"

"Reassure and scatter those people cooped up in Styles's room, and then I'll show you," Dundee promised. "Will you come in now, Ogden?" he called to the keen-eyed, sharp-faced young man whose lean body had cast the shadow across the open door of Styles's room.

Five minutes later Lieut. Strawn knocked and was admitted to the room which had been occupied by Dan Griffin, under the alias of Herbert S. Magnus. The typewriter was still tapping away steadily, but no human hands were touching the keys.

"Well, I'll be—!" Words failed the chief of the Homicide Squad as he planted himself before the desk and bent over the strange apparatus which reared itself to the left of the typewriter. "Is that all there is to it? What makes it work?"

Dundee laughed, then jerked an electric cord plugged in at the outlet behind the desk. The tapping ceased suddenly. A short, rubber-capped plunger stopped, hovering just over the letter q, which it had been striking with amazing efficiency so long as the current was on.

'Not quite all, chief. The rest of 'the perfect stenographer' is in this old trunk of electrical 'junk' which Arthur Wheeler left here. A quarter-horse-power motor, a small transformer to reduce the house line voltage and current to the field of the solenoid magnet—" And he stooped and hauled the trunk out from its resting place under the roll-top desk.

"Then Wheeler was mixed up in it?" Strawn interrupted.

"Not that he knows of," Dundee grinned. "His only crime was in beating his board bill, so that he had to leave this trunk behind, thus putting ideas for a perfect alibi into the wicked head of Dan Griffin, alias Herbert S. Magnus. But meet Mr. Clarence Ogden, electrical engineer, Lieutenant Strawn."

"Glad to meet you," Strawn mumbled. Then an idea shook him: "Say, Dundee, you haven't gone off half-a cocked, have you? Got it into your head that Magnus must be guilty, and thought up a way to smash his alibi, without any real proof that he ever used such a contrivance!"

"Hardly, chief! Every item of this contrivance was found in this room, as Ogden can swear. Even this—" and he snatched a flat black disc from the small motor which lay in the trunk.

"Looks like a little phonograph record," Strawn commented.

"Exactly! But it isn't. It's a 'bakelite' disc. See these fourteen little metal plugs, like bits of chewing-gum stuck into the bakelite? I can't explain very technically, but this disc regulated the tapping of the key, so that it wouldn't be too steady—intervals of different lengths between the tapping, you know. Oh, Griffin wasn't taking any chances! He was clever enough to duplicate almost perfectly his own slow, one-finger typing As soon as I knew that Magnus or Griffin, was my man, and that he had only seemed be typing in his room when he couldn't have been there, since he was in his mother-in-law's room, murdering her, I had an inkling of how the thing could be done, and put the problem up to Ogden here. He assured me it was mechanically possible, even easy for a man with some knowledge of electrical engineering to rig up an outfit like this. Something of which the major portion would be hidden from sight, and which could be dismantled in less than a minute. Watch!"

And Dundee laid violent hands upon the visible parts of the device, throwing them into the trunk. The dissembling of the portion in the trunk and the parts attached to the typewriter took less than two minutes.

"What are you trying, to do—destroy evidence?" Strawn demanded, outraged.

"Oh, Ogden can have it in working order in an hour, if you like," Dundee explained easily. "When I brought him to look through the trunk he immediately spotted everything required but this bakelite disc. Of course, we could have duplicated it, knowing darn well that Magnus must have used one, but I was lucky enough to find it."

"Where?" Strawn asked, rather surlily.

"Inside this tie rack," and Dundee took from the wall a round object, fitted with a hand-embroidered linen cover, to which were sewn half a dozen long ribbon loops, still crowded with cravats. "Look!" and he ripped out the big loose stitches he himself had put there the day before, and drew forth a small phonograph record. "When I first talked with Magnus he told me a lot about his family; said his little sister had made this for him before he left home five years ago. Yesterday, when I was looking for a good place of concealment for a round flat object I remembered this thing. He had remembered it, too, when he wanted to get rid of the disc. I presume there was a round piece of thick cardboard in it before, for stiffening. He simply removed the original stiffening, inserted the disc, and sewed the linen cover up again. You see, chief, the disc was the only peculiar-looking item in his contrivance, the only thing that would have looked odd in a trunk of electrical junk, even to the thick-headed police, as Magnus undoubtedly considered us. So he hid it most in his room, leaving everything else in plain; sight . . . Good 'purloined letter' psychology, eh?"

"What's that?" Strawn asked irritably. Then: "But I thought you said Bert Magnus's story of his past checked up all right. I don't see how you ever got on to him—"

"Let's amble down to Police Headquarters and while we're waiting for Griffin's confession, I'll tell you the whole story." Dundee suggested. "I promised Uncle Pat he could hear the tale, too. Thanks a lot, Ogden. You will have to appear at the trial, of course, but I'm sure the district attorney's office will be reasonable about loss of time."

"Good publicity for my shop," Ogden grinned, as he took up his tool kit and left.

Half an hour later the Police Commissioner, the chief of the Homicide Squad, and the Squad's newest recruit sat about Lieut. Strawn's desk at Police Headquarters.

"Well, shoot the works, boys," Commissioner O'Brien commanded, a broad grin of almost paternal pride on his Irish face. "Begin by telling how you found out Bert Magnus wasn't Bert Magnus."

"That part was easy," Dundee admitted. "I should have been suspicious of his identity long before I was because there was plenty to make me suspicious all along. See these?" and he took his little collection of trash bag exhibits and ranged them all on the desk-top. "Here are some torn pages of a scenario, entitled '*More To Be Pitied*.' White paper, typing perfect. But torn up and thrown away! The last page, as you see, shows signs of age, so this script must have been written several years ago by the real Bert Magnus, and typed by a professional stenographer. And here are corresponding pagos of the 'revision' on which Bert—as we'll call him still—was working the night Mrs. Hogarth was murdered. There are no changes! Get that? If I'd had my wits about me I'd have stumbled on to that significant fact days ago. When I did discover it, I asked myself why a poor man, with one hand crippled, was toiling away retyping a manuscript of which he had destroyed a perfect copy.

"Answer obviously, was that he was using his typing as a blind; that he had typed and retyped this silly scenario merely to accustom people to hearing his typewriter, even late at night. If he had been just a shade cleverer, or more gifted as a scenario-writer, he would undoubtedly, have written a new story and one of my most important clues would have been missing."

"I see," O'Brien nodded "It worked all right. Four people swore he was in his room when Mrs. Hogarth was murdered, because they heard him typing. But how did you get on to his not being Bert Magnus?"

"Well, as soon as I had reason to doubt Bert's perfect alibi, I had ample reason to check his identity, since I couldn't get that 'bad penny' business out of my head," Dundee explained. "It was ridiculously easy to check up on him, for Bert had broken his glasses and I had been lucky enough to find the broken lens in a trash bag in the basement, along with these other things—"

"Lucky?" O'Brien chuckled.

"Well, have it your own way!" Dundee grinned. "I admit it—I'm clever! Anyway, I simply wired to the Riverside optician whose name I had seen on Bert's glasses' case. He was keeping the real Bert's case, all right, but he wasn't wearing the real Bert's glasses. He couldn't have worn them, or he'd have gone blind. When the optician wired me the prescription of the real Bert Magnus's glasses I took it, along with the broken lens, to Sharp's oculist here and asked him: 'Could the man who wore this prescription five years ago, wear this lens now?' And his answer was, 'Not in a million years!'"

"And so you knew who Bert Magnus wasn't—but you didn't know who he was," O'Brien summed up, wagging his head.

"Exactly, Uncle Pat! Of course, the next step was to wire Miami, Florida, where Bert Magnus, as he had told me, had been hurt in a motor bus crash four years ago. Police there were able to supply me with minute descriptions, acquired at the time, of the dead and injured. And it was Bert Magnus who was killed, and Dan Griffin, using another name, of course, whose hand was badly cut! Not that the Miami police know the truth!

Their records show the reverse to be true, but the description of the dead man tallies exactly with our fake Bert's appearance, and if the Belton, Mo., police had been reading descriptions of the injured they might have tumbled to the fact that their much-sought Dan Griffin, under the name of Bert Magnus, was nursing a pretty badly crippled hand in a Miami hospital. The fake Bert, in his chummy way, had told me all about the accident, even told me how he'd wired his parents in Riverside to reassure them. When 1 got copies of their wire to the hospital and his answering wire, I understood why he needed to reassure them, for according to the newspaper descriptions, their son was dead, not injured—"

"You're way ahead of me," Strawn growled. "Do you mean Griffin decided then and there to take on the dead man's identity, belongings and family?"

"Exactly!" Dundee cried. "He was Dan Griffin, remember, and a fugitive from justice. Probably he had made friends with Magnus on the trip, or perhaps they had been friends for weeks. Undoubtedly he had heard all about the real Bert's family and his ambition to write scenarios. When Griffin was taken to the hospital he knew the real Magnus was dead, because they had sat side by side in the motor bus. Griffin simply claimed Magnus's name, his suit-case, and everything. Doubtless he had had time and strength, hurt though he was, to switch his pocket belongings with the dead man, in all the confusion. At any rate, the papers described the dead man as unknown, with dark-brown hair, small reddish moustache, and eyeglasses. The family, out in Riverside, was frantic, of course, when they saw their son's description among the dead, although his name was listed among the injured. But they were immensely relieved when the new 'Bert Magnus' wired them that the papers had made a mistake in the descriptions, and that he had suffered nothing worse than a crippled hand. Here are all the wires, if you care to see them."

"No, go on," his uncle directed. "What made you think of the typewriter, being worked mechanically?"

"These," and Dundee showed him the two greasy and stained wads of paper and the yellow sheets with the letter q struck over and over until the paper was cut through. "Of course, I thought of a girl accomplice, at first, but it wouldn't wash. Jewel Briggs was the only possible suspect in that connection, and I made sure she was actually at her parents' home that Saturday night. I studied these trash bag exhibits a lot, and when I found a q cut through the paper in the middle of a page of Bert's latest revision of his scenario, I was on the trail. The mechanical contrivance operated only upon the letter q, as you saw. And I knew it was typewriter oil on these wads. He used them to wedge the carriage so it wouldn't move and knock over his apparatus."

"But what the devil did he kill Cora for—if he did?" Strawn asked. "I'd have taken my oath that he was really in love with her—"

"And I believe he was," Dundee answered soberly. "I believe he had every intention of marrying her when, as he hoped, Sevier was convicted of Mrs. Hogarth's murder. But almost as soon as he and Cora had come to an understanding Tuesday night he discovered that he would have to kill her, to protect his own life. And Dan Griffin loves himself more than he can ever love any other human being."

"This is all news to me," Strawn grumbled, his brows knit in a puzzled frown. "Were you holding out on us even at the inquest?"

"I didn't hold out anything to which I attached the slightest importance at the time," Dundee answered. "I was eavesdropping when Bert became sentimental Tuesday night. I heard her say: 'Oh, Bert! Then you didn't mean what you said to Jewel?' Jewel herself called me away just then, and I heard no more, but Cora must have explained her remark pretty thoroughly, so thoroughly that Bert knew he would have to kill her, for he knew that Cora's jealousy would lead her to probe her accusations against him and Jewel. Of course, I'm only surmising, but there will be little doubt as to why Bert, or Griffin, killed Cora Barker. Later that Tuesday evening Mrs. Rhodes went up to speak to Cora, but didn't for she heard Jewel and Cora quarrelling. Cora was accusing Jewel of having been in Bert's room at midnight Thursday of week before. Said she heard Bert say to some girl—and who could it be but Jewel? 'Go to it, sweetheart! The perfect stenographer!' Of course, he was not talking to a girl at all. He was gloating over the perfection of his mechanical device, the concoction of what he fondly believed would be a 'perfect alibi.' Naturally, when Cora elucidated her remark about Jewel, Griffin was scared stiff, felt he had to kill Cora before she could charge Jewel with the 'scandal,' and thus let the cat out of the bag the cat being that if 'someone' else was typing in his room at midnight on Thursday night, 'someone' else might just as well have been typing there at midnight on Saturday night. Remember he testified at the inquest that he took a long walk Tuesday night after the little party broke up? I have a hunch he saw Sevier, who was also taking a long walk, trying to screw up his courage to go to Police Headquarters, and thought he saw a fine chance of pinning the Barker murder on Sevier, as well as the Hogarth murder. We have only his word for it that he returned about twelve o'clock. At any rate, that first murder was carefully planned to incriminate Sevier at every turn; the second was impromptu, but if the Cannons had not been trailing Sevier, it would have looked like an open-and-shut case against the poor fiddler."

"And you figured that Jewel might be his next victim, if Cora, before he killed her, told him that Jewel denied it was her in his room on Thursday night," Strawn interrupted. "Guess that's why you had a couple of men guarding her day and night."

"Right!" Dundee agreed. "I wasn't taking any chances, though I felt pretty sure that Cora hadn't had time to tell him, or Jewel would not have lived to babble about Cora's strange accusations. As for Jewel, she was too afraid of being accused of Cora's murder herself to admit having quarrelled with her." He stopped and drew a deep breath, then suddenly remembered something. "There was just one other clue, but I overlooked its significance at the time. Mrs. Rhodes had remarked casually that the fuses blew out three times last month. 'Bert' testing out his invention, of course. He had the parts made at the various electrical shops—a piece here, a piece there, but he rigged up the rubber cap plunger and the solenoid magnet himself, as well as the plugged bakelite disc. One of my telegrams, by the way, brought out the fact that Griffin had had one year of electrical engineering before he went in for banking."

"He sure played the Bert Magnus game without missing a trick," Strawn commented admiringly. "Fooled the Magnus family with his letters—"

"Because he had every intention of eventually falling heir to half of the Magnus fortune," Dundee explained. "That, as much as his need for ironclad alias, was his real reason for assuming the dead man's identity in the first place. But, of course, he didn't dare to show up in Riverside till the father was dead. The mother and older brother are already dead, and there remained only the ailing old father and the sister who was a child of thirteen. When the real Bert left home. His crippled right hand, necessitating his writing with his left, would have explained any slight dissimilarity in handwriting—"

"Wait!" Strawn interrupted, as if a great light had burst on him. "What about that crippled hand? How could he strangle two women with it?"

"In the last two days I've watched that crippled hand pretty carefully," Dundee answered. "It is true that the fingers are practically useless, but the thumb, which escaped injury, has been developed to amazing strength by way of compensation. And the thumb, pressing hard against the palm, could do far more work than the tying of a scarf, or the knotting of braids about a woman's throat requires."

"All right," Strawn conceded grudgingly. "What about Sally Graves? I suppose you've got all the dope on that, too—"

"Nothing, beyond the fact that 'Bert' admitted freely that he had come here from Philadelphia, arriving 5th June, just three days after Sally Graves or Griffin was murdered. And Philadelphia is only two hours by train from New York. Furthermore, there is no one to swear to his alibi that he was in his room at Mrs. Starrett's house on Spruce Street Saturday night and Sunday morning, 1st and 2nd June, since Mrs. Starrett was in Atlantic City at that time. Probably he had run across his former wife shortly before this, on a visit to New York, and had tracked her to her apartment. I suppose he had nursed his rage against her all these years, and cold-bloodedly set about forcing her to give him the money he had stolen and which he believed she had stolen from him. At any rate, he killed her in a red rage when she wouldn't give him the money. And when he found she didn't have it after all, he came on here, as bent on having his revenge on the old lady as on getting the money. But if it hadn't been for Cap'n and his harping on 'bad penny,' I'm not at all sure Dan Griffin would be in gaol now."

"Well, he is, and I'm due to take my turn at the third degree," Strawn said as he rose. Rather awkwardly, he thrust out a hand and Dundee gripped it. "By the way," he called from the door, "what about that other bad egg, Henry Dowd?"

"Not so bad an egg," Dundee laughed. "I got the goods on him this morning. Name of Henry Dibble. In contempt of court for non-payment of alimony, poor little henpecked devil. Probably his wife has seen his picture in the paper and is hot-footing it after him this minute."

Half an hour later Strawn returned, triumphant, to the office where uncle and nephew still sat. "Left Griffin calling for a stenographer," he exulted. "He's admitting everything—after I told him what we had on him. Told me a guy, Williams, helped him rob the bank—"

"Williams?" Dundee cried. He knit his brows, then quoted from memory an excerpt from Mrs. Hogarth's diary: 'Our good friend, J. W. is dead . . . I often wonder how S. and I would ever have got away that day if J. W. hadn't helped us pack.' Yes, J. W. was a good friend, indeed," he said bitterly. "It's plain now that accomplice James Williams found and took the $10,000 while the two young women were packing. Double-crossed his pal, Griffin, and lived to be cashier of the bank! Tell that to Dan Griffin, Strawn, and make him feel real good. It ought to cheer him up," he added with sudden boyishness savageness, "to know that he killed three women over a measly $ 10,000 dollars that neither his wife nor his mother-in-law, poor things, had ever laid eyes on it."

"Where are you going, Bonnie?" his uncle asked, as the young detective rose and started for the door.

"To shed a little sunshine and claim my reward."

"Reward?" Strawn and O'Brien echoed.

"After I tell Norma Paige that she's heiress to $2,000' instead of nothing but a parrot she doesn't like, I have every hope that she'll listen to reason when I explain that I need Cap'n, the avenging parrot, in my business. He makes the slickest Watson you ever saw, Uncle Pat!"

And he strolled away, whistling very cheerfully for a young man suffering from unrequited love.

THE END

Other Resurrected Press Books in *The Chief Inspector Pointer Mystery* Series

MORE MYSTERIES BY ANNE AUSTIN

Murder at Bridge

One Drop of Blood

The Black Pigeon

Murder Backstairs

Murdered But Not Dead

- The Problem of Cell 13 by Jacques Futrelle
- The Conundrum of the Golf Links by Percy James Brebner
- The Silkworms of Florence by Clifford Ashdown
- The Gateway of the Monster by William Hope Hodgson
- The Affair at the Semiramis Hotel by A. E. W. Mason
- The Affair of the Avalanche Bicycle & Tyre Co., LTD by Arthur Morrison

RESURRECTED PRESS CLASSIC MYSTERY CATALOGUE

Journeys into Mystery
Travel and Mystery in a More Elegant Time

The Edwardian Detectives
Literary Sleuths of the Edwardian Era

Gems of Mystery
Lost Jewels from a More Elegant Age

E. C. Bentley
Trent's Last Case: The Woman in Black

Ernest Bramah
Max Carrados Resurrected:
The Detective Stories of Max Carrados

Agatha Christie
The Secret Adversary
The Mysterious Affair at Styles

Octavus Roy Cohen
Midnight

Freeman Wills Croft
The Ponson Case
The Pit Prop Syndicate

J. S. Fletcher
The Herapath Property
The Rayner-Slade Amalgamation
The Chestermarke Instinct
The Paradise Mystery
Dead Men's Money

The Middle of Things
Ravensdene Court
Scarhaven Keep
The Orange-Yellow Diamond
The Middle Temple Murder
The Tallyrand Maxim
The Borough Treasurer
In the Mayor's Parlour
The Saftey Pin

R. Austin Freeman
The Mystery of 31 New Inn from the Dr. Thorndyke Series
John Thorndyke's Cases from the Dr. Thorndyke Series
The Red Thumb Mark from The Dr. Thorndyke Series
The Eye of Osiris from The Dr. Thorndyke Series
A Silent Witness from the Dr. John Thorndyke Series
The Cat's Eye from the Dr. John Thorndyke Series
Helen Vardon's Confession: A Dr. John Thorndyke Story
As a Thief in the Night: A Dr. John Thorndyke Story
Mr. Pottermack's Oversight: A Dr. John Thorndyke Story
Dr. Thorndyke Intervenes: A Dr. John Thorndyke Story
The Singing Bone: The Adventures of Dr. Thorndyke
The Stoneware Monkey: A Dr. John Thorndyke Story
The Great Portrait Mystery, and Other Stories: A Collection of Dr. John Thorndyke and Other Stories
The Penrose Mystery: A Dr. John Thorndyke Story
The Uttermost Farthing: A Savant's Vendetta

Arthur Griffiths
The Passenger From Calais
The Rome Express

Fergus Hume
The Mystery of a Hansom Cab
The Green Mummy
The Silent House
The Secret Passage

Edgar Jepson
The Loudwater Mystery

A. E. W. Mason
At the Villa Rose

A. A. Milne
The Red House Mystery
Baroness Emma Orczy
The Old Man in the Corner

Edgar Allan Poe
The Detective Stories of Edgar Allan Poe

Arthur J. Rees
The Hampstead Mystery
The Shrieking Pit
The Hand In The Dark
The Moon Rock
The Mystery of the Downs

Mary Roberts Rinehart
Sight Unseen and The Confession

Dorothy L. Sayers
Whose Body?

Sir William Magnay
The Hunt Ball Mystery

Mabel and Paul Thorne
The Sheridan Road Mystery

Louis Tracy
The Strange Case of Mortimer Fenley
The Albert Gate Mystery
The Bartlett Mystery
The Postmaster's Daughter
The House of Peril
The Sandling Case: What Would You Have Done?
Charles Edmonds Walk
The Paternoster Ruby

John R. Watson
The Mystery of the Downs
The Hampstead Mystery

Edgar Wallace
The Daffodil Mystery
The Crimson Circle

Carolyn Wells
Vicky Van
The Man Who Fell Through the Earth
In the Onyx Lobby
Raspberry Jam
The Clue
The Room with the Tassels
The Vanishing of Betty Varian
The Mystery Girl
The White Alley
The Curved Blades
Anybody but Anne
The Bride of a Moment
Faulkner's Folly
The Diamond Pin
The Gold Bag
The Mystery of the Sycamore
The Come Backy

Raoul Whitfield
Death in a Bowl

And much more!
Visit ResurrectedPress.com
for our complete catalogue

About Resurrected Press

A division of Intrepid Ink, LLC, Resurrected Press is dedicated to bringing high quality, vintage books back into publication. See our entire catalogue and find out more at www.ResurrectedPress.com.

About Intrepid Ink, LLC

Intrepid Ink, LLC provides full publishing services to authors of fiction and non-fiction books, eBooks and websites. From editing to formatting, from publishing to marketing, Intrepid Ink gets your creative works into the hands of the people who want to read them. Find out more at www.IntrepidInk.com.

www.ingramcontent.com/pod-product-compliance
Lightning Source LLC
Chambersburg PA
CBHW071050250626
47159CB00002B/427